Praise for Lee Goodman and INDEFENSIBLE

"Goodman takes the reader by the hand and leads them into a frightening world they will never forget. . . . This book is top-notch!"

— *Suspense Magazine*

"Complex and intelligent, fantastically well-plotted. *Indefensible* is as good as it gets."

—John Lescroart, *New York Times* bestselling author

"*Indefensible* is the kind of gem we all love to stumble on, a novel that delivers its story flawlessly. Lee Goodman has created characters we care about deeply; when he puts them through the wringer, we feel their pain. Add to this a compelling insider's look at prosecution and law enforcement, language that sings, a stunning series of plot twists, and the result may well prove to be the outstanding debut novel of the year."

—William Kent Krueger, *New York Times* bestselling author

"Lee Goodman is a rare find in a crowded field: a talented writer who knows the true intricacies and ironies of the American criminal litigation system. Before reading *Indefensible*, be sure to put on your helmet and fasten your five-point harness. You're in for a wild ride."

—Walter Walker, author of *Crime of Privilege*

"Goodman's debut legal thriller is compelling from start to finish— well-written, populated with intriguing multidimensional characters, and with many plot twists leading to a surprise ending."

—*Library Journal*

"As legal thrillers go, this one is right up there with the best of them. That's not because of its nonstop action, but because of its slow-burn pacing, unpredictable characters, and lots and lots of plot switchbacks. . . . And the big bonus is that author Lee Goodman's writing style makes me want to come back for more. And more. And more."

—*BookReporter*

"Attorney Goodman easily makes the transition to fiction writer, as have his brethren Scott Turow and John Lescroart."

—*Booklist*

"Goodman ties up every loose end in surprising ways, making for a deeply satisfying read."

—Authorexposure.com

INJUSTICE

a novel

LEE GOODMAN

EMILY BESTLER BOOKS
—
ATRIA

NEW YORK   LONDON   TORONTO   SYDNEY   NEW DELHI

ATRIA BOOKS
An Imprint of Simon & Schuster, Inc.
1230 Avenue of the Americas
New York, NY 10020

Copyright © 2015 by Lee Goodman

All rights reserved, including the right to reproduce this book or portions thereof in any form whatsoever. For information, address Atria Books Subsidiary Rights Department, 1230 Avenue of the Americas, New York, NY 10020.

First Emily Bestler Books/Atria Books hardcover edition September 2015

EMILY BESTLER BOOKS / ATRIA BOOKS and colophons are trademarks of Simon & Schuster, Inc.

For information about special discounts for bulk purchases, please contact Simon & Schuster Special Sales at 1-866-506-1949 or business@simonandschuster.com.

The Simon & Schuster Speakers Bureau can bring authors to your live event. For more information or to book an event, contact the Simon & Schuster Speakers Bureau at 1-866-248-3049 or visit our website at www.simonspeakers.com.

Cover images © iStockPhoto; Stockbyte/Getty Images

Manufactured in the United States of America

10 9 8 7 6 5 4 3 2 1

Library of Congress Cataloging-in-Publication Data

Goodman, Lee.
  Injustice : a novel / by Lee Goodman. —First Emily Bestler Books/Atria Books hardcover edition.
      p. cm.
  I. Title.
  PS3607.O577I55 2015
  813'.6—dc23
                                    2014045974

ISBN 978-1-4767-2803-2
ISBN 978-1-4767-2806-3 (ebook)

For Barrie and for Gray

Thus strangely are our souls constructed, and by slight ligaments are we bound to prosperity and ruin.

—Mary Shelley, *Frankenstein*

PART I

CHAPTER 1

LIFE IS SWEET.

That, in any case, is the opinion of a character from the funny pages, which I have taped to the stand of my desk lamp here at the cabin. Lizzy, my eighteen-year-old daughter, clipped the panel and glued it to an index card for me last July. "Dad, this made me think of you," she wrote.

But that was before the murder, and it was before my wife, Tina, suggested I find an apartment where I could live alone while she stayed home with our son, Barnaby, using my absence to "figure some things out." And it was before I discovered that the very incarnation of evil and misery had burrowed its way into the heart of my job and family.

It was on July 3, Barnaby's fourth birthday, when Lizzy gave me that cartoon, but the gesture wasn't as sweet as it sounds. The character in the comic strip wears a squiggle-mouth expression of befuddlement as if the idea of life's sweetness is an alien concept that the androgynous little freak has just stumbled upon at that moment. It taunts me, daring me to burn it, flush it, crumple it, stomp on it—whatever—smug in its certainty that anything I do to be rid of its hateful irony will only invite more calamity.

Life is *not* sweet.

Life sucks.

But on July 3 I still had a simplistic confidence in my identity as a vigilant father, a loving and beloved husband, and a shrewd federal prosecutor.

* * *

The third was a Wednesday. I remember because one of the assistant U.S. attorneys had a trial that day, which was the first event in what we, in the U.S. Attorney's Office, expected to be a wide-ranging series of prosecutions for bribery, extortion, and political corruption. This first case would be the quick trial of an unimportant player. My associate Henry Tatlock was going to try the case. Henry was a new lawyer and relatively untested in the courtroom, so I was second-seating for him.

I felt good about the trial. I liked playing mentor to new lawyers like Henry. Also, I was excited—the whole office was excited—about the burgeoning corruption investigation. This trial was the warm-up act, the first rollout.

I was also happy about the trial because of a little deception I was perpetrating on the court. The trial would take no more than one day, but when I saw that we were calendared for Wednesday, July 3, I told Henry to inform the clerk's office that we expected to need two days. Everybody blocked out Wednesday the third and Friday the fifth for trial. The fourth, of course, was a holiday. So if we actually did wrap up trial on Wednesday, and we all celebrated July 4 on Thursday, we'd have Friday the fifth completely open. Voilà! I'd created a four-day weekend!

Every year on July 4, the city has a celebration at Rokeby Park, with an evening concert by the state symphony orchestra, ending with an exorbitant fireworks display. No matter how cynical you are, it's hard not to feel some civic pride in the renaissance of this once-rotting mill town that has clawed its way back from the despair and economic desperation of the '70s and '80s.

Barnaby was especially looking forward to the fireworks. Tina kept warning him that the booms and pops could be scary, but he wasn't having it. He just ran around the house screaming "Boom!" and throwing his hands in the air.

We had invited the extended family over for a barbecue before the concert on the Fourth. On the fifth, if my scheme worked, Tina and Barn and I would drive up to our cabin on the lake for the weekend to formally celebrate Barn's birthday.

Adding to all this, Tina and I were quietly celebrating another milestone. Two years earlier Tina had had a malignancy removed from her left breast. The surgery went well, but a year and a half later, her doctor found "something of concern" in the latest mammogram. He wanted to give it six months and then look again. Now the six months were over, and the follow-up exam, done just two days before Barn's birthday, had given Tina a clean bill of health. We were confident and excited about our future.

Children; spouse; health; extended family; career.

Life certainly seemed very sweet on July 3.

CHAPTER 2

July 3 is now months in the past. I've been living up here at my cabin on the lake for several weeks, writing this summary of everything that happened. The trial will be starting soon, and I believe it will help to have things written down, especially in a case like this, where it all got so tangled up together and where, I'll be the first to admit, my own recollections and objectivity could be called into question.

I've been a prosecutor for nearly thirty years, but I still feel a moment of awe when I step into the courtroom. The polished wood of the rails and benches, the waiting seats in the jury box, the imposing altitude of the judge's bench, the smell of the carpet, and the crackle of the sound system: It is an arena, a coliseum in which great and tragic events play out. The hush of an empty courtroom is electric with incipience. Remorseless and indifferent, it awaits its gladiators.

I am a gladiator. And on the morning of July 3, pushing through the swinging gate into the courtroom proper and laying my briefcase atop the prosecutor's table, I felt that thrill.

Henry and I were the first ones in the courtroom. I had an urge to put my hand on his shoulder and ask how he was faring. He struck me as vulnerable and a bit out of his depth as a trial lawyer. My instinct was to be avuncular toward him, offering encouragement and reassurance. But I resisted. Henry deserved to be treated as an equal and a professional.

"You nervous?" I asked.

He shrugged.

"You didn't puke, did you? I've known lawyers, even experienced ones, who get so nervous they throw up before a trial."

Henry laughed. "Not my thing," he said.

"And some guys take beta blockers. They say it doesn't hamper their performance, but I don't know."

Henry took a pill vial from his pocket and shook it like a rattle. "Antihistamines," he said. "I used to get hives whenever I got nervous."

"You'll do fine," I said. I hoped it was true. Henry had more cause than most to worry about how the jury would receive him.

The judge's clerk came in. "Good morning, Mr. Davis," she said to me, then looked at Henry, paused, checked her docket, looked around the room distractedly for a moment, then said, "And this would be Mr. Tatlock?"

"Yes, one of our newer assistants," I said. "Henry, this is Paula, Judge Baxter's clerk. Be nice to her. Rumor has it that Judge Baxter is really an animatronic device created by Spielberg or NASA or something, and that Paula runs the controls."

Henry laughed. Paula laughed.

The defendant and his lawyer walked into the courtroom. The lawyer was my "frienemy" Kendall Vance.

Kendall is about my age. He's a very physical guy. As he walked to his seat, he seemed to ripple with masculine brawn. He has a weight lifter's chest and a shaved head and a "don't fuck with me" look in his eye. When he saw me, he smiled expansively. "Nick," he said—or bellowed, really—as he steered the defendant into a chair, then came and stood in front of us, overflowing with happiness at the prospect of this legal sparring match.

"Two of you versus one of me," Kendall said, looking at Henry. "Seems I ought to get some kind of dispensation to even things out: a few extra preemptives, maybe, or—I know!—I get to have Morgan Freeman come in and read my closing argument."

"That sounds fair."

"Plus, you've got another advantage," Kendall said, "because I'm dead tired. Barely slept last night. You could knock me down with a feather. See, I've been rereading some of the classics from college days. High school, even. And I got so deep into *A Tale of Two Cities* last night that I couldn't put it down. You've read it, haven't you? Anyhow, just finished it a couple of hours ago, so I brought you my copy as a gift."

This all came out in a breathless stream. He waved a tattered copy of the novel in front of us, smacked it down on the table, then went and sat with his client.

"Um. Thank you," Henry said.

"Call me after you read it," Kendall said. "We'll get together for a little book club. Just us three lawyer guys."

I knew Kendall too well to believe his generosity was inspired by sudden enthusiasm for Dickens.

When the jury panel came in, we stood and faced them. It's a trial lawyer's number one job to be liked by the jury—so I'm always trying to find just the right facial expression for meeting them—somewhere between friendliness, seriousness, and integrity. It's tough. But on this occasion, as I stood there beside Henry, the prospective jurors didn't pay me any attention. One by one I saw them curiously scan the room until they noticed Henry; then they paused and looked away for a second but quickly had to look back. Though you could see them trying not to look, inevitably they did, studying him with sideways glances.

Henry is a burn victim. His face looks as if the whole thing simply melted off and the doctors who put him back together had to re-create it from whatever they could salvage. Some things are missing; some things are in the wrong place. Nothing looks as intended. It takes time after meeting him before you can see anything beyond his disfigurement.

The one thing Henry has said to me about his appearance is that while he has come to accept it and doesn't really even mind it anymore, he wishes more than anything that he could at least have a glimpse of how he would have looked were it not for what happened to him.

Jury selection was quick. It was a small case. We had a full jury within an hour, and after a brief recess, Judge Baxter gaveled us to order. She read the date, time, and case number into the record, listed the attorneys present, stated that the defendant was charged with one count each of burglary and criminal trespass of a federal facility, and noted that the defendant was not detained but, rather, was free on bond. Then she looked at Henry and said, "Mr. Tatlock, you may begin."

Henry walked over, stood directly in front of the jury box, and with one hand he motioned a circle in the air around his face. "Don't worry," he said, "you'll get used to it within an hour or two. I was in a fire as an infant. I have no memory of looking any other way. Anyhow, consider yourselves lucky: You got to have your morning coffee at home before coming in here to look at me. Think how I feel. First thing every morning, there I am in the bathroom mirror. Yikes!" Henry laughed.

A few of the jurors laughed politely.

"But you know what?" he said. "This trial isn't about me, is it? It's about the law and the defendant. So to the extent possible, I'm asking you to disregard me. I'm just the messenger . . ."

It was a good way to open. We'd talked about it. I felt Henry needed to address his appearance outright. Let the jury gawk a moment, then let it go. He did okay with his delivery. Henry is neither a great orator nor a brilliant legal strategist, but he's likable.

I had worried about Henry's appearance when I hired him. Would the jury be put off by his disfigurement? Would it make him appear untrustworthy? I struggled over it, and while I wouldn't in a million years have discriminated against him for his appearance, it was my job to protect the public from bad people, and if Henry's disfigurement made it even an iota harder for him to convict a criminal, then my hiring him was not in the public interest.

Ultimately I decided it was a wash: Some jurors might subconsciously resist him, while others would feel compassion and subconsciously side with him.

"What the evidence will show," Henry said, gesturing at the man in the defendant's chair who sat cradling his head in his hands, "is that the defendant broke into the offices of the Environmental Protection Agency with the intention of committing a felony inside that building. The EPA is a federal agency. The defendant rifled through files of that office . . ."

Immediately I saw the jury lose interest. They wanted something juicy for their time on a federal jury. They wanted big crimes, not somebody snooping in a business office.

"What the evidence will show," Henry continued, "is that the defendant was working for a company known as Subsurface Resources, Incorporated . . ."

Now they were interested again. Subsurface is a mining services contractor. Our investigation of them was extensively reported in the newspaper. This burglary case was a tiny offshoot of a huge corruption case that could bring down some powerful people in the state. Subsurface was bribing (and maybe blackmailing) politicians to defeat new tax legislation aimed at natural gas extraction. A grand jury had been convened. Indictments were raining down.

Today's defendant, Jimmy Mailing, was known to us as a corporate security hack for Subsurface, Inc. So when he was found burglarizing the EPA offices, we tried leveraging him to get to his bosses. We offered him a walk on the burglary if he'd testify that his superiors at Subsurface had authorized the break-in.

But Jimmy Mailing wasn't playing. He lawyered up, denied having burgled the federal office, and claimed that somebody else, perhaps the FBI themselves, had planted those files in his car. So we were coming down on him as hard as we could.

While Henry gave his opening, the defendant stared down at the tabletop. This was strange. Kendall is scrupulous about getting his clients to sit up straight, pay attention, and appear engaged. But this guy seemed morose, and Kendall made no effort to jar him out of it. I figured he must be a difficult client who had already used up all of Kendall's patience.

And something else: Kendall's clients are always perfectly groomed—suit and tie, clean-shaven, conservative haircuts. But here this guy was in a dark turtleneck with black jeans and his hair falling down over his forehead. From what I could see of his face, which wasn't much because of the way he sat, he had strong cheekbones and a long chin. He looked sinister. I felt sorry for Kendall, trying to help this ne'er-do-well who apparently wasn't lifting a finger to help himself.

Henry's first witness was the security guard who had found the intruder in the building. The guard was earnest, overweight, and seemed credible. Henry led him through a direct examination:

HENRY: What was your first indication that something was amiss?

WITNESS: I heard him. I heard someone like, you know, like moving stuff around.

HENRY: And you did what?

WITNESS: I went to investigate.

HENRY: Did you approach the intruder?

WITNESS: Not at first. I watched him without him seeing me. I was behind him, and I stood behind a pillar, peeking around it to keep an eye on him.

HENRY: For how long?

WITNESS: Two or three minutes, I guess.

The security guard looked at his watch to give authority to his estimate of two or three minutes. He was a good witness. He wore his uniform, which was sharp and well fitted, even though it covered a considerable expanse of belly. And he was well groomed and sat up straight and made eye contact with Henry. He even looked over toward the jury a few times.

> HENRY: And did you, at some point, get a good look at the intruder?
>
> WITNESS: Yes, sir. As he prepared to leave, I stepped from around the pillar. I had my weapon, but I didn't draw it. I shouted at him. I said, "Halt. Turn around and identify yourself."
>
> HENRY: And then what?
>
> WITNESS: He jumped. You know, startled. And he turned to look at me a moment, or several seconds, really, then he just ran.
>
> HENRY: Did you follow?
>
> WITNESS: I tried to, but he'd already scoped out his escape route. He was fast, and he, you know, jumped over stuff and was out of there before I could, you know, um, catch him.

The witness looked down at his hands, embarrassed. He was clearly no match for the wiry and agile defendant. I wondered if he had really given chase. Maybe he'd just watched the defendant run away. The guy was just the night watchman in a federal office building. It's not the kind of place you'd expect to be called upon for heroics.

> HENRY: But you say you got a good look?
>
> WITNESS: Sure. I watched him those few minutes, then I, um, I mean, he turned right around and faced me when I yelled at him. I saw his face, like, full-on.
>
> HENRY: And how was the lighting in the room?
>
> WITNESS: Well, it was night, of course, but there was enough light from different places. It was dim but not dark. I saw him perfectly well.

HENRY: And do you see that man in the courtroom
  today?

WITNESS: Yes, sir.

HENRY: And would you point him out?

WITNESS: Right there.

The witness pointed directly at the man sitting beside Kendall
Vance.

HENRY: You're sure?

WITNESS: Positive.

Henry turned toward the court reporter and said, "Let the record
reflect that the witness has identified the defendant, Jimmy Mailing,
as the intruder he saw that night."

Kendall Vance cleared his throat and stood. "A technical point,
Your Honor," he said. Kendall wasn't smiling openly, but from his
posture and tone of voice, it was clear something had made him very
happy, and suddenly I understood why the "defendant" was not in a
suit and tie or sitting up, bright-eyed and involved.

Judge Baxter looked over her glasses at Kendall. "Go ahead, Mr.
Vance."

"Yes," Kendall said, "the record should reflect that the witness has
failed to identify the defendant."

Kendall laid a hand on the shoulder of the man beside him at the
counsel table. "This is not Jimmy Mailing but, rather, Derek Sykes.
Mr. Sykes is an actor who generously agreed to come along and help
me with my case this morning." Kendall turned and looked into the
gallery. "Jimmy, would you please stand."

Jimmy Mailing, the real defendant, stood up. He had been sitting
in a small crowd in the gallery. He was in a suit and tie, impeccably
groomed. He had prominent cheekbones, dark hair, and a long chin.
Jimmy Mailing and Derek Sykes didn't really look alike, but they
were the same type, with the same elongate faces and the same slender, athletic physique. The most striking difference was that at the

moment the imposter looked like a criminal, while the real Jimmy Mailing didn't.

"There's the defendant," Kendall said, pointing at Jimmy, "right here with us in court as required. Apparently, the witness didn't recognize him."

CHAPTER 3

There was lots of shouting.

I demanded that Kendall and the imposter and the defendant all be held in contempt.

Kendall demanded an immediate dismissal of the charges against his client because the government's witness had failed to identify him as the intruder.

I tried to place the imposter under arrest for obstructing justice.

The judge demanded we all just shut up. Then she glowered at Kendall over her glasses and ordered the jury be removed. "We're in recess for fifteen minutes," she said.

Judge Baxter is a small and ferocious woman. I don't always agree with her decisions, but I like her style of judging. She stays out of things as much as possible, and when she can't stay out, you feel her anger at being dragged in. Unnecessary objections displease her. Foolish advocacy that requires objections displeases her. Lack of punctuality and lack of preparedness displease her. She believes much more strongly in the orderliness of trial law than in the games and antics of trial law. This means she is a prosecutor's judge, not a defense counsel's judge.

When Judge Baxter's predecessor had announced his retirement a few years ago, I was approached about putting my name in for the seat. But I had no interest in being a trial judge (do boys with baseball mitts dream of being the umpire?). No, the U.S. Attorney's Office was much more appealing to me than the trial court bench. I did, however, want to be an appellate judge. I wanted to write lofty decisions that would stand for years or decades. In fact, I'd been nominated to the Circuit Court of Appeals several years earlier, but gridlock between the administration and Congress had left my nomination stalled. Technically, I'm still a nominee, though I don't expect much to come of it. Anyhow, I declined to be considered for the District Court judgeship, and Arial Baxter, a respected partner at a local firm, got the nod.

The judge returned and gaveled us back to order. "Here's what's going to happen," she announced. "I want briefs on my desk first thing Friday morning. The issues I want briefed are these: First, whether any action by either of the parties violates either the law or the procedural rules of this court. Second, whether the defendant's motion for dismissal is warranted. And third, whether this jury is now tainted. Then we'll convene at, let's say, four-thirty on Friday afternoon."

That was July 3. The murder was on July 4.

I spent the morning of the fourth at my office, writing the assigned brief. Henry had planned to write it, since it was technically his case, but I was so angry about the whole thing that I wanted to do it myself. Besides, I didn't quite trust him to get it right. I wanted to pepper it with plenty of outrage, expressed in my best legalese, against Kendall Vance. With any luck, I could get Kendall's scheming ass suspended from practice in the Federal District Court.

I didn't mind being at the office that morning. I like it when I'm the only one there. I worked with my office window cranked open as far as it would go, which was only about two inches. It was a beautiful summer day. Already you could see and hear the city getting into its holiday mood. Hundreds of baskets planted with flowers of red and white and blue hung from lampposts in the downtown section.

As I worked, the sounds of the day slipped into the office through the narrow opening. Traffic sounds seemed happier than usual. Car horns blared not with anger but with jubilation. Kids were busy with firecrackers, and I kept thinking of war correspondents on the evening news, giving their reports via satellite from conflict regions: *pop, pop, pop.* You hear gunfire in the background as the reporter recounts the action: ". . . spokesman for the rebel leaders" . . . *pop pop* . . . "says there can be no negotiations until these conditions are met" . . . *pop pop* . . .

When I got home around two in the afternoon, Barnaby exploded out the door and into my arms. Tina was rummaging in the fridge. "I thought you were going to be back at noon," she said.

"Sorry, babe, I was in the zone."

She handed me a list. "Here's what I need you to pick up."

"At the store? On the Fourth?"

"Hmm. I guess you're right," she said. "I'll serve saltines instead. And I think I have some mayonnaise I can spread on them. Won't that be nice?"

I took Barnaby to the store with me for a quick shop (brats, chicken, watermelon, ice cream). Then home.

In the kitchen I started slathering barbecue sauce on the chicken. Tina came in. "Did you finish your memo?" she asked.

"I've got a draft. It needs polish."

She chuckled. "You've got to admire Kendall. Risky tactic, but creative."

"No, I goddamn don't have to admire him. It corrupts the process and—"

"Oh, lighten up," she said. "Personally, I can't think of a better way to show the jury how flaky eyewitness identifications can be."

I started to answer but thought better of it. Tina had worked in my office as an assistant U.S. attorney for several years before resigning and going into appellate criminal defense. I hadn't thought it would be a problem, having a prosecutor and defense counsel in the same marriage. But as her heart and soul got increasingly wrapped up in her role as an advocate for the "wrongly" accused, the rift in our philosophies widened.

My cell rang. It was Lizzy, my daughter.

"Dad," Lizzy said, "Ethan and I aren't coming to the barbecue."

"You sure?" I said, making no effort to keep the hurt out of my voice. "I bought some vegetarian sausage."

"You're sweet," she said, "but we've got other stuff going on. We'll meet you at the park tonight. Okay?"

"Barnaby will be disappointed," I said, but too late. She was gone.

Ethan was Lizzy's new boyfriend. They met when they were arrested together for criminal trespass at one of the Occupy sites.

A minute later, Flora called. "Hello, Nickie," she said. "I'm afraid Chip and I won't make it this afternoon."

Flora is my ex-wife and Lizzy's mom. Chip is her FBI-agent husband. He and I are buddies, our friendship predating his relationship with Flora. "Kind of last-minute, Flora," I said.

"And I'm so awfully sorry. But we'll see you at the park tonight. We're coming with Lizzy and her friend. Oh, and I think he's such a great guy—Ethan—don't you?"

"Haven't met him yet, Flo."

"Oh, well, tonight, then, Nickie. See you soon."

Tina's sister, Lydia, arrived at about two-thirty. Barnaby rushed into her arms as exuberantly as he had into mine a half hour earlier. She carried Barnaby out into the yard, and the two of them settled into the sandbox, where she buried coins and had him hunt for them. After ten minutes of this, she came back into the kitchen, gave me a kiss on the lips, then held my hand, swinging it in hers while we talked.

"I brought a salad," she said, "except the store was out of organic spinach, so I just used Boston lettuce, which is almost as good, don't you think? And daikon, and endive, all organic, and some dill . . . oh, God, I can't stand that music . . ."

Lydia walked into the living room to turn off the stereo. I'd had an old George Winston CD playing. Lydia is the only person I've ever met who hates having music on in the house. She says it gums up her thinking. She was five years younger than Tina and had always been the black sheep of the family. She had some kind of learning disability, barely made it through high school, dropped out of college, joined a charismatic church of some ill-defined pantheistic belief, and supported herself first as a baker and then as a bookkeeper. Politically, she swung from the ditsy left to the dour right, apparently bringing unbridled verve to whichever camp she was in. She worked for the state legislature briefly in the legislative clerk's office. Now she was working for the state tourism office, producing ebullient pamphlets about the state's natural and historic attractions. Tina and Lydia were very close as children but became alienated during Lydia's tumultuous years. Now they were together again.

After Barnaby was born, Lydia started spending more and more time at our house. She was one of the family. I liked having her around. I liked her energy. It was a nice counterbalance to Tina's sober-minded reserve.

Lydia had a steady boyfriend now, and they'd just become officially engaged. I liked the guy, though I thought he was kind of plain vanilla, while Lydia was surprising and exotic.

As Lydia and I stood in the kitchen talking, we heard the front door open, and a moment later, Henry Tatlock, assistant U.S. attorney, walked into the kitchen. Lydia squealed, put her arms around him, and they had a long soulful kiss.

Yes, Henry and Lydia. He was the love of her life, she said: her hero, her savior, her husband-to-be.

We grilled the chicken and brats and corn and ate outside on the picnic table. There was too much food, so I dropped a big chicken breast onto the ground for our dog, ZZ, who snatched it up like a frog zapping a dragonfly. Barnaby named the dog himself. We'd gotten him, a bouncy Australian cattle dog pup, when Barn was two years old. He wanted to name the dog after his big sister, but in his toddler's pronunciation, "Lizzy" always came out "ZZ," and it stuck.

I went into the kitchen for more beers. On my way back, I stopped in the doorway and just watched the four of them—Tina, Lydia, Barnaby, and Henry. Barn had fallen asleep in his chair. Tina and Lydia were sitting with their backs toward me. They both had long auburn hair in ponytails, and both of them were wearing sundresses. They were slender, dark-shouldered, scrubbed women, and in the curve of their necks and the tapering of waist and erectness of posture and tilt of head as they lifted forks to their mouths, you could see they were intelligent and radiated warmth. And if I hadn't known them but was merely seeing them for the first time—eating and laughing together—I'd have recognized that they were sisters, and I probably would have envisioned getting to know them and perhaps falling in love with one of them. I picked up my phone and snapped a picture.

Across from them, facing me, sat Henry. Lydia first brought Henry over for dinner half a year earlier. I remember thinking how like her it was to not even see the disfigurement but just the man. We liked him right away. Tina and I talked about what a relief it would be if Lydia settled down with this stable and intelligent lawyer who might be able to calm the chaotic waters of her life.

It turned out Henry had just passed the bar exam and was clerking for a state court judge, but he hadn't been able to land a job after his clerkship ended. If Henry and Lydia had been married or engaged when he applied for his job in the U.S. Attorney's Office, I probably couldn't have hired him. Nepotism. And maybe if things had been better between Tina and me, I wouldn't have hired him. It wasn't because I didn't like him or that I thought him unqualified, it was just that I might have been wary of having my brother-in-law working for me. But when Lydia first introduced me to this new guy she was dating, I had already felt some ominous oscillations in the status quo of my marriage (which I attributed to the emotional impact of Tina's lumpectomy). So I was especially eager to please Tina and to do anything I could to make her see me as an indulgent and valuable husband.

At my suggestion, Henry had dropped off his résumé at my office.

I went back out to the picnic table. Henry was laughing, retelling the story of Kendall Vance's switcheroo. He was hamming it up. I handed the beers around and joined in the telling, feeding him lines but keeping him in the spotlight, making it his story.

Henry and Lydia left. Henry said he wanted to read over my draft of the memo for Judge Baxter. Lydia said she had a few errands she needed to do. We would meet at the park later. I carried the sleeping Barnaby to his bed. The longer he slept in the afternoon, the less cranky he'd be during the concert and fireworks.

CHAPTER 4

Rokeby Park lies at the southern end of town paralleling the river. The land was ceded to the city a century ago by one of the big mill families, but it remained undeveloped woodlands until twenty years ago, when a public interest group discovered that a huge chunk of money had been left in trust for the city to develop the park "for the enjoyment of all." The money was long gone. A lawsuit followed, and the resulting consent decree created a system of trails, recreational areas, groomed woodlands, and an outdoor amphitheater.

In my years as a prosecutor, I've read the name Rokeby Park in scores of police reports and investigative summaries. In different epochs of the city's tortured economic history, the park has seen homeless camps, gang wars, meth and heroin shooting galleries, and a thriving economy of drugs and prostitution. It has hosted the predictable continuum of bodies discovered under leaves or in shallow graves, sexual assaults, muggings, abductions, and suicides. How many times have I driven by one of the entrances at night and noticed the vehicle barriers removed, and seen, from deep inside the woods, the evening mist beautifully illuminated by the strobing of blue and red police lights?

But that's just a prosecutor's view of things: Exterminators probably see writhing populations of vermin where others see homes and parks and schools. Maybe prosecutors (and cops) are the same: We see the disease and the rot.

In reality, Rokeby is much more than a breeding site of social pestilence. The park is home to tai chi at noon, to joggers, to Rollerbladers, bird-watchers, picnickers, love-addled couples strolling hand in hand, kindergarten field trips, stargazers, botanizers, dog walkers, Frisbee golfers, and philosophers.

Tina and Barnaby and I spread our blanket on the grass of the amphitheater amid scores of other families. ZZ was on his leash and ecstatically trying to entangle himself with every other dog we saw. The orchestra was tuning up, creating that lovely mishmash of orphaned notes weaving themselves into ephemeral compositions. Firecrackers and cherry bombs went off in the woods, *pop, pop, pop,* and poor ZZ started trembling.

"I don't know if he'll make it through the fireworks," Tina said.

I pulled ZZ onto my lap and cradled him. Barnaby hugged him. "It's okay, ZZ," he said, "I'm here."

Pop. Pop.

We were expecting a big group, but so far it was just the three of us. Henry had called to say he was still working on the memo and he'd meet us after the concert began. I didn't know where Lydia was.

Pop.

ZZ trembled.

Flora called me on my cell. "We're just parking," she said. "We'll be along soon. Tell me how we can find you guys."

"Green plaid blanket," I said, "right near the statue. Is Lizzy with you?"

"Lizzy? No, isn't she there yet? She drove with Ethan. They should be there by now."

I hung up with Flora and called Lizzy.

"Concert's about to begin," I said when she answered.

"Okay. We're actually here already. But it's so crowded in the amphitheater. We're out walking in the woods. We'll head back now, okay?"

We hung up.

Pop. Pop pop.

Now ZZ was panting terribly. The trembling was getting worse, and he had a wild look in his eyes.

"I don't think this is going to work," Tina said.

"I love you, ZZ," Barnaby said.

"I'm going to take him home," Tina said.

"I can do it if you'd rather."

"No. You stay and wait for the others. I'll go."

"But you'll come right back?" I asked.

"Of course, sweetie," Tina said. "I'll just get him settled. It'll be quick."

"I'm going with Mommy," Barnaby said.

"No, you stay here with me, Barn. Mommy will be back soon."

"I'm going with ZZ. I'm going with Mommy," he said.

"Barnaby," I said sternly. But he was gone, running after Tina, grabbing her hand, taking ZZ's leash from her. The three of them—Tina, Barnaby, and the dog—disappeared through the crowd.

I sat by myself on the blanket. It felt odd being alone, a little surreal, as the strands of music played through the low static of all the voices chattering around me, and the screams of children playing at the edge of the woods, and a quick deafening blast of resonance when someone brought the mike too close to a speaker.

My cell rang. It was Lizzy, but when I picked it up, she wasn't there. I tried calling Tina to remind her to leave a light on in the house for ZZ so the poor pup wouldn't be left terrified and alone in the dark, but Tina didn't answer.

Pop pop pop.

I waited, expecting any second to see Lizzy and Ethan approach through the crowd and plunk down on the blanket with me; to see Flora and Chip; to see Lydia.

I mentally did the math of how long it should take Tina and Barn to weave through the crowd to the parking area, drive home, get ZZ settled, and then make it back here to be with me on the blanket . . .

Pop.

Pop.

Pop.

CHAPTER 5

There was screaming.

Then sirens.

And later the nighttime mist was illuminated from within by the strobing of blue and red police lights.

An announcement through the speakers informed us that the concert and fireworks were delayed. A little later, someone announced that the concert was about to begin. And there were rumors that seemed to spread across the crowd by invisible vectors. *A shooting. A killing.*

All around me, families like mine sat on blankets with their loved ones. Children were wrapped fiercely in the arms of parents. Lovers had their four hands knotted tightly together. People were up and walking toward the woods, toward the blues and reds flashing through the trees. A cop took the mike and shushed the orchestra and announced that the area of "the incident" was off-limits; everything except the amphitheater was off-limits, and as soon as police had facilities in place for recording our names and identification, we'd be allowed to leave the park through designated exits. Until then, we would please all go back to wherever we'd been sitting.

I'd never gotten up. I'd been clinging to my blanket on the grass, feeling it was the only place in the universe; that if there was any hope of my loved ones finding me in the chaos, I had to stay put. We had only this patch of ground.

The orchestra had started playing again. There was a vocalist.

> *. . . stand beside her, and guide her,*
> *Through the night with a light from above.*

Around me, families and couples huddled. I couldn't spot anyone else sitting alone. Just me sitting by myself while everybody I cared about was adrift in the night.

But if I was the only one whose whole family was at large, I was also about the only one who could walk right past the sentries and step over the yellow tape to part the crowd of responders, wading into the nucleus of medics and detectives and forensic technicians. I could go demand to know what had happened.

I had my badge out and with it I scythed my way into the chaos.

"I will comport myself with dignity," I whispered—as if the formality of those words could somehow create the stoicism I might need.

I had to go farther into the woods than I expected. I followed the paved path. It was lighted here and there with streetlamps, but they were few and dim enough not to overwhelm the feeling of woods and nighttime. The path wound through the trees. It led through a tunnel where another path crossed overhead. Whenever I was approached by a cop, I fended him off with my badge: "DOJ," I said, or "U.S. Attorney's Office."

There were police vehicles and unmarked cars and an ambulance. I recognized many of the enforcement personnel, but I beelined toward my target. The body was just beyond another culvert tunnel, maybe twenty yards from the trail, suggesting that the perp had muscled the victim off into the woods.

A foil blanket covered what needed covering.

When I stepped from the trail, I was again stopped by a uniformed cop. My badge failed to work its magic.

"I'm sorry, sir," the guy said, "just the evidence response team beyond here."

"But I'm—"

A strong hand encircled my arm, and a voice beside me said, "It's okay, Officer, I'll escort Mr. Davis."

This was a guy I knew. Captain Dorsey of the state troopers. He walked me forward and we stopped. Whatever the blanket covered, it was too big to be a four-year-old boy.

"Do you know who it is?" I asked.

"Adult female," Dorsey said.

One of the technicians looked up, saw Dorsey, and raised an eyebrow questioningly. Dorsey nodded, and the guy pulled the blanket back from the victim's head. She lay turned away from us and facedown in the dirt.

My first thought was Lizzy, but her hair was the wrong color. Lizzy is a honey blonde. The victim's hair was auburn.

Comport myself with dignity.

The color and texture of her hair, the shape of her head, the way she lay—it was all so familiar.

In a roar of unreality, I watched the crime scene tech squat down and, with gloved hands, gently cradle her head and lift her face from the dirt. The woods breathed with electric pulses of blue light.

"Tina," I said aloud, and the sound was odd to me and I wondered for a moment if I'd misremembered my wife's name. "Tina." But now the technician turned her head and set it back down on the dirt facing us, and my first thought was that people must look younger in death than when they're alive.

And I realized she was younger because it wasn't Tina. It was Lydia.

CHAPTER 6

That night exists in strobing pulses of blue and red. In my memory, I see stop-action tableaux. Crime scene techs placing things in plastic bags, a detective pointing out something about the geography of the crime, EMTs sliding a gurney into the ambulance.

And sound: After the ambulance moved slowly down the bike path toward the amphitheater, its siren burped once, not because it was in any hurry but to clear a path through the gawkers.

Everyone was waiting for me at the blanket in the amphitheater. The crowd swirled toward the gates. Some of the disgruntled concert-goers tried to step over the shin-high chain separating the amphitheater from the access road, but the uniformed officers were all over it.

My family: Did I tell them, or did they simply guess because they saw my face and saw Dorsey at my side with one hand gently on my bicep? It was a shock and a profound sadness for all of us, but for Tina and Henry, it was a horror beyond measure. And while I wrapped Tina into my arms, I noticed that it was Lizzy, my selfless daughter, who went immediately to Henry.

"Let's get you folks home," Dorsey says. "We'll get the information we need from you there."

Escorted by cops and leaking the sounds of grief, we skirted the crowd. I imagined that those who were so impatient to leave would catch a glimpse of how unimportant their own impatience was. But no: Some jerk tried to tag along, attaching himself to us. I hoped they'd shoot him, but one of the cops simply steered him away. "I'm sorry, sir, you'll have to—"

And then we were gone.

* * *

In the morning I drove over to police headquarters to speak with Dorsey.

"Nick. Nick," he said in a voice that strived for intimacy. He guided me to his office just as he had guided me the previous night. "You should be home with your family. We'll take care of this."

"What the hell good am I, Captain, if I can't even get my loved ones a little special attention? Thirty years as a prosecutor . . ."

"Believe me, Nick," he said, "this is getting plenty of attention."

"What do you have?"

"We're thinking it was random. Sexual assault and robbery. Her underclothes were . . ." He stopped.

"Go on," I said.

"You sure you want to know this, Nick? Maybe you should just be family on this one. Let us be the cops."

"Tell me," I said. It came out louder than intended. I shouted it, actually. Dorsey isn't the kind of guy you shout at, but he just smiled. When he smiled that way, it wasn't wide and happy, but a sad expression, the tight line of pained lips disappearing into the black of his bear-rug mustache.

Dorsey put a cup of coffee in my hands. "You like anything with that?" he asked, and the way he said it made me feel forgiven. He seemed almost as eager to give me some kind of solace as I was to give it to Tina.

"No, thanks," I said, "I like it black."

He poured himself coffee. "I like a little cream," he said, and he tipped a dollop into his cup. He sat and neither of us said anything. Then he said, "Her jeans were ripped open at the zipper, but that's as far as it went. The perp must have been scared off. Her mouth was bloody, like he punched her or pushed his hand into her mouth to keep her quiet. She was apparently too much trouble for the guy, so he just shot her, took her bag, and fled. We found the bag in a trash can at the far end of the park. Money and credit cards gone. Cell phone, too."

"Just a woman alone at night," I said.

He nodded.

"Do you have anything yet?"

"Leads, you mean? I don't know. It depends on what you call a lead. We're interviewing people. We have the usual suspects, and we're working a shitload of data from everyone we talked to last night. We're bringing a few guys in for questioning. The lab is still working the physical evidence we brought back."

"What guys? What guys are you bringing in for questioning?"

"Just guys, Nick. Ones who hang out in the park, guys known to us. Guys with records. Pervs with a tendency for violence."

"Good. That sounds good," I said. "I was also thinking we could get a couple of undercovers, a man and a woman, maybe, and they could—"

"Nick, stop."

"But I was just thinking—"

"You're not part of this investigation, Nick. It's not federal, and you're too close."

"—we could set up a sting. You know, lure the guy in."

"Listen, Nick, I'm kind of acting as a liaison of sorts because of my friendship with you."

"Who's heading up the investigation? I'd like to—"

"Let us do our jobs, Nick. Okay?" The bear rug twitched, and he ran a hand over his bald head. It was shiny, and I wondered if that was natural or if he used baby oil or something. I wanted in on the investigation, not a real hands-on job but something to keep me on the inside. I didn't want to wait at home trying to keep Tina and Henry from falling apart. I grabbed the arms of my chair. I wanted to surge to my feet and start demanding.

"So, listen," he said after we'd stared at each other a few seconds, "as long as you're here, tell me about"—he consulted his notebook, "Henry Tatlock."

"Henry? They're engaged."

"Did they fight?"

"Lydia and Henry? I thought you said it was random."

"It *looks* random. But we need to cover our bases."

"I don't know, Captain, it's hard to imagine Henry fighting with anybody."

"Does he have a temper?"

"No."

"I mean, life can't have been easy for him, the way he, um, you know, looks. So maybe he has some buried anger, and maybe sometimes it . . ."

"Everybody has some buried anger, Dorsey. I do. Don't you?"

"Nick, we're just trying to cross people off the list. Honest. Henry isn't a . . ."

"I mean, what made you go into police work, Dorsey? Smart guy like you, you could have been, I don't know, a dentist, maybe, making a few hundred thou a year with regular hours and no bullets coming at you."

"Nick . . ."

"Or investment banker. Or surgeon. Or lawyer. But no, you're going out in the night to look at murdered girls in the park. You got issues, Dorsey? You like that shit, do you? You like carrying a piece and looking at dead people in the park? Maybe you have some buried anger, Captain. Let's put your name on the list of suspects."

The bear rug twitched. I saw him recalculate. He was silent a moment, mentally flipping pages in the manual, finding the section on dealing with difficult witnesses.

"I'm sorry for your loss," he finally said.

"Not my loss, Captain. It's my wife's loss. It's Henry Tatlock's loss. I am saddened, but they are undone. They are destroyed."

"I just meant—"

"No," I blurted, "I have seen no signs of demons in Henry Tatlock. Between you and me, Captain, I don't think he'll make it as a trial lawyer for just that reason. Sweetest guy in the world, but he's milquetoast. Kind of a loner, actually, and he lacks the vortex of rage that drives a trial lawyer toward the jugular."

Dorsey considered. "Do you know where he was at the time of the murder?"

"He was at the U.S. Attorney's Office, reading over a memo I wrote for a case we're working on."

"Yes, well." The bear rug twitched again. "I'm sure it will all check out. You understand, Nick, this is part of my job. Okay?"

I shrugged.

"And I know that part of *your* job, as family, is to feel resentment at any suggestion—"

"I'm pissed that you're asking, and I'd be pissed if you weren't. No win for you. But listen to me very carefully: Henry didn't kill Lydia. Okay? And I'm sure you want to ask about Lydia too, so I'll make it easy for you: She had no enemies that I know of, but she was passionate. Emotional. Might have rubbed someone wrong."

"Would you know if she had any jilted lovers?"

"I'd be surprised if she didn't."

"Do you have names?"

"My wife might."

He nodded; he sighed. I saw his eyes move distractedly around the room, looking for the next thing to say. Dorsey knows things about me. He knows I lost a son at nine months old, he knows I was once sweet on a woman who got murdered before I had a chance to get close to her, and he knows I have a foster son in prison for murder. Maybe Dorsey wanted to say something that wasn't from the procedures manual, but he didn't really know how. Maybe he wanted to say it's hard to fathom how sad life can be. Something like that.

Dorsey's desk phone rang. "Dorsey," he said.

Pause.

"When?"

He hung up and stared at me.

"What?" I said.

"We've just apprehended someone who tried to use one of Lydia Trevor's credit cards over at MicroGiant. They're bringing him in for questioning."

"Can I watch?"

Dorsey stiffened. He wanted to say no, but I was head of the criminal division of the U.S. Attorney's Office. He had to let me.

* * *

We watched on a monitor from a separate room. The suspect looked about twenty years old, skinny with a scraggly beard and stringy hair. He sat waiting, showing no apparent fear or concern. Maybe he was on meds. He wore torn jeans with a dirty undershirt.

Two detectives walked into the interrogation room and introduced themselves. One was a large guy, the other a tiny woman. The suspect smiled happily. "Hi," he said.

The male detective spoke first. "Mr. Crane. Can I call you Tom? So, Tom, you were caught using a stolen credit card. You're in a bit of trouble here."

"Not stolen," the suspect said, "it was given to me."

"By who?"

"The Lord."

"Really?"

"I told him I needed computers. So he gave me the credit card."

"Did he hand it to you?"

The question seemed to make Tom Crane sad. "You don't know Him very well, do you? He led me to it."

"How . . ."

"On the sidewalk. I stepped on it."

"Stepped on it?"

"I had just said I need to buy computers. Said it inside my head, I mean, not out loud. Not to someone else. I just said inside my head, I need to buy computers, and right then I step on something, and I look down and there's this credit card."

"What did you do?"

"I thanked Him."

"With the credit card. What did you do with it?"

"I picked it up." Tom Crane laughed. He was pleased with himself. "Praise the Lord."

"Why computers, Tom? What did you need computers for?"

"I need many of them."

"Okay, but why?"

"For the children."

"What children?"

"Rivertown children. To teach them."

"Teach them what?"

"Everything. Everything about computers."

"Why?"

"Isn't it obvious?"

"Not to us."

"To propel them."

"Propel them?"

"On life's path. Toward learning. Toward the Lord."

The detective doing the questioning glanced up at the other and rolled his eyes.

Dorsey looked over at me and shook his head. This wasn't our guy.

The door of the observation room opened, and a cop handed Dorsey a file. Dorsey scanned it. "No criminal record," he said. "And it seems Mr. Crane was at MIT until about a year ago. He didn't graduate, just left."

"Crackers," the cop said.

Dorsey looked at the cop and frowned. "If, by 'crackers,' you mean that Mr. Crane has some mental health challenges, I think it's a reasonable, though offensively phrased, conclusion."

The cop left.

In the interview room, the female detective said, "So, you were going to have workshops or something for the kids?"

"Yes," Tom Crane said. "Something like that."

"And where were you going to do this?"

"I don't know. Outside, I guess, unless the Lord gives me a place. A vacant place."

"But you'd need electricity. And what if it rains?"

"Extension cords," Tom Crane said. "And tarps. But you're right, inside would be much better. Do you know a place?" He looked around as if sizing up the interview room for his computer workshops.

"And Tom, you don't even have a car. What were you going to do with this equipment if you'd gotten it out of the store?"

Tom Crane looked around the room again, but his movements were jerky now. He said, "I um, I um, I um, would have carried them."

The door of the observation room opened, and the same cop handed Dorsey a note. Dorsey read it, then pushed an intercom button and said, "Let's take a break."

In the interrogation room, the male detective put his hand to his ear and said, "Let's take a break."

Dorsey turned to me. "Two more of Lydia Trevor's credit cards have turned up. One at Rivertown Super. A shopper tried to use it for groceries. The other was called in to the eight-hundred number on the card. The caller said he found it on the sidewalk in Rivertown." We walked into the hallway. The interrogators came out.

"Keep working on him," Dorsey said to the detectives. "We'll detain him on credit card fraud while we check this out. Meanwhile, call social services so they can catch Crane when we cut him loose. Poor guy's family is probably worried."

Dorsey and I walked toward the exit. "What do you think?" I asked.

"I think the guy found the credit card on the sidewalk, just like he says. I think the real perp realized it'd be nuts to use the cards, so he tossed them. Or maybe he was messing with us, trying to get us going in different directions. Notice he went all the way across the city to drop them, where it's more likely someone would try to use one."

My phone jingled for a text message. I looked at the screen. It was from Lizzy: "Dad, where are you? We need you home with us."

CHAPTER 7

Judge Baxter recessed the Jimmy Mailing trial for a week, but she didn't disqualify the jury. I took over because Henry wasn't up to it. Apparently, I wasn't, either: I lost. Jimmy Mailing was acquitted of burglarizing the local offices of the Environmental Protection Agency. I hated to lose, but it was a minor loss on the scale of the big political corruption investigation under way.

Six weeks after Lydia's murder, Tina and I invited everyone over to our house for an end-of-summer barbecue. This time nobody canceled. We had reached the stage where we could pretend normalcy—the fake-it-till-you-make-it stage. We could talk about things other than the murder. Tina could laugh again sometimes. Henry was losing his hollow-eyed stare. Flora and Chip had stopped bringing over dinner in foil-covered baking dishes. If a hypothetical stranger stopped in to observe us briefly, he might leave again with no knowledge that anything had happened. But that was on the surface. Beneath the surface, we were in turmoil—one indicator being that Barnaby, who had been potty-trained for well over a year, was back in Pull-Ups.

We made shish kebabs. Tina assigned each of us our own jobs. Ethan and I were in the kitchen cutting up peppers, onions, and zucchini.

"Just between you and me, Nick . . ." Ethan said quietly as he stood studying a cube of zucchini.

"Yes?"

"I don't understand why anybody eats this stuff, do you?"

"Zucchini? That's easy," I said. "We eat it because it's easier to digest than sawdust."

"And tastes no worse than leaf mulch."

"Have you eaten leaf mulch?" I asked.

"No."

"Then don't assume."

Tina came over to see how we were doing. "Lots of zucchini," I said.

"I know," Tina said, "isn't it great?"

"Yum," Ethan said.

Chip maneuvered in beside me at the counter. He had a bowl of boiled shrimp to peel. He snatched a chunk of zucchini from Ethan's cutting board and popped it into his mouth. "Man," he said, "sure love zucchini." I looked at him for an ironic smile, but apparently, he was serious. Ethan looked at me and smirked.

"Ethan," I said, "has it occurred to you that Chip, being married to my former wife, is essentially my husband-in-law?"

Ethan studied the two of us a second and, deadpan, said, "Actually, I think that would make him your step-husband."

I liked this kid. Overlooking (to the extent possible) that he was sleeping with my eighteen-year-old daughter, he seemed to be a good kid. He was a college sophomore who, like Lizzy, had a highly developed sense of social justice. Back in the sixties, the two of them would have been aboard a bus to Birmingham. In the eighties, they'd have been sleeping in an ersatz apartheid shantytown erected on some college green. But in the twenty-tens, it was the fading Occupy movement that had earned them both criminal records. I hadn't decided if they were stupid or noble.

Ethan was a nerdy, hyperintelligent kid who talked too much about his cause, but he laughed a lot and fit in well with us. I didn't expect Liz to end up with him permanently, but it was nice having him with us, giving Liz her own support system, while I focused on being the rock that Tina and Henry needed me to be.

Chip cleared his throat several times and kept glancing at Ethan. "Ethan," he finally said, "could you give us a minute?"

Ethan took his bowl of zucchini outside.

Chip and I had been checking in with each other regularly. The

FBI wasn't involved in investigating Lydia's murder, but as a member of the extended family, Chip was keeping tabs on it. If nothing else, he could make sure that anything Dorsey needed from the Bureau—lab analysis or access to data of some kind—would get hurried through without any red-tape delays.

With Ethan out of earshot, Chip said, "Is there news, Nick? Have you heard anything?"

"Zilch, you?"

Chip shrugged. "I've made inquiries," he said, "but Dorsey is strangely quiet. It's almost like . . ." He stopped and shrugged again.

"It's like what?"

"Like there's something they're not saying."

"Why should Dorsey keep anything from you?" I asked, but I had a pretty good idea of the answer. There was only one reason Captain Dorsey would obfuscate on a direct inquiry from a special agent of the FBI: There was something the troopers didn't want our family to know. And the only thing I could imagine the police wouldn't want us to know was that one of us was being investigated.

An arm reached between Chip and me and placed a bowl of beef cubes on the table. "I . . .um . . . I marinated some beef. At home. Overnight," Henry said.

"Excellent, Henry," I said, turning and laying a hand on his shoulder. Henry had started talking this way since the murder: in disjointed phrases, as if holding all the parts of an idea together in his head was more than his traumatized brain could manage.

"Why don't you carry that meat out to the table," I said. "You can help skewer. Okay?"

"Okay."

Henry went into the backyard where Tina and Flora were sliding stuff onto bamboo skewers. The backyard was narrow, compressed between two six-foot wooden fences. It is not a nice place to linger and enjoy the outdoors: too cramped.

Tina and I lived in a renovated row house. The neighborhood was once workers' housing for a textile mill, but now it's all upscale. Granite countertops, custom hardwood cabinets, Viking appliances.

Our home is on three floors, eaves to eaves, with identical ones on either side. The tiny backyard is about thirty feet deep.

Henry and I barbecued the mound of kebabs, then brought them into the living room to eat because it was starting to drizzle, and the kitchen table is always cluttered, and we don't have a real dining room.

I banished ZZ to the kitchen because he was begging and getting his nose into everybody's plate. Lizzy's dog, Bill-the-Dog, wobbly and arthritic, watched from her bed, thumping her tail from time to time in case any of us felt inclined to free up a piece of meat.

"What I read," Chip announced, apropos of nothing anybody had said, "is that acupuncture is great for stress. I might give it a try myself." What Chip actually meant but wasn't saying, was that he'd heard it can be good for treating depression. He glanced at Henry.

Flora said, "Yes, sweetie, that's true. Maybe we could all get a group rate someplace." This got a few chuckles. "In fact, I'm thinking of getting trained. Adding acupuncture to my practice," Flora said. Flora's "practice" was in counseling: relationship and personal issues.

"Fabulous idea," Chip said.

Flora beamed at Chip. The two of them sat there holding hands like teenagers.

We were silent for a while. Chip's comment about treating stress had brushed against the reality that things were not okay in this family. Now we were caught between talking about it and not talking about it. I decided to steer us away. "Liz," I said, "how's the running going?"

She shrugged. Liz was a dedicated runner, not a star, but passionate. She didn't answer my question and avoided my eyes.

"What's the matter?" I asked.

I saw her eyes fill. Ethan put an arm around her. "She's scared," he said.

"Scared?"

"To go out on her own."

"Even at your mom's?" I asked. Flora lived outside of town in the rural suburb of Turner, where crime statistics are so low as to be barely measurable.

Lizzy shrugged.

"Yes," Ethan said, "there, too. I run with her sometimes, but I can't keep up, can I, Liz? Sometimes we go to the track at the high school and I sit on the bank and watch her, but . . ."

"But running the track sucks so bad," Lizzy said. She was tearing up.

"You're scared even during the day?" I asked stupidly.

She shrugged

"Oh, sweetie," I said. "Maybe Ethan could . . ." I stopped to think. Then I continued, but it came out in an overexuberant rush: "Yes, that's it. Ethan could bike when you run. Do you have a bike, Ethan? I have a bike. It's old, but we could fix it up. Right, Flora? It's out at your place, isn't it? We could fix it, and Ethan could ride while Liz runs. How about that, you two?"

Lizzy ignored me. "Hey, Barn," she said.

Barnaby was happily choo-choo-ing around the living room with a pull train. He looked up at Lizzy, who held her arms out to him. He got up and climbed into her lap, and she wrapped him tight in a hug that looked like it might squeeze him in two. Then she put him down on the floor, excused herself, and went upstairs. Ethan followed.

Barnaby climbed up into my lap, and my arms went around him just as Lizzy's had. I put my cheek down on his head. I felt something inside me. It was visceral; the primal drive to protect the young—to hurl oneself between the serpent and the babe; the ability (as it exists in urban legend) to lift the car off the child pinned underneath. And not just children: the clan, the tribe. We had been attacked, violated, slain. My cherished sister-in-law was dead; my beloved wife had not returned from the land of shock and sorrow. My friend and colleague Henry Tatlock was stupefied with grief. And now I saw that my daughter's life has been plundered. The killer had made off with her youth, her joy, and her ability to live at peace inside her world. And all of us, including Special Agent d'Villafranca (Chip) and Assistant

U.S. Attorney Davis (me)—we who ought to form the impenetrable bulwark against violent crime and who should guarantee a quick and vengeful response when one of us was made victim—we sat impotently waiting while Captain Dorsey conducted a witch hunt among our family, letting the real perp off the hook.

Barnaby squirmed away. "Owie," he whined. "You're squeezing too hard." He climbed into Tina's lap.

The party petered out. We weren't talking about Lydia and the hunt for her killer, but we didn't know how to talk about anything else.

CHAPTER 8

I'm going running."

"You don't run," Tina said.

I patted my stomach, where there was a slight convexity above the concavity of my belt line. "It's time," I said.

She was sitting in the kitchen paying bills. "We should just get rid of the landline," she said. "None of us ever uses that phone anymore."

"I use it sometimes," I said. "I mean, not for the phone. Just the fax when I'm working at home."

She held up the phone bill for me to see. "Is it worth forty-seven dollars a month?"

"To work at home? Definitely." I picked up my car keys from the table.

"Why not just run from here?" she asked.

"Too congested," I said. "I'll just go out along the river or over to one of the parks."

"Take ZZ."

I didn't want to take ZZ, but I couldn't think of an excuse not to.

"And plastic bags for poop," she said.

I went over and kissed her on top of the head. "Wish me luck."

"I'm impressed," she said. "Maybe I'll start, too."

"That'd be great."

Lizzy was at her mom's. Barnaby was upstairs in bed. Tina loved this time of night, when she could burrow into her work, a cup of tea or glass of wine at hand. She wouldn't mind being alone.

I drove to Rokeby Park. ZZ was dancing on the front seat, excited about getting out and zooming around in the park.

"You've got to stay, Z," I said. He sat and tipped his head at me, incredulous. "Sorry, boy."

I took my Glock service revolver from under the seat and put it in my pocket.

Lights over the paved trail made pools of amber every several hundred yards, but with stretches of darkness between. Tree trunks and leaves beside the path glowed pale, giving the illusion of openness, but not far off the trail, a crosshatch of shadows offered concealment to anything or anyone with the patience and cunning to linger.

I walked through the culvert tunnel, and on the far side, I found the site of Lydia's murder. It had been lit up with floodlights and flashing blues and reds during that terrible night less than two months ago, but now, like vines and saplings reclaiming a jungle clearing, darkness concealed the fact that anything of note had happened here.

I kept walking.

There were a few people out. Several men jogged past. Two female runners approached. I tried to smile at them, making the point that I was a friend, not a foe, but they looked straight ahead.

There was a bench off the trail. I sat there to see who would come along. A solitary woman ran past. This worried me: I watched her disappear up the path into shadow, and I thought of calling after her, of urging her to be wary.

After ten or fifteen minutes, I started walking back toward the car. I passed two guys in hoodies. They smiled. I nodded.

Morning. I left early and stopped at the FBI before work. I got buzzed in and took my Glock down to the basement. The range manager reviewed some things with me about grip and stance, and I proceeded to inflict a few flesh wounds on a paper silhouette. Nothing fatal; it's harder than it looks on TV.

I arrived at my office with the smell of gunpowder in my nose. Walking past the office that had been Tina's, I got the familiar tingle of nostalgia. While she'd worked there, three doors from my own office, the boundaries of propriety between supervisor and subordinate had collapsed into a heap like clothing at the foot of a bed. We had gotten involved, fallen in love, and gotten married. We'd been together five years now, which was approaching a record for me. We haven't had an easy time of it. I sometimes think that if she hadn't gotten pregnant so quickly, the naughty thrill she got from dating her boss would have given way, and she'd have moved on.

Henry had taken over Tina's office after she left. Next to Tina's/Henry's office was my friend Upton Cruthers. I stopped in his doorway to visit for a minute.

"How do, boss?" he said, smiling his bony-faced, jaw-thrusted, stubble-chinned grin. If you stuck a corncob pipe into that grin, I'm sure you'd be able to smell salt air and a deckload of cod.

From behind the door, a voice said, "Nick-Nick-bo-bick."

I stepped inside and saw Cicely, one of Upton's daughters, sitting in the corner at an old student desk that Upton had brought in for her. She would spend a couple of mornings a week with Upton, who kept her busy with word-find puzzles and mazes and some drawing projects until his wife came in around eleven to take her to the occupational therapist.

"Cicely-bidicily," I said.

She laughed. Her face had a smile of sublime joy. "Nickle-Nickle-fartsicle," she said.

"Sis!" Upton snapped, but she just laughed.

Cicely was twenty-two. She had overdosed on crystal meth at seventeen and stopped breathing. EMTs had revived her, but her recovery had plateaued pretty quickly.

"You keep an eye on your dad for me, will you, Sis?" I said.

"Nick-wick."

I walked past my office to the coffeepot. I loved walking through the criminal division in the morning, listening to the noises of smart people deep in their work of protecting society: the clicking of keyboards, quiet conversations, phones chirping, printers rolling out page after page of elegant legal arguments crafted by clever minds.

Coffee in hand, I went into my office and called Dorsey.

"Good morning, Nick," he said. "What can I do for you?" Did I hear reluctance in his voice, or did I just imagine it?

"You can tell me what the hell is going on," I said. "The wellspring of sharing and cooperation seems to have hit a drought, Dorsey. You're concealing something."

"Nick, it's okay. Settle—"

"Don't patronize me, Captain. You said you'd keep me in the loop."

"I said I'd keep you informed. And right now I'm informing you that I can't comment on an ongoing investigation."

"Jesus H!" I yelled. My office door was open, and Janice, my admin assistant, looked in over the top of her reading glasses.

"If you'll be patient—"

"I *was* patient. I've moved clear through impatience to arrive at irate. What aren't you telling us?"

He was silent.

"I'm coming over to trooper HQ, Dorsey, and I won't leave till you tell me a few things."

"Don't, Nick."

"I'm on my way now."

The phone went dead.

I felt powerless. I wasn't really going to go over there. I thought of calling Pleasant Holly, *the* U.S. attorney, and I thought of calling Chip. But neither of them could do anything even if they wanted to.

To calm myself, I reread some files on the political corruption case. Upton and I were scheduled to have a conference with a cooperating witness first thing the next morning.

In the early afternoon, it became clear why Dorsey had been stonewalling. Henry got a call from a Detective Philbin at trooper HQ, asking him to come in for another informal Q and A.

CHAPTER 9

I drove to trooper headquarters with Henry.

Philbin was a jowly guy with sunken, disinterested eyes. He wore a suit jacket that made me think of the tarp you throw over a baby grand when you repaint the living room. He wore a wedding band that was sunk into the flesh of his finger like fence wire through the trunk of a maple.

"If you'll just wait out here, Mr. Davis," Philbin said to me, beckoning Henry back toward the interview rooms.

"I have no intention of waiting out here," I said.

"Pardon?"

"I'm here as . . ." I stopped. I was about to say I was there as his lawyer, but for some reason, I changed my mind. Thank God I changed my mind. I was going off half-cocked, pissed at being stonewalled by Dorsey, helpless in the face of Tina's and Henry's grief, stunned by Lizzy's sudden fearfulness. My reflex was to respond with belligerence, but I checked it. "I'm here as his friend," I said. "And *he* is here voluntarily."

"Whatever," Philbin said. He asked if we wanted coffee, then pointed out soda and candy machines in case we were hungry. He led us into a windowless interview room and left the door open. The female detective stood in the doorway eating a yogurt. She looked like a much younger version of Ruth Bader Ginsburg.

"So, Mr. Tatlock," Philbin said, "you told us earlier you were home at the time of Ms. Trevor's murder, is that right?"

"Yes."

"But Mr. Davis here—lucky you came along, Nick, you can confirm this—Mr. Davis thought you were at your office. True?"

"Well, I started at the office, but I ended up taking the memo home to work on."

"What time was that?"

"Um. Five-thirty, say."

"Any particular reason you went home instead of working at the office?"

Henry shrugged. "Home," he said. "Home is home. You know?"

"Yeah," Philbin said, "I hear that. And where was Ms. Trevor when you got home?"

"I don't know. She wasn't there. We had plans to meet later at the park."

"And I think you told us last time you can't think of anyone who might be able to confirm your whereabouts between five-thirty and when you arrived at the park, about nine. Is that right?"

"Yes. By the time I got to the park, Lydia had already been, um . . ."

"Killed. Yes. How come you worked at home so long? I mean, the concert was starting at eight-thirty; Fourth of July and all, you had plans to meet your friends and family for fireworks and the concert. But you're staying home working till nine? What's that about?"

Henry looked at me for support. "Nick and I had a brief due first thing next morning," he said.

"But what I hear," Philbin said, glancing at me, "Mr. Davis had already written the brief. You were just reading it. So it takes three hours to read? What was it, like *War and Peace*?"

"I was revising," Henry said. "You know, tightening it up."

I gaped at Henry. Any other time I'd have asked him what the hell needed tightening, but I kept quiet.

"Okay," said Philbin. "Time line we got goes like this: You're at Nick's barbecue with your fiancée. Then you and her leave at about four-thirty. You drive home, drop Lydia off, then head over to your office. Brings us to about five o'clock. At the office, you pick up some work and head right on back home and get there about five-thirty, by which time Lydia has left for the park. You stay home working without seeing or talking to anybody. Then about nine, you head over to the park, where you find Lydia's sister and family sitting around wondering what the fuck's going on. That summarize it pretty well?"

"Pretty well."

"Mr. Tatlock," Philbin said, "do you know a guy named Pursley? Aaron Pursley?"

"Yes," Henry said. He sounded wary.

Philbin put a phone bill in front of Henry. Half a dozen calls to the same number were highlighted in yellow. "So, are you guys friends or what?"

"I wouldn't call us friends."

"What, then?"

"Mr. Pursley was doing some work for me," Henry said.

The Ginsburg look-alike who had been leaning against the doorframe came and sat beside Philbin.

"What kind of work?" Philbin said.

"Investigating."

"He's like, what, a private investigator?"

"Yes," Henry said.

I had trouble reading Henry's face because of the scarring. But his body language was obvious. He was squirming. If he'd been wearing a blood pressure cuff, the mercury would have blown out the end of the tube.

"Investigating what?"

"Me. I'm looking for my biological family," Henry said.

This was news to me. I'm not sure I even knew he was adopted.

"Lydia encouraged it," Henry said. "I never really wanted to before."

"Detective Sabin," the Ginsburg woman said, introducing herself. She had a heavy New York accent. "Tell me, Mr. Tatlock, do you know if this Pursley guy is a licensed PI?"

"I didn't think to ask him," Henry said.

"How did you find him? The phone book, maybe?"

"No," Henry said. "I hired someone else who I got from the phone book, but the first guy never found anything, so he gave me Pursley's number. He said Pursley cost a god-awful lot, but he used unconventional techniques, which sometimes had more success."

Detective Sabin put a rap sheet in front of Henry. "Aaron Pursley," she said. "Or at least that's one of his aliases."

I leaned over and looked at the rap sheet with Henry.

"It's a pretty good read," Sabin said. "B and E, extortion, identity fraud, oh, and right here"—she snatched the sheet away, studied it a moment, then slid it back to us with her finger on one particular entry—"possession of and sale of a firearm with the serial number removed."

Henry shook his head. He seemed surprised but maybe not surprised enough. He looked at me. "Nick," he said, "I didn't—"

"You see our concern," Philbin said. "Best-case scenario, you innocently hired a guy you thought was a legitimate investigator to legally obtain some buried information. But I've got to tell you, Mr. Tatlock, I'd think as a federal prosecutor, you'd have had the—what do you call it . . . ?"

"Savvy," Sabin said.

". . . to be suspicious. Check his PI license or something. But that's best-case. Worst-case is that this biological-family stuff is a crock, and you were buying an untraceable gun from Mr. Pursley for the purpose of shooting Ms. Trevor. Or maybe, here's another theory, you were having him arrange for someone else to shoot her for you."

Henry sat paralyzed.

"Or here's a second-to-best-case scenario," Philbin said. "The bio-family stuff is true, but you contracted with someone, knowing he intended to obtain nonpublic information through—what's the word you used, 'unconventional'?—unconventional methods of breaking and entering, records theft, and perhaps violent intimidation."

"I'm no legal expert," Sabin said, "but I think that'd be conspiracy: hiring a guy, knowing he plans to break the law." She looked at me. "Right, counselor?"

This was bad. We needed time to think it through.

"I'm not here as Mr. Tatlock's lawyer," I said, "just as a friend. So I'll merely make the observation that if I were in his position, I'd invoke my right to counsel at this point."

CHAPTER 10

Henry and I drove back to the office. I didn't believe for a second he was up to something nefarious. I could see him being stupidly innocent—hiring a scumbag without bothering to think it through—but not intentionally criminal, and definitely not complicit in any violence.

"And notice there was no talk of motive," I said when we'd ridden too long without speaking. "It's just that you didn't have anybody to vouch for your whereabouts. That's what caught their attention. They poked around, found the Pursley thing. But they'll figure out pretty quick they're fishing a dry hole. And trust me; those two are homicide dicks: As soon as they decide you're clean on the shooting, they'll drop the Pursley bullshit. But we will still need to brief Pleasant."

Pleasant Holly. Our boss. *The* U.S. attorney. Whether it was innocent or not, she needed to know that an assistant U.S. attorney had gotten entangled with a guy like Pursley.

"There goes my career," Henry said.

"It'll work out, Henry. Trust me."

I had worried about Henry imploding after the murder. He never struck me as a conqueror; he seemed vulnerable, even fragile. It was one of the things I liked about him. But he *was* surviving. He was depressed—who wouldn't be?—but he kept coming in to the office and did his job well enough not to get sent home. Maybe I had underestimated him.

Now I was concerned all over again. Because if a guy loses his fiancée and then his career, he might be left wondering who he is and what he's got left to live for.

* * *

Next morning at the Bureau, Upton and I sat in on the questioning of a guy named Calvin Dunbar. He was a former legislator who wanted to turn himself in on corruption and bribery violations. Chip was there, along with a DOJ lawyer from the public integrity section.

Dunbar showed up with his wife and his lawyer. It was perplexing. We were investigating a number of legislators for taking bribes from Subsurface, but Dunbar wasn't one of them. He'd simply called the Bureau one day and confessed.

We talked to Dunbar in the conference room. "I lost my soul," he said.

"Can you be more explicit?" I asked.

His wife held his hand, gazing at him as though he were taking the oath of president.

"I profited from the public trust. I took money for influencing legislation."

"Why are you coming forward?"

"I've been tormented," he said. "I'm not making excuses, but I was in desperate financial straits. They don't pay legislators squat. You know that, right? And the cost of campaigns; and it's a full-time job; more than full-time. And I put so much time into it that my insurance business—that's what I do, I have a brokerage—was in trouble, and I'd let my clients down, and like I say, I lost my way. The money was offered, and I took it. I mean, I'd have voted how I voted regardless; I think I would have, but I let my state down; I let my wife down"—he turned to look at her—"and I let myself down."

"Yes, Mr. Dunbar," Chip said, "but—"

"You have this corruption probe under way," Dunbar said, "and I see all these legislators I served with getting subpoenaed, getting called in, and at first I was terrified, certain I'd be next. It ate me up. I couldn't sleep, could barely eat. Then one day my phone rings and I realized I *wanted* it to be you guys. I wanted to stop being afraid, and I wanted to . . . I don't know, I wanted to confess. I'd become someone I loathed."

Calvin Dunbar wept. Then he tried to collect himself, and he gazed into his wife's clear eyes. "Whatever you do to me," he said, "it will be better than what I'm doing to myself. The night after I called you guys last week, I actually slept for the first time in forever. I mean, I'd actually thought of taking my life. And other things: It wasn't just the money from Subsurface. It's like, when you're a legislator, everybody loves you. You feel powerful. Like the rules don't apply to you. Everybody wants something, and they're willing to pay. Money, sure. But women, too. Young girls, even. I've seen it. I can name names. And I proved myself weak. I mean not the underage ones"—he looked at his wife, his eyes pulpy, his words coming out staccato—"never the underage ones. I've confessed everything to Kelly. She's heard all this. She's forgiven me."

Their hands were knit together. Kelly was small and pretty, young, with wavy blond hair. She wore a red Scandinavian vest over a white shirt, unbuttoned at the neck. On the open market, she'd be gone in a second. I wondered about Tina: If I were this transgressor, would Tina . . . ?

"I'll go to jail," he said. "I almost want to go to jail. I'll name names, tell everything I know. Not that I know much: They were clever, Subsurface was. It was all very subtle, you know? Hard to pin down."

All this came out with intermittent tears. The rest of us waited for him to finish before starting in with questions.

I had no idea whether Tina would stick by me in similar circumstances. Things were out of kilter between the two of us. It had been worse since her lumpectomy and worse yet in the wake of Lydia's death. I knew that, with everything going on, I needed to pay more attention to her and to be more present. I wanted to leave the interview that very moment, to drive to Tina's office and wrap her up in my arms with a promise of enduring love and commitment. *Save that thought,* I told myself.

Calvin's lawyer finally laid a hand on his shoulder. "Enough for now, Cal," he said. He handed around some papers. The top sheet was a bank statement showing a deposit of forty-five hundred dollars. The next two were the same.

"In good faith," the lawyer said, "Mr. Dunbar is offering this confirmation. Three years running, he received forty-five hundred dollars from someone he believes was with Subsurface Resources, Inc. And yes, we do assume that restitution will be part of whatever agreement we make here."

CHAPTER 11

Nothing happened in Lydia's murder case for several weeks. Presumably the troopers were still investigating the Aaron Pursley matter, and I assumed they had brought Pursley himself in for questioning. But if they found anything, they didn't tell us about it. Pleasant Holly returned to town. She'd been in D.C. for a nationwide meeting of U.S. attorneys. Henry and I briefed her.

Lizzy, it turned out, liked my idea about having Ethan bike along with her when she ran. They were living in Turner with Flora, biking and running every day. Ethan was starting back at the university in a couple of weeks. Lizzy was taking a gap year. She'd had big ideas about traveling and volunteering on distant continents, but with a new boyfriend, and now with Lydia's murder, she didn't seem in any hurry to leave.

Tina and Henry were both holding their own.

And me: Several mornings a week, I went to the pistol range for twenty minutes before work; a few evenings a week, I'd take ZZ to Rokeby Park, where I recorded license plate numbers in the parking lot and kept an eye out for suspicious characters. Between times I was immersed in the Subsurface matter. It was an exciting case, a big case. The grand jury was cranking out subpoenas and indictments. They had just subpoenaed Bud Billman, the CEO of Subsurface Resources, Inc.—our main target, the quarry, the trophy that we all wanted stuffed and hanging on the wall. We had also subpoenaed Jimmy Mailing, the Subsurface "fixer" who had been acquitted of burgling the EPA offices.

I often took work home. Tina and I shared an office on the third floor of our house. We each had a desk. Hers looked out the front window. The house is on a hillside, and she could see the sprawling city across the river and the rooftops of the Aponak and, slightly to the west, Rokeby mill buildings. Her desk is always tidy and clear. She keeps on the desk only what she is working on at the moment. My desk is different. I have two, actually, one pushed endwise against the wall and the second at right angles abutting the outside end of the first. It creates a cul-de-sac, a harbor where I have everything close at hand. Tina calls it my cockpit. "Are you planning to be in your cockpit all evening, or are you going running?"

It's nice when we're both working there in the evening. Barnaby is in bed a floor below; ZZ is snoozing on the rug and occasionally thumping his tail as he chases bunnies in his sleep. We like to work with the overhead light off, just our desk lamps creating two commingling spheres. I'll often watch Tina when she's at her desk, her back toward me. Sometimes, in the reflection from her window, she sees me watching her, and several times this unplanned game of peekaboo has ended in the bedroom. But not so much anymore.

I was in our office one evening a week after Henry was questioned about Aaron Pursley. Tina put Barn to bed, then came upstairs with her briefcase.

"I had a habeas petition denied today," she said.

"Which case?"

"Devaney."

"Grounds?"

"Exhaustion. The judge says we still have a remedy in state court."

"Do you?"

"Yes and no. The DA keeps coming up with procedural obstacles, so we tried going to federal."

"What obstacles?"

"Chain of custody, statute of limitations, harmless error, absence of a constitutional error. You name it. It's been going on for years. The guy languishes in prison, and the state won't let us test for DNA."

"So you're not even sure if there is DNA?"

"No, state says it's irrelevant because the guy confessed."

We continued talking in this legal shorthand. Tina works for the

Innocence Project. Actually, she *is* the innocence project here. It's a one-lawyer office, the only one in this part of the country. She's poorly paid and overworked. The Innocence Project takes cases in which justice has been subverted and an innocent person has been convicted. It's hard work, Sisyphean work. She is always pushing a boulder up the hill, always having it roll back down over her. The justice system doesn't treat kindly continued claims of innocence once the jury has ruled and appeals have all been exhausted.

I worry about her. She cares too much. New cases stack up and old ones go on for years and years. "Do you want to come on a field trip?" she said. "I'm going to talk to a witness. It's out near the reservoir."

"When?"

"Whenever you can. No hurry. The interview will be short. Just a drive in the country."

"Sure, babe."

Tina's cell phone rang. She looked at it and squinted. Then she answered, sounding perplexed, and listened for a few seconds before smiling. It was a cautious smile. "Craig," she said, "it's been a few years."

The world is full of people named Craig, but I could tell from the strange combination of familiarity and wariness in her voice that this was her ex-husband. Tina crossed her legs, shifted in her chair, brushed hair from her eyes. "Oh, you heard," she said. "Yes. It's been horrible. And we'd gotten so close again these past couple of years." Her voice cracked. Tears started down her cheeks for the millionth time since the murder. Then she laughed sadly. "I remember that. Lydia always liked you. She used to say, if I ever cut you loose . . ."

Tina laughed again, stood up, and made her way out of the room. "He's fine," I heard her say as she disappeared down the stairs. "Growing like a weed."

I waited in the office for about twenty minutes. When she didn't come back, I changed clothes and went down to the kitchen, where she was still on the phone. "Running," I said to her. She waved but didn't look up. I took ZZ and left for the park.

* * *

Saturday morning. I made pancakes in various shapes. I made a dog for Barnaby, but it looked like a pig. He started eating the head. Tina was still upstairs. I tried pouring batter in the shape of a heart for when she came down.

"Make a giraffe," Barn said. His plate was empty already, and ZZ was licking something up off the floor.

"One giraffe coming up." I did my best, but it looked more like an octopus.

"My guys," Tina said. She came into the kitchen and kissed Barnaby on the head.

"Sit," I told her. I poured her coffee and put the not-very-heart-shaped pancake on a plate in front of her.

A phone rang. It wasn't a cell phone. It sounded odd. Nobody used the landline anymore. The phone itself had been pushed back out of the way, hidden behind accumulated kitchen clutter. There were wine bottles and soda bottles around it, waiting to be recycled, and newspapers, and an old toy of Barnaby's: a red plastic train that announced in a muffled tone, "Choose a number or a color," every time someone bumped it.

I pushed things aside and answered the phone.

"This is Sun Goddess vacations with an exciting—" said a recorded voice.

I hung up, but I noticed the LED on the phone base was flashing. "New messages," I said. "I wonder how long they've been here."

"Good pancakes," Tina said.

"Message received August ten, one-fifty-two P.M.," the digital voice said. Then the message: "This is Sun Goddess vacations—"

Delete.

"Message received July seventeen, four-thirteen P.M.," "Are you satisfied with your long-distance telephone plan—"

Delete.

"Message received July four, eight-oh-seven P.M." And then the message:

"Tina! Oh my God, Tina," the recording said. It took a moment for me to recognize the voice, not only because it was the last voice I expected to hear but also because it was unnatural, choked with terror or horror or grief. "I need to tell you," Lydia said. "I can't even . . . I don't . . . The park. I'm coming to the park."

And that was all.

CHAPTER 12

Detectives Sabin and Philbin came over and listened to the message. They let us convince them that the landline had become extraneous, that the answering machine was hidden behind recyclables, and that we'd never seen the flashing message indicator. I served them coffee.

"Why would Lydia have dialed that number, though?" Tina said. "She knows we never use it." Tina looked terrible: tear-streaked again, pale, haunted.

"In moments of panic," Detective Sabin said, "the mind plays tricks. It's probably just the old number that came to mind first."

"Or else she dialed from her contact list—had both numbers entered there—touched the wrong one. It happens," Philbin said. He helped himself to more coffee from the vacuum pot on the table.

Lizzy walked into the house. She looked at me and then Tina. Barnaby was sitting in Tina's lap. For a while after we found the message, Barn had tried to mop Tina's face with tissues, but now he was just burrowing into her, deeper and deeper.

"Quickest I could get here," Lizzy said. "I was still asleep when you called." She gently took Barn from Tina. "We'll go to the playground." And they were gone.

Sabin said, "At this point, I'd say we can dispense with any idea that the crime was random."

I said, "I wonder why she didn't call nine-one-one."

Philbin played the message again: "Tina! Oh my God, Tina. I need to tell you. I can't even . . . I don't . . . The park. I'm coming to the park."

"Hear that?" Sabin said. "It doesn't sound like she was in immediate danger. Just like she'd discovered something."

"Something way bad," Philbin said.

"Something repugnant," I said.

"Something unbelievable," Sabin said.

I reached for Tina's hand. She let me take it, but her fingers didn't wrap around mine.

"You two got any ideas what it could have been?" Sabin asked.

We didn't.

Philbin said, "Maybe she, you know, maybe she finds out her fiancé is doing something on the side. What do you think? Do you think that could be it?"

"No," I said. "I don't think Henry was doing anything on the side, and—"

Tina jumped in: "—and that's not how she'd react anyhow. Lydia was strong. Ballsy. If she'd caught Henry stepping out, she'd be right in his face about it. Pissed, not traumatized."

"Other ideas?" Sabin said.

No one said anything.

The detectives wanted to talk to Henry. They took the answering machine with them. Tina and I followed in our car.

Henry and Lydia's house was a ranch with a tidy yard. They had bought it a few months before the murder. Sabin played the recording for Henry. It shook him just as it had Tina and me. He groped his way to a chair like a man who'd been socked in the gut. "What does it mean?" he asked.

"We were hoping you could tell us," Philbin said.

"No. I have no idea."

"Mr. Tatlock, we'd like permission to search your house."

"My house?"

"Maybe get a hint what Lydia discovered. Figure out who she was."

"Yes. Sure. Of course," Henry said.

"You realize, Henry—" Tina said, but I grabbed her arm and squeezed. She stopped.

"What?" Henry said.

"Nothing."

Tina was thinking like a defense lawyer. Even though Henry knew the law, and even though Tina had no interest in protecting him if he was up to no good, she'd been about to remind him that even though Sabin and Philbin were ostensibly looking for anything that could shed light on Lydia's panicky phone call, whatever they found would be admissible against Henry: Permission to search is permission to search. I was thinking like a prosecutor. I wanted to see what the detectives would find. This was working out great for the detectives, because there was no way they had probable cause to search for evidence against Henry. All they had against him was some vague suspicion triggered by the knowledge that he'd exchanged phone calls with a scumbag. But with this new discovery, the detectives were getting a freebie.

Tina sat with Henry in the kitchen while Philbin searched. Sabin helped search for a while, and then she sat in the kitchen, too. I followed Philbin around for a few minutes, and it was heartbreaking: the gloved hands of a stranger groping item by item through kitchen drawers and file boxes. In the closets, he patted down dresses; in dresser drawers, he probed the pockets of jeans and shook out sweaters that had been folded and stacked into tidy piles; he unrolled socks and oafishly invaded those little auras of privacy that clung to Lydia's bras and panties. Pocket litter, receipts, small notes, big files, and the miscellaneous accumulation of catchall drawers were collected for inspection. I went into the kitchen to wait with the others while Philbin continued his search. He searched the laundry, the bathroom, the trash cans. It didn't appear that anything of interest turned up.

Before they left, Henry pulled a box out from under the bed. "This is stuff from her office," he said. "They called a couple of weeks ago and asked me to come pick it up. I haven't looked through it."

The detectives carried the boxes of evidence out to the cruiser.

"Who knows," Sabin said. "Nothing jumps out. We might find something on the laptop."

I asked Henry if he was going to be okay or if he wanted to come home with Tina and me and hang out for the day. He said he thought he'd be okay, but maybe he'd come over later. As we drove away, he stood on his front steps, looking as forlorn as a man can look. His arms hung lifelessly at his sides, back hunched a bit. He was wearing one of his bowling shirts, which I always thought made him look dumpy. I had no idea what he'd do once we left, but from the look of him, and from what was going on in his life, it was hard to imagine him doing anything other than going inside and falling apart.

CHAPTER 13

On Monday morning, the office was abuzz with the news that Bud Billman, the CEO of Subsurface who'd been under investigation and subpoena, had died in a plane crash. He was piloting his own small plane to meet his family at some island off the coast. His youngest grandson had been in the plane with him.

I called Upton and Chip. We needed to talk about what this meant for our grand jury investigation. We agreed to meet for lunch at the Rain Tree, a local restaurant that had become my second office.

Upton and I drove together. Chip was already there. The restaurant is in a cavernous room on the ground floor of the Aponak Mills building. Aponak and Rokeby were the two biggest of the textile mills that created this city. They're huge redbrick factories rising straight up from the eastern shore of the Aponak River. Some sections are condemned. The renovated portions are taken over by office space, senior housing, a convention center, shops, and restaurants.

The Rain Tree always smells the same: the aroma of grilled burgers and onions and something else that, when you recognize it, brings back the feel of childhood summers. It is clam broth. Rain Tree's specialty is steamed clams served in the pot and accompanied by dishes of melted butter.

The restaurant was crowded and noisy, as it always is at lunch. They don't take reservations, but whenever there's a line, the owner shamelessly moves cops and veterans to the top of the list. He's a disabled vet who lost his legs in Vietnam.

We got a table and ordered some clams.

"What are they saying about the crash?" Upton asked.

"Too soon to know," Chip said. "The plane went down in the ocean. They'll probably never recover the wreckage. From what I've heard, those V-tail planes are flying coffins."

"Sad," I said. "Why would someone even . . ."

"Bud Billman was that kind of guy," Upton said.

"What kind of guy?"

"Balls to the wall; screw the niceties; don't slow down. Something gets in your way, bowl it over."

"Just like Subsurface," Chip said. "If it needs drilling, drill it. If it needs fracking, frack it."

"Yes, like that," Upton said, though I could see Upton and Chip were coming from different places. Upton was referring (admiringly) to Billman's aggressiveness and free-market exuberance. Chip was referring (disparagingly) to Billman's arrogance and disregard for environmental regs.

I said, "Billman was like, 'If a legislator needs buying, buy him.'"

"Self-made guy."

"Bootstraps."

"Didn't get where he was by following rules."

"I didn't know he was a pilot," I said.

"He was everything," Upton said. "Pilot, wreck diver, kite-boarder, big-game hunter, you name it."

"What do you think," Chip said, "death wish?"

"No," Upton said, "the opposite. He thought mortality didn't apply to him."

"Rules didn't apply to him," I said.

"Or environmental regs," Chip said.

"Anticorruption laws," Upton said.

"Lung cancer," Chip said.

"How's that?"

"He smoked like a chimney."

"Still," I said, "you hate to see it."

"Death of a legend."

"And especially the grandson," I said.

"Especially the grandson."

"Especially."

Bud Billman *was* a legend: A high school dropout, he found work with a drilling operation, poking holes through the tight gas shales underlying our region. He learned the industry and decided he could do it better. He went out on his own, founding Subsurface Resources, Inc. When fuel prices soared, the industry redefined itself around the nucleus of Subsurface's logistical know-how and Billman's political savvy. He was ruddy-faced, gregarious, profane, and apparently could be quite charming, though I never had the pleasure.

"So what do we do without him?" I said. "Our strategy is defunct. We were going to cut deals with the small players to get their testimony against Billman."

"I guess we just—"

"This looks like trouble," a woman said. She approached the table. It was a lawyer named Monica Brill, partner in a local firm. She wore spike heels, lots of mascara, and scarlet glue-ons. She specialized in criminal defense. There was a story about her that had made the rounds, though nobody knew whether it was true. She had been cross-examining a police officer, badgering and taunting him. The prosecutor was a new assistant DA who was in way over his head and kept missing legitimate objections and offering up bad ones. Monica ridiculed the prosecutor for every bad objection, then resumed hammering on the witness, who got so befuddled that his answers to the simplest questions were incomprehensible. His voice trembled, he was red in the face. Finally, the judge interceded. "Ms. Brill," he said, "I think we should take a—" But before the judge could finish, Monica Brill swung to face him and snapped, "Do you want some, too?"

"Exactly what we need," Upton said, grinning at Monica, "a little feminine charm to offset the rough-and-tumble tête-à-tête of our boy's club. Gentlemen, let's find a chair for Monica."

"Love to," she said, "but I'm meeting a client."

"Thanks for the warning," I said. "Should we evacuate now, just in case his vest goes off prematurely?"

She laughed and tugged my earlobe. "You *federales* are all the same," she said. "I defend one small-time terrorist, and now, as far as you're concerned, I'm marked for life."

She left.

"Where were we?" I said.

Where we were was that we were trying to decide what to do with our corruption investigation now that our Moby Dick had come belly-up to the surface all on his own.

The conclusion we arrived at was that there were plenty of other targets, and we should start working our way through. For any of the legislators and lower-echelon officers of Subsurface who wanted to cut deals, we'd take them first come, first served. There wasn't much more to discuss. Our plan boiled down to a simple process: Investigate, subpoena, indict, convict.

As we prepared to leave, my cell rang. I recognized the number: trooper headquarters. "Hello, Dorsey," I said. "What news do you have?"

"Wrong," a woman's voice said. "It's Detective Sabin. Have you got any time to meet this afternoon?"

"I've got right now."

"Where are you? I'll come to you."

I told her. She said to stay put, she'd be there in a few minutes.

Upton and Chip left.

CHAPTER 14

The table was a mess. Clams are like that: dishes of semi-congealed butter, soggy balls of crumpled napkins, broth and butter drippings everywhere, drinking glasses with an inch or two of scummy water.

Sabin showed up within a few minutes. She sat where Chip had been and looked at the table with a crinkled nose. The server came and started piling it all onto a tray. "Anything?" she asked Sabin.

"Just coffee," Sabin said.

"You sure?" I asked. "We could get more clams."

"Allergic."

"Poor you," I said. "One of life's simple pleasures."

Her coffee came. I got a cup as well. We talked about Bud Billman for a few minutes, then she asked how Tina and Barnaby were doing with all the trauma. "We're managing," I said, "but that's not what you're here to talk about, is it?"

She laughed. "No. There was a phone in that box of belongings from Lydia Trevor's office."

"A phone?"

"A burner. Prepaid. Disposable."

"And?"

"Used mostly for texting. Just a few calls. But always the same number. Only one number." She sipped her coffee, then put it down and patted her mouth with a napkin. "Lydia Trevor was having an affair."

"Oh. With whom?" I asked. I was pleased at my nonchalance. *Don't react, just listen.*

"We haven't figured it out yet," Sabin said. "The other party had a disposal, too. No quick way to identify it."

"What *do* you know?"

"He's married. He was cautious, referring to his wife simply as 'the W' in texts. No names. Lydia was more revealing. She texted a lot about Henry and Tina and your family."

"So this mystery lover: I guess he's our main suspect now?"

"Not exactly," Sabin said. She put a sheet on the table. "This is a printout of all the texts. If you read through, it feels like Lydia and this guy had more of a tired old marriage than a passionate fling. Very few sexual references, and the guy sounds genuinely happy for her about getting engaged."

I flipped through the pages, reading a few strings:

555-1225: Glass of wine tonight?
Lydia: Can't. Plans with Henry.
555-1225: Lucky guy.

While I was reading, Sabin chuckled. "That number," she said. "Christmas Day. Twelve-twenty-five. It's my birthday. Ironic for a Jewish girl."

"What are you talking about?"

"The phone number: 555-1225. I'm always seeing that string: twelve-twenty-five. December twenty-fifth. I used to use it for passwords and security codes."

I continued reading.

Lydia: Fun afternoon. Got to pop in my favorite CD!
555-1225: Can't believe I fell asleep.
Lydia: LOL. Passion gone. So sad.
555-1225: Passion is fine. Youth and stamina gone.
Lydia: LOL.

"You're sure it's a man?" I asked.

"Pretty sure," Sabin said.

"Any clues who it could be?"

"Not yet. We're working on it. What we're interested in—"

"What about his wife? She'd have motive."

"Possible," Sabin said. "But look at these texts we pulled out." She handed me another sheet.

Henry would fucking kill me.
Henry went ballistic.
Henry went postal.
If he ever finds out I'll be dead.
Scares me sometimes.
He's got demons like a dog's got fleas.

I handed the sheet back to Sabin. "You'd have to know Lydia," I said. "She was like that. Everything's the biggest, the best, the worst. Everything always leads to cataclysm or to paradise. It's just the way she talked."

"Yeah, well," Sabin said. She sipped her coffee. "You see where we're coming from."

"You're thinking Henry's involvement with that scumbag investigator . . . what's his name?"

"Pursley."

"Pursley. Right. You're thinking Henry had his suspicions, hired Pursley. Pursley did the digging, discovered the affair. Is that right?"

"Ten-four."

"And it looks bad that Henry was even involved with a guy like Pursley. Too cozy with the criminal element?"

"Well, it doesn't look *good*."

"And I'm sure you're thinking that when Pursley confirmed what Henry already suspected, Henry went ballistic. Postal. Whatever. So Lydia fled. She tried to call Tina, but in her panic, she got the number wrong."

"Yes," Sabin said, "that's what I'm thinking. Henry went after her in a jealous rage, caught up with her in the park, shot her, did some quick tinkering with the scene to make it look like robbery and attempted rape, then made his way to the amphitheater and sat patiently waiting with everybody else."

"He'd have to be a pretty cool customer."

"That's the thing, isn't it?" Sabin said. "His face being the way it is, he's a hard guy to read. Am I right?"

"Why are you telling me this?" I asked. "Why this sudden sharing of info?"

"Two reasons," she said. "First is that Captain Dorsey told us to keep you in the loop."

"And second?"

"Well, this one you're not going to like so much," she said, her Brooklyn accent suddenly thicker. "Philbin's out talking to your wife and daughter again, asking how Henry Tatlock seemed that evening when he showed up at the amphitheater."

She was right, I didn't like this. They were really trying to make the case against Henry. From their perspective, it all fit together perfectly.

"You'd have to know Henry," I said.

She expected me to continue, to tell her all about him, and I could see her getting ready to silently debunk whatever I said. She'd listen to me, but she'd be thinking I was like the neighbor saying that the killer next door seemed like such a nice man. A quiet man. Henry *was* a nice man and a quiet man. We were friends, but in a much different way than I was friends with Upton or Chip. With Henry, I felt like the wizened master to his little grasshopper. He had that childish innocence. He was wounded, and whether the psychic wounds came with his burns or arrived separately, I had no idea. I couldn't tell Sabin this, though. I would say, *He has a wound, Sabin. He's fragile.* And she'd start to profile him: *Yes, he has a wound, and whenever it hurts, he reacts in mindless fury.*

It was better for me to keep my mouth shut. A real investigation would vindicate him, so my strategy should be to make sure they investigated broadly, rather than myopically zeroing in on Henry.

"Sad, though, isn't it?" Sabin said.

"You're a master of understatement, Detective."

"Not the murder. Of course that's sad. I mean how screwed up it gets. Even if Henry isn't the perp. You have this couple, giddy in love, but she's got old business with some married guy." Sabin thumps the printout of text messages with a knuckle. "You can tell the guy cared for her—the married one, I mean. It reads like he's an old friend. Maybe they could have been friends, all three of them—all four of them. Henry and her and the other couple. Except for the benefits thing. Sad."

"Listen to you," I said. "The yogi detective. Sounds to me like you might have a sad story of your own."

She shrugged.

"Married?"

"Divorced," she said.

"Amicable or otherwise?"

"Amicable. That was the problem. Not enough passion."

"Got kids?"

"High school. Boy and a girl. Just about ready to fly the coop."

We sipped coffee.

"Henry didn't do it," I said.

"Somebody did it," Sabin said.

CHAPTER 15

Evening: I cleaned up after dinner and went upstairs to work in the office. Tina put Barn to bed and must have fallen asleep reading to him, because she was gone a long time. She came into the office just as I was starting to fade. There was a lot to talk about. I rallied.

"Did you know Lydia was stepping out?" I asked.

"If I'd known, I'd have told you. And I'd have told the police."

"I don't know," I said. "Sisterly secrets."

"But damn her," Tina said. There was fury in her voice. "It's so like her. I thought she'd outgrown that bullshit."

"Do you have any idea who it was?"

Tina shook her head. "I only met the real boyfriends. I wasn't privy to all the illicit ones."

I wanted to wrap Tina in my arms, but she was way too angry for that. I realized something about her relationship with Lydia: Tina was very much the big sister, and she'd spent much of her life watching out for Lydia, who could be irresponsible and immature. So with the death looking more and more like something Lydia had brought about through her own lousy choices, Tina would be left wondering for the rest of her life how she could have steered the rambunctious Lydia in a safer direction.

"It's so goddamn typical of her," Tina said. "Finally getting something good and sabotaging it."

"I know, babe."

"*Intentionally* sabotaging it." She wiped her eyes. "Fuck it all."

"How'd it go with Philbin this morning?"

"He just kept asking if Henry seemed strange when he showed

up at the concert and if there was anything notable in his appearance or behavior. I kept saying no. Philbin was like some loser representing himself in court, trying to get around a hearsay objection by rearranging the words."

"I know how this works," I said. "The detectives have Henry in their sights, and they're gearing up to prosecute. They get blinders."

"And they probably won't follow up on other leads."

"Conclusion-based investigation."

"What can we do?" she said.

"Stand by Henry."

"Of course."

"And try to come up with another theory," I said.

"I've been trying."

Silence. I wanted to jump up and do something. Investigate. Figure it out. Charge into the night and come back with the head of whoever had messed with us. I stood up and turned off my desk lamp.

"Don't go running," Tina said.

"Don't?"

"Stay here with me. Please."

I sat back down and turned on my lamp again. I really wanted to go out.

"Do you think it's possible?" she asked.

"Think what's possible?"

"About Henry." She swiveled around to look at me.

Was it possible? I'd been wondering, too. It wasn't possible for the man I thought of as Henry to kill his fiancée. But what if he had me fooled; what if he had all of us fooled? I liked how Henry was quiet and reserved and thoughtful. It was such a great counterbalance to Lydia's impulsiveness. But had I misread him? I'd assumed his placid surface concealed a philosophical core—still waters run deep, and all that. I assumed his physical scars and the events that had caused them had resulted in a heightened capacity for introspection and compassion.

Could I have been wrong? Could the placid exterior conceal bitterness? Rage? Psychosis? Did he have demons like a dog has fleas? Would the neighbors someday say he seemed like such a normal and pleasant man?

I hated to admit it, but Detective Sabin had planted some doubt.

Now, months later, I sit in my cabin up north, writing this sorry record of events. With the omniscience of hindsight, I'm amazed at how resistant I was to the idea of Henry's guilt. But back then, as revelations accumulated, I was the legendary frog in a pot. The fire had been lit, and the water would boil, but it would happen slowly enough that I wouldn't think to jump.

"Henry guilty?" I said to Tina. "Of course not. Henry is just Henry."

Morning. At work, I jogged up a flight of stairs to Pleasant Holly's office. Pleasant had been appointed U.S. attorney about three years previously, after Harold Schnair, my friend and mentor, retired. Pleasant's background is in civil law, which makes me especially valuable to her, advising her along her journey through the criminal system. We were meeting to talk about Henry's situation—his entanglement with Pursley. I doubted Pleasant even knew about the mystery cell phone and the "enraged lover" theory, so I knew I could talk her back from doing anything impetuous, like placing Henry on administrative leave. I would remind her that we have a right of free association in this country. Presumed innocence. Henry was doing fine at his job, I'd tell her. We could stick with the status quo while quietly collecting facts.

"Nick, c'mon in," Pleasant said. She motioned me to sit, but before my ass even found the seat cushion, she said, "I'm putting Henry Tatlock on administrative leave."

As a trial lawyer, I should have immediately voiced my objection and launched into argument. But I was too surprised. I gaped.

"Have to," she said. "We must avoid not only impropriety but the appearance of impropriety."

I blurted a quick version of my prepared spiel: presumption of innocence, benefit of the doubt, loyalty to colleagues. It came out garbled, and I could see she wasn't listening. "It's done, Nick," she said. "Let it go."

"Easy for you to say," I said. I glared at her. She was surprised by the hostility in my voice. I was surprised by it, too. I'm usually tactful; I usually conceal annoyance behind excess cordiality. But this was too much. Poor Henry, who just lost his fiancée, who had no family of his own, whose effort to keep coming in to the office and producing work during these traumatic months was both inspirational and pathetic. It was pathetic because I knew he had no place else to be and nothing else to do. It infuriated me that Pleasant would so callously send him packing.

Harold Schnair had let me run the criminal division as I saw fit. But Pleasant liked to stick her nose in everyplace, despite knowing a fraction of what Harold did about prosecuting.

I had liked Pleasant a lot when we were equals. But after she ascended to the role of *the* U.S. attorney, I became less of a fan. Harold Schnair had ruled the office by gut and creativity; Pleasant ruled by the book. No creativity.

I should have had her job. Everybody assumed I'd be Harold Schnair's successor, but Harold retired while my ill-fated nomination to the U.S. Circuit Court was pending, so Pleasant Holly, who had been head of civil division for only a few months, got tapped for U.S. Attorney. Now, despite my twenty-plus years as head of the criminal division, I'm her subordinate, and there's not a thing I can do about it.

From Pleasant's office, I went down to the small conference room. Chip and Upton were already there. Calvin Dunbar arrived with his attorney.

Calvin's lawyer and Upton went over the particulars of our agreement with him: Calvin was pleading guilty to three federal counts of bribery and would accept a suspended sentence of four years' prison time and restitution of fifteen thousand dollars. In exchange, he would cooperate fully with our investigation and would be immunized for any crimes incidental to the ones he was confessing to. If he perjured himself during the investigation, though, all deals were off.

The tale he told went something like this: The state legislature was reworking the tax structure for natural gas extraction. The industry argued that any additional taxes would smother production. Every fraction of a percentage point in the tax rate was worth tens of millions in tax revenue. And for every year the legislature failed to enact the legislation, the industry saved hundreds of millions. Everyone knew some bill would pass eventually—the only questions were when and at what rate.

As he described the industry and the politics of the issue, Calvin Dunbar was animated, even enthused. I could see how he'd been a good politician. He was knowledgeable and had a knack for making the complex understandable. The guy was likable. He had a boyish look; he was eager to please. There seemed always to be a smile waiting just behind whatever expression he wore. He had blond hair that was mussy, and he had shown up that day in jeans. I knew his remorse was sincere, and I admired him for coming forward. I always gave the perp's remorse and sincerity a lot of weight whenever I argued sentencing in court.

Calvin noticed me watching him. He looked down, embarrassed. He assumed I was repulsed by him. I wished he'd look up again so I could give an encouraging smile.

"Okay, we've got it," Upton said when Calvin finished with the background info. "Let's talk about your involvement."

Calvin Dunbar told us how he didn't have direct involvement in these matters. As chair of the appropriations committee, he hadn't ever seen the final bill until it hit the floor of the full house.

"Appropriations," Chip said, "which one is that?"

"We give out money for particular projects," Calvin said. "It's the opposite side of the coin from Revenue, which is where the gas tax bill was being worked up. So the only impact I had was my vote on the floor." He cleared his throat. Paused and then cleared it again. His confident manner was faltering. We were getting closer to his actual crimes.

"I was a centrist," he said. "I hadn't voiced my position on the gas tax. So you see . . ." He choked up for a moment. "You see, my vote was pivotal. They wanted to make sure I was . . ." He stopped. His eyes filled, and he shook his head. "Stupid, stupid, stupid," he whispered.

This all made sense. Subsurface was just tossing a few thousand dollars to a few state reps who hadn't declared their position. They were paying for some insurance.

"Who else got payoffs?" Upton asked.

Calvin listed half a dozen other legislators.

"How was it arranged?" Chip said.

"Subtly," Calvin said. "Maybe an envelope *accidentally* dropped on the floor, wink wink, during a private meeting in the legislator's office. And sometimes not even money. Sometimes they'd send a Subsurface work crew over to build you that new deck on the back of your house, or they'd install that new kitchen, and then they'd kind of forget to bill you."

"Specifics," Upton said. "Did Billman himself do any of these payoffs?"

"Sometimes," Calvin said, "but other guys, too."

"Names?"

"Jimmy Mailing, for one. He was the main fixer."

Mailing. Of course. That was the guy who got caught burglarizing the EPA office, trying to get proprietary information on the productivity of various gas wells. I made eye contact with Chip. We could subpoena Mailing, maybe get a second crack at him.

The questioning went on and on. Upton had prepared well. And just as Calvin Dunbar had promised, he had plenty of names to name and facts to recount.

When we were done for the afternoon and everyone stood to leave, I shook Calvin Dunbar's hand. He seemed surprised and grateful for this.

CHAPTER 16

It was late September. Things were settling down. Not that anything had been resolved, but the relentless series of events seemed to have ended. First there had been the murder, then the discovery of Henry's involvement with Pursley, then Lydia's panicky phone message. Then Lydia's affair. It all told a story, but Sabin and Philbin read the story one way, while Tina and I read it another.

Everything was in wait-and-see status. On Saturday morning, Tina and Barn and I went on that field trip Tina had talked about. The guy she wanted to interview lived near the reservoir seventy miles west of the city. We brought ZZ, of course. It was a gorgeous day, with the first bite of fall detectable in the September air. Tina seemed in good spirits, which put me in good spirits. In the car, we sang "Itsy-Bitsy Spider" and "Baby Beluga" and "All the Pretty Horses." Barnaby kept adding "Happy Birthday" to the mix, so we went with it, even though it wasn't anybody's birthday.

The guy Tina wanted to talk with had found a body eight years earlier—actually, he said his dog had found it—in a shallow grave partially excavated by animals.

I remembered the case. I hadn't been able to finish reading the news reports. It was too close to home: an eight-year-old boy had gone missing from Orchard City, a couple of hundred miles away. For most of a year they never found anything. Then, here at the reservoir, a local guy was out in the woods with his yellow Lab. He reported that the dog had found something of interest, so the man had walked over to see what it was.

Lizzy was ten or eleven years old. My foster son, Kenny, was in his early twenties, and my son, Toby, who had died, was forever just nine months old. I hated reading about crimes against children. I was okay with the legal and procedural details, but I avoided reading the narratives of what had actually taken place. As for this particular case, I was just here to hang with Tina. I didn't want to be too involved.

Tina wanted to see where the body had been found, and to ask the man if he remembered whether there had been any clothing or other evidence.

"Why don't you petition for production of evidence?" I said. "Why travel all the way out here?"

"Because I'd rather state the facts right in the petition. It's better if I can assert that there *was* testable evidence, and demand that they produce it, rather than asking if such evidence existed."

"In other words, you don't trust the state?"

"Would you?"

"I'm a prosecutor," I said.

"I know," she said. "Too much of one sometimes."

The Drowntown Café, out near the reservoir, is indistinguishable from thousands of other rural eateries. Eggs, burgers, short stack, long stack. The place is decorated with old photos of the towns that existed in the valley before it was dammed for the reservoir back in the early 1900s.

"Are you Arthur?" Tina said to a man alone in a booth with a cup of coffee in front of him.

He stood, shook Tina's hand, then mine. He seemed shy during introductions, the kind of guy who isn't sure whether he should be meeting your eyes or looking into the air to the side of your face.

"And this is Barnaby," I said. "Barn, can you shake hands with Mr. Cunningham?"

Barn confidently shook the man's hand, getting a bit goofy about it, shaking too hard. The guy laughed and loosened up a bit.

"So, what's this all about?" Cunningham said. "Are you writing a book or something? It was a long time ago now."

"Something like that," Tina said. "Doing some research."

"I try not to think about it anymore," Cunningham said. "It was pretty disturbing."

"Barn," I said, "let's you and me go look at the reservoir while Mommy has a meeting." I took him outside; we didn't need him exposed to talk about decomposed corpses. Tina and Arthur Cunningham didn't talk long. They were out within fifteen minutes. We got into our car and followed Cunningham to the site where he'd found the body.

"Do you really need to see the place?" I asked Tina.

"No," she said. "But I'd rather this guy thinks I'm a reporter or something. I've been vague with him. If he knows I'm a lawyer, he might call the state prosecutor and say that a defense attorney has been poking around. They might be tempted to hide something. Nobody wants to have their screwups uncovered."

"I think your job is making you paranoid," I said. "How was the conversation? Did you learn anything?"

She glanced over the seat back at Barnaby. "Later," she said.

Cunningham led us down old logging roads through the woods to an open area that had once been a hay field but was being taken over by weeds and willow saplings. At the edges of the clearing were alders that already had a few tinges of autumn yellow. I could see a stone wall through the trees. ZZ and the guy's yellow Lab jumped out and started sniffing each other's butts and running in growly circles. The Lab brushed against Barnaby, knocking him down, but Barn bounced back up laughing. I put him on my shoulders and started trotting after the dogs so Tina could talk to Cunningham.

Again, they didn't talk long. Tina called me back to the car. We thanked the guy and drove away.

"Cunningham told me about a paddleboat and canoe rental ten miles up the shore," Tina said.

"Barn, you want to go try a paddleboat?"

"Yeah yeah yeah."

So we drove up the shore to a place with a yard full of boats. "Just in time," a woman said, "we close for the season tomorrow."

She put us in a blue plastic paddleboat. Barn sat on my lap in his huge life jacket, and we pedaled out toward the other side of the reservoir, which was remote and undeveloped. I'd once been present at a crime scene over there when the troopers dug up the body of a young informant who'd been executed. That was a long time ago, though. Now I thought it would be fun to explore the reservoir sometime in a canoe. Maybe even bring a tent. Tina and I occasionally talked about going canoe camping. I took Tina's hand and held on to it as we pedaled our way across the water to the other side. Then back.

On the way home, we took a detour to the south through Lukus County to visit a crafts shop that Tina had heard about.

Lukus County, along with its county seat, Lukusville, is notorious in our state. Originally located fifty miles to the north, Lukusville was settled by northern European immigrants. They farmed the fertile floodplain of the Slippery River Valley. But then the river was dammed for the reservoir, and all that good farmland became lake bottom. Thousands of residents moved south onto the unfarmable wetlands the state offered them in compensation. Poverty ensued and brought with it all the predictable social problems.

State and federal officials had turned a blind eye for most of the century. Even as recently as twenty years ago, Lukus County led the state in alcohol and drug abuse, domestic assault, high school dropouts, fetal alcohol syndrome, suicide, incest, and STDs. The increasingly resentful, poorly educated, and unhealthy residents of Lukus County were suspicious of any intrusions by police, social workers, public health officials, and anyone else connected to the government. It was our own little piece of Appalachia. I knew lawyers who'd done public interest law in Lukus County back then. They had stories of the region that would curl your toes.

Things were improving, though, and Lukus County was coming into the modern age. Locals used to have to drive almost two hours to the city if they needed a hospital; school kids got bused an hour each way to high school. But now they had a top-notch medical clinic and a modern new high school. There were jobs programs. There was an extension branch of the university.

The new craft shop near the reservoir was one of Lukus County's attempts to create some regional pride. It was a tiny place off the highway. I was sure it couldn't stay open if it weren't subsidized. The crafts were old-world stuff: beaded hangings, ceramic bells, hand-knit mittens and sweaters, painted eggs, glass wind chimes, nesting dolls. Tina picked out some Christmas-tree ornaments.

An elderly woman sat behind the counter knitting with arthritic hands.

"You have some lovely things," Tina said.

"Yes, well, it's a community endeavor," the woman said. "Anybody in Lukus County can sell here."

That explained the variability of quality.

We heard a crash. Tina and I ran back around the corner and found a large stained-glass lampshade ruined on the floor, and Barn standing there, deciding whether to deflect any recriminations with a tsunami of tears. Tina snapped him up into her arms, and I started pushing the wreckage into a pile with my shoe. The woman brought a dustpan, brush, and wastebasket. "There, there," she said to Barn. "These things happen."

"We'll pay for it," Tina and I said in unison.

When everything was cleaned up, the woman went in the back and got a home-baked chocolate chip cookie for Barn.

Barnaby fell asleep on the way home.

"Okay, so tell," I said. "What did you learn from Mr. Cunningham?"

"Quite a bit," Tina said. "I learned that the boy's body was clothed and wrapped in a sheet when the dog found it. Shallow grave. Some animals had disturbed it. Dirt had been dug away, and Cunningham could see perfectly well that it was a body."

"Strange," I said. "Had he—the body—had he been, you know, sexually . . . ?"

"Yes."

"But still the perp clothed him and wrapped him up in a sheet before burying him?"

Tina nodded. "They say it means remorse. The perp felt guilty."

"Who'd they convict?"

"The guy's name is Devaney. Daryl Devaney."

"Yes. I remember that now. What makes you think he's innocent?"

"I don't. I don't have an opinion yet. But the guy's sister has been trying to get our attention for years, so I finally looked at the record."

"What's the evidence against him?"

"He lived in Orchard City, close to where the kid disappeared. Neighbors said they'd seen a red truck casing the neighborhood. Devaney's sister had a truck that fit the description. Daryl didn't have a license, but he used to drive the truck around on their farm. Daryl lived with his sister. And Daryl is odd. He has borderline intelligence and apparently was inappropriate sometimes."

"Inappropriate how?"

"Modesty, grooming, hygiene. So the police questioned him a couple of times but couldn't get anywhere. A year later, when Cunningham's dog found the body, the police immediately took Devaney in for questioning again. This time he confessed."

"So what's the problem?"

"Lots of problems: They questioned him for fifteen hours before he confessed. And his sister claimed that, given his limitations, there was no way he could have driven those two hundred miles from Orchard City up here to Lukus County to bury the body, then gotten home again without her knowing he was gone. And who knows if he even understood that he could stop the questioning and ask for a lawyer."

"Did his trial lawyer try to get the confession thrown out?"

"No. The state offered a deal. If he'd plead guilty, they wouldn't go for the death penalty."

"Ouch. So you're arguing against a confession *and* a guilty plea?"

"Right. That's the thing. The guy is persuadable."

"Was there physical evidence?"

"I don't think so. I have the impression the cops didn't look too hard once they had the kid's remains. When the body turned up, they swooped in, questioned Daryl all night long, got the confession, arrested him, pled him, sentenced him."

"What about corpus delicti?" I asked. Corpus delicti is the legal principle that someone can't be convicted solely on their own confession. The confession needs corroboration of some kind.

"Right," Tina said. "Apparently, Daryl knew details that hadn't been released to the press. Stuff about where and how he was buried."

"Then that resolves it, right? He must be guilty."

"For Christ's sake, Nick, think like a lawyer," Tina said. She was genuinely irritated. "They questioned him for fifteen hours. *Fifteen hours!* And he's cognitively impaired. How easy would it be for the cops to feed him those details, get him all confused about what he knew and what he didn't? So when they finally convince him that he must have done it, he works all this new information into the narrative. Problem solved."

CHAPTER 17

It was evening. I put Barnaby to bed and read him *Henry Hikes to Fitchburg*, his favorite—or maybe it's my favorite. I took ZZ to Rokeby Park for our run, then home and up to the office, where Tina was drafting her petition to have the state turn over all physical evidence it had collected in the Kyle Runion case.

"How's it coming?" I asked.

"Not bad."

"Do you think you'll . . ."

"Please," she said, "I just want to . . ." And she dove back into it.

I took out my file on the Subsurface probe. "Want some ice cream?" I whispered.

Tina shook her head. I went down and got a bowl for myself; back at my desk, trying not to clink my spoon against the bowl too loudly, I ate ice cream and read transcripts of the previous grand jury witnesses.

Morning. I went into the personnel records and pulled Henry Tatlock's file. Anyone applying to work in the U.S. Attorney's Office has to survive a background check. I recalled Henry mentioning some trouble when he was in his teens, but I never knew all the details. There was nothing about it in the official record. I called him at home to ask about it.

"The record was expunged," he said.

"Did you have a lawyer?"

"Yes. Public defender."

"What was his name?"

"It was twenty years ago, Nick. What's this about?"

"I'm going to stick my neck out for you, Henry. I don't want surprises."

"Okay. I guess. What happened was—"

"Wait," I said. "I just want to read the file and transcript, get the unbiased perspective. And I don't want to have to go through the court to have it officially released—I'd hate to draw anybody's attention to it. So just track down your lawyer, see if he or she still has a file, and give your authorization to let me look. Okay?"

"It was a nightmare, Nick. I'd hate to dredge it up again."

"Eyes only. Promise."

I walked into Upton's office. Cicely was at her desk doing a jigsaw puzzle. I looked at the box. It was a picture of kittens. "You like cats, Sis?" I said.

"I'm allergic."

"You like puzzles, though, don't you?"

She didn't answer.

Upton said, "She's a woman of few words today, aren't you, Sis?"

She didn't answer, just kept working.

"She gets engrossed," Upton said.

"Jimmy Mailing," I said to Upton.

"I'm ready for him." Upton took a legal pad from his desk and thumbed through page after page of questions. Jimmy Mailing was scheduled to appear before the grand jury in about twenty minutes. We'd given up trying to convict him of something; now we were hoping he could tell us who arranged the payoffs, who made them, and who received them. Jimmy would be given immunity for his testimony, so he couldn't plead the Fifth. The info Calvin Dunbar had provided was fine as far as it went, but Calvin's knowledge of the facts was narrow. He was just a legislator who'd taken a bribe; he knew little about the larger workings of the scandal. With Bud Billman gone, Jimmy Mailing probably knew more than anyone.

Upton packed his briefcase. "You stay here, Sis," he said. "Mom is going to pick you up in a little while. Okay?"

"Bye, Dad. Bye, Nickel-pickle."

In the elevator, Upton said, "I think she's doing better. Just, you know, bit by bit."

"That's wonderful."

"I mean, you know, nobody expects miracles. Right?"

"She's so sweet," I said. "Have you guys had any luck finding a group home yet?"

He shrugged. "She's such an easy keeper. I hate to."

I couldn't tell whether he didn't want to talk about Cicely or was focused on getting ready for questioning Jimmy Mailing.

Upton's footsteps and mine echoed down the courthouse hallway. It was stark but for several benches along one wall, and I saw there a familiar solitary figure: Kendall Vance, Jimmy Mailing's lawyer. Kendall stood. He smiled pleasantly and said, "Mr. Mailing has been held up."

"For how long?"

"Difficult to say."

"Do you expect him at all?"

"I have no reason to think Mr. Mailing will fail to appear."

Upton said, "You have no idea where Mailing is, do you?"

Kendall ran a hand over his knobby head. "Mr. Mailing has not been in touch this morning. But it's probably just traffic."

"I'm sure that's it," I said. I went into the courtroom, followed by the other two. The eighteen grand jurors sat waiting for something to happen, and they waited another hour until the judge released them for the day. A warrant was issued to pick up Jimmy Mailing and detain him for contempt.

"Golly darn," Upton said on our way back up in the elevator. He fanned the pages of his yellow legal pad—all his questions there in tidy penmanship and arranged by subject. "I was so friggin' prepared."

Tina, Barn, and I went to the lake for the weekend. We had planned to go the weekend following July 4, but there was the murder and everything in its wake, and then Tina and I were struggling to catch up on all the details of work and life that had gotten brushed aside. Now, mid-October, we were finally getting away.

Flora and I had bought the property at the lake when we were first married. We lived in the little cabin there for a few years. Flora was a full-time mom to our son, Toby, and I was the assistant DA, soon to become acting DA, in that small rural county. We moved to the city after Toby died and Flo and I split up. We built a second cabin for Flora, and I kept the original one.

Tina was quiet for most of the drive. Usually, she and I would chatter through the two hour trip, but not this time. I kept thinking she was asleep, but every time the music ended, she'd pop out the CD and put in a new one.

Barnaby slept the whole way. It was after eleven at night when we arrived. Barn woke up when Tina carried him into the cabin. I unloaded the car while Tina snuggled Barnaby in the bed until he fell back asleep. I fed ZZ, then he and I walked out for a quick look at the lake in moonlight, then back inside and into bed. I'd hoped to lure Tina over for some snuggling of our own, but she was apparently asleep, too. ZZ jumped onto the bed, turned some circles on the quilt, and curled up beside me for the night.

In the morning I made a fire in the woodstove. Tina made coffee while Barn and I went outside. He was on my shoulders, ordering me this way and that way. We walked out on the dock and peered into the water to see if we could spot any trout. The air was cold and smelled like fall, that combination of sodden leaves and wood smoke. It was the time in autumn—that psychological moment— when the lake goes from looking cool and inviting to seeming cold and thick and concealing.

Tina called us for breakfast. Barn zoomed inside, legs and arms pumping.

Lizzy and Ethan arrived in early afternoon. Henry showed up a bit later. They all put their overnight stuff in Flora's cabin. Hers had two bedrooms separate from the main room, while mine was one common space.

Ethan, Henry, and I went to pick up supplies in town. It's a small town where a dingy consignment shop occupies the plate-glass storefront that Woolworth's vacated several decades ago. The grocery store has changed owners and names half a dozen times. But the hardware and "dry goods" store has been a constant. The rural hub—the bigger town where you go if you need anything more than bare essentials—is forty miles to the south.

Henry and Ethan went to get beer and a few extra groceries while I went to the hardware store; some of the boards in our dock needed replacing. I collected what I needed and waited at the checkout behind a sixtyish woman with a cart full of painting supplies. She didn't look rural. Her clothes were stylish, her hair and makeup neither wholly ignored nor overly exuberant. She surveyed the store and her fellow shoppers with the inquisitive eye of a tourist.

"Are you a visitor?" I asked.

"Yes and no," she said. "Born here, but I moved away years ago. My husband and I just bought a summer place over on Tamarack Lake."

I knew Tamarack Lake. Pricy homes. Some developer had bought up lakeshore, put in a road lined with faux-colonial gas lamps, and built a handful of vacation homes. There were rumors of a golf course coming soon.

"Nick Davis," I said, offering my hand.

She shook but didn't let go of my hand. She peered at me over her half-frames, puzzling about something. She seemed to have gotten stuck in a cerebral cul-de-sac.

"And you are . . . ?" I said. I slid my hand out of hers.

"Yes, I see it now," she said. "Older and grayer, like all of us, but I see you. I, I recognize you. You were the lawyer. DA. Prosecutor. Whatever."

"Should I know . . ."

She laughed. It was a confident laugh. "No, you and I didn't have business directly. My business was with your son. I was a nurse. Retired now, but a nurse down at the hospital. Pediatrics."

A tingle traveled my spine.

"Such a beautiful boy," she said. "And so happy. So stoic." She was talking about Toby. He'd had hemophilia. Flora and I would rush him those forty miles to the hospital whenever he started hemorrhaging. "It was my first real job out of nursing school," the woman said. "Probably that's why I remember so well."

Toby had been gone for almost thirty years. I think of him as existing nowhere but in my memory, and in Flora's. But here was someone who actually remembered him. It made him real. I found her hand in mine again—my doing, I think, holding it in both my hands while I tried to figure out how to respond. I wanted to know her. I didn't want to let go.

We made a big dinner. Everyone pitched in. I grilled fish outdoors on the barbecue, but it was too cold to eat out there, so we all sat around the big pine-slab table in the cabin. I sat beside Barnaby's booster chair.

"Dad," Lizzy said, "where are you? You seem, like, far away."

"Sorry. Just thinking."

"About?"

"Family," I said. "How great it is to have us all here." This was true and false. It *was* great to have us all together, but that wasn't why I was quiet. I was still moved by my encounter at the hardware store. It was more of a feeling than a thought. It was the feeling of something having happened. It was the sense of awakening from a good dream that you can't remember but want to get back to; the feeling of being lighter in the literal world, having slipped a foot across the line into another kind of place.

Liz smiled at me. Conversation was going on around us. I don't think anyone else had heard her comment or noticed my spaciness. I would tell her about Toby's nurse when I had a chance: a story for Lizzy and me to share about her brother. I knew she would like that.

"This must be the peak of foliage," Henry said. And just that simple comment made me feel fond of him. I could see he was struggling. He'd spent a couple of weekends here with Lydia in May and June. He must have missed her terribly, but he was making an effort.

Barnaby yelled, "I want to get down," and before I got up, Henry stood and lifted Barn from his booster. Instead of putting Barnaby down on the floor, he said, "Hey, Barnstormer, how about some fresh air? I'll teach you to skip stones on the lake."

Henry walked outside with Barnaby in his arms. I watched them through the cabin window. I knew Henry needed to get away from us for a bit, to calm the mental chaos of being back here without Lydia. That he took Barnaby with him was touching: finding solace in the companionship of a child. He held Barn tentatively, lacking the self-assurance Tina and I had with our son. But that scene—the two of them together as Henry carried him to the lakeshore—elicited something. I was full of magical thoughts about Toby at that moment, my encounter with the nurse having somehow brought Toby back toward the threshold of existence, and the two boys blended in my mind. For an instant it was Toby in Henry's arms, and I got up and went out to join them. I had the thought of throwing my arms around the two of them—the wounded and fragile Henry, and the boy who was both my sons at once—but it was only an impulse.

I walked over as Henry put Barn down by the shore of the lake, and in the cool autumn dusk, the three of us threw stones into black water.

CHAPTER 18

Tina was quiet for most of the drive back to the city. I was blissed out with the feelings of a weekend with family. It was so great having Lizzy and Ethan there, having Henry along as one of us, and then to find Toby so unexpectedly summoned into my heart and mind. I felt happy, and I wondered if Tina and Henry were able to experience happiness yet. Tina didn't seem like herself, but I hoped time would eventually work its magic.

I couldn't tell if she was asleep or not. Her eyes were closed and we didn't talk and she didn't change out CDs, but she was restless, changing positions a lot, trying to get comfortable. At one point I thought she was awake and I said softly, "Great weekend, wasn't it, babe?" but she didn't answer.

We approached the city: exit ramps, lane changes, towering streetlamps above the interchanges lighting up the car.

Tina sat up. "I'm not happy," she said.

"About what, babe?"

She brought her feet up onto the seat, put her arms around her knees, and laid her head on her knees, facing away from me. "Us," she said.

I tried to get more out of her, but she kept her head turned away from me and said, "Another time, Nick. We'll talk. I just don't have the energy right now. I shouldn't have said anything."

I hardly slept. I couldn't think how to approach Tina about her unhappiness. Chip called me at six in the morning to say that Jimmy Mailing was dead. Dorsey had just called him. Police had found

Mailing's car, and a body they presumed to be Mailing's, in a parking area at Rokeby Park.

"Got to go," I told Tina, and I was out the door. I stopped at a drive-through for coffee, and then drove to the park. It wasn't at the amphitheater but at a small gravel lot at the far end of the park. A car had been driven off into the trees, where it was concealed.

My Glock was in the locked glove box. I left it there. I'd have felt silly carrying it with all the *real* cops around.

Yellow tape was already strung; the evidence response team had just arrived. Chip pulled in behind me. Dorsey briefed us: An early-morning runner had called it in. The police ran the plates, which came back registered to Mailing, who was still wanted under a federal contempt warrant for not appearing at the grand jury.

Dorsey and I approached the car, a small SUV. I'm not really used to crime scenes. I attend them only when they relate to an active case I'm involved in or when, as with Lydia, I happen to be in the neighborhood. At this scene, as with Lydia's, I was comforted to find Dorsey at my side.

The body was tipped over sideways across both front seats. There was blood spatter on the windshield and dashboard. I couldn't see the face from where I stood.

"Mr. Mailing is known to you?" Dorsey asked.

I turned away, pretending to clear my throat because I felt that reflexive constriction of throat muscles. I retched quietly, but nothing came up. "Yes, he was known to us," I said. "But are we sure this is really Mailing?"

Dorsey said, "Do you recognize him?"

There was a lot of blood. He was lying on his right side, and I could see the entry wound behind his ear. The guy's face—what I could see of it—looked out of shape, probably from dying on his side like that. His mouth sagged toward the seat, which was black with dried blood. I couldn't really see what he looked like, so I walked around to the passenger side and peered in through the windshield: narrow face, short dark hair. "Pretty sure that's him," I said.

Chip came over and looked.

"We'd better have a sit-down," I said. "Your guys and mine. Assume Mailing was killed because of things he knew."

Chip left. I stayed and watched as the crime scene techs did their work. I couldn't tell whether they found anything significant. They got the body into the coroner's van. Dorsey was alone for a moment, so I said, "What's it look like, Captain?"

He shrugged. "You saw what I saw. Doesn't look like there was a struggle, does it? Probably a prearranged meeting. Killer approached the car to talk, then pulled the gun and killed him."

I called Janice, my assistant, and asked her to set up a meeting with Upton and Chip and anyone else Chip wanted involved. Sooner, the better.

It was still early when I left the crime scene. I drove over to the FBI and took my Glock into the basement, where I dotted the paper target with holes. I was getting better: several shots to the head and heart, a few to the organs and extremities, and only a couple off into the wild blue.

Janice called back and said the joint meeting on Mailing's murder would be held at the FBI in twenty minutes.

I went up to the conference room. Chip was there with his colleague, Special Agent Isler, and their boss, FBI Section Chief Neidemeyer. Upton came and so did Pleasant Holly. Dorsey showed up; though it had gone all federal, the troopers had responded to the murder this morning.

"Let's make this quick," Neidemeyer said.

It was quick. Isler led the discussion. He said that Jimmy Mailing was reputed to be Billman's chief errand boy. "Mailing probably had the most knowledge of who was getting paid to do what."

The Bureau had no physical evidence pointing toward anyone, but based on motive and reputation, they had two suspects in mind. The first was Subsurface's VP for operations, reputed to have fanatical loyalty to Billman. The second was a state senator known to be way too cozy with Subsurface and Bud Billman.

Neidemeyer said, "Shall we ask these guys to come in and chat?"

"They're both under subpoena to the grand jury on the corruption probe," I said. "If they know they're persons of interest in a murder investigation, they might be less forthcoming. Let's hold off."

"Carry on, then," Neidemeyer said. The meeting was over.

In the evening, I read Barn a story and put him to bed, then took ZZ to Rokeby Park. Back in July, I'd only pretended I was going for a run. I had felt compelled to be in the park at night, almost as if I could *undo* something—like, if I was there and prepared and willing, I could rearrange everything that had gone haywire. It was a passing feeling, long gone now, but I kept going to the park anyway; though I was helpless against the last bad thing, maybe I could head off the next one. I felt useless hanging at home while, out in the black beyond, the next in an inevitable sequence of bad things was swirling itself into existence. I pictured these things like the nascent hurricanes you see in satellite photos: an immensity, indiscernible up close but which, if you get far enough back to look down on the whole of everything, you can discern with absolute clarity. So I kept going out into the night with ZZ, and since I was going out anyway, I actually did start running. I'd never been a runner, but now I surprised myself by enjoying it. I would go running and then get home all sweaty, and I'd peel off my clothes and take a quick shower, feeling strong and youthful, feeling that I'd *done* something.

I ran. And on this particular night I picked at the idea of Tina's unhappiness. She was prone to phases. Of course she was unhappy. Her sister had been murdered. I had asked a few times since then if she wanted to talk. She always said no, in a voice implying that her discontentment had just been a momentary thing. I had let myself think things were mostly okay now. Except that I glimpsed it in her from time to time. I decided I should keep signaling my willingness to talk, but if she kept declining, it would do me no good to pester. She would feel beleaguered. No, it was better for me to quietly work on being more attentive, more present, more "wonderful."

When I got home, I took my shower and went up to the office.

Tina was there, inhabiting the glow from her desk lamp, her back toward the door but the window above her desk making a mirror, as it always does at night. She looked at me, and I smiled and went over and kissed her on the head, then I settled into my cockpit. "How you doing, sweetie?" I asked.

She shrugged.

"We never finished talking," I said.

She turned to face me, but I didn't see happiness or annoyance or melancholy in her eyes. She looked perplexed.

I hadn't been surprised the previous night, when she'd said she wasn't happy. I realize now, looking back on it all, that Tina has never been all in. No doubt she could give you a laundry list of reasons for her reticence, but the bottom line is that I have a way of irritating her. True, when life is calm, she's not as susceptible to being irritated, but when times get tough, she seems to find me less and less tolerable.

"You told me you were unhappy," I said. "Maybe we should—"

"I didn't say I was *un*happy. I said I wasn't happy."

"And there's a difference?"

"Huge."

"Well, I'm available to talk anytime you want."

"Maybe another time," she said.

CHAPTER 19

I skipped work and went to pick Lizzy up in Turner. We drove through rural wetlands on our way to intercept the interstate farther to the south. It was early. Mist still lay on the surface of cattail marshes.

This was the first chance Liz and I had had to spend time alone since Lydia's murder. I was on my way to see a lawyer down near the state line a couple of hours away. Lizzy was along for the ride.

"Let's enjoy the morning," Lizzy said. "There's a pullout a few miles up."

I gave her a questioning look.

"Ethan and I drove down here a couple times to hike the Wishbone Trail," she said.

There was so much about this girl that I didn't know. For the past few years she'd been spending more and more time at her mom's house because her school and all her friends were out in Turner, and because Flora's house has more privacy than mine. It might also have been because Flora's husband, Chip, is more laid-back than Tina.

I pulled into the wayside where Lizzy showed me. We parked facing the marsh and sat with the car doors open, drinking coffee from to-go cups and eating carrot muffins she'd baked.

"Good muffins," I said.

"Liar," she said, making a face at her muffin. "Maybe I forgot the sugar."

Lizzy was being humble. She didn't forget anything. More likely she'd gotten the recipe from one of Flora's cookbooks that didn't believe in sugar.

I said, "You know, Liz, if you're not going traveling anytime soon, I might be able to use your help with a few things."

"What kind of things?"

"Research things. Investigation things. I was thinking if—"

"Wait, shush," she said. "Listen." She got out of the car and peered off into the cattails. "Hear it?"

"Hear what?"

"Creak creak drip. Like an old pump."

I listened. I heard it. *Creak creak drip*. "What is it?"

"It's a bittern. A kind of heron."

"How do you . . . ?"

"Ethan likes birds," she said. "Sometimes we get up early and go out looking."

Creak creak drip.

"And speaking of Ethan," I said, "how are things?"

"Okay, I guess," she said. "He really loves me."

"Reciprocated?"

She sighed. "Yes. Sometimes."

"You're still young," I said, and immediately hated myself for coming up with such pablum. "I mean . . ."

"How are things?" Lizzy said.

I didn't answer. She waited. So I said, "It's been a tough few years. And now Tina's really grieving for her sister."

Lizzy nodded.

Creak creak drip.

Renfield is a small city—the kind where you can't figure out why anyone lives there. The surrounding land is wet and shrubby. It is monotonous, lacking the mountains and picturesque lakes of the north country. The economy is depressed; towns are small and seem to run mostly on inertia. Renfield is a paper-mill town, but unlike the defunct textile mills up in the city, the economic engine of Renfield Paper, anemic though it is, still chugs.

I found the office. It was above a bank in a small business complex: HOWLAND AND HOWLAND, ATTORNEYS, it said.

"You go take in the sights," I told Lizzy. "I'll call you when I'm done."

"But if I'm going to be your investigator . . ." Liz said.

"Not on this one," I said.

Jennifer Howland was expecting me. She'd been a new lawyer at the public defender's office when she represented Henry years ago. Now she was a fiftyish small-town general-practice lawyer.

"You'll have to go over to the public defender's offices to see the actual file," she said, "but I reviewed it after Henry Tatlock contacted me. So we can talk first if you like."

She made tea for the two of us. On her desk was a picture of her and her husband and two teenage boys at a high school football game. One of the boys was suited up. There was another picture of just the boys. They each had a river kayak on one shoulder, and they were wet, wearing neoprene spray skirts.

We sat down and made small talk, then the outer door opened and the man from the photo walked in. Jennifer introduced him: "Joel, my husband and law partner." Joel and I shook. He was wearing biking shorts and fingerless gloves and shoes that sounded like tap shoes on the bare floor. He was tall and looked overjoyed to meet me, but I'm sure it was just his endorphin high attaching to anything in its path. Jennifer pushed him affectionately back into the outer office and closed her door.

"Henry Tatlock," she said. "I haven't thought about him in years. I remember hearing he went to law school, but I didn't know if it was true. Poor Henry."

"Why poor Henry?"

"Well, realize I only knew him through this one case. But he was an angry kid, and he seemed like a loner. A target, maybe. His mother was odd, and . . ."

"Odd how?"

"You know that painting with the pitchfork? A farmer and his wife?"

"*American Gothic.*"

"Right. That was her. She was older—maybe around seventy when Henry was in high school. The father died when Henry was young. The mother was well meaning, but I'm sure the kid didn't exactly have a rollicking family life."

Jennifer went on reciting what little background she knew. Then she told me about the case: A girl accused Henry of date rape and of beating her up in the process.

"Did he do it?" I asked.

Jennifer shrugged. "There were three versions of events," she said. "Henry's version, the girl's version, and mine. Take your pick."

"I'll take yours."

A girl named Sherry Butler asked Henry out on a date. She was pretty, but it wasn't always visible under all the makeup. Her home life was a mess. The crowd she hung with was always in trouble. She was sexually precocious and, Jennifer suspected, the victim of sexual abuse in the home. She had been referred to Children's Services twice for unexplained bruises. In high school she acquired a boyfriend with a complicated history of his own.

Henry and Sherry's date had been a dare: Her friends had dared her to go out with the burned kid. "I don't think those girls were really Sherry's friends," Jennifer said. "I think they were the cool crowd that Sherry wanted to be part of. So they were able to get her to do their bidding."

Jennifer said she didn't know whether the dare required Sherry to have sex with Henry or just go out with him. They did have sex; this was proved by the DNA swab Henry was compelled to provide, though the medical exam reported no evidence of forcible rape.

Jennifer stopped and shook her head. "Make no mistake," she said, "Henry was quiet and polite, but he had a temper. He broke down in my office once, sobbing that he hadn't done anything wrong. But right then, in my office, it turned to rage. Scary rage, yelling about all the things he'd do to her if he ever got his hands on her, calling her a lying whore cunt. That sort of thing. No way I'd have put that kid on the stand.

"Anyhow, I don't know whether Sherry got cold feet or whether the plan all along was to set Henry up. Or maybe the girls who'd goaded Sherry into it started teasing her after she'd been with him, so she tried to save face by accusing him. I don't know. I don't know if he really gave her those bruises or if it was her father or boyfriend. Even if it was Henry, I don't know whether it was because she got him all worked up, then tried to back out at the last moment, or maybe because she started ridiculing him at some point."

"What do you *think* happened?" I said.

"It's been twenty years," she said.

I waited.

"I believe my client's story," she said. "I think Henry went on a date with a mean girl, or at least a girl who was more of a target than he was. It was summer, and he got lucky out in some hayfield. He lost his virginity with a girl he didn't like and went home thinking that was the end of it. I believe he thought everything was fine until the police knocked on his door the next evening. As for the girl's bruises, I believe her boyfriend got wind of things and decided to educate her on the consequences of infidelity. I believe Sherry accused Henry of rape and assault to protect her boyfriend, or to try and salvage her reputation with her friends."

Jennifer delivered this testimonial in a monotone. I wasn't sure whether she really believed what she claimed, or if she just wasn't going to say anything against her client's interests.

I sat thinking my way through. What did I believe? I guess I believed Henry's story. But maybe I believed it in a monotone, like Jennifer.

"Nobody wanted to try this case," Jenifer said. "The DA knew that Sherry would be the worst witness in history, and I had no idea what her friends would come up with if I called any of them as hostile witnesses. It would have been a horrible trial, and it certainly would have played to the jurors' worst instincts. So we worked out a deal. The DA dropped the sexual assault charge, and I got Henry to plead to plain old misdemeanor assault. His record would be expunged after his eighteenth birthday if he kept his nose clean. Henry wanted to fight it, but the risk was too great. If he lost, he'd have a felony conviction and would have to register as a sex offender. It was a good deal for him."

When we were done talking about Henry, Jennifer stood and opened her office door. We found Lizzy and Joel talking in the outer office. Joel and Jennifer invited us to have lunch with them at a diner on the main street. I liked these people. We laughed a lot at lunch, and after lunch they said we should come over for dinner to meet their sons. It would have been fun, but I didn't want to be gone so late. We parted, and they promised to get in touch next time they were up in the city.

In the public defender's office, I read through Henry's juvenile file. It had been expunged as far as the court and the state were concerned, but I'd correctly assumed his lawyers would have the physical file. That was why I'd driven down instead of just talking with Jennifer Howland on the phone. However, the file added nothing to what Jennifer had told me.

Lizzy and I headed toward home, but we had one more stop to make. Alder Creek State Penitentiary was not far out of the way.

I refer to Kenny as my foster son, though I was never actually licensed as a foster parent, and Kenny never lived with me. But he'd been in my life since he was ten. I had loved him, advocated for him as he got shunted through the foster system, helped him financially, helped him find a place to live when he aged out of foster care, given him a job, and tried to make him one of the family. Now he was doing twelve to twenty at Alder Creek for involuntary manslaughter.

Lizzy and I were patted down. We surrendered our belts and all the contents of our pockets, then waited for Kenny in an antiseptic room where there were half a dozen round tables and no windows and a guard kept watch from a glassed-in cubicle. In the federal prison up at Ellisville, I was a VIP; in fact, I'd put a lot of those prisoners in there. But down here at Alder Creek, I was nobody special.

I tried to get down here to see Kenny every six months or so. In the past four years, Lizzy had been here twice with me. I didn't know whether she ever came to visit on her own or with Flora.

Kenny was brought in. A guard uncuffed him, releasing his hands from the chain around his waist. He was allowed to give us both a hug. He looked okay.

When he first arrived here four years earlier, I didn't know if he would survive. Within the first few months, he went from looking healthy to looking skeletal. His mischievous eyes had become wary and, later on, vacant. But he seemed better now. He'd gained back the weight and didn't seem on the verge of panic anymore.

"I heard about Tina's sister," Kenny said. "That really sucks."

"How are you doing?" Lizzy asked. She had picked up a game of UNO from another table and was dealing out cards for the three of us.

"I'm fine," Kenny said.

"I don't mean 'How are you?'" she said. "I mean 'How *are* you?'"

"Okay," he said. "I got a new job."

"Still in the cafeteria?"

"No. In the library. How great is that, Nick!" He beamed at me. Kenny had been my gofer at the U.S. Attorney's Office before his arrest. He had spent a lot of time in the law library.

"Pretty great," I said.

"Yup. Pretty great."

"Kenny, have you ever run into a guy named Daryl Devaney?" I asked.

"Dipshit? Yeah, he was here. They moved him, though."

"What's your impression?"

Kenny shrugged. "Just a guy. You know? He got sent to solitary a lot."

"What for?"

"I don't know. Guys teased him a lot, you know? So he'd just react."

"Did you ever stand up for him?" I asked.

"You mean with the guards or with other guys?"

"Guards."

"No."

"How about with other guys?"

Kenny gave me a complicated look. Maybe it meant that you don't stand up for a child killer. Or maybe it meant that Kenny had no capital to spend on anything other than keeping himself alive. I didn't often let myself think about Kenny's life in prison. He's a good-looking young man, and he's never been tough or aggressive, not a leader, so there were things about his reality that I didn't want to know. There were philosophical questions on the appropriateness of punishment that I didn't want to ponder.

We didn't stay very long. Lizzy and I hate going to see him there. I don't even know if Kenny likes our visits. Lizzy cried after we left.

We got back on the road and headed home. I was quiet.

"What are you thinking about?" Lizzy asked.

"I was thinking about Howland and Howland."

"What about them?"

"I guess . . . I don't know. It might be silly."

"Tell me."

"I guess I was wondering what Tina would think about moving up north and opening a practice together and living in the cabin."

CHAPTER 20

Barnaby was asleep when I came in. Tina was in the office working, so I heated a plate of leftovers and sat talking with her while I ate. I told her everything I'd learned about Henry's past.

"So do you still believe in him?" she asked.

"Of course I do," I said. "A shy and lonely and confused kid with all that trauma in his past tangles with a vicious girl. I mean, regardless of whatever *actually* happened . . . You know?"

"I know. And how was Kenny?"

"He's surviving."

"Good," Tina said. "Good. I'm glad."

Tina didn't have the history with Kenny that Flora and Lizzy and I did. She and I had gotten together right around the time Kenny was arrested, so for her, his sins weren't offset by any lingering loyalty.

"Funny thing about loyalty," I said.

"What's funny?"

"We've both seen it in court, haven't we? Parents, girlfriends, siblings. The ones who can't believe that a perp committed the heinous acts he's accused of. The ones with loyalty enough to disbelieve the laws of physics if they need to; to disbelieve that the sun will rise in the east and set in the west."

"Um, yeah, I guess."

"And then the other group. The ones who know the truth but will stick around anyway. They cry when the verdict is read. They'll be there if the perp ever gets out. But they're not fooled."

"Yes," Tina said, "I've seen some of those. They always had more cred when they argued and begged at sentencing. They're harder for a judge to ignore than the deluded ones."

"And then there are the ones who start out loyal, disbelieving all the charges, but wake up one morning and see the perp as nothing but a scumbag."

"Right," Tina said, "the ones who stop coming to court."

"I've even seen them keep coming to the trial, but they switch sides. First they're sitting on the defendant's side, the next day they're sitting with the victim."

I was loyal to both Henry and Kenny. They'd both had a difficult childhood, and they both possessed endearing qualities you couldn't necessarily see on the surface. But they had little else in common, and my loyalty to Kenny was of a different species than my loyalty to Henry. I'd known Kenny since he was a kid. I'd partially raised him and taken care of him, so though he'd done horrendous things, I couldn't wholly cut him loose. I couldn't not love him.

Henry was a different matter. I was loyal to Henry because Lydia had loved him and Tina loved Lydia and I loved Tina. I understood that this chain of devotion affected how I thought of Henry. It made it easy for me to believe that whatever the facts were of the incident in Renfield twenty years earlier, Henry was the victim in a moral sense. I believed on faith that no cruel and vicious man hid under Henry's quiet and wounded surface. But if I were ever to learn something to change what I believed—if I decided that he had wantonly beaten and raped a high school classmate and/or killed Lydia in a jealous rage, my loyalty to him would be snuffed like a match in a monsoon.

My bond to Kenny had survived his bad acts. My friendship with Henry would not.

It was nice sitting and talking this way at night with Tina. We spoke the same language. Our philosophical spheres overlapped.

"So that town of Renfield . . ." I said.

"What about it?"

"It's not so different from up at the lake. Rural, small-town, quiet."

"And?"

I wanted to tell her about my musings—the idea of opening a small private practice together. Leave the city, go back to the north country. Barnaby could grow up in a rural paradise with parents who spent quiet days overseeing real estate transactions and innocuous misdemeanors, maybe even an adoption now and then, because right now Barnaby had two parents up to their eyeballs in murder and rape and the avarice of political corruption. I thought of poor Lizzy, so traumatized by Lydia's murder and possibly by a lifetime of my bringing briefcases full of violence and terror and woe into our home. Bad enough when it was just me, but now, with Tina, I'd doubled down.

No wonder Lizzy had chosen Flora's house of crystals and incense. Flora's house is thick with an aura of peace and spirituality (albeit an ill-defined spirituality of cosmic harmony and organic groceries), while Tina's and my house reeks sometimes with the atmosphere of anguish that lies so thick in courtrooms, and that clings like cigarette smoke, hitchhiking its way through our front door and into what should have been a refuge from a world so eager to rob its children of their youthful innocence.

Those are the thoughts I wanted to share with Tina. But they were too new and unformed: *A private practice up at the lake*, I'd say, and she'd brush it away like a gnat. I needed to think it through first, to decide if I was serious, and then to make a prepared pitch.

"Nothing, never mind," I said. "It was an interesting day. It stirred up a lot of dust."

"I'm sure," Tina said. But she had already turned back to her work.

CHAPTER 21

Morning. Jake Voss, vice president for governmental affairs at Subsurface, was in front of the grand jury. In the weeks since Bud Billman's death, we had been calling him "Moby Junior." Upton was questioning him.

> MR. CRUTHERS: What was Subsurface's position on the legislation?
>
> MR. VOSS: It was bad for the industry.
>
> MR. CRUTHERS: Basically raising taxes on gas production?
>
> MR. VOSS: Yeah.
>
> MR. CRUTHERS: By how much?
>
> MR. VOSS: Half a point.

Jacob Voss didn't want to be here. What we knew of the guy was that he was rabidly antitaxation and antigovernment. He was a hunter, drinker, fisherman, and former Golden Gloves champ. He was a lot like Billman: self-made, not afraid to get his hands dirty. Being called to implicate Subsurface in a grand jury hearing was probably, for him, like being asked to collaborate with the devil. He answered questions as though he had lockjaw.

> MR. CRUTHERS: And how much is half a point worth to Subsurface?
>
> MR. VOSS: Nothing. We're not a gas company.
>
> MR. CRUTHERS: Oh, right. You're not a gas company, you're an industry service company. So how much is it worth to your clients?

    MR.VOSS: Which ones?

The questioning was dreary. It was all about guys like poor Calvin Dunbar—though most of them less likable—who had sold their souls for a few thousand bucks.

The investigation had seemed huge and juicy at first, but with Billman gone, it had lost its intrigue. We could round up a few more legislators and a few more underlings at Subsurface, but except for the part about Jimmy Mailing's murder, it all felt silly.

There was nothing silly about the murder, though. The murder was perplexing because the cash changing hands was so small: a few thousand bucks in exchange for an implied promise to oppose a tax hike that these legislators were likely to oppose anyhow. And jail sentences would be short. So maybe it was about reputation: Someone valued his or her reputation enough to kill the only guy who knew all the dirt.

    MR.CRUTHERS: When was the tax hike first intro-
        duced?
    MR.VOSS: Twenty-eleven.
    MR.CRUTHERS: It didn't pass that year?
    MR.VOSS: No.
    MR.CRUTHERS: How about in twenty-twelve?
    MR.VOSS: It never came up for a vote.
    MR.CRUTHERS: But it passed this year?
    MR.VOSS: Yes.
    MR.CRUTHERS: And the delay of those two years saved
        the gas industry how much?
    MR.VOSS: Like five hundred million, I guess.

Now I was interested again. Billman and Voss had paid chump change to a few legislators even though the tax hike would eventually pass. But by holding it back just one or two years, they had benefited the industry immensely.

CHAPTER 22

In the evening I called Lizzie. "I have your first assignment," I said. "I want you to find out everything you can about that gas tax legislation."

"Everything how?"

"Everything everything. Supporters, opponents, amendments, votes. Whatever. Start with the state's public information service, then go to the law library and have the librarian show you how to do a legislative history. Everything. Call me if you have questions."

Lizzy and I hung up. I went upstairs. Tina was in our office. "Lizzie's going to do some research for me on the corruption case," I said. "Be great for her. Be great for me."

"That's nice."

Tina was deep into her work. The state court had agreed to hold a hearing on her petition for access to all physical evidence in the Kyle Runion case. It was scheduled for the next afternoon. Probably best not to bug her, so I started on my own work and left her alone.

Tina's phone rang. She looked at the number and answered. "Oh, hey." She got up and walked toward the door. "No, that's okay. I hoped you would."

I assumed from her voice that it was Craig again. Her first husband. I'd never met him. He and Tina had met when they were teaching in the same elementary school on the West Coast. What she'd told me was that once she was in law school and looking toward an aggressive career in trial law, Craig no longer seemed enough for her. "He's kind of like a Muppet," she'd said. "Warm and cuddly and full of love, but hard to take real seriously."

* * *

The hearing in the Kyle Runion/Daryl Devaney case was a small thing, just a routine step in the process, but it attracted attention, since it was the first public event of any kind in the case in years.

Daryl Devaney's sister, the person who had pestered Tina and the Innocence Project to take a look at the case, was driving in from her farm outside of Orchard City, several hours away. Tina invited me to join the two of them for lunch. They'd never met in person, and Tina said she wanted my read on the woman. "We're meeting her at Denny's," Tina said.

"Why Denny's?"

"I don't know. I just thought she might be most comfortable there."

"You mean you thought she might be too lowbrow for the Rain Tree?"

"Ouch. That's kind of aggressive, Nick."

"Just saying."

The woman's name was Peggy Devaney. When we got to Denny's, she was seated in a booth, paging through a copy of *Better Homes*. She seemed nervous. "After all these years," she said. "And now, finally, something."

Peggy's eyes were watery. She ducked her head, pulling it down between her shoulders in a submissive gesture. Tina reached across and took her hand. "Peggy, let's not get our hopes up. The obstacles are huge, both legal obstacles and factual obstacles."

"Factual? What do you mean, factual?" Peggy Devaney snapped, her voice suddenly contemptuous, the submissiveness gone.

"No, no, no," Tina said. "I wasn't meaning he might really have done it; I just meant that even if we get access to some evidence, there might not be anything testable."

"Sorry," Peggy Devaney said. She shrank back between her shoulders. This woman was clearly one who would never believe her brother was guilty no matter what the evidence. I worried that Tina and the Innocence Project had been duped. I wanted to see clearheaded objectivity, not emotional volatility.

"Of course. Of course," Tina said. "It's an emotional day. I get that."

Peggy Devaney propped her forehead in her hand and cried for a few seconds, then sat up and wiped her eyes with a napkin. "I'm not really like this," she said.

Tina nodded.

"If you knew . . . I mean . . . I'm three years older than Daryl. And look at me." Peggy Devaney waved her fingers at her body. She was a leather-skinned woman in a Carhartt jacket. She had graying hair in a ponytail. She wasn't fat and wasn't unattractive. She was just solid and strong. "I could knock some heads," she said, "and believe me, I've knocked a few. Daryl always needed watching out for. You grow up the sister of a boy like Daryl, and you get a pretty shitty perspective of other children. They think they're clever. It's a game to them. You know, there's all this talk about bullying now. That's good. Because believe me, what Daryl endured . . . And he was such a pure soul. A beautiful soul. He wouldn't hurt a flea."

Tina reached across and took Peggy's hand again. "We'll do our best."

"I tried to protect him," Peggy said. "But bullies aren't only in the schoolyard. Do you know that? Some of them are in suits and ties. Some of them put innocent boys in jail just because they can. And I couldn't do anything, Tina. I tried, but nobody listened. Not the DA, not even his lawyer."

She cried some more. Tina let her. "How embarrassing," Peggy said. "It's been building up for eight years. I know I shouldn't hope too much."

There was a small crowd outside the courtroom. Tina and Peggy Devaney went into a conference room to talk. I waited in the hallway in the midst of everyone who had come to silently oppose Daryl Devaney—people who probably considered the hearing a further insult to the memory of Kyle Runion. Tina and Peggy might be the only ones there in support of the convict. I still considered myself neutral.

I spotted a couple I assumed were Kyle's parents. They were with a small group.

Chip came over to me. I hadn't noticed him. "I came to hear Tina argue," he said. "I thought she could use another friendly face in the room."

Henry showed up, too. He went over to one of the benches along the wall and sat down near a guy who looked familiar to me. The guy said something to Henry. Henry looked at his watch and replied.

I sat down on the other side of Henry. The guy looked over at me and said, "Hi, Mr. Davis."

Of course. It was Arthur Cunningham, the man who had found the body. I wasn't surprised he'd come; I bet the neighbors who had spotted and reported the suspicious red pickup had come, too. And maybe a teacher of Kyle's, and business associates of his father. And if his parents had joined a support group, some of those members were here as well. Perhaps detectives who had worked the case and any clergy who had counseled the grief-stricken family. The impact of a crime like this is so immense that it spreads out through the community in traumatizing waves. Kyle's abduction fractured the peace and undermined the simple assumptions held by neighbors and friends and witnesses and teachers. They had all come to watch Tina try and disrupt their private sorrow, to rip off the scab that had taken the past eight years to form.

The courtroom door opened, and people exited from the previous case.

The crowd in the hallway filed in.

This was state court; I didn't know the people over here. Judge Matsuko was presiding. I'd heard he was smart. But he'd been a state prosecutor before being nominated to the bench, and I worried that would work against Tina.

Matsuko read the details into the record: ". . . petitioner is a convicted felon . . . incarcerated in the state penitentiary . . . not present in the courtroom . . . Mr. Devaney, through counsel, petitions to have the state itemize any and all physical evidence in its custody, and to make such evidence available for testing."

Tina stood at the lectern. "May it please the court," she said. Then she delivered her argument: "A defendant's right to examine evidence is established in state and federal law." She spoke confidently. She quoted cases.

The judge stopped her. He sounded inconvenienced. "Daryl Devaney is not a defendant," he said, his Asian accent rounding out the "r" in Daryl. "Mr. Devaney is a convicted murderer. So aren't you eight years too late, Ms. Trevor? Daryl Devaney confessed to his crime and pleaded guilty. I'd say that settles the matter."

Tina was prepared and was answering before he finished the question. She talked about Daryl's cognitive impairment. She talked about how his guilty plea was irrelevant to his actual innocence. She talked about how small a burden it was for the state to allow the testing, and how immense a burden for an innocent man to live and die in prison. I was proud of her. She stood gripping the lectern, speaking with force and passion. I was sure the judge would be moved.

Tina wrapped up her argument: "Daryl Devaney faced an impossible choice eight years ago: Plead guilty or face death by lethal injection. He pleaded guilty so he could live to fight another day. This is that day." Tina's voice was deep with emotion.

She sat down. Nobody said anything. I cleared my throat, hoping Tina would turn around so I could give her a thumbs-up. But she didn't turn, and I was left looking at the back of her head. I saw that she'd gotten her hair trimmed recently; strange that I hadn't noticed till this moment. It made a tidy line across the back of her blouse and was somehow girlish and endearing. It made me think of July 4, the last few hours of Lydia's life, when we had that informal barbecue at our house and I went into the kitchen for more beer and looked out the window at Tina and Lydia sitting side by side, their backs toward me. I still had that photo of them in my phone.

CHAPTER 23

G regory Nations walked to the lectern.

Spectators shifted in their seats. They sat more erect, slid forward on the benches. Nations is the district attorney. The spectators probably wanted to break into applause for him, just as they probably wanted to boo at Tina.

I wasn't used to being in the defendant's camp. And though I professed neutrality, I'm sure I was seen as being there in support of Tina and Peggy's cause.

Through a thousand trials, I have been the one to do battle against violence and lawlessness—the one thrust into the arena to slay the many-headed beast of chaos and criminality. Even when the crowd has been against me, when a defendant's friends and family have packed the benches, I've still felt society's approval. It exists everywhere: My office is in the courthouse building; the government writes my paycheck; newspaper articles, either overtly or in subtext, laud my mission of excising moral disease from the population of free citizens. I am used to hearing the subtle stirring in the crowd when I stand to speak after the defense attorney has argued. *Now let's hear some truth!* the crowd seems to say.

But sitting in the gallery at that moment, and seeing the crowd through Tina's eyes as she took her seat and Gregory Nations stood, I caught a glimpse from the other side.

"May it please the court," Nations said.

I know Gregory Nations fairly well. Though he is a state prosecutor and I'm federal, we are frequently invited to appear together and to serve on task forces and joint commissions. We get along, though we've never been friends.

"I can make this short and simple," Gregory said. "It is the goal of the justice system to create finality in criminal prosecutions, and toward that end—"

"I thought the goal was to create fairness," the judge said.

"Naturally," Gregory said. "But this convict had every opportunity . . ."

It went on like this for a few minutes. Gregory had something he wanted very badly to say, but the judge kept heading him off, preferring a theoretical debate on the finality of conviction over whatever Gregory was itching to get to. Finally, Gregory threw his hands out to either side and blurted, "Your Honor, it's moot."

The judge stopped. Tina put a hand against her mouth.

"Go on," the judge said.

"I was informed just an hour ago," Gregory said. "The physical evidence in this case has been purged."

"Informed by whom?"

"The commissioner."

"So there's no physical evidence to test?"

"That's correct."

Matsuko thought about this a few seconds.

Peggy Devaney was sitting a row in front of me. She had her hands pressed against either side of her face.

"Mr. Nations," the judge said, "if any evidence was destroyed or discarded in response to Mr. Devaney's petition, then that is a criminal act, and I will personally order an investigation—"

"No, Judge. It was discarded over a year ago in a routine housecleaning. I'm told the department has limited space for the storage of—"

"Yeah, yeah, yeah," the judge said. He was paging through the file. "I'll just note here for the record that while the current petition was filed only a few weeks ago, I see this whole argument began several years ago. It went to federal court . . . got kicked back to us."

The judge closed his file and took off his glasses and looked at Peggy Devaney. "I'm sorry, ma'am. If, as the district attorney claims, the evidence has been disposed of, then it does appear to be moot." He looked at Gregory. "And, Mr. Nations, perhaps this was an innocent error by the department, or maybe it was intentional. I intend to find out—"

The judge was interrupted by a high-pitched note that, for a split second, sounded like an electronic warning of some kind. But it was quickly identifiable as the uncontrolled overflow of poor Peggy Devaney's grief. She had been in this battle long enough, and she knew enough about the process, to realize that this wasn't just one more setback. She had been clinging to the hope of finding DNA evidence proving that Daryl was not the perpetrator. But the absence of evidence meant her road had reached its end. She had nothing more to hope for.

Behind me, a familiar voice said, "If I may, Your Honor?"

It was Chip, with his cell phone at his ear.

"Bailiff," the judge said, flicking his head toward Chip. Cell phones are strictly prohibited in the courtroom, and in a hearing of this kind—oral argument on a petition—the only people speaking should be the two lawyers and the judge.

The bailiff started toward Chip, and Chip audaciously held up a hand to stop the man, and in the hand was his FBI badge. Chip spoke a few more words into the phone. Then he said to the judge: "Special Agent d'Villafranca, Federal Bureau of Investigation."

It worked its magic. The bailiff stopped and looked at Matsuko for guidance.

"I may have information," Chip said. "I don't know anything about evidence in this particular case, but I do know that a few years ago, the Bureau tried to close several child abduction cases by linking unsolved cases to ones where a perpetrator had been identified. We collected evidence in cases of this sort from several jurisdictions."

Judge Matsuko blinked a few times. Gregory Nations looked back and forth from Chip to the judge. The quiet siren of Peggy Devaney's sorrow stopped. "Are you telling us the FBI is in possession of physical evidence pertaining to Kyle Devaney's murder?" Matsuko said.

Chip held his phone up to the judge. "That's what I'm trying to find out."

"If you would, sir, please step into the hallway and find out what you can. Then come back and let us know." The judge turned toward Gregory Nations. "Have you finished with your argument?"

"No, Your Honor, I—"

"Yes," the judge said. "I think you have finished. It seems the state has done one of three things: It has disposed of evidence that was the subject of a convict's legitimate petition for postconviction relief; or it has transferred the evidence into federal jurisdiction without keeping adequate records of that transfer; or it has failed to keep track of whether there was any evidence in the first place. In any case, Daryl Devaney's petition for access to any and all physical evidence existing in his case is hereby granted. An empty victory, to be sure, if it turns out no evidence exists. Now we'll just wait to see."

The judge didn't smack his gavel—we were still in session—but nothing was said and nobody moved. It took about five minutes before the courtroom door opened again. Chip came in and stood at the back.

"Do you have information, Mr. FBI Agent?" Matsuko said.

"I don't have an inventory yet," Chip said, "but it does seem we have a box."

CHAPTER 24

I called Chip the next afternoon to ask if the FBI had gotten anywhere in investigating the murder of Jimmy Mailing, the fixer for Subsurface, Inc. Chip said no, no developments. There had been a few things in Mailing's home that might help our corruption inquiry, but nothing pointing to a suspect for Mailing's murder.

"We have the log from his cell phone, though," Chip said. "The night before the murder, there was an incoming call to him that we can't identify. We're thinking it might have been the killer setting up the meet."

"Keep me informed," I said. "In fact, send over the list of stuff you think might be useful for the Subsurface case. Let me have a look."

"Will do."

"And what's the time frame for testing the evidence in the Devaney case?"

"I don't know," Chip said. "What I hear is that we're arguing over who gets to test it, us or the state."

I worked on other matters, but I was restless. After a few hours I went and bothered Upton. If it had been morning, I'd have brought coffee, but as it was late afternoon, I took a flask from my bottom desk drawer and knocked on his door.

"Who?" he said.

I opened the door a crack, stuck my arm in, waving the flask.

"Granddad," Upton said, "you're always welcome here."

I went in and poured us both a shot. Neither of us is really a drinker, but in each other's company, we like to flout propriety with this act of rebellion. It has become more important and more frequent since the schoolmarmish Pleasant Holly replaced the crusty Harold Schnair. Harold used to have a nip with us sometimes.

Pleasant, if she knew, would send us photocopies from the relevant pages of office "regulations and guidelines" and would probably refer us for alcohol screening.

Janice knocked on Upton's door. "Fax for Nick," she said.

It was from Chip: the summary of evidence relating to Subsurface that the Bureau had found in Jimmy Mailing's place. Upton and I read through it together. Chip had been right. There were a few things we might be able to use. The last page of the fax pertained to items found in Mailing's car and on his person, including his phone.

I tipped us another shot. The workday was over.

The next morning I got up and went downstairs to make coffee. Tina showered and came down a bit later.

"I'll get Barn up," I said.

"Wait."

"Wait for what?"

Tina poured herself coffee and sat down at the table. She didn't say anything.

"What's up, babe?"

"It's not your fault," she said.

"What isn't?"

"Everything."

I waited.

"I can't find it," she said.

"It?"

"How it used to be."

"How it used to be?"

"Yes."

"It's still how it used to be, isn't it?"

"Maybe it never was," she said.

"That's wrong. It definitely was."

"Maybe it was for you and not for me."

"It was, Tina. It definitely was. And it still is. Trust me. It really is. There's just too much happening right now. With Lydia and your health. And the corruption investigation that's kept me so busy. But things will—"

"I know," she said. "It *is* too much. I'm not very good at being me right now."

"It'll be back to normal soon. I promise."

She got up and walked around tidying the kitchen. "I'm aware of loving you," she said, "but I can't always find it."

"Be patient," I told her. "Don't panic." I told her we'd live our lives and things would get back to normal. I told her she was still in shock, that it would be unwise to make big changes. She said she had tried being patient, but the feeling just got bigger. She said she'd tried not to panic, but the panic kept coming to find her. I said I probably hadn't focused on her enough, with all she was going through. She said I'd been okay, that wasn't it. I said I'd do better. She said I'd done fine.

"I have ideas," I said. "Plans. Plans about us. Well, no, not plans, thoughts. I was going to tell you. I was waiting, though, until things settled down, but I'll tell you now. I had wanted to tell you sometime when we were curled up on the couch with wine, talking, and I'd say it as, like, some hare-brained scheme, and we wouldn't have to take it real seriously but just toy with the idea and see if it took root. So this isn't what I pictured, both of us about to leave for work and you feeling how you're feeling. But I just thought . . ."

"What?"

I cleared my throat, sipped my coffee, and told her my thinking about moving up to the lake and opening a private practice together. It came out urgently, desperately. It sounded preposterous even to me.

She laughed. But where a minute ago she'd been remorseful and compassionate, her laugh was caustic. "Unbelievable," she said.

"What?"

"Your solution to my feeling alienated is to ignore everything I've said and move to a cabin in the woods." She poured the dregs of her coffee into the sink. "I should have known better," she said to herself, but plenty loud enough for me to hear.

CHAPTER 25

On Saturday Lizzy met me at Jo Mondo's. We had a latte together and drove to a building on the edge of downtown. It was in plain sight at the intersection of two busy roads but hidden from notice by its shoe-box architecture and by the fact that there was nothing about it you should ever need to know: FRIENDLY CITY EXECUTIVE SUITES, the sign says: DAY, WEEK, MONTH. I once spoke at a law enforcement conference there ("Recent Changes in the Law of Search and Seizure"), and though I'd driven past the building a thousand times, I had to look up the address that day because I couldn't place it on my mental map of the city.

I remember when it was built. I had worked in construction a couple of summers during college, and the experience left me with an interest in how buildings are put together. It's a disappointing thing to watch: two-by-fours, plywood, pipes, wires, Sheetrock. Then siding—plastic or aluminum or fake stone or, in this case, tan stucco. At every step, you expect to see something to make it seem less disposable and less transitory. But no: It is always just one fire, or one earthquake, or one bankruptcy, or one termite infestation, or one design flaw, or one economic downturn away from being a pile of rubble or a vacant derelict.

"This is nice," Lizzy said. We were looking at a suite. "Suite," as used in the context of an empty, undifferentiated, impersonal hotel room, meant it had an extra room where Barnaby or Lizzy could stay sometimes. Barnaby would have no say in this, but as for Lizzy, it is probably a fiction I tell myself that on some evening she may actually choose this joyless warehouse of displaced spouses over the goofy and cinnamony country home where she and Ethan play at being married in the laughter-filled, no-questions-asked haven of Flora's spare room.

Lizzy volunteered to help me find a place. There were lots of one- and two-bedroom apartments available around town, but the act of renting a real apartment instead of a joyless hotel suite would give this sorry chapter greater weight than it deserved: DAY, WEEK, MONTH.

Day: certainly.

Week: worst case.

Month: not a chance.

I pulled the curtain aside from the balcony window and saw that I had a view of office buildings and parking garages.

Lizzy helped me carry things in from the car. I said, "How about if we go out for dinner, Liz? There's probably an acceptable restaurant nearby."

"Love to, Dad, but I told Ethan and Mom I'd be home."

"That's okay."

"Come have dinner with us. Mom and Chip would love to have you."

"No, I'll stay and get settled. You go."

When she left, I turned on the TV and found a show about people who clean out abandoned storage units and then sell the shit they find.

I woke up in the night. I tried watching TV or going back to sleep. Eventually, I got up and drove over to my house, parked in front on the street, and dozed off in the car.

CHAPTER 26

Monday morning. I got into the office early and reviewed my list of current cases, taking notes on what needed doing for each one. Then I got coffee for myself and wandered around chatting with people. I stopped in on Upton. He asked about my weekend, and I said it had been fine.

Detective Sabin called me later in the morning to talk about Lydia's murder. "Let's meet," she said.

"Do you have anything new?"

"No, we keep hitting dead ends. So Philbin and I thought it might be good to put our three heads together again, come up with some new ideas."

I met with Sabin and Philbin at Jo Mondo's. There were no tables open, so we sat three across at the counter along the window.

"Haven't heard from you in a while," I said. "Do you have any new theories?"

"We know who the perp is," Philbin said. "It's Henry Tatlock. We have tons of circumstantial. We're working on finding something physical."

"Well, no," Sabin said. "It's not so cut-and-dried as Philbin claims."

Philbin was sitting between Sabin and me. He is huge and she is small. She leaned way forward over her coffee, head almost down on the countertop, to see around him while she spoke.

"Of course it's cut and dried," Philbin said.

"Get up, Philly," Sabin said, appearing behind him, on her feet now. She shoved him on the shoulder. "Move over. Let me sit there."

Philbin moved over. Sabin sat next to me.

"We have enough circumstantial to make a case and put that freak away where he belongs," Philbin said. "And I'm sorry if you're feeling all sentimental about the murderous Henry Tatlock. Honest, I really am." (This said sarcastically.) He held up his fist and peeled back his index finger so it was pointing straight up. "First, Henry Tatlock, the fiancée-killer, can't account for his whereabouts at the time Lydia Trevor was shot. Second—"

"Christ's sake, Philly," Sabin said, "he's accounted for his whereabouts. He just doesn't have anyone to confirm it yet."

"Second," Philbin said, pulling another finger from his fist to stand beside the first, "the saintly Mr. Tatlock was consorting with underworld figures, to wit, one Aaron Pursley."

"For which Henry has a credible explanation," Sabin said.

"Credible, my ass. And Aaron Pursley is known to be in the firearms-procuring business," Philbin said. "What a coincidence. Lydia Trevor was shot in the head with a firearm that somebody must have procured from somebody."

"Have you questioned Pursley?" I asked.

"Gee, never occurred to us." Philbin said. "Hey, Sabin, you ever think of asking Pursley about any of this?"

"For Christ's sake, Philly, simmer down," Sabin said. To me, "Yeah, we spoke to Pursley. At first he wouldn't say anything. So I told him what Henry had said about looking for his bio family, and Pursley says, 'Well, I wouldn't dispute Henry Tatlock's version of events.' That's all he'd say."

"*Known* underworld figure," Philbin repeated. He peeled another finger from his fist. "Third, it turns out Mr. Tatlock's fiancée was out bucking someone else's bronco, which, for her being engaged to a guy as explosive as Henry Postal Tatlock, is kind of like playing Russian roulette with five bullets in a six-shooter."

"Unless I'm mistaken," I say, "you don't even know if Henry was aware of Lydia's affair."

"Fourth," Philbin said, and he freed a fourth finger. Sabin, who was sitting with her back to Philbin, rolled her eyes in exasperation. "Lydia left a panicky message for her sister minutes before she was killed, making it clear she was running from someone. And fifth . . ."

" 'And fifth,' " Sabin mocked, using a cartoon voice.

Philbin extended his thumb and waved his open hand at me. "Fifth, Lydia's texts with her illicit Romeo made frequent and repeated reference to Henry's violent temper and unpredictability and to Lydia's fear of him. Wherefore, to put it in legalese you might understand, counselor, we got it scientifically proved that Henry Tatlock did, with malice aforethought and desirous in his heart to splatter her head like an overripe melon, shoot her with no more compunction than if she was a rabid skunk."

"Oh, for Christ's sake, Philly," Sabin said, "all that is—"

"The guy was a powder keg," Philbin said. "We've asked around. He's bad news."

I hadn't realized what a volatile jerk Philbin was. I had hoped to talk with these two about other theories for the case, other directions to go with the investigation. Now I was pissed.

We were all facing out the window. I'd been watching the sidewalk across the street, where a guy in a gorilla suit was handing out fliers. It wasn't a busy time of day, so the gorilla spent a lot of time leaning against a building and staring at the sidewalk. The costume was cheap and ratty. The guy seemed tragic.

Philbin pivoted on his stool. "If you'll excuse me," he said, and made his way to the men's room through the thicket of laptop and iPad and smartphone and tablet users.

"Sorry about him," Sabin said. "He gets like that."

"Henry didn't kill Lydia," I said.

"I kind of believe you," Sabin said. "I mean, you know him. We don't."

"Thank you," I said. "I wasn't sure you two recognized that fact."

"Tell me about him," she said in an intimate voice. "There are rumors about him. That he went off on some girl once."

"Where did you hear that?"

"We've been talking to people. Have you heard about anything like that? People talk about him like he's got one foot in the psych ward. And Philbin always believes the street talk. I like to think I have a more balanced understanding of how rumors work. So help me out here, Nick. What's the real story?"

I liked Sabin. I liked her Brooklyn accent and her no-bullshit approach, and now I liked that she was more interested in getting some facts than in jailing the first possible suspect. She was attractive, too, not that I was looking, but a guy can't help noticing. Maybe if I could explain Henry to Sabin, she could get Philbin to back down. "Here's what I know," I said. "I know that Henry—"

My cell rang. It was Lizzy. "Hi, Dad. I was just wondering how you're doing. Are you okay?"

I held up a finger to Sabin and mouthed, "Be right back." I walked toward the restroom hallway, which was quieter than the café area. "I'm okay, sweetie. Can't really talk right now, though."

"Mom says you should come over for dinner tonight."

"I don't know," I said. "Let me think. I'll call you back in a half hour?"

"Sure, Dad."

"Bye, honey."

Before returning to Sabin, I went into the men's room and found Philbin there, also talking on his phone. He nodded. I nodded. I took care of business and walked out, weaving back through the crowd of zombified screen-gazers. I realized that Philbin was just hanging out, delaying to give me time with Sabin, and it struck me like a sledgehammer that I was being played: Philbin had gotten me worked up and indignant about Henry, then he'd gone off to piss, leaving me to be comforted and cooed at by the compassionate Sabin. And I *fell* for it! Me: hard-bit prosecutor, ready to cozy up, stool to stool at the coffee counter, our heads all but bumping as I spilled Henry's secrets to the calculating Sabin. She had plied her feminine charms, and I was ready to believe we were allies in trying to wrest the investigation from the oafish Philbin.

Good cop/bad cop. Damn them both. I'd take what I knew to Chip. Let him be the one to crack it open.

I sat back at the counter beside her. "You were saying," she said.

The gorilla paced the sidewalk across the street. Sometimes

he'd hand out a flier and sometimes he'd let people pass without interruption.

I said, "Well, you remember that kid you questioned the day after the murder? The one who found a credit card and wanted to buy computers? What ever happened to him?"

"I don't know," Sabin said, "but what I want to know—"

"Be right back," I said. I went up to the counter and ordered a coffee drink, then took it outside and crossed the street. The gorilla offered me a flier. I offered him the cup. "Been watching you," I said. "Thought maybe you could use a pick-me-up."

He took the cup warily.

"Vanilla latte," I said.

He took off the gorilla head. I was expecting a kid like the confused credit-card finder. But the gorilla was closer to my age and unshaved. Homeless, perhaps, impersonating a gorilla to make a few bucks. "Okay," he said.

I crossed back to the café.

"A humanitarian," Sabin said.

"Not really. It was just a notion."

The gorilla sipped the coffee. I tried to catch his eye—I wanted to hold my coffee up in a salute—but he didn't see me.

"About Henry Tatlock," Sabin said. "You have information."

"Oh, right. Sorry. My information is that Henry is innocent."

"I know. But something about a girl. Something about people misunderstanding and about careless accusations."

"No," I said. "I wouldn't know about anything like that." I looked at the flier I was still holding. BLOWOUT LIQUIDATION SALE!!! It was for one of those places that's always going out of business but never actually goes.

CHAPTER 27

I tried to get work done in my office, but I couldn't focus on anything. The meeting with Sabin and Philbin had me too upset. It had started me thinking about Lydia again. I thought how furious Tina had been at her dead sister when we found out about the secret romance. I'd been pissed, too. I was still pissed. Was it really asking so much for Lydia to keep her panties on and to revel in her good fortune at landing a guy like Henry? Damn her. Because not only did it screw up her own life; the shock waves were still spreading out like a tsunami rising up from the surface of a placid ocean.

I was thinking about my own marriage, of course. Tina and I were just finding our groove. Things had been tough. Tina had gotten pregnant as soon as we'd gotten together. It was a difficult pregnancy, followed by life with a colicky infant and the torturous deprivation of sleep—much less sleep for her than for me—followed by the breast cancer scare, then waiting for results, then more waiting during those months when the doctor didn't like the looks of things. Then the week before Lydia's death, Tina's follow-up exam came back clean. It should have been our independence day. Barn had been sleeping through the night for over a year. Tina felt great and loved her work. We were finally free to get on with the long-delayed business of being newlyweds. But Lydia fucked it all up, smiting Tina with this unmanageable sorrow at the very minute we'd thought ourselves delivered.

Damn Lydia. I pulled out my phone to look at that last picture of her. Though it was taken from behind, Tina and Lydia were turning to look at something, so the camera captured a quarter profile each: a cheek, an eye, the jawline, and part of the forehead. They looked very alike except for the texture of skin and crinkle of eyes and neck. You could tell that Tina was several years older.

I felt the realization in my veins and then in the prickle of my skin. I felt it in scattered bits, then the bits became a stone that stuck in the middle of my chest. I couldn't breathe for a second.

I took my phone to Janis's desk. "Can you help me print this picture?"

Janis got me set up. I printed the picture and quickly ripped it in half, right down between the two women. "Who is this?" I asked Janis, showing her one half of the picture.

"Your wife, of course."

I took it to Upton. "It's Tina," he said.

Tina had worked in this office. She was known to everybody here, and everyone I asked identified her in the photo. But they didn't identify her. The picture I showed around was Lydia. Lydia, a younger version of Tina: Tina the way she'd looked five years ago, pre-marriage, pre-childbirth. Anybody might have mistaken them, but especially someone who knew Tina only before she'd acquired that ineffable look of motherhood and maturity, before lines of character and worry and sun exposure began to surface in the predictable spots around her face.

The conference room at the FBI is a cheery place. It has a big sky-light. Upton was there with me; Isler and Sabin and Philbin, too. The two halves of the Tina and Lydia photograph were on the table.

"So if you're right," Philbin said, "if it was a case of mistaken identity and your wife was the target, who would want to kill *her*?"

"You know the federal prison out at Ellisville?" I said. "It's full of people who would love to kill her."

Upton said, "Tina specialized in gangs and drug prosecutions and crimes against children. Mostly it's little guys, users and losers, and the last thing they want when they're sprung is any new problems with the man. But a few are megalomaniacs who take it all real personal."

"You got any names?" Sabin asked.

"I've got every case she worked on." I waved the list Janis had printed for me. "We can go through it a name at a time. Cross off the ones still inside. Focus on the ones who are out and have a history of violence."

Tina walked into the room. Chip had sent over an agent to pick her up at her office. There were half a dozen empty chairs around the table, and she picked the one next to me. I slid the list to her. Without hesitation, she flipped through and found the name she wanted. Tony Smeltzer.

"This guy would be my first choice," she said. "But I assumed he was still inside. Corrections is supposed to inform me when he's released. You remember him, Nick? He's the one who screamed at me in the courtroom, said he was coming after me when he got out. We all just figured someone had slipped him some angel dust in lockup and that he was high as a kite during trial."

"But if he's still inside . . ."

"He isn't," Chip said. Chip was typing on his laptop as we talked. "It says here he successfully appealed his sentence, shortening it by five years. And that he did every day of the shortened sentence, so he was released outright. No parole."

"When was he released?" I asked.

"Last January."

The timing was right. The guy had taken a few months to get on his feet and up to speed on Tina's whereabouts and habits. Then he'd made his move.

"Tell us about him," Chip said to Tina.

"Drug case," Tina said. "We didn't know where he fit in—whether he was running his own enterprise or working for someone else."

"He was suspected in a couple of killings," Isler said. "Vicious jobs, but unfortunately, we couldn't find anything solid. We took him down in a drug sting, but things went wonky, and we could only make a case on possession. He did seven years."

"Tell us about the threats," Chip said.

"He was a surly son of a bitch," Tina said. "You could feel the rage. He wanted to testify, and his lawyer couldn't dissuade him. He really hurt himself, opened the door to all kinds of shit: priors and even some domestic dirt. I went at him hard on cross. He almost lost it a couple of times. Then he really went berserk during my closing. He'd given me so much to work with that I was going on and on about what a worthless piece of shit he was, and he finally came out of the chair. Guards jumped on him before he did any damage, but the whole time he was screaming how he was going to kill me and kill the people who testified against him, blah blah blah. Like I say, he seemed to be on PCP."

"Tony Smeltzer," Chip said. "Last known address is over in Rivertown."

"What I remember best," Tina said, "after he was restrained, after he calmed down and the jury delivered its verdict, they were taking him out and he looked right at me and said, 'You'll be hearing from me.' That's what gave me the willies."

"What does he look like?" Sabin asked.

"He looks sinister," Tina said.

"Sinister how?"

"Kind of round and hunched over. And creepy eyes that seem to bulge even though they're always half closed."

"I'll have a picture in a minute," Chip said.

"I remember him," I said. "I remember wondering if he had a spine problem or something, because his neck seemed to come from his body frontward instead of upward. Kind of vulturelike."

"It says here that Mr. Smeltzer was mostly a good boy in prison," Chip said, reading info from the computer. "He was involved in the prison ministry and doing correspondence classes in . . . um . . . here it is . . . business administration. But they put him on suicide watch a lot."

"So what do we do about this?" I said. "It's almost four months since Lydia was killed. Is he lying low before trying again, or is he not our guy?"

"Let's pick him up and find out," Isler said.

"Can I go back to work?" Tina asked.

Nobody answered at first, then Chip picked up the phone and arranged for a female agent to keep Tina company back at her office. "Just till we have him in custody," Chip said.

The meeting broke up. Philbin and Sabin got up to leave. "Are either of you guys going back to trooper headquarters?" Isler asked them.

"I am," Philbin said.

"Great. I need you to bring something over there for me. Come on down to the evidence room."

Philbin left with Isler. I rode with Chip to Tony Smeltzer's apartment building. Since the guy was a murder suspect, and since he was also believed to have intended the murder of a former federal prosecutor—namely my wife—we took a SWAT team. The address in Rivertown was a dilapidated apartment house. The downstairs hallway was dark. It smelled of piss and cigarette smoke, and it seemed to vibrate with rap blasting from one of the ground-level apartments. The bulb was burned out in the stairway. I heard a child crying. There was no elevator. Smeltzer's apartment was on the second floor. The team trotted up the stairs and spread out in the hallway, covering the exits. Chip had a Kevlar vest, like the SWAT guys, though he didn't have the helmet and assault rifle. I had a vest on, too, and I had my Glock, and I felt that at any second someone was going to tell me to knock it off and go back to my office, where I belonged. Sabin and Philbin had tagged along, but this was a federal operation now, so they waited outside. Chip walked past the artillery-clad SWATs and, standing to one side, knocked on the apartment door.

"Tony Smeltzer, FBI. Open the door."

The lock clicked. Everyone stood ready.

The door opened. The SWATs tumbled into the apartment. I heard a scream. Then a little later I heard "Clear." Chip walked in. After a minute or two, I followed him.

Chip was questioning a woman. She stood in the room with a child on her hip. She was Caucasian and slender and wore an em-

broidered T-shirt and jeans. She looked at us all with curious eyes,
concerned but not terrified. "If you'd called ahead, I'd have made
fresh coffee," she said. She wasn't hostile, but not friendly, either. She
was the way you'd expect someone to be when five heavily armed,
Kevlar-clad commandos drop in and take up positions around the
living room. "Smeltzer?" she said. "Yes, I believe that was his name.
You'd have to ask the landlord. I never met him."

The room was nice. It had a futon couch and an IKEA dining
table. The radio was on. I heard classical music.

". . . moved in on August first," the woman was saying.

I noticed a tall bamboo plant in a raku pot near the window.

"AmeriCorps," she said. "My husband's a nurse."

"Were any of Smeltzer's things still here?" Chip asked.

"No, the place was clean."

I looked out the window into an alley. Young kids were down
there playing. A couple of mothers stood watching.

"No, we love it here," the woman said. "We love the vibrancy,
the diversity."

Chip handed her his card.

"Very exciting," the woman said. "I've never been swarmed by a
SWAT team before."

We all left. The commandos piled back into their van and drove
off.

"All dressed up and no place to go," I said.

Chip and Isler ignored me. They were both on their cell phones.
I pulled mine out, too, and called Upton with the update. Then I
called Tina. "Are you okay?" I asked her.

"Just fine," she said. "I have my new best friend here: Agent
Agnew from Augusta. I've tried to put her to work reading trial
transcripts, but she—"

"Dammit, Tina, take this seriously."

"I *am* serious," Tina said. "Her name is Agnew, and she's from
Augusta. And, Nickie, the guy has had nearly four months since he
killed Lyd. I'm not expecting him this afternoon."

"What about Barnaby?"

"We don't think he'd be a target," Tina said, "but Captain Dorsey sent a statie over to guard him at the day care."

We hung up. Chip dropped me back at my office.

Tina called me around four-thirty in the afternoon. "They still haven't found the guy," she said. "He seems to have gone missing right about the time Lyd was killed. Chip doesn't want me to go home till they find him."

"Gee," I said, "by the sheerest of coincidences, I have some extra room at my place, if you need somewhere to stay."

"It was nice to see you today," she said. Her voice signaled sincerity through its absence of inflection—businesslike: just the facts.

"So?"

"So let's give it more time to work. It's working. I'm more relaxed . . ."

". . . despite having a psychopath after you."

She laughed. "So, sticking with our plan . . ."

"*Our* plan?"

"Okay, *my* plan—thought maybe I could co-opt you—sticking with my plan, I'll go stay at Henry's. Is that okay?"

I wanted to rebel. I could have wailed and pleaded and maybe guilt-tripped her into coming to stay at Friendly City Executive Suites (Day, Week, Month). She was vulnerable. I could have prevailed, but she'd have resented it.

"Henry's," I said. "Sure, the poor guy would probably love the company. Besides, it's really your sister's place, isn't it? So it seems appropriate."

"Thanks, sweetie," she said.

Chip called me just before five to say they hadn't found Smeltzer. It was looking like the guy had gone invisible.

"What about Lydia?" I asked. "Have you found any real evidence that Smeltzer was the shooter?"

"Nothing actually pointing to him, but we haven't found any-thing to exclude him, either. And not finding a way to exclude him is almost the same as implicating him."

"It is?"

"Definitely. Give me ten names at random, good guys or bad guys or names from the phone book. And give me a crime. By the end of the day, assuming none of the names is the perp, we can usu-ally find a way to exclude all of them. So in a case like this, where we have good reasons for suspecting a guy to begin with, and he *coincidentally* goes missing right about the time of the crime, and the Bureau can't seem to locate the guy in a whole afternoon of looking, I'd say the chance that he's our perp hovers in the hundred percent range."

"Okay. Now what?"

"Well, since our suspicion of him as Lydia's killer has gone biospheric—"

". . . Stratospheric."

"—I'd say we need to take the threat against Tina pretty god-damn serious."

CHAPTER 28

Over the next few days the Bureau remained unable to locate Tony Smeltzer. Chip and I drove up to Ellisville Max to interview his former cellmate.

Like Smeltzer, the cellmate was in on narcotics charges. He turned out to be nondescript: white, fortyish, plain. Chip did the preliminaries, explaining to the guy why we were there. "So we're not looking for anything incriminating," Chip said, "we're just trying to get a feel for Tony, to assess whether he might present a danger."

"Oh. I see."

"For example, did Tony Smeltzer ever talk about his trial?"

"I can't say that he did."

"Or about the prosecutor?"

"No. I can't say that he did."

"Did Tony Smeltzer talk about places he liked? Other parts of the country—places where he had connections?"

"No. No, I can't say that he did."

"Friends on the outside?"

"Nope."

"Did he get any mail?"

"I really wouldn't know about that."

"Visitors?"

"Not that I heard of."

"A girl on the outside?"

"I can't really say."

It went on like this for some time. Finally, Chip said, "Is there anything you *can* tell us?"

The cellmate thought a few seconds, then said, "His shoulder hurts him sometimes."

"His shoulder?"

"It got broke in a motorcycle accident. It's lower than the other one. Like this." The cellmate stood and let one shoulder droop, the arm hanging limp. "Made him walk kind of sideways."

"Well, that's something," Chip said. "Thank you. Is there anything else?"

"No. Can't say that there is."

Chip and I left. I said, "That was a god-awful waste of time."

"Do you think so?" Chip asked.

"Don't you?"

"I thought it was valuable. I learned a ton."

If Chip had been anybody else, I'd have thought he was joking. But he isn't one for irony. "Learned what?" I asked.

"I learned that Mr. Smeltzer is able to command fear and/or respect. That he's a serious person."

"Serious how?"

"Think about it," Chip said. "The guy was willing to tell us that Smeltzer has a broken shoulder, but nothing about his actual behavior. Obviously, the guy wasn't going to tell us anything important about Smeltzer. He could have said, like, Smeltzer loved watching football, or Smeltzer read novels, or Smeltzer loved to go fishing. But no. The only thing the cellmate would comment on was physical description. It tells me that saying anything about who Smeltzer really is, how he acts, what he likes or hates, is off-limits—no matter how unimportant it seems."

"Okay. So what does this mean?" I said.

"I'm not a profiler, right? But what I see is a guy who is good at controlling his environment and controlling his image. He's in charge, and people aren't likely to cross him."

"And?"

"And so he takes things pretty seriously. I'd say he definitely could have held on to a bit of homicidal rage for the past seven years."

Morning. At the office, everything felt relatively normal until I settled in at my desk and the phone rang. It was Tina. "I guess things have calmed down," she said. "But they're still not sure if it was him last night."

"If what was him? If he was who?"

"The prowler."

I waited.

"Are you telling me you didn't hear about it?"

"About what? What prowler?"

"Oh my God. No wonder you didn't come over. I thought you were just being you: roaming the village with a torch instead of coming over to be with me. Henry got up in the night to go to the bathroom and he saw somebody in the backyard. He woke Agent Agnew, and she got on her radio, and next thing you know, there were cops and agents everywhere."

"Why didn't *you* call me?" I said.

"Like I said, Nick, I thought—"

"You have my son with you. You're my wife and you have my son, and you didn't even bother checking in with me?"

Tina hesitated a few seconds, and then laughed. "I thought the same of you. I couldn't believe you hadn't bothered to come touch base with me."

I was silent.

"Nick?"

"Goddammit," I yelled. "If you were living with me, I wouldn't have to touch base, would I?"

"Nick, calm down, I—"

"Don't tell me to calm down. I don't . . . You don't . . . Don't even think about telling me to calm down."

"Nickie, relax, it's okay . . ."

"Go to hell," I shouted. I slammed the phone down. My office door was open. I got up and slammed it, shaking the wall, maybe the whole room. I wished I were at home instead of my office, because I wanted to smash something: some plates, maybe, or put my foot through a wall or window. I wanted to rampage. At the office, my options were limited. I picked up Tina's picture, a five-by-seven behind glass in a fancy frame, and threw it against the wall. Broken glass went everywhere. I stood in the middle of the room, panting. There was a knock on the door.

"Nick, you okay, buddy?" Upton said.

"Fine. Go away."

"Okay. I'll check back."

I picked Tina's photo out of the wreckage. It was torn, but I flattened it on the desk and taped up the tear on the back, where it wouldn't show.

CHAPTER 29

The Bureau gave us two cars for the trip. No one thought Smeltzer was actively tracking Tina; rather, that he was waiting for an opportunity. He was probably on his own, without much money or technical sophistication. But to be cautious, we drove to the FBI building, left our cars there, and took the cars they offered. Henry drove one; Tina, Barnaby, and I went in the other. Agnew followed in a third.

The Bureau had been looking for Tony Smeltzer for a week without success. The midnight prowler had never been identified or located. Chip and Isler thought it would be best if Tina stayed out of sight for a while. They talked about using a Tina look-alike (a law enforcement professional, carefully surveiled) to lure him into the open.

We thought of going to our cabin, but if Smeltzer had done any research at all, he already knew about that getaway. The Bureau was taking the guy pretty seriously. They considered him a lone wolf and a little psycho, but they also believed he was organized enough, smart enough, angry enough, and vicious enough to, say, go after one of Tina's friends or coworkers, violently extract information on Tina's whereabouts, shoot the informant, and come after Tina. Thus, Tina's whereabouts would be need-to-know only.

Chip proposed some locations; the Bureau kept a few places around the country for this type of situation. Tina kept vetoing every place he proposed. In the end, she settled on a cabin in the lake system several hundred miles northwest of the city. Tina's cousins owned it. In summer the region was bustling with canoe campers, but in early November, with freeze-up imminent, the place was perfect. Tina would feel right at home because the environment was similar to that of our own cabin. In fact, she seemed excited.

There'd be wood fires, flapjacks, canoeing on the lake—at least until freeze-up—and long evenings of contemplative silence. There would be red plaid wool jackets, rubber boots and hiking shoes, and if she got lucky, she'd hear loons calling across the lake at sunset and maybe, just maybe, the far-off song of wolves howling at the moon. Tina loved that stuff.

I wouldn't be going into hiding with Tina and Barn. There was too much to do at my office, and we didn't know how long this would last. Besides, the simple threat of a vengeance-fueled assassination wasn't enough to overcome Tina's need for a marital time-out. I did go along on the trip to get them settled. I refused to let her take Barnaby off into exile without having some part in it.

We left from the FBI early on Friday morning. I promised myself that on the long drive, I wouldn't keep asking her about "us." Instead I would focus on being the perfect coparent and traveling companion. We'd sing "Old MacDonald" and "Baby Beluga" and we'd read *Henry Hikes to Fitchburg* and *A Light in the Attic*. I felt if I could just chill, then our conversation would quietly and lovingly and organically stretch out into a map of the next thirty or forty years—about work and play and kids and grandkids; about places we hoped to travel, books we wanted to read (and write), and all the other unconquered items on the to-do list of life. I knew Tina wanted to remove the partition between the kitchen and dining room in our home to give it a more open and airy feel. We'd talk about that. I wanted a sailboat. We'd talk about that.

The drive takes seven hours without a four-year-old. With a four-year-old, it took ten. Barnaby needed to pee. He had to poop. He got carsick. He cried. He was hungry. Tina rode in the backseat with him for hours. We never got to talk. When Barn finally fell asleep, Tina said, "Pull over at the next wayside. I'll ride with Henry for a while. I need a break."

* * *

Henry would be staying with Tina and Barn as my stand-in. He had nothing better to do, having been put on suspension by Pleasant Holly. There was a second cabin he could live in, and now that he'd been so decisively delivered from the role of prime murder suspect, he was the natural choice. Also, since he'd been engaged to Lydia, he was family. Henry had grown up in the rural country around Renfield. He knew the rural lifestyle, and as an AUSA, he was a law enforcement professional. Barnaby loved him, and Tina was comfortable around him.

It was dark when we arrived. The night sky was an explosion of stars. It was well below freezing. The cabins were great; actually, the big one was more of a small log house than a cabin. Agnew and Henry went to claim spots in the little cabin behind the main house. The bedroom of the main house had a double bed and a bunk bed. I got Barnaby snuggled into a sleeping bag on the bottom bunk. Tina looked at the double bed and at the top bunk of the bunk bed and weighed her options. We shared the double.

Saturday was fun. We all slept late. We had breakfast and then went out canoeing. Agnew was a solid young woman with her hair in a French braid, and she seemed dour, like enforcement people do sometimes.

"Agent Agnew," I said, "how do you like working for the Bureau?"

"I like it," she said.

I waited for more, but there was no more. We were in two canoes, paddling side by side. Agnew and Henry and ZZ were in one; Tina, Barn, and I in the other. The day was gorgeous: blue sky, no wind, golden leaves lying on the surface along the shoreline. The lake had a feeling of unboundedness. Vastness. It felt like it beckoned us into the great beyond, and I imagined that Agnew was not Agnew but Lydia or some other woman—Henry's girlfriend or wife. Without meaning to, I imagined her pregnant and we two couples and Barnaby bravely and exuberantly paddling into the vastness.

"Have you had any word about the evidence in the Kyle Devaney case yet?" Henry asked Tina. He was definitely interested in the Devaney case. He had gone to hear the oral argument at the state Superior Court. He'd asked me for updates several times.

"Nothing yet," Tina said. "You should come over to my office when things are back to normal. I'll set you up with a case of your own to work on. We need pro bono lawyers."

"Yes," Henry said, "maybe I will."

Henry was coming back to life. I'd grown to admire him. He had handled his fiancée's murder and his status as a prime suspect with amazing dignity. I thought of how poorly I'd behaved on the phone with Tina the other day, exploding because I hadn't been notified about the prowler. As far as I knew, Henry had never acted out like that during his whole ordeal. I felt embarrassed.

Henry liked to fish. He trailed a line behind his canoe, and by dinnertime he'd caught two big trout. I didn't know whether the fishing season was open, and Henry probably didn't have a license, but we were refugees who had fled from a killer and landed here on the edge of civilization. We didn't worry about a fishing license.

Back onshore in the evening, Henry filleted the trout. He knew his business with a fillet knife, handling it with practiced confidence, producing four clean and bloodless fillets in just a few quick motions. We pan-fried the fish, made a salad, and opened some beers.

Agnew left on Sunday. I drove back to the city on Monday.

CHAPTER 30

I moved back into my house. Inside, I found the lingering vapors of my previous exile, and of Tina and Barnaby and ZZ's absence. The house felt like a discarded shell; the life I had lived there was dried and gone. I actually considered returning to the Executive Suites, where I'd at least achieved the bunker mentality of digging in, holding on, and making do until the siege ended.

There was plenty to keep me busy, though, so I got busy. If I could have everything running like a well-tuned machine when Tina and Barn returned, Tina couldn't help but revel in our return to normalcy. I called a contractor to come over and give me an estimate for removing that wall she'd talked about. If I'd known for sure when she was coming home, and if the contractor could have promised to have it done by then, I'd have gone ahead. But I didn't want her returning home to a construction zone.

At work, I tried to focus on Subsurface, but I was distracted. Days passed slowly.

On Friday afternoon I drove over to Turner to have dinner with Flora and Chip and Lizzy. It was nice. I always liked being there because the house is homey and Flora has the knack for making everyone feel like a valued member of the family. Her marriage to Chip has been great for her. She had been well on her way to becoming the stereotypic old lady in purple: half a bubble out of plumb, as they say. Now with Chip, she seems well shored up, though not completely righted. As for Chip himself, he's my buddy, though I admit I get miffed with his newfound smugness. He acts like he invented the whole idea of contentment. (As if, following the collapse of his previous marriage, I'd never heard him wailing to me over the phone about the agony and futility of life.)

Dinner was curried stir-fry over rice stick noodles. I asked Chip if he'd heard anything about the physical evidence in the Kyle Runion/ Daryl Devaney case.

"Actually, the evidence went back to the state," he said. "They're testing it. But no, nothing yet."

Lizzy said, "Devaney? Is that the one with the little boy they found near the reservoir?"

Immediately, I regretted mentioning it. Lizzy might be almost nineteen with an occasional live-in boyfriend, but I still didn't need to be making dinner conversation about the most vile human depravity.

"Chip, what do the profilers say about a perp like that?" Ethan asked.

Chip cleared his throat and sat up straighter. "The fact that the victim was clothed and wrapped in a sheet tells us the perpetrator felt remorse. The nature of the crime suggests a shy perp, probably not real confident among peers, and especially shy with women. They say he was probably abused as a child, both sexually and generally, and that owing to the traumas of his upbringing, he has no self-esteem. He is meek. He may or may not be intelligent. The remorse he feels would cause him to—"

"Does Daryl Devaney fit this profile?" I asked.

"I don't know," Chip said.

"Dessert," Flora said. She clapped her hands and started clearing. Everyone jumped up to help. Lizzy playfully hip-checked Chip out of her way. Chip bumped her back. They tussled.

After dessert, Flora said, "Nickie, let's walk."

We took Bill-the-Dog on a leash, and the two of us walked the road. She linked her arm through mine. "How come you're not with Tina and Barnaby?" she said.

"I figured I'd be more valuable here, keeping tabs on the hunt for this Smeltzer guy."

"I see."

"What?"

"That's your pattern, Nickie. It's what you do."

"What pattern?"

"It's how you deal. You rush out and take charge."

"What's wrong with that?"

"Who's with Tina?"

"Henry."

"Exactly. And who was with her after Lydia was killed?"

"I was."

"That's not how I heard it. I heard you were everyplace but. Running, shooting, meeting with Captain Dorsey."

I stopped and stared at her.

"I know you, Nickie. Better than anybody. I bet I know you better than Tina does. You're always charging into battle."

"Don't shrink me, Flora," I snapped. Flora is a couples counselor. Flora and I had been a great couple once, but our marriage collapsed along with everything else in the wake of our son Toby's death. She likes to get me under her microscope, but everything she comes up with is hogwash.

I drove home alone. I envied Chip and Henry. Chip was living in the rural suburb of Turner, being a family man in the cinnamony home of my ex-wife, and standing in as dad to my daughter, Lizzy. Henry was with my current wife, Tina, and with my son, Barn. None of this meant anything, of course, it was only owing to the exigencies of the moment, wasn't it? But still . . .

CHAPTER 31

Yes, still. That conversation with Flora was well over a month ago, and I'm still not back with Tina. I'm up here in my own cabin on my own lake, preparing for the trial by writing this account of everything that has happened—especially what happened in the days after I left Tina and Barn in the supposed safety of that wilderness retreat.

In my solitude here at the lake, my mind sometimes drifts away from all that criminal unpleasantness, landing instead on the unpleasantness of my personal life.

Naturally, I've asked Tina for more information about her unhappiness: What went amiss? She talks about my not being there for her in the right way at the right time. I ask what I can do to fix it. She shakes her head and sighs. When I try fixing it on my own, being more attentive, she says I'm hovering and that she needs more space.

During the times in our marriage when everything else in life is smooth sailing—when we both have energy and time to absorb each other's more irksome traits—we do great. Love blossoms. But in tough times, the incompatibilities come to the surface. And most of our marriage has taken place during tough times.

I stayed in the city, leaving Tina and Barn with Henry in their wilderness hideout. Days passed without news. Sometimes I'd run in the evening and sometimes I'd shoot in the morning and between times I'd work long days on Subsurface and other cases. Tina had a satellite phone with her, and she'd call at night and tell me in a few clipped sentences about their day—how great it was to have Henry with them in "hiding," how Barnaby loved the lake and canoeing and being "home" with his mother all day instead of having to go to preschool and day care.

Sabin called me about a week after I got back. "Let's swap notes," she said.

"What's to swap? Tony Smeltzer killed Lydia."

"Still and all," she said, "let's make sure there're no dangling threads."

We arranged to meet after work at the Rain Tree.

Late in the afternoon Dorsey called. "Nick, I just got off the phone with someone from the state crime lab. I have news you may want to pass along to your wife: They've recovered a few hairs from the Kyle Runion remains. Not his hairs, someone else's. And get this—they also found a stain."

"A stain?"

"Semen."

"On what?"

"Not sure. Underpants or the sheet he was wrapped in or something."

"Are they good samples? Testable?"

"Yes, they're very good. The stain especially. Not too much degradation."

"I'm amazed," I said. "After all this time."

"I know. Apparently, he was wrapped up. Protected from the elements. Tough stuff, DNA, if it's out of the weather."

"What all was in that box of evidence?"

"I never saw it. Detective Philbin saw it. He transported it from the Bureau over to the state lab. He said it was just the boy's clothes and that sheet."

"When will you have results?"

"Soon. I'll let you know."

* * *

Sabin got to the Rain Tree before I did. I found her at the bar with a glass of red. I ordered the same. We clinked. She said, "The real reason I called you was to apologize."

"For what?"

"Trying to hustle you with that good cop/bad cop thing. Philly and I really thought Henry was the one. We thought you had a blind spot."

I shrugged. "Just doing your job, I guess."

"And Philly, he thought you might be susceptible to some female compassion."

"Oh, and you played no part?"

"Guilty," she said.

"Why did Philbin think I'd be so susceptible to your charms?"

"Just rumors, Nick. Word is that you and the Mrs. are in a rough patch. But no hard feelings?" She held her glass up again. We clinked again. She sipped her wine, wiped her mouth on a napkin, stretched, and sipped again. "I did a year of law school," she said.

"Dropped out?"

"Got pregnant. I thought I could go back later, but you know how it is. Everything gets complicated."

"Yeah, tell me about it."

She laughed. "I mean, I love police work, but sometimes I have regrets."

"Careful of your scarf," I said. It was silk; earth tones with fringed ends. Some of the fringe was dangling above the wine. She looked nice. The scarf was elegant, and she wore earrings of tourmaline. She was attractive. She must have changed her clothes and tidied up before coming to meet me, because she always looked more gritty and detective-like when she was on the job. "You'd be a good lawyer," I said, though I had no idea if that was true. "And you're young enough. You could go back and finish."

"Don't be silly." But a second later, she said, "You really think so?"

We talked about lawyering and about the investigation of Lydia's murder. She ordered more wine. She looked at her watch. "We could get a table," she said. "Have some dinner."

It sounded nice, having dinner with Sabin. There was nobody waiting for me. Even ZZ was away. It was lonely at home, and I felt good here in the lively atmosphere of the Rain Tree. There were couples all around us clinking glasses and holding hands and reaching their forks across the table to try a taste from each other's plates. Sabin was attractive and exotic, and I liked how she could flip between being a shrewd detective and being an engaging dinner date.

We got a table. Sabin went to the ladies room. My cell rang. It was Isler.

"I think we've located Tony Smeltzer," he said. "The guy is in San Francisco. He's been using an alias. He isn't in custody yet, but I expect we'll catch up with him pretty soon."

"Are you sure he's physically there?"

"No," Isler said. "Until we have cuffs on him, we can't be sure."

I stood up and put some bills down on the table for the wine and the dinner that I wouldn't be eating. I wanted to call Tina on her satellite phone to tell her it was almost over. And I didn't want to be having dinner with Sabin when I talked to her. I liked Sabin okay. But I was a married man and didn't want to send any false signals.

"Critical developments," I said when Sabin got back to the table. "I'll explain when I can."

She was gracious. Cops understand things like this. I walked toward the exit and turned around to wave before stepping through the door.

I called Tina. "The Bureau wants you to stay put until they actually have their hands on Smeltzer," I said, "but that will probably be before morning."

"Come get us," she said. "We'll stay a few extra days. It's so nice here." I agreed to leave the next day to go pick them up. I'd swing by the office midmorning, drop a few things off, and be on the road by noon. Tina put Barnaby on the phone before I hung up.

"I miss you, Daddy."

"I miss you, too, Barn. I'll see you tomorrow night, okay?"

"Can we go canoeing, Daddy?"

"Of course."

"I want to be in Henry's canoe."

"We'll see, Barn. I love you."

"And Henry's car. I want to ride home in Henry's car."

Isler called in the morning: "We've had Smeltzer all night. We're releasing him."

"Releasing him!" I yelled.

"It wasn't him, Nick. The guy was an open book. He hasn't left Frisco since he arrived there in April."

"Maybe he hired someone to kill Lydia."

"Yeah, the guys out there thought of that. It's hard to rule out, of course, but there are no indicators. He seems more like a derelict than someone who's hiring contract killers. Believe me, the team in San Fran is good. The best. They sweated him hard. They assured me it wasn't him. So I'm assuring you, it wasn't him."

Isler convinced me. He told me they'd get back to work figuring out who killed Lydia. They'd go through all of Tina's prosecution cases, looking for anybody who might have a vendetta to settle. For now, without the specter of an enraged Tony Smeltzer on the loose, it was probably okay to bring Tina and Barnaby home.

I packed what I needed for the drive, then headed over to my office. I kept the car radio off. I needed to think. If Isler was right about Tony Smeltzer—that he wasn't involved—then we were back where we started; and where we started was that Henry was the main suspect in Lydia's murder. We'd gotten so fixated on the idea of the murder as an act of mistaken identity that we'd forgotten about the possibility of somebody intending to kill Lydia as Lydia. And in that version of reality, Henry was still the only *identified* suspect.

I thought of Philbin's five fingers waving at me: the five points of his certainty that Henry was the perp.

Maybe I'd been too quick to dismiss it all. I hadn't been able to see Henry as an enraged killer even though, in my business, you learn that anybody can fool you. Henry was quiet, brooding, and seemed contemplative. If somebody had claimed that he was a quiet psychopath with dark secrets, maybe I could have believed it. But that he was a time bomb of violent rage—it didn't fit him.

On the other hand, who knew what indignities Henry had suffered? Who knew the psychological component of his physical scars? Who knew the accumulated bitterness of all the rejection and humiliation he must have endured in his life? First was the rejection by his natural parents, then by the girl in high school (whatever the actual facts of that fiasco), and then maybe every day of his life by schoolmates and pretty girls and professional colleagues. Who knew the emotional toll of being gawked at, feared, reviled? I had no idea what it would be like to live in Henry's body. But for a second, as I drove to the office and happily anticipated going to pick up Tina and Barn, I thought of Lydia stepping out on Henry. And I asked myself the question that Henry must have asked himself a million times: If he looked normal, would it all be different? I thought about how it might have felt to Henry, thinking he'd finally found, in Lydia's arms, a safe haven from the inevitable cruelty of life. And then to discover that her supposed love was not the deliverance he had thought but, rather, the cruelest ruse of all. It must have felt like a repeat of his high school humiliation, played out on a grander scale: to be sucked in by a desirable woman only to find he was merely the ridiculed victim of a hoax. For that second, as I pulled into the parking garage beside my office, all these thoughts swirled in my imagining—the trauma, the rejection, the humiliation, followed by the relief, the surrender to love, and then full circle back to betrayal and rejection.

I'd have killed her, too.

I wouldn't tell Tina that Smeltzer had been cleared of suspicion until she and Barnaby were well away from Henry. I'd let her go on thinking Smeltzer was the killer and everything would be fine. I wanted to get to them as fast as I could. I'd drop off some things at the office, and then I'd get right back in the car and drive. I wouldn't stop until I could position myself between Henry and my family. Because if he *was* the killer, and if, on hearing that Smeltzer had been cleared, Henry figured the gig was up and we were closing in, who knew what desperate measures he'd resort to.

When I stepped out of the elevator, the criminal division felt different. Down the hallway by my office, I saw Chip standing with Pleasant Holly and Upton. Without saying a word, Chip tipped his head toward my office door. Something was very wrong. Something terrible had happened up at the lake. Upton and Pleasant and Chip stood like mourners as I walked past them into my office. They followed. Upton closed the door.

"We've got DNA results in the Kyle Runion case," Chip said. "The lab tested both the hair and the semen stains. They're from one individual, and that person is not Daryl Devaney. My guess is Devaney will be cleared of Kyle Runion's murder, as well as involvement in two similar disappearances."

This was good news. Tina would be excited. I'd been sure they were about to tell me that Henry had gone on a rampage, or maybe that a canoe had tipped over. I made my way to the desk and tried to look like I was sitting down in the chair as opposed to falling into it. But the three of them, Upton, Pleasant, and Chip, were still staring at me, as somber as undertakers. It didn't take the three of them and a closed door to tell me Daryl Devaney had been vindicated.

"What is it?" I said.

"The lab ran the DNA results through the national database of violent offenders," Chip said. "They got a match."

"And?"

"They were clean samples. At my request, they ran the test a second and third time. It's conclusive."

I waited.

"The hair and semen from Kyle Runion's clothing and remains matched a DNA sample from a date rape case twenty years ago down in Renfield. The offender's name was—"

"Henry Tatlock," I said.

CHAPTER 32

The second most important thing was to make sure Barnaby didn't witness anything. I didn't want him seeing Henry handcuffed and thrown in the back of a cruiser, didn't want him watching SWATs tackling Henry from behind, didn't want him watching a dozen gun barrels appearing from nowhere. I didn't want him seeing agents tackling Tina to get her out of the way. I didn't want Barn himself being scooped from the ground, terrified to find himself in the arms of an artillery-clad commando, and I especially didn't want him seeing his uncle Henry getting gunned down if things got nasty. Barn had to be taken out of there before we moved against Henry.

Henry was an unpredictable psycho. He had not only perpetrated unspeakable crimes against Kyle Runion and, in all probability, several other disappeared juveniles, he'd also wantonly shot his fiancée in the head, probably when she stumbled upon the truth about him. So the first, most important thing was to make sure Henry never felt threatened until Tina and Barn were far away.

We went in two helicopters and were met at the other end by local law enforcement. I was given a car. It was decided that instead of our driving multiple cars to the cabin, and instead of my bringing officers or agents in the car with me, two SWAT-trained agents would crouch under a blanket on the backseat floor.

It was early afternoon. I turned onto the windy road that dead-ended at Tina's wilderness hideout. The escort vehicles hung back out of sight. Most of the leaves had fallen; we could see the cabin from far off. The car lent to Tina by the FBI was parked outside.

"Almost there," I said to the blanket behind me.

"Signs of activity?"

"Not yet."

I pulled up beside Tina's car.

"Be careful," the blanket said. I had my Glock in my jacket pocket. We had discussed many versions of how this might play out, and how I should respond in different scenarios. If I could get Tina and Barn out of the house with Henry inside, I'd pick Barn up and tell Tina "Run!" and get back to the car as quickly as possible. The agents would have climbed into the front, and we'd go spinning out the driveway. If Tina and Barn were in the house and I could get Henry out, I'd slam and bolt the door, and agents would come from the car and take him.

I got out of the car, walked to the cabin, and went in. Everything was orderly. The woodstove was warm, coffee cups on the table, dishes in the sink. Nobody home. I went back out and updated the agents, then walked to the bunkhouse. Ditto: It was lived in but currently vacant. I went to the shore and counted canoes. I was pretty sure one was missing. I went to the car and consulted. One of the agents radioed the status to his reinforcements. More agents arrived and took up positions in hiding.

"Now we wait," Chip said.

"You wait," I said. "I'm going out looking."

They tried to talk me out of it, but sitting around waiting felt like the worst idea. If another gargantuan cyclone was swirling into existence, I'd be damned if I was going to sit around waiting for it to make landfall. Henry might have caught wind of something. He might have fled out the road with my family as hostages, or maybe he'd decided on some warped survivalist tactic, taking to the woods, perhaps even heading for the Canadian border in a bizarre attempt to flee from justice at two miles per hour in the stern of a canoe. Or maybe he was taking Tina and Barnaby off into the woods to indulge his unspeakable proclivities. Who knew what his festering wounds would cause him to do when he was playing family with Tina and Barn a zillion miles from anyone else's eyes? I pushed a canoe into the water, jumped in, and went.

I had been on the water about an hour, well out of sight from the house, when I saw the tendril of smoke rising from the trees on a tiny island. I tried Chip on the two-way radio he'd given me, but his response was unintelligible. I told him I'd found them, though I doubted he understood me; I switched the radio off so it wouldn't give me away.

When I got close to the beach, Barnaby ran to the water and started jumping up and down, screaming, "Daddy, Daddy!" ZZ barked. Tina and Henry stood on the beach shoulder to shoulder, waving.

"Cooking hot dogs," Barn yelled, and the second I was out of the boat, he had me by the hand and pulled me to the fire, where they had everything for their cookout ready to go.

"I hoped we'd have some fish," Henry said. "I guess I'm not such a great provider." He laughed. Tina laughed. She grabbed Henry's arm and said to me, "He's been so great."

They wanted to know if there was news: anything new about Smeltzer; anything about Lydia; anything about Kyle Runion.

"Nothing," I told them. "Nothing about anything." But Tina saw how agitated I was. She went from happy and affectionate to wary and standoffish. They'd been in their own world, the three of them, far from the horrors of Lydia's death and of Tina being stalked by a killer. From Tina's perspective, she and Henry had a bond in their grief over Lydia that I didn't share. It made me the outsider, the intruder. They'd put on a good show for a few moments, but with my conspicuous agitation, I'd brought all the unhappiness of the outside world to this wilderness paradise of theirs. I was unwelcome.

I had allowed myself to forget that Tina and I were on the outs. Now I remembered loud and clear. Her body language and tone of voice said it all. In subtle ways, she oriented toward Henry, not toward me. The connection between them was palpable. I was sure, as fellow refugees and partners in grief, they'd found solace in each other's company that felt better to her than her fraught relationship with me.

But Henry would be on his way to life in prison (or worse) within the hour.

"We should go," I said.

"Why?" Tina said, her voice heavy with resentment.

I had no answer for her. I should have thought something up ahead of time: *We have to go because . . .*

Because there's a storm coming?

Because Lizzy was in an accident?

Because I ate a bad burrito, which is about to be ejected from both ends at once?

Because if I'm gone too long, the FBI is apt to send one of the helicopters out to look for me, perhaps causing your new best friend, Henry, to go off like a Roman candle, forcing me to shoot him right here by the shore as our four-year-old son looks on?

"Henry, can I have a word?" I said. I walked away from the fire, beckoning him to come with me.

"What is it, Nick?"

I walked until we were out of sight from the campfire. "Everything okay, Nick?" he asked, brimming with innocence. In his tone of voice, in the pronunciation of every syllable, every inflection, and in the way he walked, the swing of his arms, the solicitous bend of his back, the way he now stopped and turned toward me, the way he blinked at me questioningly, the lifting of his arms in a "what gives" gesture, I felt his calculating, remorseless psychopathic deception. I thought about the excitement he must have felt at first snatching up young Kyle Runion, and of his self-congratulatory efficiency at dealing with Lydia when she became a threat, and I thought about the smug satisfaction he must have gotten these past two weeks while lavishing fatherly attention on Barnaby and husbandly compassion on Tina.

I had my hands in my jacket pockets. My Glock was in the right-hand pocket. I held it. I wanted to use it. It would have been so much easier than keeping up the charade, pretending all was well.

I could do it. I could save everyone a lot of trouble. *He knew something was up,* I'd say. *He jumped me. We wrestled for the gun. I won.*

Nobody would doubt me. Nobody would care.

"Nick," Henry said. He touched my shoulder. I jumped backward—now would be the moment . . .

The moment passed.

"It's Lizzy," I said. "I just got word. There's been an accident."

"Oh my God. How . . ."

"I don't know anything yet. I don't want Barnaby to know. You tell Tina," I said. It was easier lying to Henry like this than to Tina. If I'd tried lying to Tina, everything would have gotten too confused. The emotions in that lie would have overcome me. But it was easy with Henry. My hatred for him masked everything else.

We loaded the canoes and left. Tina and Henry went in one boat. I took Barn and ZZ with me.

CHAPTER 33

We hit the beach in record time, propelled by the urgency of my lie about Lizzy. I hurried Tina and Barn into the cabin, asking Henry to secure the boats.

Within minutes Henry had been handcuffed, loaded into a helicopter, and was gone.

The detention hearing was two days later. Henry shuffled into the courtroom, chained up like Marley's ghost. I sat in the gallery behind Gregory Nations, hoping my presence would add federal gravitas to the proceedings. The judge was Wendell Ballard, a former private lawyer, new to the bench, and not expected to last long because he was already talking about how much he missed being a combatant in the tooth-and-claw grappling of trial law.

He called court to order: ". . . detention hearing of Henry Tatlock on one count of murder in the first degree . . ."

Just murder? I wondered why they weren't charging him with kidnapping or any of the possible sex crimes. So I almost missed it when the judge said: ". . . for the killing of Lydia Trevor."

Lydia? I looked around in the courtroom, and yes, a couple of rows back, Detectives Sabin and Philbin were there to watch.

Henry's lawyer stood. "We believe there is insufficient probable cause for an arrest in Lydia Trevor's murder, and so—"

Judge Ballard interrupted: "Ms. Brill, are you moving to quash the arrest warrant?"

"I am, Your Honor."

"Fine. Submit your motion. We'll schedule arguments. But today's hearing is on the question of whether Mr. Tatlock, being charged with Lydia Trevor's murder, should be detained or freed on bail."

It took me a few moments to realize what a shrewd move it had been for Gregory Nations to charge Henry in only Lydia's murder right now, not Kyle Runion's. Prosecutors *never* want to admit they've convicted an innocent man. It causes the public to lose confidence in the system. Some of the old-school prosecutors claim that no innocent man or woman has ever been convicted in their jurisdiction—though I doubt they believe this. What they *really* believe is that a few wrongful convictions are a small price to pay for a society that trusts the police, prosecutors, and courts. So Nations would resist caving on Daryl Devaney's eight-year-old conviction as long as possible. If the DNA evidence against Henry held up, Daryl would go free, and the state would write him a big check for his trouble. But Gregory Nations wasn't giving up this bone without a fight, especially seeing as he could, for now at least, keep the new suspect—Henry—in jail for something else.

Monica Brill, Henry's lawyer, argued that considering his good reputation and ties to the community, he should be free on bail. She said there was no good evidence linking him to Lydia's murder, and it was an atrocious misuse of the system that he'd been charged for the crime. She said he posed no danger to the community.

But we all knew about the DNA results. So even though Henry was being arraigned for a crime having nothing to do with the Kyle Runion killing, there was no way a judge was going to put him back out into society. "The suspect is to be detained pending trial," Judge Ballard said. His gavel hit the bench.

The officers got Henry to his feet and started walking him toward the exit, but he swung around violently, jerking his arms from the guards' hands. He looked toward all of us in the gallery. I saw savage terror in his eyes. He barely looked human. It was a split second before the officers had him facedown on the floor. He screamed in pain at having his arms wrenched up tight behind his back. But there were words in the shrieks; "I didn't do anything."

I doubted Henry would ever again spend a day as a free man.

PART II

CHAPTER 34

My cabin feels different this morning. I didn't stoke the fire last night. It burned out hours ago. I stick my head out from under the quilts and can see my breath. But it's not only the temperature. The light is steely white and cold, and I know before even looking out the window that it snowed last night. Probably not much, just an inch or two, but enough to blend the landscape into a startling blur of sameness. It will melt by noon, as early snows always do, its flash of clean renewal turning immediately to gray and brown. But for now, everything feels erased.

I wish Tina were here with me.

I wish Barn and Lizzy were here.

I'd even settle for Flora and Chip showing up at the other cabin to irritate me with their abundance of good cheer.

I have spent the past month writing down everything that has happened. I'm done now. Finis. I have caught up to the present. This process has helped me keep it all straight in my mind, and the discipline I had to exercise, sitting here methodically going back through the murder, the investigations, the revelations about Henry, and the realization of how I'd so naïvely invited him into all corners of my life, has helped me traverse the emotional quicksand.

Henry Tatlock is the very incarnation of evil and misery. He inserted himself into my life. He killed and debased the innocent Kyle Runion, he murdered my sister-in-law, he corrupted the integrity of the U.S. Attorney's Office, and with who knows what malevolent intentions, he positioned himself as ad hoc husband and father into my relationships with Tina and Barnaby during their time in hiding.

I hate him. But "hate" is too weak a word.

* * *

I get up and make a fire in the woodstove. Then coffee. I walk out to the end of the dock. The snow is nice. I take a deep breath of cold air and spend a minute reflecting on the feeling of renewal that arrived with the new snow.

I go back into the cabin and sit at the pine-slab table. I have some of the Subsurface files with me. It's time to climb into the saddle; time to do some work. I open one of the files, but the startling whiteness of the light distracts me. I get up and close the curtains partway.

Better.

But now it's too cold, so I throw more wood into the stove.

Better.

But now it's too hot. I damper the stove and crack a window.

Better.

But it's a little dark, so I open the curtain.

I call Tina. "What are you and Barn doing today?"

"Birthday party for a little girl from day care. Remember I told you? It's at the pool. Cake, ice cream, and lots of little bodies running around in water wings."

"Sounds great. Maybe tomorrow I'll—"

"Oh, crap," she says, "gotta run. I'll call you back."

I try working again, but after about twenty minutes, I scoop everything into my briefcase, shut down the stove, get in my car, and leave.

I arrive in the city around four in the afternoon. It's a ridiculous notion, but I drive over to the rec center, where the pool room reverberates with the ecstatic din of children who are deep into a sugar high. The event room is filled with ten-year-old girls. The kiddie pool is full, but I don't recognize a single face among either the kids or the parental horde lining the edges. The party I'm looking for has been over for hours.

It's getting dark. I stop on my way "home" and pick up a pizza to go, then drive to Friendly City Executive Suites (Day, Week, Month).

* * *

I call Sabin. We haven't spoken since before Henry's arrest. I want to know whether they've gotten any traction at all—any real evidence—connecting Henry to Lydia's murder.

"How about coffee?" I ask.

"Do you one better," she said. "How about a walk? We'll go to Rokeby, linger at the site, see if the wind and trees will whisper their secrets to us."

We meet at the amphitheater parking. She has a brown bakery bag. I stopped over at "Tina's" house to get ZZ. The sign says to keep dogs on a leash, but ZZ is obedient, and as long as you bag the poop, nobody seems to care. It is cold out. Yesterday's puddles are today's ice slicks. ZZ, zooming around happily, tries switching directions at the wrong moment and goes down on the ice, sliding across with four paws in the air. We both laugh.

"I want to get another dog," Sabin says.

"You used to have one?"

"Always did. But now, you know, work and everything."

"I know."

We find the site of Lydia's murder and linger there.

"Are the trees whispering?" I ask.

"Not to me. Are they to you?"

"You're the detective."

We continue down the path and stop at the bench where I hung out sometimes in the weeks after the murder. Sabin hands me a chunk of coffee cake.

"Have there been any developments?" I ask.

"No, Henry was careful. I don't think we could convict him of Lydia's murder without the Kyle Runion thing. But now Lydia is just icing. You knew we searched his house again, right?"

"Find anything?"

She shook her head. "We hoped to find a memento."

"Memento?"

"Of Kyle Runion. You know, pervs and psychopaths sometimes keep something of the victim's."

"Maybe Lydia found the memento. Maybe that's how she figured it all out," I said.

"That's what we think. She took the memento, he chased her down, killed her. Took the memento back, whatever it was, and got rid of it."

"It all fits," I say. ZZ is barking at a squirrel on a branch. "ZZ, shut up."

"Now it makes more sense that Lydia was stepping out," Sabin says.

"How do you mean?"

"Her affair: It fits the profile," she says. "Guys like Henry, lots of times they have a girlfriend or wife for cover, but it's never sexual. So Lydia Trevor was finding comfort someplace else."

"I didn't think of that. You're right. It all starts to make sense," I say.

"And the other thing," Sabin says, "a lot of them were bullied as kids. Socially isolated."

"I think that fits him. It seems to, from what I know."

"Everything fits," she says. "You still can't think of who she might have been having the affair with?"

I consider this in the context of our new information. It doesn't have to be someone she was in love with, just somebody who could fulfill that need of physical intimacy. Nobody comes to mind.

We get up from the bench and start walking back. Sabin has gloves on but no hat. She is wearing a waist-length jacket, looking more like a skier than a detective. When we reach one of the frozen puddles, she takes my arm. When we're back on solid pavement, she doesn't let go.

"Do you have a first name?" I ask.

She laughs. "Rachel. But Sabin works just fine."

* * *

In the afternoon Lizzy comes to my office to talk about the gas tax legislation that caused the Subsurface scandal. "I'm a little stuck," she says.

"How's that?"

She hands me her notes. "I've learned all the easy stuff about who sponsored the legislation, who supported it, who opposed. How everyone voted. It's all public record. Easy breezy."

"Well, that's all I was looking for, Liz."

"No, it's not," she says.

"It's not?"

"No. You want to know the backroom stuff."

"Not really; I mean, sure, if you hear anything, I'd love to know, but I'm not asking for that. That's the Bureau's job. I just want to make sure I understand the basic who, what, and where of this legislation."

She gives me the look of a long-suffering daughter. "Boring," she says. "I could have had that to you in one afternoon. It's all right here." She waves her sheaf of notes at me. "But let me keep going. It's interesting."

"Sounds like maybe politics is your calling."

"Oh, please!" she says in a voice of exaggerated revulsion. She sits here in my office looking happy and confident. It bothered me at first when she bagged her plans to go traveling. I worried she'd mope and let a year pass without anything to show for it. But now she seems to be in gear again. She is planning to fly off someplace within the next month or two, though she hasn't settled on a destination. And she says she intends to start college a year from January.

"How's it going with Ethan?" I ask.

"I thought this was a business meeting." She laughs.

"You're right," I say. "So let's get dinner later? We can dish then."

"It's a date. Now back to business?"

On a slip of notepaper, I write a name and phone number. "Call this guy. He'll be the best source to start with if you really want to go deep into the sausage factory."

"Sausage factory?"

"The old saying: The two things you never want to see being made are laws and sausages."

"Calvin Dunbar," she says, looking at the note. "Isn't he one of the legislators who got charged in the whole mess?"

"He is. But he's remorseful—turned himself in. We've become friendly. Just tell him you're my daughter."

Lizzy pockets the note and gets up to leave. I walk her out. Upton's office door is open. "Hi, Upton," she says.

"Hi, Lizzy. Come say hi to Cicely."

Lizzy goes into the office. Cicely is busy at something on her desk. "Hey there, Sis," Lizzy says. The girls have known each other for years, though they were never friends.

"Are you in college yet, Lizzy?" Cicely asks.

"Not yet. Next year, maybe."

"Me, neither," Cicely says. "Maybe next year for me, too. Right, Dad?"

"We'll see, sweetie."

"Do you have a boyfriend yet?" Cicely asks.

"Yes. Do you?"

"No. Maybe next year." She laughs.

Lizzy hugs her good-bye, and we leave. I walk Liz out to her car.

CHAPTER 35

Not long after she got back from hiding, Tina petitioned the court for a trial in the Daryl Devaney case. Usually, when you find undiscovered evidence like the DNA implicating Henry and vindicating Daryl, you ask for a *new* trial. But since Daryl confessed and pleaded guilty, there was never a trial in the first place.

The morning of the hearing is déjà vu. The hallway fills again with Kyle Runion's family and friends, all of them still seeking justice for his memory. But there aren't as many spectators as last time, and the ones who do show up are less sure what to think. At the first hearing, they were quietly outraged at the idea of Tina manipulating the system to get Daryl Devaney out of prison on some technicality. But today I see uncertainty in their faces, and I hear it in their voices. They don't want to go through it all again. They *want* to be convinced of Daryl Devaney's guilt; they *want* to go to bed tonight convinced that he is justifiably rotting in prison. Kyle's parents, neighbors, aunts, and uncles, they're all eager for Gregory Nations to tell them the DNA thing is a hoax.

Among the people waiting for the hearing is a familiar man. Not Arthur Cunningham—he's here too—but a fortyish guy who looks out of place. He has made an effort to dress appropriately, but he missed the mark. He wears khakis, clean running shoes, and a shirt that looks like he came from yoga class. His hair is shaggy, and he has an almost invisible blond goatee, more peach fuzz than whiskers. I can't place him.

We all enter the courtroom. Judge Matsuko comes in and announces the case: ". . . petition to reverse guilty plea . . . new evidence . . . DNA analysis . . ."

Tina stands. Again I see the tidy line of her hair across the back of her dress. For a split second I puzzle over why I can't seem to remember her picking out that dress. Of course I can't: I don't live with her, I live at Friendly City.

I see Tina's hands on the lectern. (*Grab the lectern,* they told us in law school. *When you don't know what to do with your hands, grab the lectern.*) I slide over a few inches to get a better view of her left hand. I see she still wears her ring, but things feel different; she feels more *gone* than before. I suddenly realize who the guy outside the courtroom was. I turn in my seat and see him in the back row, far off to the side, trying to be invisible. It is Craig, Tina's first husband who lives on the West Coast. I recognize him from old photographs.

Tina gives her argument: "While DNA evidence is not always able to identify who *should* be considered a suspect, in many cases it can determine with absolute authority who is *not* among the population of possible perpetrators. In the Kyle Runion case, DNA testing has conclusively eliminated Daryl Devaney."

She goes on to describe the DNA results in technical language: short tandem repeats; alleles; markers; tetranucleotide repeats. She goes into a bit too much detail but moves quickly and then summarizes with an aggressive conclusion: "All of which means there is a zero percent possibility that Daryl Devaney was the source of the DNA."

"But, Ms. Trevor," Judge Matsuko says, "not only did the defendant—or strike that, he's not a defendant, he's a convict—not only did he confess to this crime, he also pleaded guilty. And then he slept on his rights, he failed to make timely appeals, and the statute of limitations for the introduction of new evidence expired long ago. In your own brief, you cite no controlling statute allowing me to consider this evidence."

I watch Kyle Runion's supporters. Family and friends of a victim usually like to see the defense take a scolding. But this is different. They don't want legal complexities, they want their doubts quieted. I see the woman I assume is Kyle's mother. She watches Tina, listening with her head cocked sideways. She looks like a PTA mom in skirt and blouse, her blond hair showing enough of a wave in front that you can't be sure if it's natural, kept out of her eyes by a quick comb-through with her fingers, or done at a salon. She is serious-looking, her face revealing that she understands most of what she hears. I have no doubt that she reads everything Gregory Nations sends her and calls him up with questions when something doesn't make sense.

Peggy Devaney sits near me. A striking contrast to Kyle's mother, Peggy is burly, has raw, chapped hands, and the complexion of an old shingle on the side of a barn. Her hair is white and braided. She wears new jeans and two button-down shirts. The inside one is white and buttoned one shy of the top. The overshirt is blue plaid and quilted and opened to the waist, tucked into the jeans, giving her more bulge below the beltline than she can take credit for. She is very much a farm girl. Both women listen as Tina answers the judge's comments, and I wonder if they could ever be friendly. What if Daryl's "conviction" is overturned; what if Henry is legally proved to be the perp? These two have endured such trauma—not just losing a loved one but also the agony of clinging for so long to the most meager scraps of hope. Until Kyle's remains were discovered by Arthur Cunningham a full year after the boy disappeared, his mother clung, no doubt, to the hope that he might yet be found alive. And Peggy Devaney has clung for eight years to the hope of a reversal that will vindicate her brother and set him free. I wonder if, when it's all over, one will ever reach out to the other.

Now Gregory Nations stands to argue. He talks about protecting the finality of verdicts.

The judge interrupts. "But in the case of newfound compelling evidence of innocence—"

"Your Honor, while analysis of this new evidence indicates that it was not Daryl Devaney's DNA, we would argue that the person who kidnapped and murdered Kyle Runion might not be the one who actually left the DNA. Additionally, there could have been a laboratory error in analysis of the sample, or chain-of-custody problems, or contamination of the sample. So if—"

Matsuko interrupts again. "So why not have a trial? Let a jury decide those questions?"

"I'll tell you why, Judge," Nations says. He squares his shoulders and straightens to maximum height. The message of his body language is obvious: He wants to remind us that he speaks for the people. For *society*.

Gregory Nations is an empty suit. He is unimaginative and unexplored. He is a zealous prosecutor, and he believes that being a prosecutor means he is also philosophical, and wise, and insightful about the human condition. But whenever we get together, our conversation withers the second we get off the subject of current prosecutions. As far as I can tell, he doesn't think about anything besides convicting accused perps, and he doesn't ponder or anguish over the tragedies that we are called upon to redress. It doesn't surprise me that he seems unmoved by the possibility of Daryl's innocence. "It's not about innocence," I heard him say once, "it's about order and consistency."

Gregory Nations says in a voice a bit deeper than a moment ago: "As you just pointed out, Your Honor, there was a confession, a guilty plea, a sentence. Mr. Devaney never requested, within the prescribed time frame, to withdraw his plea, and he never filed a timely appeal, and there is no statute or case law specifically allowing a new trial."

"Yeah, yeah, yeah," Matsuko says, "but I'm not talking about points of law, I'm talking about innocence. *Actual* innocence."

Gregory shakes his head at the judge's apparent naïveté. "Your Honor," he says, "do you really want to open your court docket to every convict who claims he didn't do it?"

CHAPTER 36

The hearing ends. Judge Matsuko is in no hurry to make a decision. He and Gregory Nations are playing the same game. They want to be certain *somebody* fills the prison cell of Kyle Runion's murderer. They'd prefer it to be the right person, but until they have more confidence in the case against Henry, they don't want Daryl Devaney going anywhere.

At the last hearing, Kyle Runion's people got out of the courtroom as quickly as possible, not wanting to risk an encounter with Tina or me or Peggy Devaney. This time they are in less of a hurry. They're uncertain what to think.

I go to Tina and give her a hug. "Great work, babe," I say.

She responds with a tepid one-arm hug. "Thanks. I think it went okay."

Peggy comes and stands with us. She has a small handbag clutched against her waist. It seems incongruously dainty against this hefty woman, whose eyes are comically magnified behind thick lenses. She is different than the last time I saw her. With the DNA results, she has been stunned by the first blinding rays of optimism. It must be terrifying.

I step away to let the two of them talk. Craig is gone from the room. Too bad. I wanted to introduce myself to him. I was going to shake his hand, hold on to it too long and squeeze too hard, and stand too close, holding his hand near my stomach, breathing on him, and being all inside his personal space. But he slipped out. The coward.

Lizzy met with Calvin Dunbar. She calls me up, full of excitement. "He was so nice," she says. "He explained the whole process to me.

I took civics, like everybody else. I thought I knew stuff. But I guess I didn't know anything about how it really works. Back-scratching. You know? What Calvin said—get this—he said that except for how there's no smoke anymore, the smoke-filled rooms are as smoke-filled as ever, metaphorically speaking. Isn't that great?"

Lizzy chatters on about her meeting. She's as happy as I've heard her in a long time. She feels grown up and useful. She says she'll write up her notes for me. We make a plan to meet for lunch the next day, when she'll "debrief" me.

Chip calls. "I just forwarded you that report," he says.

"What report?"

"From the SF station. You know, when they investigated Tony Smeltzer?"

Smeltzer. I've scarcely thought of him since the DNA results from Kyle Runion's murder. We had thought he killed Lydia and was after Tina. We were wrong. Now he was just a dead letter. I open the email from Chip. The report comes up with a couple of photos. One is an old mug shot, the other was surreptitiously snapped by the agent who investigated Smeltzer. Doughy face with eyes that are hooded and bulging. He reminds me of the old actor Peter Lorre. The report says Smeltzer got out of Ellisville back in January, showed up in San Francisco in April, and spent some time in a hospital there in June.

The report states that Smeltzer hasn't left the Bay Area since he first arrived. He had surgery for colon cancer this past spring, and his health appears frail. He has a job working in an auto parts store just outside of San Francisco, and he spends much of his free time in a local bar called the Fog City Tap. Occasionally, he'll find a woman to leave with. The reporting agent, a guy named Laird, says he engaged Smeltzer in conversation and they shot some pool together. "The subject makes no bones about being fed up with everyone and everything," Laird writes. "He makes frequent reference to taking a walk halfway across the Golden Gate Bridge one day soon." According to the report, Smeltzer headed for the West Coast after getting out of Ellisville because the feds had nabbed both the stash and the cash when they arrested him years ago. Apparently, some of his old crowd has heartburn about that loss of assets, so Smeltzer figured he'd keep his distance.

Lizzy and I meet at the Rain Tree. The place is packed. We stand inside the door, waiting for a table. Several parties are ahead of us, and within a few minutes, several more come in behind. New arrivals blow warm breath into their hands and stuff woolen hats into overcoat pockets. *Wow! Brrr!*

Steve, the owner, comes over in his wheelchair. "Sorry for the wait, folks. We'll seat you as soon as we can."

He spots me in the crowd and we exchange nods, then he goes over to the hostess and says something to her before rolling away to wherever he came from. A minute later, the hostess comes up to me and says quietly, "Mr. Davis, your table is ready." Lizzy and I follow her to a table for two over by the windows.

"Geez, Dad," Lizzy says.

I shrug modestly.

We order a small pot of clams as an appetizer. Steve brings them on a tray balanced across his prosthetic knees. "Davis," he says. We bump fists.

"Thanks for the table."

He brushes the comment away with a flip of his hand.

I say, "I'd like you to meet my, um . . ." I glance at Lizzy. She looks professional. She has obviously prepared for this meeting and wants be taken seriously. Her clothes are businesslike, her hair is brushed, and she wears a touch of mascara and muted lipstick. (Who *is* this girl?) She has a black folio in which, I assume, are the notes and the report she has prepared for me. In her left hand she holds a pen, dexterously twirling it through her fingers in a way I've never mastered.

"I'd like you to meet my associate, Elizabeth Davis," I say to Steve.

"Elizabeth," Steve says. He holds up a fist and Lizzy bumps it. She smiles, and I try to think whether I'm surprised to see a mouth of even white teeth instead of silvery hardware and colorful rubber bands. The passing of time made more sense to me back when I saw Lizzy regularly throughout the week. Now that she's living full-time with Flora, weeks pass without a meeting in person. I haven't gotten my mind around the new Lizzy.

"Associate?" Steve says. "An associate with the same last name. And it looks like you and her are from the same cookie cutter, different batch."

"You caught us," I say. "Lizzy's my big sister."

"Daddy," she says, and in her smile, I imagine the ghost of those braces. How many years have they been gone?

"Anyhow," Steve says, "honored to make your acquaintance, Elizabeth," and he leaves us.

Steve has done well with the Rain Tree. I hear him mentioned on the radio, and I see bits in the paper about his generosity to nonprofits involved in drug and alcohol rehab, social service projects, and veterans' assistance. But his appearance hasn't caught up with his economic and social standing. If he lingered in his chair on the sidewalk beside a tin can, you'd be tempted to drop coins into it.

We finish the clams. I order a Reuben. Lizzy gets the Thai sesame salad with no chicken.

"So, about Calvin Dunbar," Lizzy says. "I've written up a report for you, just like a real investigator would."

"Aren't you a real investigator?"

"I don't have an investigator's license."

"Then let's call you a consultant. They write reports, too. For now, how about you give me a narrative, and I'll read your report when I get back to the office."

She takes her report from the folio. It's inside a plastic cover, and I see it has a title page. She flips through. "The first thing is, I like this Calvin Dunbar guy. I can see how you two hit it off. He's interesting." She scans the first page. Reading it upside down, I see it says, "Background info on Source." "He grew up in the South; went into the army after high school and trained as an airplane mechanic," Lizzy says. "And he's a diver. He went wreck diving in the Seychelles last year. I told him I was interested in diving, too, and he said maybe we could all meet up someplace for a diving vacation sometime. Anyhow, he went to college part time after the service. Prelaw, but somebody offered him a job in insurance, so he went that way even though he was more interested in public policy. The statehouse thing—him running for office—it was a whim, he didn't expect to win. Et cetera."

She looks up at me. "It's sad he got involved in all that Subsurface stuff. He says it was so stupid. He didn't even think of it as payoffs or anything. The Subsurface people liked him and just kept giving him money. So he ended up wanting to please them."

"You're right, it's sad."

"He really likes you, Dad. He says you treated him with respect and fairness. He never expected that. Anyhow, he even thought of killing himself when all this stuff came out and he felt so disgraced. But he says that was for cowards, so he decided to face the music."

Our meals arrive. Lizzy watches me bite into my Reuben. "How's your cholesterol?" she says.

"Are you planning to ruin my lunch, Liz?"

"Just saying."

I watch her with the salad. She has always been interested in nutrition, in a crunchy, hippie kind of way. She gets this from her mom. I used to make fun of her for it, but now that I've become a runner, I'm more interested in all her dietary notions.

"So, about the legislation," I say.

Lizzy puts down her fork and pats a napkin against her mouth. "Some people wanted to raise taxes on the—quote-unquote—extraction and production of natural gas. And they get at the gas now by fracking, which is a whole 'nother ball of wax. But this bill didn't address environmental stuff. Not at first, anyhow. It was all taxes."

"Who proposed it?"

"A bunch of guys with backing from the governor. Their names are in here." She taps the report. "Calvin says our taxes are way below the national average. Then Bud Billman and Subsurface Resources,

Inc., started campaigning against the tax, and they wrote all these checks to legislators, and it got bogged down in committees and stuff."

"Which committees?"

She taps the report again. "Here's where it got kind of interesting . . ."

Lizzy stops. Captain Dorsey has just walked over to us. He stands a few feet away, waiting for an opening to approach. Things got awkward between Dorsey and me when the troopers zeroed in on Henry and I still thought he was innocent. I haven't seen Dorsey since before the DNA revelations.

"Dorsey," I say, trying to sound as if there's no weirdness between us. "Where you been lately?"

"This looks like a nice father/daughter lunch," he says pleasantly. "I won't interrupt, I just wanted to say hello."

"I guess you guys were right about Henry," I say. "I should have listened."

Dorsey shakes his head at the sadness of it, his bald expanse sparkling with reflected light from the windows. "Very bad business," he says. "You have my sympathy."

"Thanks, Captain."

"But I do want to give a little heads-up." His eyes shift toward Lizzy. "If you could call me when you're done with lunch."

"How about I just go to the girls' room?" Lizzy says. She gets up and leaves.

Dorsey looks around, spots an empty chair, and pulls it over. He sits, leans in close. "We're working together with the Bureau on this Kyle Runion/Henry Tatlock thing. There were unsolved cases in other states: disappearances that looked similar to the Runion abduction. We tried to fit them to Daryl Devaney but never got anywhere. One of them actually took place after Devaney got convicted. So now we're trying to fit them to Henry Tatlock."

"And?"

"Expect a call from one of my detectives," Dorsey says. He stands and slides the chair back where he got it. "Good to see you, Nick."

Dorsey leaves, and Lizzy is back a minute later. She senses the shift in my mood, and we eat in silence for several minutes.

The waiter comes to take our plates away. "Did you save room for dessert?"

"The cheesecake," I say.

Lizzy clears her throat, camouflaging the world "cholesterol" within the cough.

"Second thought," I say to the waiter, "just decaf. What about you, Liz?"

"Tea, please."

"Subsurface," I say to Liz. "You were about to say?"

"Right. That first year, the tax increase has all the votes needed to pass, even though Subsurface was fighting against it. But at the last minute some rep nobody ever heard of tags on an amendment. The rules let them do that. And the amendment has all these environmental restrictions, even though they already decided against all that. So it got kicked back into a committee, and it was dead for the year."

"Who's the representative who added the amendment?"

Lizzy tapped the report once more. "His name is Porter. And the next year the very same thing happened again. Same legislator, same amendment, same result."

"Did you talk to Porter?"

"Not yet. I called his office and left a message. I'll keep—"

"No," I say, "you have to lay off of it for now."

"But, Dad, I—"

"Liz, we think something big might be going on. Until we've figured it out, I don't want you getting any closer to it. You can work with what you already have, but don't go interviewing anyone new. Okay?"

She scowls at me, and then she nods.

CHAPTER 37

Judge Matsuko denied Tina's petition for a trial in the Daryl Devaney case. He wrote a lengthy opinion that talked about how Daryl had confessed and pleaded guilty and never filed any attempt to withdraw his plea or appeal within the time limits. Matsuko wrote: ". . . furthermore, seeing as there has been no constitutional error and no malfeasance on the part of the state, our focus shifts from protecting the defendant to protecting the criminal justice system itself . . ."

It went on discussing the importance of finality, and of the crushing burden to the court system if all convictions became "negotiable."

Tina is stoic. "It's pretty much what I expected," she says.

I am over at "our" house, picking up Barn for a father-and-son Sunday. Barnaby is in the living room, watching cartoons. Tina and I drink coffee in the kitchen. I look through the mail on the kitchen counter while we talk. I've already been upstairs to get some clothes, all the while scanning the landscape for evidence of my new nemesis, the Muppetish, granola-crunchy, wife-stealing playground monitor named Craig. I've found nothing.

"You expected to lose?" I ask.

"Definitely," Tina says. "Matsuko would be way out on a limb. If somebody is going to overturn this 'conviction,' he'd much rather see the state supreme court do it. Or the federal court. If you study this decision, he kind of gives a blueprint for how the next court should decide in Daryl's favor."

I'm amazed. I hadn't appreciated how strategic Tina was. When she says that Matsuko provided a blueprint, what she isn't saying is that she provided him the pieces of that blueprint in her brief and her argument. She apparently knew just what she was doing, knew she was going to lose at the superior court and was setting up the game for the next round.

"More coffee, Nick?" She comes over with the pot and fills my cup. This second cup of coffee is a good thing. She's inviting me to linger.

What the fuck is going on with you and Craig?

I almost say it. I'm aching to say it. She is a clever legal strategist, mother of the best little boy in the world, and wife of an adoring husband who is head of the criminal division of the U.S. Attorney's Office and former nominee to the U.S. circuit court of appeals. And while I may be kind of bovine in tending to the emotions of my fair feminine flower, I think I'm trainable. I think I've shown myself willing to learn, to listen, to strive. Would she trade me in for *him*, captain of nothing but a third-grade classroom? Really?

I hold my tongue. No sudden moves. No demanding she give me answers. As with Tina's strategy for Daryl Devaney, I must play with my eye on the next round. While that may be how appellate lawyers think, it isn't how we trial lawyers think. We want to be up in everybody's face. We want to shout, wave our arms, put on a show.

I manage to hold myself back. "Good coffee, babe," I say. "Are you going to appeal within the state system or habeas back to federal court?"

"Not sure," she says. "Probably state."

I nod. I wish I could stay here, talk legal strategy in the kitchen with Tina, play Chutes and Ladders with Barn. Maybe all of us go out for burgers later.

Barn and I had a good day. We did some shopping, went to the library, where I read him a zillion books, then went "home" to Friendly City. I made him dinner and put him to bed.

Morning now. I consider playing hooky and hanging at home with Barn, but there is way too much going on at the office. So I drop him at day care, and I collect a hug and a kiss before releasing him into the melee.

I'm back at the FBI for a conference. Upton and I arrived together. Isler is here. Chip plays host, pouring coffee for everybody. Gregory Nations is here, too. Philbin and Sabin show up. I say, "Hi, Philbin, how you doing? I guess you were right about Henry, and I was wrong."

"Forget about it," Philbin says. "The guy was family. Nobody expects you to be objective when it involves family."

"Thanks," I say. I look at Sabin and say, "Hi, Rachel."

I'm watching Philbin out of the corner of my eye. I can tell he notices this bit of familiarity and lodges it in his mental file cabinet. Obviously, I'm enjoying strutting my new, special friendship with Sabin. Then, like a slap, I realize he's probably not the least bit surprised. Rachel Sabin might have told him all about our meeting at the Rain Tree, and about our walk in Rokeby Park—how she took my arm, holding on to me, rubbing her shoulder against mine as we crossed the ice and made our way slowly back to the cars, and how the cadence and pitch of her voice changed as we walked—from crisp and businesslike to warm and confidential—and how the change in her voice was timed to the tightening of her hand on my arm and the slowing of her pace. She probably told him, too, how my voice had changed in response to hers, and how my hand came up briefly and squeezed her hand where she held my arm.

They were playing me again. I can't believe I fell for it twice. I'm just their listening device inside the U.S. Attorney's Office. Damn them both. I turn away and sit at the conference table. "Let's get this started," I snap to nobody in particular. "I've got work to do."

Chip brings us all up to speed. The investigation of other juvenile abductions is federal because it involves interstate crime. Chip summarizes what they know of those other disappearances and how frustrated they've been, trying to develop a lead. He gets into a lot of detail, but I have trouble following. I'm not sure if my problem is that I'm so angry after realizing that Rachel, this smart, attractive, age-appropriate woman who befriended me at the moment of my marital upheaval, is using my woebegone state to play me like a fiddle. Or maybe I'm put off by what I'm hearing from Chip. It's too horrible. The man who was my friend, colleague, and very nearly my brother-in-law not only killed Lydia and committed unspeakable acts against the innocent Kyle Runion, he apparently also traveled to other states to pick up other boys who were never heard from again. A year before Kyle disappeared, a kid in Ohio disappeared, a seven-year-old named Nathan Miller. Another case: a boy from New Hampshire. Although the Bureau hasn't been able to put Henry in Ohio or New Hampshire, neither can they exclude the possibility.

"Has anybody asked Henry Tatlock to account for his whereabouts at those times?" Isler asks.

"Negative," Philbin says. "His attorney, Monica Brill, won't let us anywhere near him."

Except for Gregory Nations, everybody in the room thinks it is time to charge Henry with Kyle's murder. Gregory resists because he's trying to hold on to the Daryl Devaney conviction. But Gregory is outvoted.

"You feel okay, Nick?" Rachel Sabin asks me as we all get ready to leave.

"Of course," I say. "Why wouldn't I?"

I get out of the conference room and out of the building, and I walk the mile back to my office, liking the shock of cold air. I don't bother zipping my jacket.

"Messages for you," Janis says as I pass her desk on the way into my office. I grab the notes she proffers.

"No interruptions," I tell her. I close and lock my door. I think about the cartoon figure Lizzy clipped for me from the funny pages of the newspaper nearly six months ago, on Barnaby's birthday. LIFE IS SWEET, it said.

But life isn't sweet. Life sucks.

I lie down on my office couch and pull my jacket over my head. Someone knocks on the door.

"Nick, it's Upton. You okay, buddy?"

"No," I say. "Go away."

It's late. I'm "home" at Friendly City, trying to sleep. I give up. I go down to my car and drive to my real home. I park in front of the house where Tina and Barnaby are sleeping. I pull the sleeping bag over myself—I keep it in the car for this reason—and eventually doze off.

Dawn. I sit up and rub my eyes. I take a minute to clear the cobwebs, then drive back to Friendly City for a shower and coffee.

CHAPTER 38

G regory Nations holds a press conference in the lobby of the state courthouse. He announces that former assistant U.S. attorney Henry Tatlock has been charged with the murder, kidnapping, and sexual assault of Kyle Runion eight years ago. The evidence to be presented by the state, Nations says, is Mr. Tatlock's DNA, recovered from the exhumed remains of young Kyle.

Reporters start yelling questions: "What about Daryl Devaney? Isn't he doing life without parole for that murder?"

"Good question," Gregory says. "The issue of a new trial for Mr. Devaney is currently on appeal to the state supreme court."

As usual, Gregory isn't wearing his suit jacket but has it hitched over his shoulder. Though this press conference has been scheduled for hours, he gives the impression of being unexpectedly caught by the cameras on his way from one important obligation to the next.

"But if you are charging someone else with the crime . . ."

"Daryl Devaney's status is in the hands of the supreme court and the state attorney general's office," Gregory says. "It is no longer my case, so it would be improper for me to comment."

"Do you think Henry Tatlock is guilty?"

"If we didn't think he was guilty, we wouldn't have charged him."

"So Daryl Devaney must be innocent."

"Sorry, it's not proper for me to comment."

"Any evidence besides DNA?"

"That will be revealed at trial."

"Will you seek the death penalty?"

Gregory ponders a moment before answering. He waits for quiet, then says, "Several other children have disappeared under circumstances similar to Kyle Runion's. If Mr. Tatlock were to help us bring closure and peace to the families of those boys, we would be open to discussing a sentence of life without parole."

"Is it true he killed his girlfriend?"

"Mr. Tatlock has been held in the murder of Lydia Trevor, to whom he was engaged. Being a former law enforcement official, Mr. Tatlock was adept at covering his tracks. In all frankness, the investigation of that murder is stalled. So at this point, I'm announcing that charges against Henry Tatlock for Ms. Trevor's murder have been dropped. But I stress that jeopardy has not attached, so Mr. Tatlock can still be tried for that crime when more evidence comes to light. And I firmly believe that more evidence *will* come to light."

It is a masterful performance. Gregory manages to look confident, authoritative, and victorious in admitting that, while Daryl has spent eight years in prison for Kyle's murder, they're now charging somebody else for it without letting Daryl go free. He made the state supreme court and the attorney general's office sound like bureaucratic fumblers preventing Daryl's release, and he managed to make the dead-ended investigation into Lydia's murder sound like a nonissue.

He's smooth. And now that we're on the same side—both of us wanting to remove Henry Tatlock from society—Nations looks to me more like a dedicated public servant and less like the overzealous, politically ambitious, unenlightened automaton I considered him just a week ago.

The case is big news. It has everything. It involves a former federal prosecutor; it involves the most despicable and revolting kind of crimes; it involves digging up—literally and figuratively—a conviction that was settled years ago; there is evidence that the incident being charged is just one in a series; there is a sympathetic and wrongfully convicted man serving the defendant's time; there is a murdered fiancée. And for the unenlightened and prejudiced among the public and press, there is a disfigured defendant.

The sensationalist paper in town wastes no time in putting a photo of Henry on the front page, alongside a picture of Freddy Krueger. Of course, this ignites a firestorm of outrage that forces everybody to choose up sides before a trial date has even been determined. People seem to want Henry convicted based on nothing but his disfigurement. One hatred-spewing windbag on talk radio comments that "the good Lord saw fit to brand Henry Tatlock with the mark of Cain so we would recognize him for what he is."

These two nicknames, "The Freddy Krueger Killer" and "The Mark of Cain Killer," catch fire among Neanderthalic reactionaries inhabiting the booger-eating fringes of talk radio, sensationalist print, and the wack-a-do free-for-all of the blogosphere.

Not to be outdone by the wing-nut end of the law-and-order crowd, the hypercorrect, bunny-hugging, criminal-coddling, blinded-by-the-light do-nothings have decided that Henry Tatlock was chosen to take the fall for Kyle's killing for no other reason than his scars. Never mind the DNA results; Henry is pure victim. They believe his prosecution reflects society's obsession (driven by Hollywood and Madison Avenue) with physical beauty. Beauty equates to goodness and morality; absence of beauty equates to evil. We have plucked Henry from innocent obscurity because he is the perfect embodiment of everything our superficial society despises. End of story.

The court holds a pretrial conference to talk about evidentiary issues. Gregory Nations looks more lawyerly than usual. He has been to the barber. The jacket hitched over his shoulder has been pressed. And if I'm not mistaken, he has applied some Grecian Formula around the temples. He is an athletic-looking guy, handsome, I guess, though I would think any intelligent woman could look right through his transparent exoskeleton to see, plain as day, the frighteningly un-complicated levers and pulleys of his workings.

Gregory is sitting at counsel's table in the front of the courtroom. Monica Brill isn't here yet, so I walk up and sit beside Gregory. I want to tell him not to be fooled by Henry's apparent disinterest in everything going on around him: It's just shyness, and it's how his face works, I want to say. He's wicked smart, and he notices everything.

While I'm sitting there with Gregory, Monica comes in. I nod to her cordially, but she scowls and looks away. It's odd. I was unaware of any unpleasantness between us.

Henry is brought in wearing an orange jumpsuit.

The judge comes in. I go sit in the gallery. The two lawyers and the judge pick a trial date. It's a month away. "Other matters?" the judge asks.

Monica stands and hands some papers to Gregory and the judge. "I have several evidentiary matters, Your Honor. I'm moving to exclude any mention of my client's juvenile record, which, as you know, was expunged almost twenty years ago. I'm also asking to prevent any reference to the investigation of, or even the existence of, crimes against other children in other states."

The judge scans the papers. "That's fine," he says. "Mr. Nations, you'll respond to these motions, and we'll set the matters aside. When and if they become an issue in trial, we'll boot the jury from the room and have ourselves a little evidentiary hearing. Until then, Mr. Nations, these details will be off-limits as far as the jury is concerned. Understood?"

"Understood, Judge."

"Other evidentiary issues, Ms. Brill?"

I expect that Monica will move to prevent any mention of Lydia's murder. But she doesn't. "No, Judge," she says.

Gregory and the judge are as surprised as I am. It is the first thing any of us would do in her position. If the jury hears that Henry's fiancée was murdered recently and that the killer is at large, they'll make the connection regardless of whether anything is said about Henry being a suspect. I know that Gregory hopes to make frequent and pointed mention of Lydia if he can get away with it. And if Monica Brill is somehow able to muddy the DNA evidence, the whole verdict could hinge on whether the jury connects Henry to Lydia's murder, even though that isn't the case being tried. Of course, if Lydia's murder is mentioned, the judge will tell the jurors, emphatically and repeatedly, not to assume from it anything about Henry. But jurors are only human.

Maybe Monica has a reason for not raising the issue now. She'll have a chance later. She's cagey. It's hard to believe she hasn't thought about Lydia, but I'm squirming with glee at the possibility that, while accusing Henry of Kyle's murder, Gregory might be able to subtly convey the certainty that Henry followed up his crimes against Kyle with a quick execution-style offing of his fiancée.

Along with my frienemy Kendall Vance, Monica occupies the tip-top stratum of criminal defense lawyers in this town. I don't know whether Henry tried to hire Kendall, but I do know he wouldn't have taken the case. He won't defend anyone charged with crimes against children. Monica has no such qualms.

She is tall and slender, made taller by heels. Her fake nails would give her a better than even chance if she ever got locked in a cage with an angry ocelot. And while I generally dislike perfume, Monica wears something subtle that I never notice until, after being near her a minute or so, I find myself thinking of seashores and rose gardens. Perhaps that fragrance, whatever it is, has a subconscious effect, because while there's nothing about Monica that I particularly like, I kind of like her on the whole. She has spunk and wit.

She's the most irritating kind of defense lawyer, though: She's unnecessarily confrontational, gloats over victories, and weaves every defeat into a vendetta. I think her style of advocacy carries over into her personal relationships, because she's never been married. I assume (with no evidence to back this up) that she is lonely and that her law practice substitutes for family. I see her around town sometimes with different men, though I doubt any of them stay for long.

"Anything else before we adjourn?" the judge asks, his gavel poised.

"Yes, Your Honor." Monica stands again. "It looks like the U.S. Attorney's Office has an interest in this case." She stares at me for a couple of seconds. "I've moved to prohibit mention of crimes from other jurisdictions. So in the interest of fairness, I'm requesting that

Mr. Davis and all other lawyers from the U.S. Attorney's Office be prohibited from any participation in this trial."

Damn. If I had my way, I'd prosecute Henry myself, and I'd strap him to the gurney and stick a needle in his vein and push the red button without a qualm. I hate him. He wounded me and my loved ones. He murdered innocence. He murdered family. I wanted to offer Gregory my assistance and input, to talk strategy with him and put my staff at his disposal. Now dragon lady wants me sent to Siberia.

I stand up, about to argue with her. But it's not my place, and Gregory is probably thrilled with Monica's request. The last thing Gregory Nations wants is to share this limelight (and our inevitable victory) with anybody at all, much less a fed.

Judge Ballard smiles. He likes the idea that there might be some fireworks in this trial. He likes the fact that several reporters are already busily writing in notepads, even though pretrial hearings are usually as boring as it gets.

"Mr. Nations?" the judge says.

Gregory stands. He looks at Monica. I see something in his expression that I didn't notice before: contempt. I think back to the look Monica gave me when she first walked into the room, and I recognize it wasn't meant for me, except to the extent that she linked me to Gregory. They despise each other. The judge probably knows this already. He probably relishes it. It gives him a chance to get involved. He can wade in and pull them apart when he needs to.

". . . preposterous request," Gregory says. "Frivolous. Mr. Davis is licensed to practice law in this state and it's none of the defense's business who I have on my team."

Monica is still standing. "Considering Mr. Davis's personal relationship to the defendant," she says, "I may want to call him as a witness."

"Hogwash," I say. "I'm trying to convict the son of a bitch. You won't call me."

"Don't be too sure."

"I am sure."

"I'm adding you to the witness list right now," she says. She starts to write something.

"Bullshit," I say. "You're just doing that to keep me off the prosecution."

"Order," the judge says. For good measure, he smacks the gavel. "How about we do this: Ms. Brill, you drop your objection to Mr. Davis being on the prosecution team. And, Mr. Nations, Mr. Davis, you agree not to object if Ms. Brill calls Davis as a witness. You'll still be protected by privilege, Nick, you just can't refuse to take the stand. Agreed?"

We don't like it, but we agree.

CHAPTER 39

I drive to the house to pick up Barnaby for the night. Tina is in the kitchen cutting up vegetables. The TV is on. She mutes it when I come in.

"Whatcha making?" I ask.

"Just a stir-fry for myself. Or for Barn and me. Or for . . . I don't know, you want to join us?"

"Sure."

"Okay."

"Okay." She takes a beer from the fridge and hands it to me. She pours herself a glass of wine. "How'd it go today?"

I tell her all about the pretrial hearing.

"How'd Henry seem?" she asks.

"He just stared at the tabletop. He never looked up and didn't say a word. He wouldn't have known I was there if they hadn't been talking about me."

"Who was talking about you?"

"Gregory and Monica."

"Why?"

I tell Tina about the dustup over my involvement in the trial.

"So you're part of the prosecution team now?"

"Kind of," I say. "Ex-officio, maybe."

She takes a long weary breath.

"What?" I say.

"I wish . . ." She stops.

"Wish what?"

"That you were less like you sometimes."

I have no idea where to go with this comment. But before I figure out how to respond, I see Henry on the TV screen. I grab the remote and unmute it. ". . . being called the Mark of Cain Killer . . ."

Some cameraman staked out the rear entrance of the courthouse. It's a split-screen picture. In half of it, Henry is being led into the transport van, trying to look away from the camera. He can't shield his face with his hands because of the manacles. The other half-screen is Henry's mug shot, and I feel an unexpected twinge of something other than hatred. "I guess people are just who they are," I say. I have no idea what I mean by this.

Tina is beside me watching. She is crying silently.

"Babe," I say. I stand up and put my arm around her shoulders. She tolerates it but stiffens when I try to pull her close.

The TV cuts to a clip from Gregory's press conference a week ago: Gregory says: ". . . if Mr. Tatlock were to help us bring closure and peace to the families of those boys, we would be open to discussing a sentence of life without parole."

Now it cuts to Monica Brill. She is in the hallway outside the courtroom. "Henry Tatlock is innocent of these charges," Monica says. "Even if he wished to plead guilty, which he doesn't, he would be unable to meet the district attorney's terms because Henry knows no more about any of these crimes than you or me or Gregory Nations himself."

Monica looks good on camera. I wonder if she does her makeup with an eye toward how it will look with TV lights blasting in her face.

The news moves on to another story. I turn it off.

The kitchen fills with the smell of sesame oil and soy sauce. It is dark outside. So far, I've seen no evidence of Craig in this house. I can hear the other TV in the living room. Barn is watching the show where a cartoon dog has a team of real kids (like Mouseketeers of a new generation) who have a scavenger hunt.

"I guess what I was thinking," I say, "is I know he's guilty, but I don't believe he sat here with us scheming and hating. I think he loved it here and at the cabin and even at the office. I think he loved being part of something real. I think he wanted to be normal, but the demons always got the better of him. You know?"

"No," Tina said, "I don't know. I don't know what to think. Lyd loved him, we cared about him, Barn loves him. Maybe I even loved him a little. When we were in hiding together, I understood why Lydia loved him. Honestly, I did. And if Lydia was so wrong, and I was so wrong, then I have no idea what to think about anything. Like . . . like who is Henry? Who are you? Who is Chip, or Ethan, or Upton? And if I follow that far enough, I end up thinking, *Who am I? Who is Lizzy or Barn?* I feel like some junior high schooler discovering, I don't know, sex or marijuana or e. e. cummings and realizing I never knew anything about life till this moment. You know? It's crazy-making, Nick. And all I can do is keep the TV on to create noise, and to work my cases and play with Barn and try not to think about any of it. But you're making me think, goddammit. So what I need you to do, sweetie, is I need you to talk about something else and eat dinner with me, and take Barn for the night if you need to—though I'd rather you not, but it's your night, so you can if you want—and then go away, but call me up in the morning so I know you're still alive, and Barn's still alive, and I'm still alive. And you can ask me in the morning if it's okay for you to come over for coffee, but you need to be okay with it if I say no. Can you do that?"

When I go home after dinner, I leave Barnaby with Tina. But in the middle of the night, I get up and drive over to park outside the house.

If Tina and I survive all of this as a couple, I'd love to take her someplace special. Italy, Hawaii, or maybe Baja, where we could see whales. Or the Galápagos. Yes, she'd love the Galápagos. I'd love the Galápagos. Barn would love the Galápagos: It doesn't get any better than giant tortoises and seagoing iguanas when you're four or five years old. Maybe Lizzy could come, too, and she'd take Barn off our hands for a few days so Tina and I could split the difference between a family vacation and a late honeymoon. Maybe if I offer to pay for Ethan . . .

These thoughts are triggered by staring down at the earth from thirty thousand feet. It always makes me sentimental, especially when I'm alone. And I'm alone on this trip, winging off to the annual conference of the FLSPC (Federal, Local and State Prosecutors Coalition) in San Francisco.

As I suspected, Gregory Nations doesn't want my fingers in his pie, but having won that tiff with Monica, he now feels compelled to parade me around as a way of gloating his victory. "Nick, I have another press conference," he said a few days ago. "Come stand with me."

I did. It was awful. Rather than giving him the gravitas of federal enforcement, I felt like stage dressing. From now on, I'll keep my distance. And in furtherance of that intention, I decided to get out of town for the week.

Henry Tatlock's prosecution won't be a complicated trial. The state's case will look something like this: Kyle's mother will take the stand to talk about her son going missing, and about the search, and about their family's torment. Arthur Cunningham will talk about finding the body. Expert witnesses will talk about recovering and analyzing the DNA. Someone from the FBI will describe matching the crime scene DNA to Henry Tatlock in the national CODIS databank, which collects DNA profiles from all perpetrators in violent crimes. Gregory Nations will ask the FBI witness why Henry happened to be in that database. Monica will object because it refers to Henry's expunged juvenile record, which is inadmissible. Gregory will shout. Monica will shout. The judge will shout. The jury will be removed. Everybody will shout some more. The judge will rule. The jury will be brought back, and the judge will instruct them about what to disregard and what not to disregard. The state will rest, and Monica will put on an unsuccessful defense that neither negates the DNA evidence nor overcomes the emotional testimony of Kyle's family. The jury will convict, and then, sometime later, there will be a sentencing trial.

I fall asleep. I wake up when we start the descent toward San Francisco. I am scratching my cheeks. It's Tuesday. I didn't work yesterday, except to spend an hour on the phone with Gregory Nations's DNA guy. Last Thursday and Friday, I had no important meetings and no courtroom appearances. I haven't shaved since last Wednesday. Nearly a week.

I'm still groggy as we come gliding in over the bay. I doze in and out. We bank around. Looking out the window, I see the spires of the Farallon Islands far offshore. They look like shreds of a fantasy hovering in the mist. I know of the Farallons from a report Lizzy wrote in middle school about great white sharks. A population of them likes to stop by the islands every year to enjoy the annual seal-pup smorgasbord.

Now we bank the other way, and I can see Alcatraz right in the middle of the bay. It hasn't operated as a prison since the early sixties, but the buildings are still there, stark and ugly. It is nightmarish. I've read a bit. I know how the bureau of prisons operated a boat—a water taxi for the damned—taking prisoners out to Alcatraz and, in significantly fewer cases, returning them to the mainland at the end of their sentences. In drowsiness, I imagine myself captain of that unhappy ferry, transporting load after load of transgressors to their new life of exile, isolation, and futility.

Why do I imagine this? Why not imagine myself captaining a boat out to the Farallons, where, though the waves on its beaches turn crimson whenever sharks are on the hunt, at least it's not about captivity? It is about the dramas of nature, not the pathologies of man.

Or the Galápagos: Why not captain a boat to the Galápagos? I'll fill it with Barn and Tina, Lizzy and Ethan, maybe even Flora and Chip, and in happy familial sublimity, I'll transport them all out to Alcatraz . . .

No, *not* Alcatraz: the Galápagos.

I wake up again when our wheels hit the tarmac.

CHAPTER 40

The conference badge has my name and city in letters too big to be missed, so I keep it in my shirt pocket and show it only when needed. It turns out I need it a lot, because a six-day growth of beard has me looking like nobody's image of a federal prosecutor. *Sorry, sir, attendees only in this area.*

I skip the afternoon keynote and the evening reception. I go to my room, change into dirty jeans, a stained T-shirt, and an ancient fatigue jacket. I take a cab to a section outside the Tenderloin District.

I saw Tony Smeltzer in court once, but it was over seven years ago, and I was sitting back in the gallery. The likelihood of his recognizing me is nil, but for good measure, I take an eye patch from my pocket and put it on. Then I walk into Fog City Tap.

It isn't what I expected. I had in mind a place like the Elfin Grot back home, where I've gone a few times to connect with a guy who was connected into the underworld. But where Elfin Grot is dark and reeks of spilled beer, cigarette smoke, and the body odor of nighttime drinkers who pack its narrow, low-ceilinged space, Fog City is bright and open and smells of charbroiled burgers. It is on the second floor, above a plumbing supply store. The altitude gives a view of the bay and the city lights through big windows. There are two pool tables.

I take a stool where the bar bends around the corner, so I can see the door and most of the room. My damn eye patch throws me off, though. I keep moving my head around to compensate. The bartender puts a cardboard coaster down in front of me. "Drinking?"

"What's on tap?"

"Right there." He points to a chalkboard on the wall behind the bar. It's a long list of microbrews. Some names are familiar, most aren't. I pick one: "Wet Snout Stout."

"My favorite, too," he says.

It isn't that I don't trust the Bureau and the local agent who sussed out Tony Smeltzer and deemed him a nonissue. It's just that things don't seem to be tumbling into place quite right. I don't doubt that Henry killed Kyle Runion, so I don't doubt that he could have killed Lydia, too. But the fact that they haven't nailed Henry for Lydia's murder leaves the possibility, however tiny, that someone else killed Lydia. Tina is my wife and I love her. Since I'm a law enforcement professional (albeit the white-collar kind) and I know a few things about how these people think and work, and since the FLSPC was meeting in San Fran this winter, and since Gregory Nations wants me as far away as possible, I decided to fly out here to this barstool and decide for myself whether or not Tony Smeltzer is, as the local FBI agent claimed, a feckless and sickly, washed-up ex-con who is letting bygones be bygones.

Unfortunately, whatever Smeltzer's intentions, they don't include a drink at Fog City tonight. After three beers in three hours, I drop some bills on the bar and head for the door.

"See you again, buddy," the bartender says.

I sleep late and get to the conference about nine in the morning. I attend a seminar on social networking for prosecutors, a yearly update on SCOTUS rulings, a discussion on prosecuting elder abuse, and another on injuries in infants and children. I browse the exhibitors' booths. I'm not interested in any of this right now. What I am interested in is anonymity (because how do I explain to anyone why I've shown up without shaving for the past week?) and in not getting worn down by too much listening and talking, because I need to be sharp and alert for my evening of barstool sitting.

* * *

Fog City again. I sit on the same barstool, and my friendly bartender slides the coaster in front of me and says, "Wet Snout Stout?"

"Please."

I feel good here. He brings me my beer. "Anything to eat, buddy?"

"Yeah, a burger?"

"How?"

"Medium."

"Fries?"

"Definitely." I sip my beer. A little later, a waitress comes over with the burger and fries. Later, when the bartender brings my second beer, I reach across the bar and offer my hand. "Nick," I say.

He shakes. "Malcolm."

We exchange snippets of conversation for two hours. After a third beer, I put some bills on the bar—the tip is generous—and I leave.

In the morning I sleep late again, then attend two seminars ("Identifying, Recovering from, and Preventing Burnout in Emotional and High-stress Jobs" and "Reaching Out to Your Public").

I get to Fog City earlier this time. I sit on the same stool. Malcolm points at the tap. I nod. He draws the beer and brings it over with a coaster. "How was your day, Nick?"

"Unremarkable. Yours?"

"Awesome. I surfed all morning."

A half hour later, Tony Smeltzer comes into the bar. I recognize him before I can see his face. He has that drooping shoulder and sideways walk. He joins some guys at a table. When I get a look at him from the front, I see his soft oval face and bulging eyes. I stare at him, willing him to turn and look at me, but he doesn't, so I call the waitress over. On a bar napkin, I write "Ellisville," and I say, "Tell that guy over there I'm buying his next drink, whatever it is, and give him this."

A few minutes later, Tony Smeltzer is on the stool beside me. "I don't recognize you," he says.

"I was in transit," I say, "coming out of Alder Creek on my

way to Leavenworth. I was only in Ellisville for, like, a month. I'm Nick."

"Tony," he says. "But I still don't remember you."

I tap my eye patch. "I didn't have this. But I remember you. You got that shoulder thing."

"You live here?" he asks.

"I guess I do now. I got a brother here."

He is silent for a few moments, then says, "Well . . ." And he stands up.

"Wait," I say, and in a quiet voice so nobody else can hear, "I'm, um, looking for something to get involved in. You got anything going on?"

"Shit," he says.

"Or do you know of anything?"

"I'll tell you what I got going on," he says. He lifts his shirt. There's a bag strapped to his stomach. "This is what I got going on. They pulled out half my plumbing, but not soon enough. Chemo is what I've got going on: puking, drinking Pepto, and shitting out a hole in my stomach is what I got going on."

"Whoa. Sorry, man, I didn't mean to—"

"Soon as I got out of Ellisville. I'm not so old, you know? I could still do some things. I'm smart, you know? And career people always used to tell me: They'd say, 'Tony, you got management potential.'" He makes quotation marks in the air with his fingers. "So I could have done stuff. Had a family. Been in charge of something. But no. Before my feet even hit free ground, I could feel my insides going haywire. Fucking prison docs missed it back when it wasn't too late. You know?"

"Jesus, that sucks," I say. "When did they, um, you know, operate?"

"When? It was last June, but that's not the point. The point is, to hell with them all: To hell with prison docs, COs, everyone. Hell with all that cold weather back there, hell with the rotten stinking economy back there, hell with the junk and the users and the sup- pliers. Hell with cops and lawyers and judges and inmates. Hell with bitches who say they'll stick around but don't. You know? Hell with you. Hell with me."

I say, "I know what you mean, brother."

"No, you goddamn don't know what I mean. When you're like this"—he taps his stomach—"and like this"—he shows me bandages on both arms from IVs—"then you'll know what I mean. But I'll tell you this, man: If *you* find some action and you need a guy, come get me. I was going to try straight, I shit you not. Keep my ass out of trouble. But the hell with *that*. I'll do anything now. I don't care. It's not like I got anything to lose. I'll go in with barrels blazing and not think twice. Because if you ask me, it's better than a long walk on a short pier. You know? Go out with gusto. Am I right? Better than a walk on the Golden Gate. Right? Halfway across and all the way down. And I'll tell you this: It's sure as shit better than what's in store. Tubes sticking out every hole I got and a few extra besides. You know? So come find me if you hear of something and you need a guy. I don't care what the hell it is, I'm in."

"Yeah, okay," I say. "I'll keep it in mind."

"Do that," he says. He gets up and goes back to his table.

"You ready for another?" Malcolm asks.

"No. I'm good. Do you know that guy?"

"Tony? He's here a lot. He's always venting. But he's not a bad guy. He buys rounds. He tips good."

I toss the eye patch into a trash can outside Fog City. At the hotel, I take a shower and shave. Smeltzer didn't kill Lydia. The poor schmuck was just out of surgery for a colostomy, and he certainly wasn't dragging women off into the woods and shooting them. I'm not worried about him. I doubt Tina still holds a spot anywhere near the top of Tony's long list of hated people.

CHAPTER 41

Trial. News vans with telescoping microwave antennas park in front of the state court building. Judge Ballard has announced a ban on cameras in the courtroom, but reporters and cameramen populate the hallways looking for anyone to interview.

Yesterday was jury selection. Monica Brill tried to exclude anybody who had experienced a violent crime or sexual assault, either themselves or through a friend or relative. She excluded anybody who had recently lost a loved one or who had ever lost a child. She excluded anybody who watched horror movies and anybody who worked in child protection or law enforcement and anybody with young children at home. Gregory Nations excluded anybody who, either themselves or through a friend or relative, had experienced a disfiguring injury. The judge excluded anybody who had read about the case or who knew any of the lawyers, cops, or likely witnesses. And he excluded anybody with ethical objections to capital punishment.

Now, the first real day of trial, I look at these twelve jurors and two alternates. They're curious and nervous and eager to do the right thing. Each of them thinks of himself or herself as more insightful, more ethically balanced, and more earnest than the other thirteen. Each of them either pays attention to no news at all or only to national news. They know what DNA is but have no training in either human genetics or forensic science. They believe themselves capable of understanding a discussion of probabilities. And they all claim to be able to judge someone on the evidence regardless of the way the person looks.

Among the fourteen of them, there are five college degrees, one graduate degree (fisheries management), two GEDs, six women, eight men, three African-Americans, three retirees, no Asians, two

Hispanics, four divorcées, no Native Americans, four of predominantly northern European descent, four of predominantly southern European descent, one of Eastern European descent, no Australians or South Pacific Islanders, no Scandinavians, one stamp collector, five with some degree of obesity, two with health concerns that could require brief absences from the courtroom, one who confesses to a drinking problem, two who work in retail, one in food service, two in office work, two in construction, building trades, or labor, none in factory work, none in health professions, two unemployed, and two in management.

Gregory gives his opening statement: The state will prove that Henry Tatlock kidnapped and killed Kyle Runion.

Monica gives her opening: The defense will prove he didn't.

Gregory and I are getting along okay because a few days ago I declined my seat at the prosecutor's table. He doesn't have to worry about my elbowing in on his moment in the spotlight, and I don't have to worry about putting up with his suffocating self-aggrandizement. Though I'm sitting in the gallery, as far as the judge is concerned, I'm allowed into the club anytime there's a conference between judge and lawyers.

Gregory's first witness is a police detective from Orchard City, where Kyle Runion lived. He talks about getting the call regarding a minor who was several hours late getting home from school, and about mobilizing the missing child response procedure, and about how his department pulled out all stops trying to find Kyle. Gregory does a good job directing the detective through all this, eliciting a description of the urgency and emotion when a child goes missing, and I find myself picturing the whole thing. I picture police cars screeching up in front of the house and the school and the bus stop. I see tracking dogs hurried to the scene and given items of Kyle's to sniff. I picture high-intensity lights set up in the field to look for clues, I see detectives and officers hurrying in and out of the Runion home without knocking and without wiping their muddy shoes on the mat. I see Kyle's parents sitting in shock at the kitchen table as relatives and friends arrive. I picture cops knocking on the doors of friends, teachers, and neighbors.

I feel the chill. Sitting there in the courtroom imagining all this, knowing how it ends, I ache to steer it differently.

Gregory doesn't keep the witness long. He just wanted to lay the foundation. But on cross-examination, Monica Brill has other ideas. "Remind us how many years ago the events you described took place," she says.

"About eight years ago," the detective says.

"And why is it just coming to trial now?"

"Objection."

"Sustained."

Monica keeps working on this, and by the time the detective leaves the witness box, he has told us he believed for years that it was Daryl Devaney who killed Kyle Runion, not Henry Tatlock, whom he'd never heard of until a month ago.

Gregory's second witness is Kyle's mother. She gives a wrenching testimony. Many in the courtroom, including jurors, are unable to hold back tears. When Gregory finishes with the witness, Monica stands up and says, "Mrs. Runion, I'm so very sorry for your loss. I have no questions, Your Honor." She dabs her eyes with a tissue and sits down.

Gregory calls John Farquar, the DNA expert from the state crime lab. He's the one who headed up analysis of the samples once they were retrieved from the FBI. Explaining DNA to laypeople can be tricky, but this guy is good. First Gregory runs him through his credentials: PhD in molecular genetics, fellow of the American College of Medical Genetics, diplomate in forensic biology, author of fifty-seven peer-reviewed articles in genetics and forensic science. Et cetera. Farquar's credentials are bulletproof. Now Gregory leads him through the most basic explanation of genetic analysis. From my perspective as a trial lawyer, watching these two in direct examination is like watching an Olympic couples figure-skating team. Gregory feeds him just the right question at just the right time for Farquar to respond with a lucid explanation that uses enough jargon to give the jurors the thrill of feeling on the inside without ever going over their heads.

MR. NATIONS: So what I hear you saying, Doctor, is that we can ignore the entire molecular structure of the DNA except for these "base pairs," as you call them.

DR. FARQUAR: Correct.

MR. NATIONS: And there are four bases that make up these base pairs, represented by the letters C, G, T, and A?

DR. FARQUAR: Right. It helps me to think about Morse code. With only two symbols, dot and dash, the early telegraph operators could transmit twenty-six letters and ten numerals, and from there they could spell out all the works of literature ever created. Now consider that in the human genome, there are four symbols instead of two. And there are three billion base pairs. That is how we can have the staggering diversity in humanity. You know, Mr. Nations, people often ask me whether the scientific structure of DNA supports a creationist or an evolutionary view of life. And I always answer, "Both." It is equally miraculous whether you believe it originates with the good Lord Himself, or through endless millennia of trial and error.

Gregory asks about the DNA recovered from the Runion remains. Dr. Farquar says they were good samples, and the degradation due to weather and exposure was minimal. Gregory asks about the probability that the DNA of someone not responsible for the semen and hair at the crime scene would match the sample.

"I think you're asking about what we call the RMP, or the random match probability," Farquar says. "This is the probability that a person selected at random, and whose racial heritage matches the perpetrator, will have the same DNA profile. In this instance, the RMP is about one in one hundred and fifty billion."

> MR. NATIONS: Okay, Doctor, so after you've isolated
>   a subject's DNA from the evidence and performed
>   the "electrophoresis," as you've called it, how
>   then do you find out whose DNA it is?
> DR. FARQUAR: Well, we have a database of—

"Objection," Monica says. She isn't loud or emphatic. She doesn't bother getting to her feet. Her objection was anticipated.

Judge Ballard has the jury removed, and then he says, "I'll meet with counsel in my chambers."

"All rise," the clerk says.

"Wait," Henry says. It is the first sound I've heard from him since his outburst at the arraignment, and his voice has startling authority.

"Mr. Tatlock?" the judge says.

"I want to be present for the conference in chambers," he says.

Monica is clearly surprised, but I can see she's ready to make sure he gets his way.

The judge hesitates. The request is unusual, and superior court judges aren't in the habit of inviting murdering pedophiles into the inner sanctum of their jurisprudential brain vault. It will require chaining Henry again and leading him like livestock into the judge's private office, which, with its dark wood and profusion of bookshelves and elegant carpet, resembles the library of an English lord (I'm guessing) more than a prisoner's holding cell. Still, it could be argued that Henry has a right to be present while Gregory and Monica argue over how much the jury gets to hear about why Henry

Tatlock's DNA profile happens to be in a database of convicted violent offenders. "Mr. Tatlock," the judge says, "it's just a chambers conference, off the record. It would be out of the ordinary for—"

Henry interrupts: "Isn't the persecution of an assistant U.S. attorney itself out of the ordinary?"

"I think the word you're after, Mr. Tatlock," the judge says, "is 'prosecution.'"

"You use your word, I'll use mine," Henry answers. His voice is sharp and angry, which probably isn't the best way to speak to the guy who has such power over your life or death. This infuriates me, and I think, *How dare he?* How dare he feel entitled to his petulance? If I hated him a moment ago, now I hate him a hundredfold. Until now I held on to the idea that the Henry whom Lydia was in love with, the one who was my colleague, friend, and perhaps protégé, was a Jekyll and Hyde—that there was a man of integrity tragically shackled to a monster he couldn't control. I could have had compassion for that Henry. I wouldn't want him free in society, I wouldn't want him to escape the consequences of his crimes, but the idea of him would have been easier for me to live with into the future. If there were, in fact, a *good* Henry, then he could join Lydia and Kyle Runion and (to a lesser extent) Tina, Barn, Lizzy, and me as a victim of that monster who shared his body. I could grieve for him and someday forgive myself for being so blind to the enemy in our midst. But now he has shown us that there are not two Henrys. There is only one: Henry the murderer. And like all the other sociopaths and psychopaths, he dares to feel indignant. He dares to flip this case on its head and imply it is *we* who do an injustice to *him* by removing his rotten, stinking existence from our midst.

In the lines of Monica's face, I can see that she is furious with him. She would probably walk away right now if she could.

Judge Ballard stares at Henry a few moments, deliberating, I assume, whether to vent his own outrage at this smug prick of a defendant. He doesn't. "Well, vocabulary aside, Mr. Tatlock, I'll honor your request. We'll stand in recess while the bailiff clears the courtroom. We'll have our conference right here."

It is a judicious decision. Spectators and court personnel are shooed out, leaving only the judge, lawyers, and bailiffs.

Henry points at me and says, "What about him?"

It is the first time our eyes have met since I hurried Tina and Barn away from him moments before the FBI took him down as he pulled the two canoes up onto the sand. I don't know what he sees in my face right now, whether I'm as transparent as he, but the look I get from him is one of sheer, unadulterated abhorrence.

CHAPTER 42

It is a windowless courtroom with five rows of benches for the spectators. The jury box, witness box, and judge's bench are all made of maple, the carpet is tan, and the lighting is subdued and recessed. I can hear the sound system crackle.

"We're off the record," the judge says, "so please spare me any speeches. Here's the issue: I've already ruled that Mr. Tatlock's juvenile record, which has been expunged according to law, is not admissible at trial. So we need to resolve how the prosecution should make reference to Henry Tatlock's DNA being present in the database of violent offenders. My own preference is that we make no reference to a database at all. The prosecution witness merely testifies that the crime scene DNA matches Mr. Tatlock's DNA. Period. Paragraph. Does that work for you, Mr. Nations?"

"No, Judge," Gregory says. "It waters down the authority of the science and undermines the very conclusions of Dr. Farquar's findings, and therefore it egregiously—"

"Counselor," the judge interrupts, "did you hear me a moment ago when I said no speeches?"

"Yes, Judge, it's just that—"

"It's just that you're still trying to get the defendant's expunged juvenile conviction before this jury, and I'm telling you, counselor, that ship has sailed. Now, Ms. Brill, what do you have to say?"

Monica stands up. "I have—"

"Sit down," the judge says, "we're just chatting here."

Monica sits. "Sure, fine," she says. "I have no objection to your proposal, except for one thing."

"And that would be?"

"I'm moving to have any reference to my client's DNA, and thus the identification of him as a suspect in this case, excluded from trial as violative of the Fourth Amendment to the U.S. constitution and—"

"Oh, Christ," Gregory says.

"And your grounds, Ms. Brill?" the judge asks.

"Under the law, once Henry's juvenile record was expunged, his DNA should have been removed from the CODIS database of violent offenders. This provision was implied by law and expressly stated in his plea agreement on that conviction."

Gregory is on his feet: "Your Honor, that's—"

"Sit down, Mr. Nations."

Gregory sits but rants about the ridiculousness of the motion. He is enraged. I sit there trying to mentally pick out the flaws in Monica's argument. I can't find one. If Monica is right—if, under the law, Henry's DNA profile shouldn't even be in that database, then the state's whole case against Henry is faulty. He would go free, in which case I'm sure he'd move away where nobody knows him, becoming more cunning and insidious as he perpetrates a hideous career of murder and abasement against the children of whatever country and continent he chooses.

I'm on my feet. "It's bullshit!" I yell.

Monica, Gregory, and Henry all swivel in their seats. I hear the gavel smack the bench, and I see the judge's pinched smile. "Mr. Davis," he says placidly, "maybe you missed it when I told everyone to stay seated. So sit down and shut up. Okay?"

I sit. I'm breathing hard, and I feel how red my face is—with fury, not embarrassment. I collect myself a moment, then I say, "I'm sorry, Your Honor."

"No, don't speak. Nod for yes. Shake for no. Can you keep your ass in the chair and your piehole shut?"

I nod.

"Excellent," he says. "Now, let me tell you all what's going to happen here. First I'm going to call the clerk and court reporter back in, and Ms. Brill is going to put her motion to suppress DNA evidence on the record. Then Mr. Nations is going to oppose the motion on the record. Then I'm going to deny the motion, and this trial will resume. Mr. Nations and his witnesses will say that the defendant's DNA was found at the crime scene, blah blah blah, Henry Tatlock's juvenile offense will not be referred to, and the jury will draw their own conclusions. Understood?"

We all nod, except for Henry, who shows no sign of having heard any of it.

Trial resumes. Farquar returns to the witness box.

> **MR. NATIONS:** Tell me how closely the DNA sample taken directly from the defendant matched the DNA recovered from among the victim's remains.
>
> **DR. FARQUAR:** It matched perfectly.
>
> **MR. NATIONS:** So you're saying there is a probability of approximately one hundred fifty billion to one that it is this defendant's DNA.
>
> **DR. FARQUAR:** Correct.

Gregory finishes with Farquar. Monica stands. "Just to be clear, Dr. Farquar, how did you obtain these DNA samples you tested?"

"They were given to me by—"

"They were given to you?"

"Yes, by—"

"So you didn't recover them yourself?"

"No, the way this works is—"

"That's okay, Doctor, no need to go into all that. But tell me, to the best of your understanding, the hairs and semen stains that you have linked to Mr. Tatlock, these were collected from items recovered at Kyle Runion's burial site. Is that right?"

> **DR. FARQUAR:** Yes.
>
> **MS. BRILL:** And is it scientifically possible, Doctor, that the semen you attribute to Henry Tatlock could have been found someplace else and, I don't know, maybe rehydrated or something and introduced into the evidence you tested?

DR.FARQUAR: Well, that's kind of far-fetched.

MS.BRILL: I'm sorry, Doctor, I thought you were a scientist.

DR.FARQUAR: I am a scientist.

MS.BRILL: Then please give me an answer based in science and not your opinion of whether someone wants my client to appear guilty of something he didn't do.

Farquar and Monica glower at each other. He isn't used to being slapped down like that. He looks to Gregory for help but doesn't get any.

DR.FARQUAR: Well . . .

MS.BRILL: It's a simple question, Doctor. Could the sheet and underclothes you tested have been contaminated, intentionally or not, with Henry Tatlock's DNA after they were removed from the crime scene?

DR.FARQUAR: Yes. It's possible.

MS.BRILL: Is it also possible that semen stains from, let's say, Mr. Tatlock's own underclothes or bedsheets could have been rehydrated and introduced as the source of DNA found among Kyle Runion's remains?

DR.FARQUAR: Yes, technically, I suppose.

MS.BRILL: Correct me if I'm wrong: You were given evidence to test for DNA, but whether that DNA has anything to do with the crime is not your bailiwick. You rely on others for that. Correct?

DR.FARQUAR: But standard procedure—

MS.BRILL: Standard procedure, Doctor, involves actions you never see undertaken by people you never meet. Is that correct?

DR.FARQUAR: Well, technically, but—

MS.BRILL: That's fine, Doctor. We all understand you tested Mr. Tatlock's DNA and found it to be Mr. Tatlock's DNA. I have nothing further.

Monica has something in mind. There are only a few ways to defend against DNA evidence. Either you argue that the laboratory made an error (usually a losing strategy) or that the defendant, despite astronomical odds against it, happens to have the same DNA profile as the perpetrator (always a losing strategy), or you make a case that someplace in the process, the evidence was somehow contaminated with DNA from an innocent party. Monica is obviously basing her defense on this third scenario.

CHAPTER 43

Morning. Gregory Nations plans to call several witnesses to establish chain of custody for the evidence. This is what Monica was harassing the poor scientist about yesterday. From the overgrown field where Arthur Cunningham found Kyle's body, crime scene techs collected the evidence, transported it to the evidence room at headquarters, and logged it in. According to protocol, there should be a record of every time it was moved or handled.

This isn't usually an issue at trial, but since it looks like Monica is planning to attack the chain of custody, Gregory wants to call a witness or two who can head her off. They'll testify that, according to records, the evidence spent about five and a half years in the state evidence room without being disturbed. It was then transported by agents to the FBI for their wide-ranging investigation into abductions with MOs similar to the one in Kyle Runion's case. The Bureau's intended investigation was never pursued, and the evidence languished another couple of years. After Judge Matsuko granted Tina's petition for production of evidence in the Daryl Devaney case, it was retrieved from the Bureau by detectives and submitted for analysis at the state crime lab. Every step has been documented.

I don't go to court for this chain-of-custody stuff. Instead, I go to another meeting about the Subsurface probe over at the Bureau. I get there just as the meeting is starting. Isler seems to be running things today. "We still haven't figured out where that five million went," he says.

"What five million?" I ask.

My question makes them all uncomfortable. Nobody wants to point out that I've been AWOL for the past week or two. I found updates from Isler and Upton on my desk when I got back from San Francisco, but I haven't read them yet.

Upton steps into the silence. "When you were gone, boss, Special Agent Isler updated us on the forensic accounting of both Subsurface's books and Bud Billman's personal finances. Between the two, there's about five point two million unaccounted for."

"Lots of money," I say. "Are there any hints where it might be?"

"I was getting to that," Isler says. "From the raw numbers, just looking at the books, no, nothing points anywhere. So I thought we should kick it around. Come up with some theories."

"Great idea. Let's have theories," I say in a stupid attempt to sound on the ball. Because not only have I been out of town and not reading my messages, but even at this moment I'm way more focused on Henry's trial than on Subsurface. I'm trying to appear present while the cogs and gears labor to bring me back.

"Yeah, well," Isler says.

I tip back in my chair and stare up through the skylight. Nice day. Puffy clouds, blue sky.

". . . Jimmy Mailing," Chip says, "and if he—"

"Excuse me," I say. "What about Mailing?"

"I think it's a no-brainer," Chip says. "Mailing was Subsurface's fixer. Mailing knew where the bodies were buried. He probably buried a lot of them himself. Then Mailing gets killed. Now we discover Subsurface and/or Billman diverted five million to who knows where. So do we think maybe Mailing knew a little too much?"

"Yes," Isler says. "Either he knew too much, or maybe there was an ownership dispute over the five mil."

"Have we looked through Mailing's finances?" I ask.

Again, this brings things to a momentary halt. Maybe they talked about this while I was admiring the sky.

Upton to the rescue again: "Isler and his guys did a quick look after he was murdered, but they're planning another look with combs of a finer tooth."

"Superb idea," I say, trying to use energy and enthusiasm to give the impression I'm engaged and up to speed. I feel ridiculous, and

I resolve to go back to my office, read all the messages and reports piled up there, and try to reenter the loop with more momentum.

We adjourn. I walk back to my office alone. Finally, when I'm out in the open air with my legs moving, the idea of Subsurface catches wind in my mind again. I remember Voss, the Subsurface VP for governmental relations, telling the grand jury that the proposed tax legislation would cost the industry hundreds of millions. I know that Subsurface, Inc., lives or dies on the financial well-being of the whole industry, and while the piddly bribes paid to Calvin Dunbar and his ilk were easily folded into the accounting of a business the size of Subsurface, five point two mil kind of sticks out.

Obviously, somebody over at Subsurface was paying somebody to do something. And the two guys most likely to have been involved, Billman and Mailing, are dead.

My Volvo wagon is in the shop. It keeps overheating, and the mechanic I spoke with on the phone made the armchair diagnosis of a blown head gasket. So I'm sans Volvo for the next week or two. Kenny had a Toyota pickup that rides high off the ground and has shiny chrome bumpers and knobby tires. Flora and I offered to sell it for him when he went to prison, but he declined. I think it represents something to him: the promise of getting out and picking up his life where he left it. So I parked it out behind Flora's garage, and we keep it under a tarp. Flora, Lizzy, and I use it anytime we need a truck, and we deposit a few bucks into an account for Kenny each time we take it out.

Chip picks me up at my office after work. "How was Frisco?" he asks as we weave through town toward the highway.

"I think it was great," I say. "But I've been back three days, and with this trial and the Subsurface thing, who can remember that long ago?"

"That's like me," he says. "I've got a good memory, it just doesn't last very long."

I laugh.

Traffic is jammed up. Daylight saving time ended a month ago. It has been dark out for an hour, and we're getting a heavy, wet snow that clings under the wipers. "You should come over and spend Christmas with us," Chip says. I don't say anything, so he adds, "If you're not . . . you know."

Five years ago Chip leaned on me during his marital upheaval. He's aching to repay me now that my own domestic harmony has gone flat. His eagerness is disconcerting (and Christmas is several weeks away). "Thanks, Chip," I say. "Very kind of you. But I expect I'll be home with Tina and Barn."

"Oh, how wonderful," he says, irking me even more.

When we get to their house, Chip announces to Flora in a booming voice, "Look what the cat dragged in."

Flora comes over and hugs me. "You'll stay for dinner," she says. I protest feebly. She insists. I agree.

Chip goes upstairs to change clothes, and I go back outside to pull the tarp off Kenny's truck. I drive it around into the driveway.

Poor Kenny. The truck was two years old when he went to prison. So even if he gets out at the first possible moment, it'll be fourteen years old by then. He should have let us sell it.

I go back inside. Chip comes downstairs and opens a beer for me and one for himself. "So who killed Jimmy Mailing?" he says.

I say, "Until today, I didn't really care who killed him. I figured it was the price he paid for living on the wrong side of the law. But now, considering the five million, I kind of like Voss for the perp."

"Voss? Which one is Voss?"

"Bud Billman's protégé. Vice president for governmental affairs. He's an angry, entitled prick. I think he saw the corruption probe coming and figured the company would break apart when everything came out into the open. He'd lose millions when the company either got sold or filed Chapter Eleven, so he decided to take his share out now."

"But why—"

"And since Mailing seemed to know everything that went on, Voss needed to keep him quiet."

"That makes sense, I guess."

"Who do you think killed him?"

"I don't know. That's more Isler's area than mine. But if I had to guess . . ."

The front door opens. Lizzy and Ethan come in, and my conversation with Chip gets derailed. After initial greetings and a big hug from Lizzy, she pulls me upstairs to her room, pushes me into her desk chair, and sits cross-legged on her bed flipping through some notes. On the desk beside me is a travel guide to Southeast Asia, another for Africa, a bunch of paperwork from the state legislative information office, and two books, one entitled *Private Investigator's Handbook*, and the other *Great Wreck Diving Around the Globe*. (Lizzy has been talking about taking scuba lessons for years.)

"I haven't written a supplemental for my report," Lizzy says, "but I thought I'd update you. Okay?"

"Sure. Let's hear it."

"Remember I said how that tax law got delayed two years because someone kept hanging an amendment on it? It's really weird. The amendments were about environmental stuff. They were antifracking regulations. And the legislator who proposed them, Porter, he's a big environmentalist and way in favor of this tax increase."

"So the amendments make sense, don't they?"

"It only looks that way at first. They were too last-minute. There wasn't enough time left before the recess to decide anything, so all they did was kill the bill for that year. Twice. So why would this antifracking, pro-tax, pro-environment representative do that? Why kill a bill you want, disguising it as environmental policy?"

"Are you thinking he was in on something? Maybe getting a payoff?"

"I don't have a clue, but I thought we could think out loud . . ."

Lizzy goes on chattering confidently, but I'm not very interested. I don't want background, I just want conclusions. I nod pensively while she talks, trying to keep an ear open for anything significant, but what I'm really doing is conducting an archaeological survey of her room, visually uncovering the strata of her journey from little girl into this young woman who has the combined sensibilities of an academic, a sophisticate, a hippie, and a child. Among the books on her bookshelf, I spot a couple of old Nancy Drew books I bought for her at a yard sale long ago; a Bradford Angier book on wilderness skills that was mine as a kid; numerous books by her favorite authors like Jane Austen and the Brontës, and a well-read copy of Naomi Klein's *The Shock Doctrine*. On the wall is a framed photo of the cabin up at the lake, taken from a boat offshore. There are posters tacked up on the walls publicizing some of the Occupy events, and a poster of the Dixie Chicks, and an artistic poster of a ballet dancer working at the practice barre. On the desk is a photo of Flora and me and baby Toby, taken about eleven years before Liz was born. An old trophy from some equestrian event is on the windowsill, dirty clothes are piled in the corner, a painting she did of Bill-the-Dog sits on the dresser with a papier-mâché volcano, a book on the Analects of Confucius, and a copy of *West with the Night*, by Beryl Markham. In the open closet are her Dr. Martens and a pair of high heels with open toes. Sticking out from under the bed, I see a pair of Ethan's Jockeys. I don't *want* to see Ethan's Jockeys, so I slide my chair over to where they're blocked by the corner of the bed.

"Anyhow," she says, "are you passing my reports along to Chip?"

"No, honey, they're just for me, so I can keep up with the Bureau."

"I thought I'd talk to CD again. See if he has ideas about Representative Porter: why Porter added that rider two years in a row."

"CD?"

"Calvin Dunbar. That was his nickname when he was younger. It's what his wife calls him. And I guess his close friends."

"Okay, fine, babe. Talk to CD. See what he says. But I only want you researching the legislation and only public information. Nothing about Subsurface and nothing behind the scenes. Okay?"

"Why not? I'm having fun. I want to pry it wide open."

"Well, honey, to use the vernacular, new shit has come to light. So I'm stressing the fact that you're just briefing me on some already public information. I'm impressed with your enthusiasm"—I pick up the *Private Investigator's Handbook* from the desk—"but I don't want you prying anything open. You're just educating yourself and then me. You're not uncovering anybody's secrets. Agreed?"

"But I think I could—"

"Lizzy. Promise me: just research, no sleuthing?"

I get her to agree, but she doesn't like it.

CHAPTER 44

Morning. Barn was with Tina last night, and I spent part of the night parked in front of the house, sleeping in Kenny's truck. Now I drive back over there to pick Barn up for preschool.

"Coffee?" Tina says.

I sit in the kitchen. She pours coffee for us and sits down.

"How was the first day of trial?" she asks.

"I don't know. No surprises. You should come today."

Tina stares at me over her coffee cup. She is thinking it through. Her face is a map of unreadable emotions.

"Are you okay, babe?" I ask.

She shrugs. "Okay, I guess," she says. Her face gets stony, and for a second nothing changes. Then it gives way. She is sobbing.

Tina lets me hold her, but we're standing in the kitchen, and when, after a few moments, I try to tug her toward the other room where I can snuggle her properly on the couch, she finds her composure and disentangles herself from me. "You go. I'll be fine."

I know that she won't come to the trial. It's too fraught. Besides the way it intersects with Lydia's murder, besides her having gotten so close to Henry when they were in hiding, there is the seesaw dynamic between Henry and Daryl Devaney. Tina's petition for a trial in the Devaney case is in the state supreme court. If Henry is convicted (as he certainly will be), that court will issue a quick one-page decision granting Daryl a trial; the case will get kicked back down to Matsuko's court; Gregory Nations will dismiss the charges; and Daryl Devaney will get to go home. But if Henry is somehow acquitted, anything can happen, because now even more than before, with Kyle Runion's murder of eight years ago becoming the biggest news in the state, nobody wants to get blamed for leaving empty the cell that should house his murderer. Gregory, Matsuko, the supreme court judges, and the cops will do nearly anything to make sure that doesn't happen.

News vans are at the courthouse again. Photographers snap, videographers film, reporters scribble. Most of them have no idea who I am, so I get into the courtroom without much interference.

Gregory didn't finish with his chain-of-custody witnesses yesterday. It turns out Detective Philbin had been the one to transport the box of evidence from the FBI back to trooper headquarters to be evaluated in the state crime lab. These facts create the opportunity Gregory needs to let the jury know all about Lydia's murder. We expect Monica to object at any mention of Lydia's murder, on the grounds that it is overly prejudicial. But if Gregory can get any mention of it before the jury, it will have the effect we want: Henry had a fiancée, she was murdered, the murder remains unsolved, and Henry stands accused of other heinous crimes.

The jury will put it together.

Philbin takes the stand. He is sworn. Gregory leads him through a terse summary of his involvement with the Kyle Runion case. Philbin tells us his only involvement was a couple months ago, when he was at the FBI for a meeting and was asked to transport a box of evidence back to trooper headquarters for testing in the state crime lab. Gregory asks whether, according to protocol, Philbin signed for the box when he picked it up at the FBI and again when it was left with the evidence clerk at the troopers. Philbin confirms that he did. Gregory shows Philbin the two ledgers documenting these exchanges. Philbin confirms his signature.

With the chain of custody established, Gregory could dismiss the witness. But he doesn't.

MR. NATIONS: And what was your reason for being at the FBI to begin with?

> DETECTIVE PHILBIN: Like I said. A meeting.
>
> MR. NATIONS: A meeting about what?

Philbin and Gregory and I all know that Philbin's meeting was when we theorized that Tony Smeltzer had killed Lydia by mistake, intending to kill Tina. I assume the judge and Monica know this, too. But either I'm wrong about Monica, or again, she's up to something. In any case, when she doesn't object to the testimony, Philbin sees his chance:

> DETECTIVE PHILBIN: We were discussing the murder
>   of Henry Tatlock's fiancée.

The effect in the courtroom is electric. The jury is riveted. All eyes shift to Henry. Reporters scribble.

> MR. NATIONS: The murder of his fiancée? What about it?

Monica finally gets to her feet and objects. She seems tired and disinterested. In fact, she seems inept, and I suddenly know what the matter is with her. She, too, is repulsed. Monica knows Henry killed Lydia and that he committed unspeakable crimes against Kyle. She took this case intending to be Henry's zealous advocate, but the facts have overwhelmed her. Lawyers run this risk—that they'll be so disgusted by a client that they can't go on. It happened to Kendall Vance once, but he dealt with it more creatively. Monica, it appears, has simply thrown in the towel.

I'm bothered by her behavior, though not because I give a damn about Henry. Rather, I worry that Monica's lackluster defense will leave Henry's inevitable conviction vulnerable to an appeal based on ineffective assistance of counsel.

Monica's halfhearted objection is sustained. Gregory asks Philbin a few more innocuous questions, then he says, "Nothing further," and sits down.

Judge Ballard says, "Ms. Brill, do you wish to cross-examine?"

"Not at this time, Your Honor, but I would like the opportunity to recall the witness later on."

Gregory opposes Monica's request, but the judge says he'll allow it. Philbin is allowed to step down. As he exits the witness box, I see a twinge of satisfaction in his jowly and generally unsmiling visage. He knows he got in a few good body blows against Henry, whom he seems to loathe so intensely.

Gregory is finished with the chain of custody. He calls Paula Myrtle, director of the Orchard City branch of the state legal assistance corporation. She is a Birkenstock kind of woman, with salt-and-pepper hair hanging to her shoulders in untamed waves. Gregory asks about her organization, and she tells us they provide free legal assistance to low-income clients, particularly in child and family matters. Gregory questions her:

MR. NATIONS: In your position at the legal assistance corporation, did you ever come in contact with the defendant, Henry Tatlock?

MS. MYRTLE: Yes.

MR. NATIONS: And can you tell us about that?

MS. MYRTLE: Well, yes, Henry was in law school. He interned with us the summer after his first year.

MR. NATIONS: What year was that?

MS. MYRTLE: I checked my records before driving here today because, you know, we get scads of interns. And it's hard to keep them all straight, but it's a little easier with Henry because of, well, you know.

MR. NATIONS: No. Tell us.

MS. MYRTLE: The way he, um, looks. Memorable. So I remember him really well. Really, really well. But I had to check on the year, because, well, like I said. And it was 2006. Summer 2006.

MR.NATIONS: And what were the dates he worked there?

MS.MYRTLE: Right. Yes. I looked that up, too. He joined us on June fifth, then he left again on August twenty-fifth.

MR.NATIONS: And when you say he left, you mean he left your employ on that date?

MS.MYRTLE: Yes.

MR.NATIONS: But do you know the date he actually left Orchard City to return to school?

MS.MYRTLE: I guess I don't.

MR.NATIONS: And do you happen to know the date Kyle Runion disappeared?

MS.BRILL: Objection.

JUDGE: Sustained.

MR.NATIONS: Or the date classes resumed at the law school here in town?

MS.BRILL: Objection. Your Honor, how is this—

JUDGE: Sustained. Mr. Nations, behave.

Everyone knows Kyle Runion disappeared on September 4, and I'm sure we'll learn that school started for Henry sometime after that. The time line is perfect. Henry had all summer to find a victim, learn his schedule, and then nab Kyle and be two hundred miles away within a few hours, never to return.

CHAPTER 45

It's Friday afternoon. Barnaby, ZZ, and I drive up to the lake in Kenny's truck. He's four and a half, talking in complete sentences. Toddlerhood is behind him. He's a little boy now.

"Are you going to live in my house again, Daddy?"

"Don't you like Friendly City?"

"Yeah."

"You like the pool, right?"

"Yeah."

"And the big TV?"

"Yeah."

"Okay. So."

"Lizzy says maybe you won't."

"But maybe I will."

"I gotta pee."

We take a bathroom break and get an ice-cream cone for Barn and one for me, and a tiny vanilla one for ZZ, which Barn gives him on the sidewalk in front of the shop. Barn and ZZ are the cutest boy-and-his-dog pair you'll ever find. Sometimes this ice-cream cone shtick gets people out of their cars taking pictures. Not today, though.

It's cold out. When we get to the cabin, the lake looks frozen, but I don't trust it. I warn Barn against walking out on the ice. He listens, looking very serious. "Okay," he says. Then he eyes ZZ and says, "If ZZ runs on the ice, I'll yell, 'Bad dog, ZZ. Bad dog. The ice is too thin.' Okay, Daddy?"

"Good plan, Barn."

We make a fire to get the cabin warmed up, then we go over to Flora's cabin and heat that one, too. Lizzy and Ethan will be along later to stay in Flora's. I want to make it welcoming.

Tina arrives as it's getting dark. I'm making dinner, and Barn is watching a movie about penguins on my computer.

"How was your drive?" I ask her.

Tina says her drive was fine, and I say that mine was fine, too, and we talk about how it's cold, but not really cold for this time of year, and how it's nice to have snow but there's not much snow compared to last year, and then I say finally, "What's the deal with Craig?"

"You mean my ex?"

"Yes, that's who I mean."

"I don't know," she says. "We've reconnected. He heard about Lyd and got in touch."

"And came to visit," I say.

She studies me a moment.

"I recognized him at that hearing," I say. "From your photos."

"I should have told you," she says.

I shrug. "We don't talk that much anyhow. Probably slipped your mind."

"It's not anything."

"Whatever," I say. "You're a free agent."

She stares at me a few seconds. "No," she says, "not really."

Tina mixes some dinner for ZZ and puts it in his bowl. I watch her. The past several years have taken a toll: postpartum depression; breast cancer; Lyd's murder. Then we believed Lydia's killer was coming after Tina. And now the horror of Henry. I should be glad she's doing as well as she is, and maybe she's beyond the worst of it. She is opening up to me again in minor ways: coffee sometimes in the morning when I pick up Barnaby for school; a beer sometimes at night. Now this weekend. "Don't walk out on the ice," I tell her. "It's still not safe."

She comes over to where I'm sautéing vegetables at the stove and gives me a kiss on the cheek, just below my eye.

Lizzy and Ethan arrive. Bill-the-Dog comes in with them and, after some butt-sniffing with ZZ, curls up by the woodstove. We get dinner on the table.

"Daddy," Lizzy says, "I've got more info on Subsurface."

"You want to brief me later?"

"It's all public knowledge," she says. "Remember, I promised. No sleuthing. Just researching."

"Okay. Tell."

"That representative who added the amendments . . ."

"Porter," I say.

"Right. Turns out he got, like, these huge construction projects in his district. Tons of jobs."

Across the table, Tina and Ethan are talking between themselves. I'm able to hear a little: "She might meet up with me in June," Ethan says to Tina.

"You haven't talked to Porter directly, have you?" I ask Lizzy.

"Only CD," Lizzy says. "I called him to talk it through. He's going to call me back."

Tina overhears Lizzy. "CD," she says. "Who's CD?"

"Calvin Dunbar," Lizzy says. "He's a friend of Dad's. He was a legislator."

Ethan says, "Of course, we'll miss each other between now and June, won't we, babe?"

"Wait a second," I say. "You'll miss each other when? Meet up where?"

"In the Andes," Ethan says.

"Ethan's leaving soon," Lizzy says. "Didn't you get my email?"

"Who's Andy?" Barnaby says.

"Andes," Lizzy says to Barn. "They're mountains. We're going to hike in the Andes. At least to start. Not sure after that."

I'm dumbfounded. It sounds like everybody else knows. "When, Liz? When are you leaving?"

"Ethan is leaving in a week, Daddy. I'm meeting him in, like, a month or two."

"I never got an email."

"I'm sorry, Dad," she says. "I'm pretty sure I sent one. I figured you were just, you know, stressed about your little girl growing up, so you didn't say anything."

"Have you told your mom?"

"Of course."

Tina pats my hand. "Don't worry, Nick, you've been busy with Henry's trial."

I'm disconcerted to know that there's a bit of truth in Lizzy's assessment of me. I *am* choked up. My little girl *is* growing up and going away. "We'll have a party," I say.

"Okay," Liz says, "but Mom's planning something, so you should just combine."

After dinner, we get the place cleaned up. When Barn falls asleep, we all play Scrabble. Then Lizzy and Ethan get their boots on for the walk over to Flora's cabin. "C'mon, Bill," Liz says. Bill-the-Dog gets up. ZZ goes along, too. They leave. I shut the door behind them. Then I open it. "Stay away from the lake," I say. "The ice isn't safe."

I can't see them, but Lizzy answers from within the darkness: "We know, Dad. You told us."

CHAPTER 46

G regory calls Arthur Cunningham, who steps into the witness box and takes the oath. The sequence of Gregory's witnesses was thrown off by Dr. Farquar's schedule. Normally, Farquar would have been called at the end to give his ironclad scientific proof of Henry's guilt after all the background testimony of his motive and opportunity. No matter. This order of presentation will work just fine. Instead of ending with the rock-solid scientific proof of Henry's guilt, we started with it. And instead of introducing the gut-wrenching description of unearthing Kyle's decomposed remains at the beginning of the case, we can present it at the end. Either way, it tells the story.

Arthur is taller than I remember. He's average height and average build, but in my memory from when I went with Tina to the reservoir, I see him as small and unobtrusive.

Gregory takes extra time putting Arthur at ease with background questions. "Where do you live?" (Right there outside the reservoir preserve.) "What do you do for a living?" (He calculates bids for a large construction firm.) "And are you married?" (He's divorced.) Et cetera.

Gregory is good. He gets Arthur settled in and even gets him to chuckle by commenting on his own ineptitude with numbers when Arthur explains his job. And then Gregory begins in earnest:

MR. NATIONS: Living near the reservoir as you do, do you spend much time in the woods there, walking or hiking or anything?
MR. CUNNINGHAM: Almost every day.

MR.NATIONS: Doing what?

MR.CUNNINGHAM: Well, I'm . . . I'm . . . I have dogs,
you know. I've always had a yellow Lab. That one was
Bo-Jangles. Not that I hunt. I don't hunt, but I work
them, and you know how energetic Labs are.

Cunningham seems shy and fragile, traumatized by having to
remember finding Kyle's remains. I understand why I thought of
him as small and slight. He has a paunch and sits bent over and
avoids eye contact with Gregory. He tends to inflate his cheeks like
a chipmunk when thinking. Gregory handles him gently: "On the
day we're talking about, Mr. Cunningham, what did Bo-Jangles do
that caught your attention?"

Arthur inflates his cheeks. "She dug."

"Oh," Gregory says, "you mean like with her front paws?" He
imitates a digging dog.

"Yes. Like that."

Gregory nods. "And she didn't do that often, is that right?"

"Not often. No."

"So she wasn't a digger by nature. I mean, some dogs are. I had
a dog once that dug up my whole backyard. Dug till his paws were
bloody."

Nobody here cares about Bo-Jangles, and we care even less about
Gregory Nations's backyard. We care about Kyle Runion's remains,
and I'm enjoying watching how deftly Gregory lures the skittish
Arthur Cunningham into the open. Jurors like shy witnesses. Some
identify with them, and others enjoy feeling superior. Gregory works
Arthur slowly at first, and then he hands him photographs from the
scene, evoking from him the slow and horrific recognition of what
Bo-Jangles had found.

Arthur tells us how, when he walked over to where Bo-Jangles
was busily tugging and excavating, the dog tore some of the shroud
free from around the child's face. Nothing can prepare you for the
first glimpse of the leering skeletal grin, dried flesh clinging in places

and dirt filling the eyeholes. It is vile. The joy and love and hope that once lived there seem not merely to be gone but to actually be undone. It makes you feel that all of life might be no more than a cruel hoax. As the photos are passed around, jurors press hands against their mouths. I hear gasps. And though she is in the gallery and can't see the photos from where she sits, Kyle's mother weeps openly. The jurors, I'm sure, wonder how they'd have reacted if they'd been in Arthur's place that day. They gaze with watery eyes at Kyle's mother and at poor Arthur, who had to unearth this horror.

And they look at Henry. This case has stopped being about the molecular structure of DNA and strings of nucleotide pairs. It has stopped being about the handing off of evidence from the state to the feds and back. It has stopped being about semen stains, hair follicles, electrophoresis, and random match probabilities. It is now about evil. And evil sits in the courtroom with us. Henry wears the mark of Cain. He comes to us in a nightmare.

"I have nothing further," Gregory Nations says.

Monica Brill cross-examines. She asks some questions about Bo-Jangles and about the bit of forest where Arthur and the dog walked that day. There is nothing she really wants to know about the dog or the woods. She just wants to try and replace this horrific vision of Kyle's remains with the image of a happy dog and peaceful woods.

Gregory's last witness is the medical examiner, who reminds me of Lurch: tall, gaunt, eyes deep in gray sinkholes. His responses to Gregory's questions, though monotonal, are quick and confident. He is not the doctor who examined the remains eight years ago, but he tells us he has performed a complete review of the record: Cause of death was undeterminable, and though the date of death couldn't be pinpointed with any accuracy, it was probably quite soon after Kyle's abduction. No foreign DNA was recovered from the remains, but seeing as there had already been a confession, a guilty plea, and a sentencing by the time they were recovered, they hadn't been examined as closely as they might have been otherwise.

Gregory turns the witness over to Monica for cross-examination. She has no questions.

The state rests. Henry is as good as convicted.

CHAPTER 47

It's almost noon. Judge Ballard announces that trial will resume first thing in the morning. I go to my office. Work has been piling up. I install myself at the desk and make a list of priorities as I drill down through the piles, delegating as much as possible, writing memos to assistants and status updates to Pleasant Holly. Everything on Subsurface and all related matters, including the annoyingly unsolved Jimmy Mailing murder, stays with me. There isn't much on Mailing: mostly updates from the Bureau confirming that they've made no progress but they expect to soon. I think this is code for the fact that it's been deemed low priority. True, Jimmy Mailing had found semi-legitimate work as Bud Billman's fixer at Subsurface, but I'm sure he was still involved in nefarious moonlighting. The hit on him looked professional, making it nearly impossible to solve. Also, since Mailing was a player in the scandal, there was no innocent victim in whose "defense" we needed to bring the perp to justice.

I write a quick email to Isler over at the Bureau about all of this, and I cc: Chip and Upton.

Last I knew, the Bureau was going to look at Voss for Mailing's murder. I know I'd have heard something if anything had turned up, but just to be sure, I send a quick follow-up email asking if investigation of that possible suspect is proceeding.

A moment later, Upton is in my office. "I've been wondering the same thing," he says.

"About Mailing?"

"Yes. How about if you and I sit down and take a fresh look?" Upton has a mischievous twinkle, because what he's really saying is that maybe he and I can find something that the Bureau missed. This is like Upton: He's cocky and audacious. He's a good lawyer, but I've often thought he'd be a better agent or detective because he seems to have an intuitive sense of human behavior—or to put it less discreetly, he can think like a criminal.

He almost was one once. He was a juvenile delinquent who caught a few lucky breaks that steered him onto a safer path before his youthful "ethic" of self-serving expedience had fully taken root. With his innate intellect, his physical coordination, and a good high school football coach, he landed himself a brief career as an NFL kicker instead of what could have been a long career in prison. I'm sure he's clean now, but he does seem to know an awful lot about the shadowy side of things.

He sits now in one of my office chairs, tipping back on two legs, feet on my desk.

"A fresh look?" I say. "Yes, let's. We ought to be able to outsmart the Bureau."

"It wouldn't be the first time," he says.

I'm not sure if this is true, but I agree with him anyway, and the two of us sit there a few moments, feeling like old cowboys talking about swinging up into the saddle to ride again. He looks very content.

I still see evidence in Upton of the unusual path he took into legal prosecution: He sometimes sees rules as things not to be guided by but to be danced around when needed. If he were a cop, he might turn off the video recording anytime a suspect needed some extra persuading. He is lenient and sympathetic with youthful defendants in nonviolent crimes. He thinks of them as less fortunate versions of his younger self. Conversely, he is remorseless with the ones he calls "the disrupters of our urban utopia." These are the real criminals. They are the powerful ones—kingpins, people of violence with no regard for the lives they ruin along the way. This is a thing with Upton: He talks about the shining city on the hill. He's a true believer. He's a little kooky about it, and I used to worry that his zealous belief in the urban utopia could get him into trouble. But years have passed, and for the most part, he has colored within the lines.

I say, "I can't do this fresh look right now, unfortunately. I kind of need to get caught up. How about tomorrow, after Henry's trial ends for the day?"

"Not tonight?"

"I have Barnaby."

"Tomorrow, then. It's a date." Upton sits there smiling at me, fingers interlaced across his stomach. He does this occasionally, just stares at me with an affectionate grin. He means well, but it's unnerving. Upton feels he owes me, because a few years back I did him a good turn when an old gambling problem came back to haunt him. I kept it quiet for him. I don't feel like he owes me anything, but it's nice to know if I ever need him, he'll show up.

He leaves. I continue drilling into the stack of paperwork. It's all humdrum except for a memo Chip sent along to me:

TO: Agent d'Villafranca
FROM: Stan Taylor, NTSB inspector
RE: Billman fatality

Agent d'Villafranca: in response to your recent inquiry, we have little hope of recovering the wreckage of Bud Billman's V-tail Cirrus. As you know, it was lost offshore in an area where ocean depths exceed 500 feet. The chances of locating it are slim. In circumstances like this, the most common cause of aircraft accidents is pilot error. I'll be in touch if we get any more information.

I'm amazed. I had no idea Chip was looking into Billman's crash. I don't know if this is standard or if Chip suspects something.

I go home to Friendly City. I have Barn. He has a stomach bug, and I stay in the bed with him, keeping a pot close at hand for him to puke into and getting cool rags for his forehead. We're up most of the night.

CHAPTER 48

Monica Brill's first witness is Ron Bauer, a police detective from Orchard City. He is African-American, bald, and has beefy forearms, which we can see because he's wearing a long-sleeve T-shirt with the sleeves pushed up above his elbows. He tells us he has been retired from police work for the past five years, and that he now spends most of his time working in his wife's florist shop. Monica smiles as Ron Bauer tells us this. She speaks to him amiably. It all seems friendly.

MS.BRILL: And before you retired, Detective, were you involved at all in the investigation of Kyle Runion's disappearance?

DETECTIVE BAUER: I was.

MS.BRILL: At some point the police zeroed in on one Daryl Devaney as the prime suspect, is that right?

DETECTIVE BAUER: Yes.

MS.BRILL: What evidence or facts made you suspect Mr. Devaney?

DETECTIVE BAUER: Well, that was back then. It was based on what we knew then. But with what we know now, it's obvious that—

MS.BRILL: Please answer the question, Detective. What made you suspect Daryl Devaney was responsible for Kyle Runion's disappearance?

DETECTIVE BAUER: He was known to us.

MS.BRILL: Known how?

DETECTIVE BAUER: Always in trouble.

> MS.BRILL: Can you elaborate on that?
>
> DETECTIVE BAUER: No.
>
> MS.BRILL: Had you ever arrested him before?
>
> DETECTIVE BAUER: I don't know. Maybe.

It continues like this. Detective Bauer, who apparently once was the tenacious pursuer of Daryl Devaney, now wants to disown the case. Monica keeps after him; he keeps dodging and feigning ignorance. She keeps asking. Gregory keeps objecting that she is leading the witness. Finally, long after I expect it, Monica says, "Your Honor, I'd like permission to treat Detective Bauer as a hostile witness."

The judge agrees.

Monica resumes, but now with leading questions. Her tone is aggressive, sometimes even mocking.

> MS.BRILL: Isn't it true, Detective, that you'd ar-
>   rested Daryl Devaney twice in the past?
>
> DETECTIVE BAUER: Maybe. I don't remember how many
>   times.
>
> MS.BRILL: One of which was for indecent exposure?
>
> DETECTIVE BAUER: Um. Maybe. Yes. The kid wasn't
>   quite right.
>
> MS.BRILL: And isn't it true that neighbors you in-
>   terviewed reported seeing Kyle speaking to some-
>   one in a red pickup truck the day he disappeared?
>
> DETECTIVE BAUER: Maybe. It was a long time ago.
>
> MS.BRILL: Well, let me refresh your memory.

Monica reads a police report about the red pickup truck. Then she shows Bauer the report.

> MS.BRILL: Is that your signature, Detective?
>
> DETECTIVE BAUER: Yes.
>
> MS.BRILL: So I'll ask you again, Detective. Is it
>   true that neighbors—

    DETECTIVE BAUER: Apparently it is. If I wrote that
      report, it is true. Yes.
    MS.BRILL: And did you also determine that although
      Daryl Devaney didn't have a driver's license, his
      sister, Peggy, owned a red Ford F250 pickup that
      Daryl drove around on their farm and occasionally
      out onto the street?
    DETECTIVE BAUER: Um. Yes.

Monica keeps at it. Her intention is obvious: to create doubt over
Henry's guilt by proving to the jury that Kyle Runion's killer has
already been identified, apprehended, and sentenced.

Bauer grows more and more compliant as she wears him down. But
while he started out relaxed and affable, he becomes monotonal and
wooden. He admits that when Kyle disappeared, investigators immediately suspected Daryl Devaney and took him in for questioning, but
they didn't have enough to charge him. He admits that they kept him
under surveillance the entire year, from when Kyle disappeared until
his remains were found near the reservoir some hundred and fifty miles
away. Bauer is a big man, the kind you wouldn't want to mess with.
But in the witness box, he's struggling. He seems no match for Monica.

    MS.BRILL: And when Kyle Runion's body was discov-
      ered nearly a year after his disappearance, you
      again brought Daryl Devaney in for questioning,
      isn't that true?
    DETECTIVE BAUER: Yes.
    MS.BRILL: And Daryl confessed to abducting Kyle?
    DETECTIVE BAUER: Yes.
    MS.BRILL: And sexually assaulting him?
    DETECTIVE BAUER: Yes.
    MS.BRILL: And killing him?
    DETECTIVE BAUER: Yes.
    MS.BRILL: And driving up to the Reservoir District
      to bury the body?

DETECTIVE BAUER: Yes.

MS.BRILL: Isn't it also true that Daryl Devaney, in his confession, was able to accurately describe what Kyle Runion was wearing that day: camouflage pants and a T-shirt that said EVERGLADES?

DETECTIVE BAUER: Yes.

MS.BRILL: I have a copy of that confession here, Detective. It has two signatures on it. One purports to be Daryl Devaney's, the other purports to be yours as witness.

Monica shows the document to Bauer. He concedes that he signed as witness and that he did in fact witness Daryl signing the confession.

MS.BRILL: Were you called to testify at Daryl Devaney's trial?

DETECTIVE BAUER: No.

MS.BRILL: Why's that?

DETECTIVE BAUER: There wasn't a trial. He pled guilty.

MS.BRILL: And do you know the sentence he pled to?

DETECTIVE BAUER: But that was before the DNA.

MS.BRILL: DNA? Do you want to talk about DNA? Did you find DNA at the scene?

DETECTIVE BAUER: No. We—

MS.BRILL: And are you a scientist? Do you have training in DNA analysis?

DETECTIVE BAUER: No, but I know that—

MS.BRILL: And was DNA testing available seven years ago when Kyle's body was discovered?

DETECTIVE BAUER: Yes. But—

MS.BRILL: But you never searched for DNA evidence because you had your perpetrator?

DETECTIVE BAUER: Well, we thought—

MS.BRILL: And he confessed?

DETECTIVE BAUER: Well, yeah, but—

MS.BRILL: But what?

DETECTIVE BAUER: I don't know.

Bauer stares at his hands. He is taking a beating. What he isn't say-ing—what he can't say—is that he and the other cops knew from the start that Daryl Devaney was trouble. They *knew* he was the one. In the torturous days and weeks after Kyle disappeared, they worked with the grief-stricken family. They made promises; they let the parents think progress was being made when it was stalled; they sat in the Runions' living room, holding the mother's hand and pretending not to notice as the father sobbed in the next room; they kept the pictures of Kyle on their bulletin boards at the station. Their lives became all about Kyle Runion and his family. They came to love the Runions in that paternalistic way you can love someone who is so thoroughly and helplessly at your mercy, as doctors might love patients, lawyers love clients, owners love pets. Bauer and the other investigators probably went home at night to their own children and felt physically ill at the knowledge that horrors like this were afoot in their own town, and it was only a roll of the dice that made this about the Runions instead of the Bauers. Sometimes they wished they'd never gone into police work. All the while, they knew with a cop's sense of knowing that the weird kid, the troublemaker, the continuously inappropriate, surly, angry, hormone-ravaged Daryl Devaney was just beyond reach. They knew he wasn't bright. He was a special-ed kid. So how dare he outsmart them on this? How dare he keep the Runions and everybody else in town waiting for the arrest, the conviction, the closure? Bauer and the other cops watched Daryl Devaney going about his life, not giving a shit about Kyle's parents or anybody else, feeling superior and believing he could get away with anything. But they knew he'd screw up eventually. He'd screw up, and when he did, Detective Bauer and the others would be there.

When Kyle's body was found, they swooped. They took Daryl in, held him, grilled him, threatened him, threatened his sister, pretended to have evidence they didn't have, and used every trick in their arsenal. They fed him information without his even real-izing it. Maybe they didn't realize it themselves: the camouflage pants; the Everglades shirt; the contents of Kyle's backpack. Maybe they mentioned particulars of Kyle's anatomy. They didn't let him sleep, didn't let him rest. They did the good cop/bad cop rou-tine. And though he had only borderline intelligence, maybe he'd watched enough cop shows or understood his Miranda rights well enough to ask for a lawyer. These were experienced cops, so maybe they saw it coming and were able to shut off the video before the request actually crossed his lips. Or maybe he never did ask. Or maybe he did ask, but that part of the video got erased.

Years have passed. I have no doubt that on the long night of Daryl Devaney's interrogation, Bauer and his colleagues believed in what they were doing. On one side they had a bereaved family, and on the other they had a perverted, murderous half-wit without enough sense to know when the game was up. Bauer and the others probably thought of themselves as janitors of a sort. Tears had been shed, blood had been spilled. Now it all needed cleaning up. Some stains just take more scrubbing.

But Detective Bauer can't say any of this in court. Bauer knows DNA doesn't lie. And as a retired detective, he has probably read articles and exposés about false confessions. Maybe he understands now that poor Daryl was so confused and panicky and exhausted and desperate and in need of a kind word that he finally said what-ever the detectives wanted him to say just to please them and get them to stop yelling at him and let him sleep and, yes, maybe get them to like him. To love him. Maybe Detective Bauer understands now that the boy he thought was a smug and calculating killer was really just a terrified child.

Detective Bauer is in a no-win situation. He has to either stand by Daryl's conviction or renounce it. If he stands by the con-viction—if he professes his continuing belief in Daryl Devaney's guilt—he could be helping the real killer, Henry Tatlock, get away with it. But if he renounces Daryl's conviction, he is admitting to his part in forcing a confession from this developmentally delayed teenager who had no lawyer and little understanding of what was happening to him.

> MS. BRILL: Detective, where is Daryl Devaney today?
> DETECTIVE BAUER: I think Fullerton State Pen.
> MS. BRILL: Doing life without parole?
> DETECTIVE BAUER: Yes.
> MS. BRILL: For the murder, kidnapping, and sexual assault of young Kyle Runion?
> DETECTIVE BAUER: Yes.
> MS. BRILL: Detective Bauer, when you took Daryl Devaney's confession, were you absolutely convinced of his guilt?

Bauer doesn't look at Monica or at anybody else. He stares at his hands. He doesn't look big and burly anymore. He looks haunted. His voice is barely audible. He bends toward the microphone like an old man. In answer to Monica's question, he says that yes, he had been absolutely convinced of Daryl's guilt.

Monica is too good a lawyer to ask the next question: whether Bauer still believes that Daryl was guilty. She ends her questioning. It was a good show. She got Bauer to confirm that he believed Daryl was the actual perp, and she got to hammer home the fact that Daryl confessed and pleaded guilty to the crimes that Henry is charged with. I'm impressed with her. She is earning her paycheck, after all. But she'll need a lot more than this to trump the DNA evidence against Henry.

Gregory Nations tries to smooth over some of the doubt Monica might have created.

On the way out of court, Monica hands me a document. I have been subpoenaed to appear as a witness for the defense the next day of trial.

CHAPTER 49

Upton and I meet in his office to talk about Subsurface and the Jimmy Mailing murder. It's around six in the evening. Most everybody has gone home. I bring beer. Ties are loosened, collars unbuttoned. We have two boxes of files.

"Where shall we start?" Upton says.

I open two beers and hand him one. "I've been otherwise involved," I say. "You take the lead, brother, show me what you've got."

"Well . . ." He takes a long drink of his beer. "What I've got is a question."

"Fire away."

"None of my business, really," he says.

He drinks.

I drink.

"What's the deal with you and Tina?"

I embark on a halting monologue about what seems to be going on between Tina and me, but I repeatedly interject a disclaimer that I know only what I know, which might be fundamentally different from what Tina knows. And what either of us thinks we know might have little in common with what is real and true if, in fact, there are such things as reality and truth.

"Reality and truth," Upton says. "Aren't you and I, as ass-kicking federal prosecutors, the guardians of reality and truth?"

"I don't know," I say. "Maybe we're just practitioners of illusion and deception. Besides, marital relationships and criminal law aren't exactly interchangeable."

"No?"

"No."

"Beg to differ," he says.

"Go ahead," I say. "Differ."

"Here's my thinking. What really matters in both crime and love is intention. Am I right?"

"No."

"Like If you could see into someone's heart, would we need trials? Would we even have lovers' squabbles?"

"Yes."

"No," he says, "but since we don't have that window, that crystal ball, we confuse actions with intentions. We forget that they're not the same thing. We assume actions are always evidence of intentions. We make it all about actions, right?"

"Wrong."

What Upton and I are doing here, blurting out half-baked philosophies of love and law, is an unconscious attempt to start a chain reaction—priming the pump for an effusion of insightful and heartfelt observations. But no effusion ensues. The observations become increasingly sophomoric.

Upton goes to piss. When he comes back, he says, "Are you going to save it?"

"Save what?"

"Your marriage. Relationship?"

"Don't know."

"Do you want to?"

I pretend to be thinking it over, but what I'm really doing is steeling my composure. I grab two more beers and open them. My thoughts flit between Tina and DNA. Farquar said that only a small percentage of those mind-boggling strands have any genetic meaning; the rest is just filler. And of the tiny percentage that *do* have relevance, we're interested in only two molecules, the base pairs, which form the connecting rungs of the double helix. He said the laboratory process of electrophoresis is essentially clearing out all the junk to get at these base pairs and reveal the source's true identity.

So maybe what Upton and I are doing here, having beers while we talk about love and crime, is like electrophoresis—hoping to clear away the junk so that something real can emerge. I'd like to explain this burst of insight to Upton, but it feels too complicated for me to hold in my head as we talk.

"Do you?" he asks again. "Do you want to save it?"

"My marriage? Of course."

"Wasn't sure."

"What do you mean you weren't sure? What should I do? Should I cry like a little girl?"

"Please don't."

Upton looks deep in thought. I'm deep in thought. I'm rummaging through the conversation, both what has been said and what remains in my head. I want to find a meaningful nucleotide strand, but it all looks like junk to me. A meaningful strand would be any shred of an idea that might bring Tina back.

I leave Upton's office for the men's room. When I return, I lift a handful of files from my box and plop them on his desk.

"Subsurface," he says.

"Jimmy Mailing," I say.

"A bubble chart," he says. He walks over to his whiteboard, which is mounted on a flimsy aluminum tripod.

"Bubble chart?" I say. "What the hell is a bubble chart?"

Upton bumps against the tripod, and it tips over. He rights it. "It's about relationships," he says.

"I really think I'm done talking about my marriage. I want to do some work."

"Yes, yes. Relationships between facts: evidence; events." He writes on his board "Mailing murdered" and draws a circle around it. Then he writes the names of the legislators we're investigating or prosecuting for taking bribes: O'Leary, Thomas, Alvarez, and a few others. He draws smaller circles around these. He writes "Calvin Dunbar" and circles it.

"No," I say, "Dunbar jumped ship. Copped to everything. He's with us."

Upton erases Dunbar but writes it in small letters way off to the side, then puts a little circle around it.

"Stubborn," I say.

He chuckles. "I'm the bubble master," he says, "you can't argue with me."

I say, "Accounting of Billman and Subsurface shows five point two million missing."

Upton writes "5.2 Mil" near the center of the board and puts a big circle around it.

"Gas tax legislation," I say. "Worth hundreds of millions to the industry."

Right in the middle of the board, he writes $$$ and draws the biggest circle of all.

I say, "Last-minute amendments delayed the bill two years in a row."

"How do you know that?"

I tell him about Lizzy's work and about Representative Porter.

Upton grins. "Aha!" he says. "Lizzy! We have a secret weapon." He writes "Amendments" on the board. Medium-sized circle. Then he writes "Porter" and draws a circle overlapping the "Amendments" circle.

I tell Upton about the big construction projects that Porter landed for his district.

"But there's nothing illegal about horse-trading like that," Upton says. "One guy gets a pork barrel project for his district. In exchange he tags an amendment, a rider, on a bill for someone else. It goes on all the time."

"I guess."

"It's only illegal if payoffs are involved. But there's no evidence of any payoff to this schmuck." Upton writes "Pork" and puts a medium circle around it abutting the Porter circle.

We're at a standstill. Both of us stare at the board. Upton says, "You know what we need to do now?"

"No, what?"

He opens two more beers and hands me one. "This is what."

I study the whiteboard. I like how the circles are spread out in a pleasing pattern. I like the arrangement and how he balanced size and space. "I think you have some serious artistic talent," I say.

He nods gravely. "Yes. I must."

"Because that puddle chart . . ."

"Bubble shark."

"Puddle shark?"

"Yes. The puddle shark is, like, a masterpiece."

"I know. Right?"

"I know."

I gaze at the bubble chart. I pick up my cell phone and take a photo of it. Upton lifts some of the Subsurface files and starts flipping through. I take the Jimmy Mailing documents from the box, but its contents slide out of the manila folder and onto the floor. I get off my chair and kneel on the floor collecting all the pages, then sit back down and start going through them one by one. Some are upside down. I try arranging them back into order. The page on top now is a list of phone numbers, and without thinking about it, I start scanning down.

Suddenly, I'm thinking about Detective Sabin. She's very nice. And attractive. I don't think she was conning me in the park that night. She took my arm and I patted her hand and we walked together.

I think about Tina. I miss her. But she is barricaded in her fortress of emotional withdrawal, making me sleep at Friendly City like Napoleon in exile at Elba.

I chuckle out loud. "Napoleon," I say.

Upton ignores me.

But Sabin: The reason I'm thinking of her right now, I realize, is because I'm staring at her birthday. (*Christmas Day*, she said. *Twelve-twenty-five. It's my birthday. Ironic for a Jewish girl.*) It was when we were looking at the texts from Lydia's prepaid cell phone: Lydia and her secret lover. The Christmas number belonged to the lover: *Something something something twelve-twenty-five*. Right now I'm looking at a list of numbers from . . . I don't know what.

I flip to the first page of whatever I'm holding. It is the call log from the phone found in Jimmy Mailing's car after he was killed. The phone was an untraceable, prepaid disposable. I get up and go into my office for my file on Lydia's murder. I get the printout of texts between Lydia and her lover. The lover's phone number is 555-1225. The number of whoever called Jimmy Mailing on the evening before his murder was 555-1225.

"Upton, look at this." I push the printouts in front of him and go to the coffee machine and brew a fresh pot. By the time I'm back with two steaming cups, Upton is upright at the desk studying the printouts.

"Do you realize what this means?" he says.

"It means my sister-in-law's secret lover, who is a person of extreme interest in the investigation of her murder, is also an associate of Jimmy Mailing's—maybe the last one to see him alive—and a person of extreme interest in *his* murder."

"Why didn't anybody catch this before?"

It's a rhetorical question, a place holder while he gets some coffee into his system.

"Three phones," I say. "Lydia's, Mailing's, and the Christmas one."

"Christmas?"

"Twelve-twenty-five. They are all burners. Prepaid. No owner info. And since the investigation of Lydia's murder is in the hands of the local cops, and Dunbar's is the jurisdiction of the Bureau . . ."

"The only place the investigations meet is right here with you," Upton says.

"We should assume that whoever called Mailing late on the night of his murder was setting up a meeting to kill him."

"And if the mystery caller is who killed Mailing . . ."

"Maybe he killed Lydia, too," I say.

"And the shootings have the same MO," Upton says.

"Single shot to the head."

"But I thought Henry killed Lydia," Upton says.

"Of course he did."

We drink coffee and try to think our way through this. I'm having trouble holding it all in my mind.

"Puddle shark," I say.

Upton gets up and turns the whiteboard around. It's double-sided. He writes "Christmas number" and circles it. He writes "Bullet to head" and circles it. He writes "Henry" and "Murdering pedophile" and "Subsurface fixer" and "Lydia's lover" and circles them all. We draw arrows between the bubbles, we erase them, we move them around. But we can't make it all make sense.

"Is Henry involved somehow in the Subsurface mess?" Upton says. We ponder. It doesn't sound right. Henry is about perversion, not money.

"We have to find out who the Christmas number is," I say. I dial Chip and ask if he can jump in his car and drive to my office. He was on his way home but says he'll turn around.

"What about those state detectives?" Upton says. "You should call them, too."

I *should* call them. That was actually my first thought: *I should call Sabin.* But I wasn't sure whether I was calling her because of this new discovery or because I just wanted to call her. I could call Philbin, but with Henry's trial going on and Philbin and me both being called as witnesses, it isn't a good idea. I call Sabin.

Chip, Upton, Sabin, and I sit in Upton's office for over an hour, talking it through, but we don't come up with much. The only thing we're certain of is that these two cases, Lydia's murder and Mailing's murder, have just become entangled.

CHAPTER 50

In the witness box, I raise my right hand and swear to tell the truth, the whole truth, and nothing but the truth.

Will I?

I assume Monica has called me as a witness because she hopes to make Henry look as human as possible. She wants it known that he was my friend; that he was a good prosecutor (albeit inexperienced). That he cared about his career and displayed empathy for victims, integrity in his work, compassion in his relationships. That despite being initially shy and awkward, he was witty and fun-loving and relaxed once you got to know him. And that he was part of my family.

I remember the weekend at our cabin on the lake. It was after Lydia's murder. I have in my mind the image of Henry and Barnaby standing in the fading light of evening, throwing stones into the water. I was glad Henry was with us, pleased that he seemed to be recovering and moving forward.

I see the two of them side by side. Henry and Barnaby.

Will I tell the truth?

No. I will say anything to convict that man—to condemn him to hell. To remove him as far as possible from Barnaby, and from Tina and Lizzy and me, and from every other decent person on earth.

Will I tell the whole truth? Nobody wants the whole truth. The court doesn't, and Monica definitely doesn't. Court cases are icebergs: The jury sees only a small tip of facts poking above the surface. Monica will try to elicit a few select truths that she can weave into one big lie that Henry is innocent. She doesn't want the truth that he date-raped a girl in high school. She doesn't want the truth that his fiancée had a lover because Henry, as a violent pedophile, had no interest in a normal adult relationship with a committed partner. And Monica definitely won't want the truth that Henry killed Lydia because she had discovered his secret. Monica will pick and choose the truths she asks for, so maybe I'll pick and choose the truths I give.

She starts with basic questions: name and address. Then she asks what I do for a living:

> **MR. DAVIS:** I am an assistant U.S. attorney, head of the criminal division.
>
> **MS. BRILL:** And can you describe for the court your duties in that position?

I give a brief narrative of my job.

> **MS. BRILL:** And did you at some point have occasion to meet the defendant Henry Tatlock?

I say that yes, I did. She leads me through a history of my relationship with Henry and his work at the office. But she moves quickly, and the questions are superficial. Where I expect her to slow down and delve into something that could make him sound human and likable, she just pushes forward, seeming to barely hear my answers.

> **MS. BRILL:** So you're saying he'd become part of the family?
>
> **MR. DAVIS:** Yes.
>
> **MS. BRILL:** And he was engaged to your sister-in-law?
>
> **MR. DAVIS:** Yes.
>
> **MS. BRILL:** Are they still engaged? Are they married?

I'm astounded. Lydia's murder was mentioned briefly by Philbin in his testimony. Now Monica has offered me another wide-open door to talk about the murder. She definitely has a plan, but I have no idea what it could be.

> **MR.DAVIS:** No. Lydia was murdered last July Fourth.
> She was shot in the head at Rokeby Park. It was
> nighttime, and the killer made a halfhearted at-
> tempt to make it look like sexual assault and rob-
> bery. Her killer has not been found.
>
> **MS.BRILL:** I'm so sorry for this loss that your fam-
> ily experienced, Nick.
>
> **MR.DAVIS:** Thank you.
>
> **MS.BRILL:** So tell me, do you believe Henry Tatlock
> killed Lydia Trevor?

Before answering, I look at Gregory Nations. The question is out-
rageously objectionable for several reasons. But the answer can only
help the prosecution. Of course I think he's guilty. I *know* he's guilty.
Gregory Nations makes eye contact with me. He shrugs. So I answer:

> **MR.DAVIS:** Yes. I believe with all my heart that
> Henry Tatlock killed my sister-in-law.
>
> **MS.BRILL:** And when did you come to that belief?
>
> **MR.DAVIS:** When we got the DNA results from Kyle
> Runion's remains. That's when I finally recog-
> nized what a monster Henry is. I guess I had a
> blind spot until then.
>
> **MS.BRILL:** And that was in late October, wasn't it?
>
> **MR.DAVIS:** Yes.
>
> **MS.BRILL:** And so for almost four months, you held
> on to the belief that Henry had nothing to do
> with Lydia's death?

Gregory finally objects. The question is leading, and my belief isn't
relevant. Judge Ballard sustains the objection.

> **MS.BRILL:** Let's go in a different direction, Nick.
> Let's talk about the investigation into Lydia's
> murder. Were you involved in that investigation?

MR.DAVIS: Not directly, no.

MS.BRILL: But did you follow it?

MR.DAVIS: Of course.

MS.BRILL: And did you meet with investigators to discuss it?

MR.DAVIS: Yes.

MS.BRILL: Can you name them?

MR.DAVIS: Captain Jerome Dorsey and detectives Patrick Philbin and Rachel Sabin, all with the state troopers.

MS.BRILL: And did these officers tell you who their main suspect was?

This is another open door, and again I bolt through.

MR.DAVIS: Because of my relationship with Henry, they were hesitant to be real direct with me. At least Sabin and Dorsey were. But I knew they were looking at Henry.

MS.BRILL: Are you implying that Detective Philbin made no bones about suspecting Henry Tatlock?

MR.DAVIS: Yes. He was direct about it. He knew from the start that Henry had done it, and he was quite open about pursuing Henry.

MS.BRILL: Did you think he was too focused on Henry, and that he wasn't open to looking for other suspects, and that the real killer was getting further and further beyond reach?

It's too much for Gregory. He objects again. The question was leading. Monica reponds by asking to have me declared a hostile witness, just as Bauer was. The judge calls Monica and Gregory up to the bench. They talk in whispers.

I've never been a witness. I never get to see the courtroom from this perspective. I'm usually sitting at counsel table, or watching from the gallery, or standing addressing the jury. It's different from here in the front, looking out into the room. It's what the judge sees (though his view is more elevated).

I look at the jury, but none of them looks directly back at me. Their eyes avoid contact with mine. They might note my proportions, my appearance, my demeanor, but they go no further. To them I'm an exotic, not unlike something at the zoo. To be fair, they're little more than cattle to me: I see them for their usefulness, their willingness to convict, but I find nothing else of interest in their presence.

I look out into the gallery. It is full. I see reporters, and I see Kyle's parents with the entourage who came to the earlier hearings about Daryl Devaney. I see Peggy Devaney. Of course she'd be here; she knows full well that Daryl's fate is inversely linked to Henry's. I see Arthur Cunningham. I see Lizzy. This surprises me; I don't know whether she came the past few days, unobtrusively slipping in and out, or if she's just here today for my testimony. Either way, I feel something unexpected when I notice her in the crowd. I feel relief, as if, in sitting here with the eyes of so many spectators on me, I almost forget I'm not the one being judged. To see her trusting face among all those looks of skepticism and curiosity and contempt (how could I possibly once have been Henry's friend?) is energizing. I sit straighter. I feel confident in my ability to field whatever Monica hurls my way.

I look around the room—the hardwood doors and wainscoting and decorative molding, the elaborate bench for the judge, the polished rails corralling the spectators apart from us, the impeccable orderliness of it all. I have said that as a prosecutor, I am a gladiator and this is my coliseum. But glimpsing it now as a witness, imagining for a second that I'm the defendant, I can see how crushing it might be. Henry entered in chains before the jury was brought in, and he'll depart in chains once they leave. Bailiffs stand ready to pounce. The jury is ready to judge, the judge is ready to decree, and the spectators are ready to cheer—to rise up in jubilation at the slaughter. All these bits of splendid formality are props to make it seem legitimate: the robes, the oak rails, the finials, the polish, the hush, the flags, the gavel, and yes (though not visible from here), there are those walls of diplomas and certificates in Gregory's office, and Monica's, and the judge's, and mine—props for creating legitimacy, just like those powdered wigs of old.

Don't get me wrong, I believe in this. My career has been about promoting the orderly prosecution of crime and about rejecting the anarchy of vigilantism. But sitting here, deprived for once of my elite position in this room, and despite my hatred for him, I can't help but think of how it all must feel to Henry. How must it feel to be so (deservedly) despised? How might it have felt to Daryl Devaney to be so wrongfully accused?

Something I know from my years as a trial lawyer is that every defendant who has ever sat here feels less guilty than his accusers accuse him of being. Maybe a few really *are* innocent. But all the rest—the multitudes who've actually done something—know in their hearts a million reasons they're not as vile as we think. They were provoked; they were goaded; they were abused; they were cheated; they had an unscratchable itch, an unquenchable thirst; they bore the scars of violence and abuse and deprivation and subjugation. They were merely leveling the field that, owing to their disability or limitations of intellect or opportunity or poverty or self-esteem, had been tilted against them. They were acting at the behest of their voices or their demons, or maybe they were reacting instinctively to the incessant and inescapable complexity of life. Even the ones who've sat here hating themselves for what they've done must believe on a subconscious level that if we knew the pain of their own self-loathing, we'd loathe them less.

The oppressive authority of this court, its massive fascistic weight, must taunt them. It is the final card in a rigged game. It is the smooth walls of the arena, which, when the gate is raised to release the lions, turn out to be unscalable.

Is this how Henry feels? Does he feel less guilty than he is? Does he blame his biochemistry, his genes, his scars, his fucked-up childhood? Does he believe that if we only knew what he knows, we'd loathe him less? I look right at him now. If he looked at me, I'd meet his gaze with this question: *Do you feel less guilty than you are?* But he doesn't look up.

I find Lizzy in the crowd again. How wonderful it is to see her here.

The sidebar ends. I have been declared a hostile witness. Monica can ask me leading questions and, if she chooses, try to impeach anything I tell her.

She goes to the lectern and flips through her notes. "Back to where we were," she says. "Mr. Davis, did you originally feel that in his investigation of Lydia Trevor's murder, Detective Philbin was overly focused on Henry Tatlock as a suspect?"

I'd love to deny this, but I think I expressed that view to many people early in the investigation, including Lizzy.

"Yes," I say. "I thought he should broaden his investigation."

> MS.BRILL: To the best of your knowledge, did De-
> tective Philbin ever broaden his investigation?
> MR.DAVIS: Not until we came up with Smeltzer.
> MS.BRILL: Oh, right, let's talk about that.

She leads me through an explanation of the Smeltzer diversion. Then she circles back around:

> MS.BRILL: It was you who came up with the Smeltzer
> theory. Is that right?
> MR.DAVIS: For the most part, yes.
> MS.BRILL: And it's your testimony that until Smelt-
> zer, Detective Philbin was focused exclusively
> on Henry as the perpetrator?
> MR.DAVIS: Yes. I guess so.
> MS.BRILL: And you tried to get him to look else-
> where?

MR.DAVIS: Yes.

MS.BRILL: Without success?

MR.DAVIS: Not until Smeltzer.

MS.BRILL: You've testified, Mr. Davis, that until the results of the DNA analysis in the Kyle
Runion case, you continued to believe Henry was
innocent of Lydia Trevor's murder. Is that right?

MR.DAVIS: Yes.

MS.BRILL: So is it fair to say that you, a federal
prosecutor, didn't feel there was compelling evidence against Henry for Lydia's murder?

MR.DAVIS: Yes, as far as I was aware.

MS.BRILL: And as far as you knew, all the evidence
was either vague suspicion or merely circumstantial?

MR.DAVIS: Many convictions are made on circumstantial evidence.

MS.BRILL: Yes, I'm glad you mentioned that.

Monica puts aside the legal pad she is using and picks up another.
She flips through and finds the place she wants.

MS.BRILL: To the best of your knowledge, has Henry
Tatlock been charged with Lydia Trevor's murder?

MR.DAVIS: No. I mean yes. Yes and no.

I describe how, after the DNA results came back in the Runion case,
Gregory charged Henry with Lydia's murder.

MS.BRILL: And can you tell us why Mr. Nations
picked that moment to charge my client?

This elicits an explosive objection from Gregory Nations. Gregory
and Monica and the judge talk openly for a minute, then they talk
in sidebar, and then Judge Ballard allows Monica to lead me through

a lengthy controlled explanation of how it appeared to me that Gregory charged Henry in Lydia's murder because it would keep Henry detained in jail while the DNA results were authenticated and while Gregory got his ducks in a row for charging Henry in Kyle's murder.

Monica continues:

> **MS.BRILL:** And to the best of your knowledge, how was the case against Henry for Lydia's murder resolved?
>
> **MR.DAVIS:** It was dismissed by the state.
>
> **MS.BRILL:** By which you mean the DA, Gregory Nations himself, dismissed the charges.
>
> **MR.DAVIS:** Yes.
>
> **MS.BRILL:** And is it fair to say the charges were dismissed for insufficient evidence?

Gregory objects again.

I still can't figure out what Monica is doing. Obviously, she wants the jury to see how flawed the case is against Henry for Lydia's murder. But no amount of weakening that case can make up for the damage of the jury knowing about the murder to begin with. Monica could have kept the whole thing from them if she wanted to.

And all the stuff about Philbin: Maybe he *was* going off half-cocked. Maybe he was responding too much to his hunch and not enough to any real evidence. This would all be relevant if Henry were being tried for Lydia's murder, but bringing it up in this trial seems nonsensical. I'm willing to bet, though, that Monica knows exactly what she's doing. It makes me uneasy.

Gregory's objection is sustained.

"Let's talk a little more about Tony Smeltzer," Monica says. She asks a series of questions to fill out what the Bureau learned about him and why they, and I, decided he wasn't a threat. I never admitted going to meet him at Fog City Tap. Nobody knows about that. Monica asks if it's expected that Tina, as a former prosecutor, would have people wishing her harm. I tell her it's not *unexpected*. Monica shows the photo of Tina and Lydia to the jury for them to see how much they looked alike. And then she's done.

Gregory cross-examines me, but it's hard for him to know where to go because it's so unclear where Monica has been. If Henry were being tried for Lydia's murder, Monica's strategy might have been okay. She got me to say that I thought Philbin's investigation was biased and inept. And with her questions about Smeltzer and about disgruntled defendants in general, she could allow the jury to believe that someone else *could* have killed Lydia. But it's hard for me to imagine what she might have up her sleeve that would be better than the jury never knowing about Lydia's murder to begin with.

The most common way of defending against DNA evidence is for defense counsel to hire its own scientist to attack the state's analysis. It's seldom successful, but at least it's something. Monica has hired no expert.

Gregory finishes with me quickly. Trial is over for the day.

I have an evening meeting with Chip, Isler, Upton, Sabin, and Philbin at the Rain Tree. I'm the first one here, and I manage to snag the table in an alcove that gives us the most privacy. There's a candle lamp on the table, and Steve dims the overheads. The lunch crowd is long gone, and the dinner crowd is sparse. Maybe this is when average Joes have PTA meetings, or replace faucet washers in the bathroom, or pick up a bottle of Shiraz to go with the pot roast, or maybe even agree—after dodging for weeks or months or years—to watch the DVD of *On Golden Pond* with the wife. Whatever: They're not at the Rain Tree.

Outside, I notice that ice lines both sides of the river, but there's open water out in the middle. Steve has installed a floodlight aimed at the dam, and the blackness of the water is smooth and golden where it falls over the lip, reminding me of Lizzy's hair when it has just been brushed. I wish I were going home to pot roast. Or I wish Tina were meeting me here: wine; dinner; home to put Barn to bed, kiss him good night and linger a second, my lips on his cheek, breathing in the little-boy innocence of his breath. Then up to bed with Tina for sleepy snuggling and the sexy sweetness of *her* breath.

I dig my phone from a jacket pocket. *I miss you? I love you?* I don't have it planned out yet; I call her and hope the right words will come. But her phone goes right to voicemail without ringing. "Hi, this is Tina. Leave a message, I'll call back." She's either on the phone or has it turned off. She used to call me every afternoon. We used to plan dinner or talk about the day. Sometimes we'd "carpool," which was what we called it when we talked on the phone together as we drove, each of us in our own car.

"I'm just trying to reach you," I say to her voicemail, in a voice as full of blame as I can make it.

Chip arrives. Then Rachel Sabin. "Where's Philbin?" I ask.

"Home, I guess," she says. "He's probably sulking. Monica Brill is calling him as a witness tomorrow. The thing about Philly: He hates court. Hates it. Now twice in the same trial." She reaches over and taps my hand. "And how are you?"

It was just last night that we sat around talking about Lydia and Mailing and the Christmas number. She drove me home.

Isler takes the lead. "A few things seem to be falling into place," he says. "Here's the backdrop: A lot of money has gone missing from Subsurface, Inc.; the tax legislation would have cost the industry—and by extension Subsurface—hundreds of millions; Subsurface was paying penny-ante bribes to a few legislators to lock in their votes; and then the anti-gas, pro-environment representative Porter delayed the gas bill two whole years by pushing his environmental amendment."

"Did any of that five point two mil find its way into Porter's hands?" Upton asks.

"Doesn't appear so," Isler says. "Here's the foreground: Jimmy Mailing was murdered, and we assume it was because he knew too much. Bud Billman, who was probably the only other person to know the whole story, died in a plane crash a few months ago. The wreckage hasn't been found because it's at the bottom of the ocean. But NTSB is taking a fresh look at radar and radio records."

"You're thinking sabotage?" Sabin asks.

"Realize we have no actual evidence," Isler says. "It's just a thought. But if some serious money was changing hands, Billman and Mailing would have been the ones to know about it. We've been sweating Voss, Billman's right-hand man. So far, he looks clean."

"What does Porter have to say about all this?" Upton asks.

"Yes, well, that's what I want to tell you," Isler says. "We tried talking with him yesterday, but we haven't been able to find him yet. His wife says he drove home to his district for some constituent events, but he doesn't answer his phone. We're concerned. I've initiated a search."

"And here's the twist-a-roonie," I say. "My sister-in-law's illicit lover seems to be the one who lured Mailing over to Rokeby Park the night he was killed."

Everyone starts talking around the table. We lose focus. I find it hard to concentrate. I liked it better the other night when it was just Upton and me with the puddle shark. Maybe if this isn't solved by tomorrow after trial, I'll try diving into it again with one other person. Upton, probably. Or maybe Sabin. Right now my mind is back in the courtroom. And I'm exhausted. Last night, after drinking a little too much with Upton, I tossed and turned all night. Alcohol has that effect on me. And the night before that, Barnaby was sick and I was up with him for hours.

Sabin puts a hand on my knee. "You okay, Nick?"

"Sure, fine."

"Bullshit."

CHAPTER 51

This should be the final day of trial. The jury is seated by the time I arrive. Everybody except the judge seems ready to go. I walk to the front bench, where a seat has been saved for me behind Gregory Nations. I turn to see if Lizzy is here. I don't spot her.

I feel good. I finally got a full night of sleep and woke to the smell of coffee and the noise of someone moving around in the suite. It was Sabin.

After leaving the Rain Tree last night, she and I met for a glass of wine at the bar in Friendly City. We talked briefly about Subsurface, but I was too bleary to make much sense. "You're not much of a date," she said, though her voice didn't ask to be taken seriously. "Do you have an extra key card, Nick?"

I nodded.

She put her hand out. "Give it here."

I hesitated.

"Relax," she said. "I'll come for coffee in the morning—make sure you're up and alive."

This thing with Sabin: If I were single, I'd explore the chemistry she and I seem to have. But what I want—what I'm desperate for—is to be home with Tina and Barnaby. Sometimes I wish Sabin would get bumped from the investigation so I don't have to deal with her. But then I go "home" alone to Friendly City, spending the evening in the cold isolation of that cell, devoid as it is of Barnaby's giggles and hugs, and I climb into bed alone without Tina beside me to talk through the events of the day and to snuggle with through the night. Tina has sent me to Siberia, and out here in these frozen barrens, I have found some guilty pleasure in this new and ill-defined friendship.

* * *

The judge enters the courtroom. Monica calls Philbin back to the stand. His contempt for her and his anger at being called as a witness for the defense is palpable. He is more jowly, more hulking, and more surly than usual. The pits of his eyes are darker.

Monica starts right in, asking about his involvement in the investigation of Lydia's murder.

Gregory is on his feet immediately. "Objection. I've been patient about the defense's fishing expedition, but I don't see how Detective Philbin's part in an unrelated investigation has any relevance whatsoever."

Gregory's objection means that he was happy to let Monica spend a day talking about Lydia's murder, knowing the jury would assume that Henry was her killer. But now he's nervous that Monica might be going someplace with it.

Monica answers the objection by claiming that this is all extremely relevant, and with a bit more latitude, it will soon be clear.

I'm watching the judge. He's intrigued. He was never a prosecutor and is reputed to side with the defense. I get the impression that he's enjoying Monica's bizarre handling of this case and is itching to see where it goes. "Overruled," he says. "You may proceed, Ms. Brill, but you're on a short leash, understood?"

Monica leads Philbin through the investigation of Lydia's murder. She has him tell us why he was so certain Henry was guilty of Lydia's murder. Point by point, under Monica's scorching questions, all the supposed evidence sounds shallow. Her questions and Philbin's answers sound like the conversation Philbin and Sabin and I had in that coffee shop months ago before the DNA revelation. "He couldn't account for his whereabouts at the time of the murder," Philbin says, and Monica gets him to admit that Henry did account for his whereabouts—he was working on the brief he and I had due in court the next day. It's just that Henry had nobody to confirm his alibi.

"And he'd been consulting with Aaron Pursley, a known felon," Philbin says. Monica elicits the explanation that Pursley was an investigator—albeit an unlicensed one—and that Henry claimed to be looking for his biological family. (Neither side is willing to have Pursley himself testify about this. Gregory Nations doesn't want any witness who might confirm Henry's story about searching for his family; nor does Gregory dare risk triggering the empathic reaction a jury might feel for a quiet and disfigured man who goes hunting for his roots. Monica, conversely, wants to avoid shining a spotlight on Henry's association with someone as shady as Aaron Pursley.)

Monica succeeds in making Philbin's suspicion of Henry look hollow. Hunches may be the engines of investigation, but when the case falls apart and the investigator has to account for it, the hunches sound foolish and the detective's perseverance appears irrational or, worse, like a vendetta.

> **MS.BRILL:** Despite a total lack of physical evidence, and with nothing more than some flawed circumstantial suspicion, you were still convinced Lydia was killed by her fiancé, Henry Tatlock?
>
> **DETECTIVE PHILBIN:** Yes.
>
> **MS.BRILL:** So you were worried Henry was getting away with murder?
>
> **DETECTIVE PHILBIN:** I figured we'd get him sooner or later.
>
> **MS.BRILL:** And you were committed to making sure that happened?
>
> **DETECTIVE PHILBIN:** Yes.

Monica pretends to be discouraged, as if she expected Philbin to admit that his investigation of Henry was ill advised. "Well, let's move on," she says.

I was fooled by her at first. No longer. Monica is not discouraged. Her hangdog look is an act. She is baiting a trap. I'm worried. I'm intrigued.

"Did you ever have occasion to search Henry's house?" she asks, as if she's curious how thorough Philbin's investigation of Henry was.

DETECTIVE PHILBIN: Yes, after the DNA results . . .

MS.BRILL: But before that, before the DNA. When it was just about Lydia.

Philbin tells us how he and Sabin conducted a search of the house after I found the phone message Lydia left on the answering machine of our unused landline.

MS.BRILL: And you were involved in the search yourself?

DETECTIVE PHILBIN: Yes.

MS.BRILL: And it was thorough?

DETECTIVE PHILBIN: Pretty thorough.

MS.BRILL: As I recall, you weren't searching subject to a warrant but, rather, with Henry's permission.

DETECTIVE PHILBIN: Right.

MS.BRILL: And you searched the usual places? Under beds, in the laundry pile, in the bathroom, in trash cans?

DETECTIVE PHILBIN: Yes. It was a search. You know?

MS.BRILL: Find anything useful?

DETECTIVE PHILBIN: No.

MS.BRILL: Did you take anything from the house?

DETECTIVE PHILBIN: No.

I don't like this. I can see Gregory doesn't like it, either. Philbin, though, is gaining confidence. He's looking up at Monica. I notice him staring at Henry with a satisfied smile.

Gregory gets to his feet. "Your Honor, I think we've let this go on for long enough—"

MS.BRILL: And just to clarify, Henry Tatlock lived alone?

DETECTIVE PHILBIN: Yes.

MS.BRILL: Do you think he was lonely?

MR.NATIONS: Objection.

JUDGE: Sustained.

MS.BRILL: Do you think he missed sleeping with his fiancée?

MR.NATIONS: Objection. Your Honor—

JUDGE: Ms. Brill. You've reached the end of that leash. This whole testimony is—

MS.BRILL: I'm sorry, Judge. I'll wrap up now. I just want to ask the witness who Karen Philbin was.

Gregory objects again, and the judge smacks his gavel. But Detective Philbin is staring at Monica, his mouth half open as if waiting for words to come out.

I think Philbin sees that he has played it all wrong and Monica played him just right. Philbin is not a strategist or a deceiver. That is Sabin's job. Philbin is just who he is: the hulking, obtuse, undereducated, overcompensating "bad cop," which is why Sabin finds it so easy to play the role of good cop. During the investigation of Lydia's murder, and during this trial, his intention was—as in every other case he is involved in—to bring others around to his point of view through sheer boorish obstinacy. Now he's starting to see that Monica Brill has bested him. She is about to make his certainty look like delusion, his perseverance look like a vendetta, and his diligence look like criminality.

No, I doubt he has thought this through yet, but he senses it coming. It is a storm, a force of nature, and like wild animals that burrow or flock or flee in the advent of cataclysm, Detective Philbin tries to find a spot of safety. But there is none.

"Karen Philbin was my sister," he says.

MS.BRILL: And is it true that Karen Philbin was murdered over twenty years ago?

DETECTIVE PHILBIN: Yes.

MS.BRILL: And that the killer was her fiancé?

DETECTIVE PHILBIN: Yes.

MS.BRILL: And that he killed her in a jealous rage when she split up with him and started seeing someone else?

DETECTIVE PHILBIN: Yes.

MS.BRILL: And that he pled to manslaughter and only served eight years?

DETECTIVE PHILBIN: Yes.

MS.BRILL: Detective Philbin, isn't it true that when people ask why you chose a career in police work, you refer to this family tragedy?

DETECTIVE PHILBIN: I don't know. Maybe I've said that.

MS.BRILL: And would it surprise you to hear somebody quote you as saying you want to catch every, um, "murdering motherfucker who does to some other woman what that man did to Karen"?

DETECTIVE PHILBIN: I don't know.

MS.BRILL: Because I can call more witnesses if you like.

DETECTIVE PHILBIN: Maybe it wouldn't surprise me.

MS.BRILL: Detective Philbin, you testified earlier that you transported a box of physical evidence from the FBI building to the state crime lab, is that right?

DETECTIVE PHILBIN: Yes.

MS.BRILL: And that the box contained physical evidence from Kyle Runion's remains?

I hear voices behind me. Gregory is on his feet yelling "Objection," and in the witness booth, Philbin sits gaping at us. He says something, but I can't hear it.

Judge Ballard says, "Mr. Nations, what is the objection?"

"Relevance. And hearsay," Gregory says.

"Overruled."

MS.BRILL: And isn't it true, Detective, that when
you transported the physical evidence from the
FBI to the state crime lab, you were alone in the
car, and this was after you had searched Henry
Tatlock's house?

Philbin sits looking back and forth from Monica to Nations. Finally, he looks at the judge and answers in a voice barely audible: "I didn't do anything." His voice is soft, and everything about him changes. He morphs into a child—a little boy entrapped in the oppressive flesh of a fiftysomething. I've noticed in the past that he has a way of looking to Sabin for approval in the middle of a conversation. Sabin complains about him and criticizes him, but I have little doubt that she would step between him and a bullet. I hadn't formed the thought before, but I see it now. She treats him like a little brother. I think of Peggy Devaney's ferocious love and support for Daryl. I think of Tina and Lydia: how exasperated Lydia used to make Tina and how bottomless Tina's grief is. I'm an only child. I haven't experienced this kind of devotion, but I've noticed how even Lizzie has a special tone of voice for referring to baby Toby, her brother who died twelve years before she was born.

MS.BRILL: Detective Philbin, will you answer the
question?
DETECTIVE PHILBIN: I didn't do anything wrong.
MS.BRILL: Did you take any DNA-bearing substance
from Henry Tatlock's house during your warrant-
less search . . .
DETECTIVE PHILBIN: No.
MS.BRILL: . . . and plant something in the box you
took to the state crime lab . . .
DETECTIVE PHILBIN: No.
MS.BRILL: . . . to convict Henry Tatlock for Kyle
Runion's murder because you hadn't been able to
convict him of Lydia Trevor's murder?

The judge pounds his gavel and yells for order. But order is elusive. Both lawyers are on their feet, speaking over each other. Spectators are talking and gasping, Philbin is repeating, *No, no, no.* Even the jury is whispering among themselves. And the defendant, Henry Tatlock, after several days of sitting impassively, at last responds. He gapes at Philbin. Then, with his elbows on the table, he puts his head down into his hands.

CHAPTER 52

The trial is over by noon. Judge Ballard announces we'll resume for closing arguments at three. I call Tina to tell her all about Monica's tactic and Philbin's testimony.

"What do you think?" she asks. "Is it all strategy, or is it really possible?"

"Possible that Henry is innocent, you mean?"

"Yes. That Henry is innocent and Philbin is a dirty cop."

I'm surprised by the question. I hadn't believed for a second that Monica's tall tale could be true. I don't answer her. I just say, "Why don't you come to closing arguments with me, Tina?"

"I can't, Nick. I just can't."

"That's okay."

"It's not because of you, though. You know that?"

"Sure, Tina."

"Maybe, um, let's have dinner tomorrow night. You want to? Come over here?"

I agree. We say good-bye. I call Lizzy. We talk about the trial, and I try to rope her into dinner tonight. She says she can't make it because she's meeting with Calvin Dunbar again to ask him for some clarification on parliamentary procedure. She wants to know how Representative Porter was able to add those amendments onto the gas tax legislation.

"Yes, good idea," I say. I'm not really listening. My mind is on the trial. "Would you like to come for closing arguments?"

"Maybe, Dad. I don't know. Probably not. I'm pretty freaked out by the whole thing."

"I'm sure you are, sweetie."

"Did I tell you I did a bunch of background research on Porter?"

This is what Lizzy does. She deflects things. Henry's trial is difficult for her to talk about, so she fills the conversation, and her mind, with unrelated minutiae to fend it off. "He's a Democrat in a Republican district, so he keeps getting almost voted out," she says.

"I can't wait to hear what Monica comes up with for a closing," I say.

"He stays in office by bringing a lot of pork projects to his district," Lizzy says.

"I'll get you a seat up front with me," I say.

"Some huge ones," she says. "He's kind of the pork master."

"That's good, Lizzy. I have to go."

"Love you, Dad."

"Love you, Lizzy."

Gregory Nations argues first. He speaks in bullets: The defendant, Henry Tatlock, was living in Orchard City working as an intern at a family-law clinic—a job that, naturally, would bring him into contact with young children. The defendant left Orchard City just when Kyle disappeared. The defendant returned here to the city to resume law school. Kyle's remains were ultimately found just west of here at the reservoir. The evidence from Kyle's remains was tested specifically because doubts had arisen about Devaney's guilt. Testing revealed the defendant's DNA, from both hairs and semen, among the evidence in Kyle's burial site; Philbin is a respected detective; Monica's version of events requires too many leaps of logic. It is a desperate defense that Henry and Monica Brill concocted in response to the absolute, definitive, and scientific proof of Henry Tatlock's guilt.

Gregory sits. It was a workmanlike closing: facts; conclusion; summary. The way he organized it, characterized the testimony of the witnesses, and built fact upon fact, and the way he juxtaposed the incontrovertible proof of Henry's DNA against Monica's desperate fantasy, I know the jurors are ready and eager to deliver a guilty verdict. I also know that Monica will deliver a formidable closing.

* * *

Monica stands. "Make no mistake," she says, "the DNA comes from Henry Tatlock. The fact is undisputed. The only question is how it got into the evidence from Kyle Runion's remains. But before we talk about the evidence, let's talk about Henry Tatlock himself. Recall that in my opening statement, I asked you to overlook Henry's disfigurement. You've all probably heard or read the atrocious names the press gave Henry. 'The Freddy Krueger Killer.' 'The Mark of Cain Killer.' Now think back to when you were picked for the jury. The questions Mr. Nations asked, the questions Judge Ballard asked. And the questions I asked. Do you remember that many of the prospective jurors were released for mysterious reasons? Let me tell you a secret: I used a jury consultant for this case. That's a person whose job is to advise the lawyer on which jurors will be most receptive to that lawyer's argument. Depending on the facts, maybe we want a more conservative or more liberal jury, or a jury with lots of book learning, or more OJT kind of smarts. Maybe we want more analytical thinkers or more emotional thinkers. Et cetera. But I told my jury consultant I don't care about how much education you all have, or your economic circumstances, or your ethnic origin or work history or marital status or where you go on vacation or any of that. I just wanted jurors who are capable of not judging a man by his appearance. I told the consultant, 'Henry Tatlock is innocent, and I can prove it. So I just need men and women who can hear the evidence instead of ones who would walk into the courtroom on day one and, maybe without even realizing it, decide he's guilty because of the way he looks.' I told the jury consultant I wanted jurors who understood in their bones that the tragic accident this man experienced in his early childhood has absolutely nothing to do with the facts of this case. I said I wanted jurors who are free of that kind of prejudice."

Monica walks the length of the jury box looking at each one of them with a knowing smile. "And you know what?" she says. "I really do believe that I got the jury I asked for."

This is brilliant. Monica has made these jurors feel special for having been selected, and she's turned Henry's disfigurement into an advantage: the only way for the jury to reward her confidence in them, and to prove they weren't motivated by small-minded prejudice, is to acquit.

"Let's talk facts," Monica says, and she reminds us of every positive thing said about Henry: He's hardworking and dedicated; he overcame an inauspicious home life and excelled in school and put himself through law school.

I realize that most of these flattering things, she got from my testimony. I tried too hard to sound fair-minded as I proceeded to condemn him to hell.

I'm impressed with Monica. I wonder if her case has a chance. I wonder if even I have been snowed by her salesmanship. She stands in front of the jury box, butt poking out because of the heels she's wearing, skirt too tight, nails too long, lips too red, hair too perfect. She is exactly the kind of woman I never did and never would ask out. Worst of all, she is the advocate for my evil enemy. But I find myself sitting here feeling fond of her, almost smiling at the idea that I, along with the jury, am the kind of guy who, prior to the DNA results, saw Henry for his inner self and his good points instead of prejudging him for his disfigurement.

She gets into the meat of her argument. It is a simple story, and it makes perfect sense. Daryl Devaney killed Kyle Runion. He confessed. He is, even at this very moment, doing life in prison for the crime.

She lets this sink in, then continues: "And now Devaney, this killer, is trying to get out of jail on a technicality."

(I'm glad Tina isn't here. I doubt she could keep her mouth shut at hearing Monica refer to Daryl's vindication by DNA evidence "a technicality.")

Monica continues: "Enter Detective Patrick Philbin, a man so tortured by his sister's murder at the hands of her fiancé that he made it his mission in life to avenge her death."

Monica goes on to say that Philbin became obsessed with convicting Henry for Lydia's murder even though there was no evidence. "You heard Nick Davis—head of the criminal division of the U.S. Attorney's Office here, husband to Lydia Trevor's sister, Tina—tell you he believed Philbin was on a fool's errand. And if that's not enough, as further proof of the wrongheadedness of Philbin's investigation, when my client was finally charged with Lydia's murder, the district attoney himself, Mr. Nations, whom you see right here at this table"—Monica walks over to Gregory and points right at him—"he realized there was no basis for prosecuting Henry Tatlock for Lydia's death and dismissed the charges."

Monica goes back to counsel table and takes a drink of water. Then she's back at it: "You heard Dr. Farquar testify that, yes, it is perfectly, scientifically reasonable to believe that DNA-bearing substances could have been introduced into the Runion evidence from other sources. You heard testimony that Detective Philbin had the run of Henry Tatlock's house during a warrantless search for which Henry himself granted permission. And keep in mind that this search was conducted when it had become obvious to everyone else that Philbin's case against Henry was ridiculous. Most important, you heard testimony of how Detective Philbin himself was *coincidentally* available to transport the box of evidence from the FBI back to the state lab."

Now Monica wraps up: Philbin obviously opened the box of evidence and introduced a few of Henry's hairs into the evidence from Kyle's remains. Philbin further contaminated the evidence with minuscule smears of rehydrated semen salvaged from the underwear or bedsheets or discarded tissues in the home of this lonely and heartbroken man. Monica paused, then said in a tone of blunt honesty, "Without going into too much detail, I'll just ask you to consider for a second how a shattered man might comfort himself at night in the wake of his fiancée's murder."

She lets that thought sink in, then continues: "Detective Philbin wasn't able to save or avenge his sister, and the way he saw it, he wasn't able to do anything about Lydia Trevor, either. So he decided to take matters into his own hands. He'd get Henry convicted of something else. He planted DNA from Henry Tatlock in Kyle Runion's remains. He had the motive and the opportunity, so he took it. There is absolutely no evidence that Henry killed his fiancée, and other than this vicious and pathological frame-up, there is no evidence that he had anything whatsoever to do with Kyle Runion."

Monica talks a few minutes about the presumption of innocence and reasonable doubt. When she sits down, our minds are muddled with the question of whether this version of reality is possible. Is it just clever advocacy, or could this be a nightmarish frame-up by a psycho cop with a vendetta? I have resisted Monica all through this trial, but as she ties everything together into this logical package, even I—I who have been wanting more than anyone to snuff Henry from memory and existence—have a moment of doubt.

Is it a *reasonable* doubt? Is it rooted in honest possibility or merely the momentary disorientation of Monica's eloquent bullshit? If I were a juror at this very moment, I can't say for certain how I'd vote.

Trial is over. I hurry out of the courthouse. I don't want to be interviewed, and I don't want to have to talk to Kyle's family or Peggy Devaney or Monica or Gregory or Philbin. I feel off balance by that moment of doubt. I'm afraid it will come back.

I go to my office and sit at the desk, wondering if there's really a chance the jury could find Henry not guilty.

Upton knocks and comes in. I knew he'd be here. I was waiting for him.

"Quite a show," he says.

I nod. Upton settles deep into one of my chairs.

"She made a horse race out of it," I say.

"Indeed she did. Do you have a prediction?"

"Toss-up," I say. "Gregory was able to right the listing ship. He has science and logic on his side. Monica has fantasy."

"Not a toss-up," he says. "It's a done deal. They'll convict."

"So confident?"

"There was a huge hole in Monica's case," he says. "Lydia's murder.

Monica told us how Henry's DNA got into Kyle Runion's remains, and she told us how Daryl Devaney really did murder Kyle, but she needed to offer a better alternative for who killed Lydia. She tried to resurrect the Tony Smeltzer theory, but that's a loser because the Bureau debunked it. So the jury is left asking themselves, if Henry didn't kill Lydia, who did? She didn't need a bulletproof theory, just some alternative to Henry as killer."

Upton and I exchange a look. We both know that it now looks like Lydia was somehow connected to the Subsurface mess, and that she was in a liaison with whoever killed Jimmy Mailing. Does this mean Monica's theory might have had legs that she didn't even know about?

CHAPTER 53

D ay over. I head "home" to Friendly City, and by the time I
get there, I have to piss so bad from all that coffee that I'm
in danger of embarrassing myself.

"Nick," someone says as I hurry across the dark parking lot. He's
hurrying toward me, but I can't see who it is. "It's Calvin," he says.
"Calvin Dunbar."

"Amigo," I say. "What brings you to this dreary outpost of abandoned husbands?"

He laughs. "I like the lounge," he says. "It's quiet, and I can sit
with a martini and get some work done."

"Wish I'd known. We could have been having nightcaps these
past few months," I say. I'm just being friendly. I like the guy, but
realistically, I'm not sure how appropriate it would be for me to get
too involved with him. Of course, a drink now and then wouldn't
really hurt.

"Listen," he says, "I was going to call you. I found a bunch of
documents that might help your investigation. I've got them in the
car." He turns for the parking lot and tries to pull me in his wake.

"Let me just run in and piss," I say. "My back teeth are floating."
I start jogging for the building. "Bring them inside," I yell over my
shoulder, "we'll have a drink."

I scoot into the fishbowl lobby of Friendly City. It'll be nice to
have a drink with Calvin. He's interesting; he knows a lot about
the political workings of the state and who's who. And he's humble, though I don't know whether that's an actual personality trait,
or it results from his having gotten caught accepting money from
Subsurface. The more I think about it all, the more forgivable the
Subsurface stuff is. The line between legitimate political contribu-

tions and bribes can be pretty damn fuzzy. The guy was on the ropes financially. He didn't actually *do* anything for Subsurface; he merely allowed them to show their support and gratitude for his position on gas tax policy.

Tina calls while I'm in the men's room. I let it go to voicemail but call her back as soon as I'm done.

"So we're on for dinner tomorrow?" she says.

I confirm that we are. She asks about the trial, and I give her a quick summary as I walk out into the lobby and around the lounge, looking for Calvin. He's not there, so I go back out toward the parking lot.

"Is there really a chance they'll acquit?" Tina asks.

"Upton doesn't think so. I'm less certain."

I see Calvin coming from his car. It's a small blue Audi TT. I can almost envision driving something like that myself.

"I should have been there," Tina says. "But it was all just too . . . you know?"

"I understand, babe."

"But you know what, Nick?"

"What?"

"I'm feeling better," she says. "A bit. Kind of."

She means she is working on coming out of her seclusion, which means opening up to me again. "I'm glad to hear it, sweetie," I say.

"Just don't . . . okay? Don't."

Don't hurry her, she means. Don't come on too strong. Don't create any stress.

"Noted," I say.

We end the call. Calvin is standing waiting. "Sorry," I tell him. "My wife."

"No problem," he says. "How is Lydia, anyway?"

"Wrong sister," I say. "I'm married to Tina." I don't bother getting into the whole thing about Lydia.

"Of course," Calvin says. "Tina. I knew that."

"So about those documents," I say.

"What an idiot I am," he says. "I thought they were in my car.

Wrong. They're at home. I'll try to get them to you tomorrow, okay?"

"But tell me what you've got. Is it significant? I can send someone over to get them."

"Oh, no," he says. "It's just some old notes and files. I mean, I'm not a lawyer, but I doubt there's anything important there. I just thought you guys should have them."

"Okay. I'll get them tomorrow. Now, about that nightcap?"

"You hurried inside too quick," he says. "I called after you. Can't tonight. The wife is expecting me."

"Too bad. 'Nother time?"

"For sure."

He gives me an affectionate two-handed handshake and heads to his car. I go inside.

I forgot to thank him for helping Lizzy with her research. Darn.

Morning. No word from the jury, so I try to call Calvin to tell him I'd like to get the documents he spoke of. He doesn't answer. I remember that Lizzy is going to see him soon, so I call her to have her pass a message. She doesn't answer, either, so I leave a voicemail and get busy on other work.

People often confused Lydia's and Tina's names the way Calvin did last night. Maybe it's because they looked so similar, or because they were both beautiful and lively and smart, or because both names end in "A." I like that it still happens sometimes, as though something of Lydia lives on through Tina.

I wonder how Dunbar knows of Lydia, though. I'm sure I never mentioned her to him. But her murder was big news, and since Calvin and I were already entangled through Subsurface, it might have caught his attention when she was killed.

And Tina's name: I don't remember ever mentioning Tina to him, either. Of course, Calvin *is* a politician and an insurance agent, so maybe remembering names and sending regards to people's spouses is his stock in trade.

But no. Something in the way he said their names was too familiar: *How* **is** *Lydia?* And then the goofy forehead smack when I cor-
rected him: *Of course. Tina. I knew that!* It sounded like he actually
knew at least one of them. Something's odd.

Upton is in trial, so I try calling Chip and Isler, but they're both
unavailable, which may be just as well. I'll think my way through
this Tina/Lydia/Calvin issue, then I'll go to my colleagues with ideas
instead of bewilderment. The question I ask myself is how Calvin
and Lydia could be connected. As soon as I form the question in my
mind, I've answered it, and it's an answer I should have thought of
months ago: Lydia worked for the state legislature several years back.
I never put it together before because these two investigations—
Subsurface corruption and Lydia's murder—were entirely separate.
Lydia's murder was under state jurisdiction and we assumed it was
about violence or jealousy or rage. It was about Henry Tatlock or
Tony Smeltzer. No way could it be about white-collar crime and
greed.

Subsurface, though, is under federal jurisdiction, and it is about
greed. It is about politicians and businessmen behaving poorly, not
about shooting innocent women in the head. So it's not like I forgot
that Lydia worked for the state legislature half a decade ago, it's more
that it didn't seem important enough to remember.

I pull out my files about Calvin Dunbar and Lydia and compare
dates: Lydia worked for the legislature—in the house clerk's office—
for only four months, one legislative session. Calvin, as chair of the
house appropriations committee, probably had plenty of business
to take care of in that office. They would have come into contact,
and I can easily imagine them hitting it off: Calvin with his Nordic
good looks; Lydia with her easy and flirtatious exuberance. Calvin
with that vulnerability and capacity for self-reflection he showed in
our discussions about his legal transgressions; Lydia with her lifelong
search into the dark corners of her own soul.

I remember the texts Lydia and her lover sent each other. They
sounded so comfortable. I had the impression they'd known each
other a long time and that the sexual urgency of new love had had

years to quiet down and was replaced not with indifference, as often happens, but with a deeper and quieter kind of affection.

Could that lover have been Calvin?

Maybe.

I start rereading the printout of their text messages again:

Lydia: Fun afternoon. Got to pop in my favorite CD.

555-1225: Can't believe I fell asleep.

Lydia: LOL. Passion gone. So sad.

555-1225: Passion is fine. Youth and stamina gone.

Lydia: LOL.

The part about the CD had confused me because of Lydia's aversion to recorded music. But now I remember something Lizzy told me about Calvin not long ago: CD for Calvin Dunbar. That's his nickname. He told her it's what his friends call him.

Maybe popping in the favorite CD wasn't about listening to music but about the anatomy of sex.

My instinct is to be repulsed by this adulterous union that has led to such woe. At the same time, I'm thinking of how this affair, amid all the assignations that go hand in glove with the other kinds of bartering so common in state politics, apparently lasted for years on a trajectory similar to that of a real marriage, real love. But this isn't about love, it's about Lydia's murder. And Jimmy Mailing's. And maybe some others.

I puzzle over it all a while longer. I really do need another perspective, so I call Isler, but he can't talk right now. He says he'll be over as soon as he's free.

I call Sabin. "I'm at a scene, Nick," she says. "Can I call you back?"

"I think I've found Lydia's secret lover," I say.

It takes her a moment to make the mental leap from whatever she'd dealing with, back to Lydia's murder. She says she'll hand off what she's doing as quickly as possible and be right over.

"Is Philbin with you?" I ask.

"Philly," she says sadly. "He's really shook, Nick, getting accused like that. He's taking a few days off."

We hang up. I get Upton's whiteboard and set it up in my office. I try writing out hypotheses and conclusions, but that doesn't work, so I start listing things I know, but I end up with a forest of seemingly unrelated bits. I wish Isler were available. He's the analytical thinker.

I erase the board and write at the top: "Assumptions: Calvin is secret lover." Then underneath: "Evidence: 1) Calvin and Lydia worked in legislature at same time," and "2) Lydia's CD reference." Under this I write: "Questions: If Calvin and Lydia were lovers, did he kill her, and if so, why?"

Then I stare at the board. Dead end.

I write: "Things about Calvin."

This time I get further. I write: "1) Legislator; 2) Insurance agent; 3) Remorseful about Subsurface bribe." I stand back and look a moment, then add quotes around the word "bribe," because I still don't think he really did anything for the money. Then I continue listing everything I know, going through all our information about him and through my notes: "Veteran; political centrist."

I stop and think. I don't know much about him at all. I flip through the files again. I read Lizzy's reports: "Chair of House Appropriations Committee; former airplane mechanic."

I go back to the file.

Scuba diver . . .

I stare at the board some more. Nothing.

Janice buzzes me. "Detective Sabin here to see you, Nick."

I go out and meet her. As always, Sabin wears a scarf that looks nice with her dark, wavy hair. I lay a hand on her shoulder. We go into my office. I don't think the hand on the shoulder would seem inappropriate if I did it to Upton or Dorsey or Janis, but I worry that maybe it was inappropriate, and now I'm wondering if I want to be appropriate. I say, "How is your morning so far, Rachel?"

"Sad," she says. "I just came from an apparent suicide. Guy all alone in a motel room."

"Yes," I say. "That is sad. How did he . . . you know?"

Sabin sticks a finger in her mouth like a gun.

"Family or anything?" I ask.

"We don't know. He isn't identified yet. He checked in under a fake name. Been dead a few days."

"Coffee?"

She says she'd like some, so we walk out to the coffeepot and I pour us both a cup, and we go back into my office. I bring her up to date on everything, then we stand drinking coffee and staring at the whiteboard.

"Well, I don't have any great theories," she says, "but I do have a plan."

"Being?"

"I think it's time to go talk with Calvin Dunbar. Want to come?"

We go together in her unmarked police car. Calvin and his wife live in a town about thirty miles east of the city. It's the next town beyond Turner, the kind of community that elects people like Calvin: pleasant, not flamboyant, middle-of-the-road. Outgoing but not effusive. The insurance agency is in his home. Sabin wants to show up without warning, hoping he'll be more candid.

The door to Dunbar Insurance is locked and the lights are off, so we ring the doorbell. Kelly Dunbar comes to the door. I remember her from when she and Calvin came for that first interview following his unprompted confession to accepting money from Subsurface: slender, pretty, blond. She tells us Calvin isn't here. She doesn't know where he is.

"Mrs. Dunbar, could we come in and look around?" Sabin asks.

"Gosh. Yeah, no, I don't think so. I mean, not without me talking to Cal first," she says.

"Please have him call me," Sabin says. She hands Kelly a card and we leave.

*   *   *

Sabin and I drive back toward town. Her phone rings and she answers it hands-free. "Sabin," she says.

"Hi, Detective. Captain Dorsey here."

"Hello, Captain. I have Nick Davis with me."

This catches Dorsey off guard. Nothing wrong with it, it's just unexpected. Dorsey and I exchange niceties, then he says, "Convenient, actually—this will be of interest to you, too, Nick. We've identified that possible suicide you covered over at Mill Town Motel, Detective."

"Go ahead."

"He was *somebody*," Dorsey says. "A state representative. The guy's name is—um, was—Representative Ted Porter."

"Porter?" I say, except it comes out as a yell. "Lizzy interviewed the guy. Or maybe she never did. I don't remember."

I explain to them what I know—how Porter was the one to hang an amendment on the gas tax legislation two years in a row, thus effectively delaying the tax those two years.

"Was the guy in trouble?" Dorsey asks. "Financial, legal, marital?"

"I'll ask Lizzy," I say. "Maybe she'll know something."

Sabin says, "Has the ME said anything yet? Are we sure it was suicide?"

"I don't know," Dorsey says. "We should have a report tomorrow."

We end the call. We're coming up on Turner, where Flora and Chip and Lizzy live, so I know the area well and I know we're about to enter a cell phone dead zone. I want to talk to Isler again, so I say, "I'll buy you lunch, Rachel. There's a cool little diner right up here."

I direct her to the Shipwreck Diner, one of those old bus-shaped diners. It has a menu tailored to Turner's more moneyed residents.

We get a booth. Rachel orders the pear salad. I get the seafood stew. I reach Isler on the phone, and since the place isn't crowded, I put him on speaker in the middle of the table. We lean in close.

". . . falling into place," he says. "In this whole corruption investigation, who has gotten the least attention? Whose dirty laundry never got looked into because he packaged it all up and brought it to us?"

"Dunbar?" I say.

"Right. He came to us confessing his guts out, copping to an illicit fifteen K, so we never dissected his finances and personal life like we did with everyone else. Basically, all we know about Dunbar is what he has told us."

As Isler talks, I'm staring at an art print on the wall at one end of the diner. I used to eat here when Lizzy was young and we'd transport her between Flora's house in Turner and mine in town. I've always found the painting mesmerizing. Up close, it looks like meaningless and random splotches of color: white, yellowish white, gray and yellow, gray and brown. But when you back up enough, it resolves into the frenzied and motion-filled image of a ship dashed on the rocks in a storm.

"What was he trying to hide?" I ask.

"How about five point two million?" Isler says. "Here's how it works: Dunbar was chair of the house appropriations committee. He's the one who got to dole out pork projects. And let's say there's this weak legislator who's in constant danger of getting voted out of office, and the only way for him to hold on to his seat is to keep bringing his voters truckloads of pork."

"You mean Representative Porter?" Sabin says.

"Yes. Porter. All Porter has to do to get this pork—all those special projects for his district—is to keep hanging his anti-fracking amendment on the gas tax legislation."

"And nobody thinks it's strange because Porter is a greenie anyhow."

"Right," Isler says. "So all the amendment accomplishes is it keeps delaying the tax legislation."

The waitress brings our lunch plates. She eyes the phone and listens for a second; the speaker is loud enough for others to hear. She says, "We don't really allow . . ." but Sabin and I both smack our badges down on the tabletop before she can finish her sentence. She retreats, and I see her whispering to the manager.

The phone beeps for a waiting call. It's Lizzy. Good. I'll call her back as soon as I finish with Isler.

". . . saving the industry and Subsurface hundreds of millions of dollars," Isler says.

"And Calvin Dunbar, as chair of the appropriations committee, was the only one in the state who could offer Porter those pork projects. So Billman slipped Calvin Dunbar five mil, and Dunbar gave Porter the pork projects in exchange for killing the gas tax with his amendments. Everybody comes out looking clean," I say. "But where's the five and a half mil?"

"My guess," Isler says, "is that it's in the Seychelles."

Of course it is. It all makes sense.

"We're getting the warrant," Isler says. "Then Chip and I are going to get Dunbar."

"He's not home," I say. "Sabin and I were just there."

"We'll find him."

"How's the salad?" I whisper to Sabin. She gives it a thumbs-up and puts a pear slice on my bread plate. I motion for her to try some of the stew if she wants. It's really good. Spicy.

". . . killed Lydia," Isler says. I snap back into the moment. Like Henry Tatlock, Dunbar seems too gentle for all of this. My subconscious must have resisted following Isler's theory out to its obvious conclusions.

"It all would have worked out for him if we hadn't started the corruption probe," Isler said. "Dunbar wasn't even on our radar. But as things started unspooling, he must have panicked and decided to eliminate anyone who knew about the deal."

"Mailing," I said.

"And now Porter," Sabin said. "I'm betting the ME declares Porter's death as a homicide."

"And Lydia must have discovered something," Isler said. "Maybe a balance sheet or maybe an overheard phone call. Or maybe Calvin told her. Pillow talk, you know? Maybe he whispered his secret, hoping she'd sail away with him or whatever."

"But Lydia freaked," I say. "She went running off, and Calvin went after her."

We discuss the particulars a while longer, then Isler speaks to someone who must have come into his office. Then he's back: "Oh, good. We have the warrant," he says. "Now I've just got to go find the son of a bitch."

The phone call ends. Sabin and I sit in silence. The soup is really too spicy, and I have to keep taking breaks to let my taste buds recover. I stare at the shipwreck painting: horror and death painted in such soul-stirring beauty.

"You okay, Nick?" Sabin says.

"How could I be so wrong about people? First Henry. Now Calvin Dunbar."

"Yes, hard to believe."

"He seemed so normal last night."

"Last night?" Sabin says.

I tell her about seeing Calvin last night at Friendly City. As I narrate the details of our brief crossing of paths, Rachel stares at me more and more intently. "But when you saw him, he wasn't coming *from* the building?"

"No," I say. "He'd already left. He just happened to see me as he was leaving to drive home."

"He didn't go back inside with you when you ran in to piss?"

"No."

Her dark eyes are fierce. Everything about her just changed. She stares at me, and I wait for her to say something. She is making me uncomfortable.

"Rachel?"

"Nick, Calvin Dunbar had not been in the lounge having a drink, and he had no documents to give you. He was there in the parking lot waiting for you, to ambush you, to get you to his car without being seen, and to kill you. If you hadn't run inside to piss, you'd be dead now. And probably if you hadn't been on the phone with your wife when you came out, you'd be dead."

"Bullshit," I say. But it's a hollow response, and it comes out sounding shrill. Sabin is right. It's so obvious. Like Lydia, like Mailing, like Porter, maybe even like Bud Billman, I know too much. I threaten his millions. Rachel is right. If not for my full bladder and a call from Tina, I'd be gone.

"You okay?" Sabin says.

I play with the phone on the table, spinning it distractedly. "I'm so stupid," I say.

"Don't beat yourself up. I'm the detective. You're just a lawyer."

"*Just* a lawyer, says the law school dropout."

She looks up at me and I see hesitancy in her eyes. I'm afraid my attempt to lighten things up has hurt her feelings. "I'm sorry. I was just . . ."

She shakes her head and reaches across the table. She quickly squeezes my hand, then lets it go. "I'd hate it if you were dead," she says. I have enough sense to leave it at that.

This detective knows a lot. She knows there is this chemistry between us, but she also knows I'll be back with Tina the moment it's possible. And I think she can also see that, given the state I'm in, I'd be defenseless against her if she forced the issue right now, but all three of us—Sabin, Tina, and me—would end up . . . I glance around the diner and spot the print of the shipwreck.

Right: That's how.

I'm suddenly self-conscious and feeling awkward. I pick up my phone, and to occupy my jittery hands, I play Lizzy's message. I put it on speaker: "It's me, Daddy. I got your messages. I'll tell CD you asked about whatever it was you wanted from him. I'm getting with him today: got a couple questions about those amendments. He's meeting me here in . . . um . . . this afternoon sometime. Love you."

Lizzy: the one who discovered the essential pieces; the one who knows the most; the one who, right now, is interviewing Dunbar about it.

CHAPTER 54

I'm aware of knocking the seafood stew off the table as we leave the booth—fish and scallops like brain bits, clamshells like skull fragments in the tomato broth as it spreads out across the floor.

Sabin drives. I call Lizzy, then Flora. Neither answers. I try Chip. He doesn't answer, either, so I call Isler again. I try explaining, but it comes out in an unhinged rant.

"Hang up!" Sabin yells. I obey. She calls Isler back on the hands-free system. When he's on the line, she says, "Dunbar tried to kill Nick last night. Now he's after Nick's daughter." She explains it in a coherent way that I wasn't able to.

Isler listens, then says, "If you're right, Dunbar is becoming unpredictable and explosive. He might do anything. Where are you? Where is Lizzy?"

"We're in Turner, driving toward their house." The word "driving," as Sabin uses it, means I am directing her along windy back roads as we round bends and make turns with tires screaming.

"Do you know for sure Lizzy and Flora are in the house?" Isler asks, and I notice how his voice has changed from its nerdy and conversational drawl to robotic and clipped. He is suddenly an agent directing an operation.

"Negative," Sabin answers in the same voice. It is a voice that body-checks me out of her way. She and Isler are running things, and I'm along for the ride. "We haven't made contact with anyone in the home."

(Meaning they all might be dead.)

I can hear voices and activity in the background of the phone call. "I'm putting together a team," Isler says. "We can be there in twenty."

Now I hear shouting on the phone. I hear chaos. I hear Chip, who has apparently just been notified that his wife and Lizzy are in the path of this unhinged killer. Hearing Chip settles me a bit: He's obviously in no condition to be running the operation, so the same has to be true about me. I feel myself surrender fully to Sabin. If Lizzy and Flora survive, it'll be Rachel and Isler who pull it off. Chip and I are just obstacles.

"Give me Lizzy's cell number," Isler says.

I do.

"One second," he says, "we can locate her phone . . . okay . . . one more second. And hold on . . ."

"Turn right up here," I tell Sabin. She doesn't seem to hear me, because she's approaching the turn without slowing. I think we've already passed it, but she does something with the brake and the wheel, and we've abruptly made a ninety-degree right turn, and if I hadn't had my shoulder strap on, I'd be in her lap.

"There, we've got it," Isler says. "It looks like Lizzy—or her phone, at least—is at home."

I think this is good. We know where she is, even if Dunbar does, too.

"Do you have a cell number for Calvin Dunbar?" Isler asks.

I find Calvin's number and give it to Isler.

"Good," Isler says. "Now let's see if we can locate him. How far are you from the house?"

"About a minute," I say.

"Don't approach yet. We'll have his location in a second."

"Turn left up here," I tell Sabin.

The town is zoned rural estates. There are tracts of woods and horse pastures and hayfields. Flora's house is out of sight from others. The road is serpentine.

"I'll drive past at normal speed," Sabin says. "If he's really melting down, anything could set him off. We'll get a quick look."

"Got it," Isler says. His voice startles me. I'd forgotten he was on the phone. "We've located his cell phone, and apparently he's—"

And the call cuts out. Cell signal lost. We're on our own.

"Up around the next curve," I say.

Sabin slows to normal driving speed. Flora's house is on the right. We approach the house like Sunday drivers. Three cars are in the driveway: Flora's, Lizzy's, and parked askew and halfway onto the grass, the little blue Audi TT I saw in the Friendly City parking lot last night.

Sabin cruises past, but the second we're out of sight, she pulls over.

"He's in there," I say. "We've got to do something."

Sabin unclips her seat belt and turns to face me. "If he came to kill Lizzy, there's no time to wait for SWAT. He's clearly not a sentimentalist. And if he's really in full meltdown, it means he's unpredictable and irrational." Sabin reaches over to the glove box and takes out her gun and a folding knife. "I'm going in," she says. "You wait here. When reinforcements show up, brief them."

I start babbling protests, but she ignores me. She unfolds the knife, then reaches up and presses the blade against the top of her head. "Scalp wounds," she says, "they bleed like a son of a bitch."

With one unflinching motion, she draws the blade forward through her hair as though she's defining the part. She waits a second, then musses her hair with both hands and rubs her face and arms until she's covered in blood. She gets out, tucks her gun into the back of her slacks, and runs toward the driveway shrieking. "Help me!" she screams.

I get out of the car and, keeping out of sight behind trees, watch her sprint toward the house.

"I think he's dead! Oh my God, he's dead! I called 911. Oh my God, help me, call 911!"

She gets to the door. Pounds on it, then disappears inside. Half a minute later, I hear a shot.

I burst into the house. There's blood everywhere. Calvin lies near the kitchen door with blood pouring from his right shoulder. Lizzy is hysterical. "She killed Calvin! She killed Calvin!" Lizzy screams, but this clearly isn't the case, because now Calvin is sitting upright with his hands cuffed behind him. Flora is just screaming. And Rachel Sabin, looking like Carrie at the prom, is packing towels around Calvin's shoulder.

"It's okay," Sabin keeps yelling, "it's okay. I'm with your dad. I'm with Nick." She sees me and stands up. There's a gun on the table. She points to it. "Calvin's," she says.

I move Lizzy and Flora into the living room and try to calm them, then go to help Sabin with Calvin Dunbar. Soon—though it doesn't feel soon—the yard fills with ambulances and police cars. Calvin gets packed into an ambulance with a couple of cops to babysit him and heads for the hospital. Rachel gets a head bandage. Flora and Lizzy get sedatives.

The medics want to take Rachel to the hospital, but she refuses. "It's just a scalp wound," she says. "Scalp wounds bleed like a son of a bitch."

Dorsey shows up. Rachel tells him what happened. Flora is talking to another cop while she sits in Chip's lap with his big arms around her. He looks awful. I sit in the living room with Lizzy and a detective I don't recognize while Liz gives her version of events.

"I was just here talking with Calvin when Detective Sabin showed up," Lizzy says. "But I didn't recognize her; she'd been in an accident."

"Talking about what?" I ask.

"My research. My investigation," Lizzy says.

"Was Calvin acting strangely?"

"Not really."

"What did he say?"

"He wanted to know who else I'd talked to about this legislative research."

"How long had he been here?"

"Only a minute."

"Go on," the detective says.

"So Calvin started talking about how nice this house is, and he asked if it had a basement, because he's doing research on furnace systems and energy efficiency. He wanted Mom and me to show him our heating system. And right then was when we heard the screaming."

"You mean Detective Sabin?"

"I guess. And she was at the door and just came inside, and Mom was like—you know Mom—she was trying to help this woman who was hysterical and covered in blood. Then suddenly there was a gun."

"Detective Sabin's or Calvin's?"

"Detective Sabin's. And Calvin: He was standing beside me, but then he grabbed me and pulled me in front of him, and before I even knew what happened, there was a gunshot and Calvin was on the floor. It was all so fast."

"Did you ever see Calvin's gun?"

"Not till you came in, Dad."

The detective keeps working Lizzy for details, and then this detective and Dorsey and the detective who was questioning Flora compare the stories. The only significant difference among the three versions is that Sabin says Calvin grabbed Lizzy and pulled out his gun. Flora and Lizzy say they never saw Calvin's gun until after Sabin shot him.

Things settle down. The driveway clears out. Sabin takes me aside and says, "They want me in town, Nick. I'm not supposed to drive. Shall I have someone else drive, or do you want to take me?"

Good question. I want to be here with Lizzy, but I want to get home and see Tina and Barnaby and to feel the belonging I feel with them. Maybe Tina will invite me to stay. Chip can watch over Flora and Liz this afternoon. I'll come back out to check on them this evening.

I walk to the street to get Sabin's car. I bring a towel for all the blood. I have no doubt that Rachel saved their lives. Calvin came here wanting to kill Lizzy and anyone else who happened to be home; Rachel arrived with no more than minutes to spare. Calvin would have preferred to kill them in the basement, but if they'd re-sisted, I'm sure he wasn't going to quibble.

I don't care whether Calvin had already pulled his gun when

Rachel shot him. And if I have to, I'll go into court and swear under oath that I saw the whole thing and that Calvin was waving his gun like a madman before Sabin drew her weapon.

I wipe down the steering wheel and seat of Rachel's car. On the seat, I find a thick full-length lock of Rachel's dark, wavy hair that got sliced off by the knife. I wipe it free of blood, then ball it up and press it to my cheek. I sniff it for the now familiar scent of her shampoo. I straighten the hair, coil it, and put it in my billfold. I'll find a safe place where it won't bother Tina but where I can have it—this memento of Sabin, who, whatever else she means to me, is now my daughter's savior.

I drive Sabin's unmarked car into the driveway and walk into the house. The crime scene techs are in the kitchen, while Flora, Chip, Lizzy, Sabin, and Dorsey sit in the living room, appearing uncertain what to do next.

I sit beside Lizzy on the couch. "Was he really going to kill us?" she asks.

"I think so."

"Daddy," she says. She pulls her feet up on the cushion and curls in toward me. I wrap my arms around her. We sit that way for a while. Neither of us speaks. We're both in shock. Later this will pack the wallop of a nuclear explosion, but right now I'm having trouble making sense of it all. I need someone to tell me what to do.

Lizzy sniffles and pushed me away. "I'll be okay," she says. "You're wanted in town."

"I am?"

"Yes," Chip says. "The jury is back in the Kyle Runion murder."

CHAPTER 55

S abin sits beside me. Her head bandage makes her look like a
Civil War soldier. She pulls down the visor and bobs around,
trying to get a good look at herself in the mirror. She laughs.
"What?"

"There's no good way to bandage a scalp wound," she says. "But
there were so many medics, I finally had to let one of them do
something."

After that, there is too much to talk about, so we don't talk
about anything. As we get farther from Turner and closer to the
city, I think less about Calvin Dunbar and more about Henry
Tatlock. I'm thinking about the defense Monica Brill put on.
Upton was right: The weakness in her case was that she never
offered the jury a good theory for who killed Lydia if it wasn't
Henry. So even though the case technically has nothing to do with
Lydia, and even though Monica came up with a believable story
of how Henry's DNA got mixed up with Kyle Runion's remains,
I'm certain the jury has voted to convict Henry. They will convict
him because they think he killed his fiancée, which makes them
disbelieve Monica's carefully constructed story about Philbin and
Philbin's sister and Philbin's simmering, festering rage toward
violent men.

Timing is everything. It was everything last night in the Friendly
City parking lot. It was everything today in the kitchen of Flora's
house, and it is everything in Henry Tatlock's trial. If today's events
with Calvin Dunbar had taken place a week ago, or if Henry's trial
had ended a week from now, Monica Brill would have had a perfect
defense: Henry Tatlock was just the innocent cuckold in Lydia's
long-term affair with a homicidal psychopath. If the jury had known

this, then Philbin's dogged pursuit of Henry would have looked irrational and, worse, just plain mean. The jury would have eaten up the idea of Henry being twice victimized—once by Calvin Dunbar, once by Detective Philbin.

It's too late now. Nothing about what happened today is grounds for a new trial. And even if Henry were to get a new trial for any reason, Monica's defense required the element of surprise. Now that the surprise is spent, Gregory Nations would have a thousand ways to head her off. Her case would be dead before the first witness is sworn.

Timing is everything. The trial is over. All that's left is the reading of the verdict. Henry has lost.

"So, about Philbin," I say to Rachel.

She looks over at me and smiles sadly. She knows what I'm asking. She doesn't want to talk about it. She doesn't want to answer my question, and maybe she wouldn't have had to yesterday, but many things have changed between us now.

"Could he have done it?" I ask.

She doesn't answer me for a few seconds. Then she sighs. It is her surrender. The resistance goes out of her. "Philly's complicated," she says.

I wait.

"He pretends he's Gibraltar," she says. "Pretends nothing shakes him. But believe me, that man bleeds. If he ever got onto the couch, he'd never get up again. But talking about shit isn't his style. Philly's too old-school to get shrunk."

She's silent. I wait.

"If I knew something, I'd tell you," she says. "Philly knows I would. And you know it, too, right?"

I smile at her. I guess I do know it. At least in a case like this, where the only evidence against Henry is what Philbin is accused of planting, I believe Rachel would rat him out if she knew. "So the next logical question," I say, "is whether you think Philbin is *capable* of planting the evidence."

She doesn't smile at me this time. She just looks at me with a pained expression. Her answer is clear: Of course he's capable. Maybe she even suspects him of it. But it's all too late.

News vans are in front of the courthouse again. It's just after seven in the evening, but nobody is heading home. The judge has scheduled court to resume at seven-thirty for reading the verdict. There are more black sedans than usual. I add Sabin's to the line of cars in the POLICE ONLY parking, and we walk the gauntlet of reporters into the building. With her bandage, and some of the dried blood crusted brown on her face, a cameraman runs after her, shouting questions.

Inside the courthouse, I see Tina. She sees me. She sees Rachel. She runs back through the metal detector and into my arms. She clings to me. Tears run freely down her cheeks. "Lizzy called," she says. "Flora called. Everybody called."

Tina steps back and looks at Sabin. "Look at you," she says. She touches the blood on Rachel's face and strokes the bandage like it's a puppy. "Thank you," she whispers.

I hand Rachel her car keys, and she leaves us. Tina and I get into the elevator and go up to our floor. Everything about this feels wrong, and I don't know what to do or what to think. Is Henry *actually* guilty or not? Calvin Dunbar killed Lydia; Patrick Philbin may well have planted Henry's DNA with Kyle's remains. I want to slow things down, but this train has lost its brakes. Halfway down the hallway, I stop and face Tina. Fear and tears streak her face. I want her in my arms again, but I don't want us to be a spectacle.

"I think Henry is innocent," I say.

She nods.

Everyone is outside the courtroom. There are many FBI agents; too many. This is a state case, but Isler and several of his colleagues stand around with suit jackets bulging at holster level.

All the usuals are here: the Runions and their entourage, Peggy Devaney, Philbin, Upton, cops from Orchard Grove, and the local cops. Oddly, the one I gravitate to is Arthur Cunningham. He seems so hapless, so uninvolved in the whole thing. He was a simple man out enjoying the woods when his dog led him to a front-row seat for this special pageant of hell. I'm like Arthur. I didn't ask for any of this. I didn't want any of this.

"Hi, Arthur," I say.

He puts his hand out and I grab it in both of mine and our eyes meet and I think he understands what I'm saying. I'm saying that poor Kyle Runion is the central victim, but in a way, all of us have been scarred. Arthur is a victim and I'm a victim and Lydia and Tina and Detective Philbin and maybe even Henry Tatlock—all of us whose lives will never really get back to normal.

"Nick," someone says. It's Upton. My moment of reverie with Arthur is broken. Upton has Isler with him. Isler sees something in my eyes—gratitude for his part in today's drama—but it will have to wait until later. "Step over here," Upton says. They guide me away from the crowd.

"Do you remember Nathan Miller?" Upton asks.

"Miller? Is that the kid from Ohio who disappeared a couple of years before Kyle?"

"Right," Upton says. "There were similarities to the Runion case. And you might recall there was some trace . . ."

"Mitochondrial DNA," Isler says.

"Right," Upton says. "Mitochondrial DNA that may or may not have come from the perp. It didn't really matter who it was from, because it was such a poor sample . . ."

"Really degraded," Isler says.

"So degraded it was useless for identifying a suspect in a database of any size," Upton says.

"It was forgotten about," Isler says. "Until now. But a short strand like that can be a good indicator for testing against a single known suspect."

"You tested it against Henry?" I say.

Isler nods.

"And?"

Isler motions with his head toward the FBI agents just now

walking into the courtroom. "Crossing state lines makes it federal," he says.

"It was a match?"

"A perfect match," Isler answers.

"So Henry's definitely guilty?"

"Yes."

"Thank God," I say.

"It doesn't matter what this jury decides," Isler says. "We're arresting Henry Tatlock as soon as the verdict is read: federal charges for the murder, kidnapping, and sexual abuse of Nathan Miller."

We are called into the courtroom. I sit beside Tina. She grabs my hand and intertwines her fingers with mine, squeezing with everything she's got. The jury is brought in. For the FBI agents and for Upton and for me, there is no suspense. The verdict has become nearly irrelevant.

Judge Ballard smacks the gavel and goes through the formalities. Then he has the jury foreman stand: "Mr. Foreman, has the jury reached a verdict?"

"We have, Your Honor."

The judge has Henry stand and says, "Mr. Foreman, would you please read the verdict."

The foreman unfolds his scrap of paper and says, "On the charge of murder in the first degree, we the jury find the defendant . . ."

PART III

CHAPTER 56

It hasn't been easy. I still have my suite at Friendly City, but I'm spending more and more time at home. The important thing, according to Tina and the couples counselor, is to avoid any more upheavals until we can establish a rock-solid rhythm and flow to our lives. I don't understand any of this, but what they (Tina and the counselor) tell me is that we had a toxic mix of *Tina's issues* combined with a series of traumatic events, combined with my response to those events, which were the product of *my issues*.

Whatever.

I'm halfway back through the door of the house, my slow and steady advance detectable only in time-lapse.

It's springtime. The ice is off the lake up at the cabin. The days are warming and lengthening. Everything is settling down.

Daryl Devaney is a free man. In the wake of Henry's conviction, Gregory Nations joined Tina in petitioning for Daryl's full pardon. The petition was granted, and now Daryl's civil lawyer is negotiating with the state for a hefty "wrongful conviction" award. Daryl may emerge from the whole thing a modestly rich man, which will be useful for him as he keeps paying lawyers to defend him in minor crimes like driving without a license and shoplifting. We're hoping Peggy can keep him under control.

Peggy invited Tina and me down to Orchard City for Daryl's coming-home party. I wish I could say we enjoyed it, especially since Tina, along with Daryl, was a guest of honor. But it was a sad affair. A few neighbors came, plus a few guys Daryl was in school with, and one elderly teacher from one of Daryl's remedial classes in high school. Peggy rented a function room at the Orchard City Inn, and even though the room wasn't large, the party felt as lost inside it as a BB in a boxcar. Peggy asked whether anyone had any comments to offer. One guy said something about remembering Daryl from school, then talked about his own children for several minutes, then said, "Let's get drunk."

Tina stood up and talked about Peggy's perseverance and devotion to Daryl. To keep things going, I stood up and praised Tina for her dedication to the case. I talked about how she'd worked so hard, often late into the night, to "right this terrible wrong." Then I said that now, though I was only meeting Daryl for the first time, I could see how her efforts were well spent and how certain I was that Daryl would put this all behind him and make up for lost time in living a good and happy and productive life. People clapped politely.

Calvin Dunbar is awaiting trial on three first-degree-murder charges. His gun, which was picked up at the scene in Flora's kitchen, was identified as the weapon that killed Jimmy Mailing and Lydia. The NTSB is still hoping to locate the wreckage of Bud Billman's plane, and possibly adding two more murders—Billman's and his grandson's—to the tally.

Over in the civil division of the U.S. Attorney's Office, several eagle-eyed lawyers are trying to find a way to get the five million back from the Seychelles. I have a personal interest in this because Tina, as executor of Lydia's estate (and sole beneficiary), has brought a wrongful-death action against Calvin Dunbar. Tina says if she ever gets any money, she'll probably put most of it back into the Innocence Project.

Rachel Sabin and I get together for lunch sometimes. She is respectful of my ongoing attempts to reconcile with Tina. She tells me Philbin is doing well: Since Henry was found guilty in state court and also charged in federal court, nobody even remembers Monica's Hail Mary attempt to blame Philbin for the whole thing. Detective Philbin has emerged unblemished.

As for Lizzy, things aren't all sunny. After coming so close to being another of Calvin's victims, she got scared again and canceled her travel plans. Flora and I (along with Chip and Tina) are being attentive. We try including her in whatever we're doing. I think she'll be okay if we can keep her out of harm's way for a change. She just needs to huddle a bit longer under the parental umbrella. She was always so smart and independent that she got ahead of herself. Mature and sophisticated though she is, she's not quite done being a little girl. She is conflicted, though. She loved being my investigator/researcher, even though it almost got us all killed. She wants more projects.

Barnaby, too, is showing the effects of all this family trauma. He has bitten a few kids at preschool and has had a couple of tantrums that seemed to have no discernible trigger. We have him seeing a therapist who says he is responding to the stress the rest of us have exhibited. Secondhand PTSD, she calls it. It is absolutely essential, she says, to keep things as calm and predictable as possible. Tina and I have both reduced our work schedules to four days a week. She takes Friday off, I take Monday. So Barn is in day care only three days a week.

Chip and Flora are fine. Flora is resilient and shows no ill effects from her brush with Calvin Dunbar.

The Subsurface corruption probe is winding down. Not much has happened. A few legislators paid fines and are spending several months in jail. The public has lost interest. After the revelations about Calvin Dunbar, everything else is anticlimactic.

As for me, I'm mostly okay. But sometimes I wake up in the night in my bed at Friendly City, and my mind plays back to me when Sabin ran up the driveway and into Flora's house covered in her own blood. I try to tweak this in my mind. I try assigning myself some role in that demented scene, because the awful truth is that Sabin concocted the scheme, drew the knife across her own scalp, and hurled herself into harm's way, while I stayed safely back at the car. This gnaws at me. I want to have been the protector; the savior.

* * *

There's one more postscript to the sorry saga of Lydia's murder. It came yesterday in a call from Chip. "I've got more news," he said.

"What news?"

"I talked to one of the agents from San Francisco," Chip said. "City police just found an abandoned rental car in the parking lot at one end of the Golden Gate. Apparently, that's a common thing, somebody renting a car and ditching it in the parking lot before taking the plunge. Turns out the car was rented to Tony Smeltzer."

This made me unexpectedly sad. Not sad for Smeltzer, so much, he was bad news. Just sad at the futility of everything. *Halfway across and all the way down*, Smeltzer had said to me in the Fog City Tap that night. Poor guy. In my mind, the futility of his worthless life blends into all the other waste and sorrow. Now that he's gone and apparently was never a threat to us anyway, I'm able to feel some pity for him.

"Did they find his body?" I asked Chip.

"Nope," Chip says. "I guess the great whites got a free meal."

This makes me uneasy, but I push the feeling aside.

And so it ends. The pathetic Tony Smeltzer has apparently written his own story, while the two monsters, Calvin Dunbar and Henry Tatlock, have been put away. The legacy of their crimes is hard to comprehend. So many lives are permanently changed by these murderers, and my family has borne the brunt.

CHAPTER 57

Lizzy calls me at work: "Dad, can we meet for lunch?"

"Definitely."

"Rain Tree at one-thirty," she says.

She looks great. Professional and confident. She has her briefcase with her, but I have no idea what she's packing in it. We get a table and order clams. The springtime sunlight makes the river and the dam and the dining room look fresh and full of promise. That's how Lizzy looks, too.

"About the sentencing hearing," she says.

Henry's sentencing, she means. It's coming up in a few weeks. The only real question is whether he'll live out his natural life as a wretched animal in a cage, or if the state will stick a needle in his arm and end the whole thing. Gregory Nations is asking for the death penalty because Henry refuses to give up any information about where he buried his other victims.

"Do you have a position?" Lizzy asks.

"No."

"You could have a lot of influence," she says.

Now I'm worried. I know this girl. She opposes the death penalty, and I know she wants to bring me over to her side. But I've already decided not to think about it anymore, and definitely not to get involved. I don't have the stomach for it.

She's right about my influence. Other than Judge Ballard, I probably have more influence over what happens to Henry than anybody. I'm a federal prosecutor, his former supervisor at work, and his former friend. I was nearly his brother-in-law. I'm family, and I am married to the lawyer who brought the Kyle Runion case back to light, which is what exposed Henry in the first place. Judge Ballard will make the ultimate decision, but he'll want input (and cover). If I take a strong stand at the sentencing hearing, my perspective could sway the decision.

"What are you proposing, Liz?"

"Lydia loved him," Lizzy says.

"Well, that doesn't justify—"

"Nobody's talking about justifications. I'm just wondering what made him how he is."

"Everyone wonders that, but . . ."

"We know he got burned in a fire and was abandoned at the hospital."

"We do?"

"Yeah. He told me. They dropped him at the hospital and never came back. That's got to mess with the head of a two-year-old. Right?

"He was two?"

"My God, Dad."

"How do you know all this?"

"I asked him about his scars once. Didn't you?"

"I, um, didn't want to pry. But none of that justifies Kyle Runion," I say. It's a stupid comment, because that isn't what she's talking about. She's talking about whether cruel blows dealt him at an early age triggered his psychopathic behavior, and if so, whether that's enough reason for me to advocate life instead of death.

A couple of months ago, I'd have said absolutely not. I wasn't interested in compassion, and I'd have happily plunged the lethal syringe myself. But that was back in the thick of things. Maybe I'm more objective now that Henry is put away and can't hurt us again. I don't feel as vulnerable.

But compassion?

My job isn't about compassion. It's about consequence and responsibility and protecting the public. Lizzy is the one with compassion: If a perp ever had so much as a hangnail, she's all about how rough his life has been. She's a pushover.

"What are you suggesting, Liz?"

"I thought I'd do some research. Maybe write something up for you to read to the judge."

"Anybody can submit material," I said

"Really? I can submit it myself?"

"Sure."

"Will you help me?"

Not in a million years, I think.

"Sure," I say.

CHAPTER 58

I don't know where to find Aaron Pursley, but I have an idea where to start looking. Pursley is the crooked, unlicensed investigator Henry hired in hopes of locating his biological family (or so he claimed). If that's true, maybe Aaron Pursley can point Lizzy and me in the right direction.

I didn't tell Lizzy I'm going to Rivertown, because she'd have wanted to come. I'm done bringing her along on my forays into the jungles of human corruption.

I know of a bar over in Rivertown: the Elfin Grot. It's small and below street level, and on weekends it fills with the sounds of working-class drinkers trying hard to replace with beer everything that pours out of them as sweat and piss and revelry. I like the place. But now, midweek, it's a different crowd. They don't hang out; they pass through. The place is like a hub or a roundhouse for the comings and goings of people whose business, like the bar itself, is dark and subsurface. The place is long and narrow. Most of it is taken up with barstools and standing room, but there are a few tables in the very back. Business gets conducted at those tables.

I show up around five in the evening. I recognize the bartender from when I was here several years ago: a woman in her sixties, cadaverous, bluish hair. Maybe she owns the place.

"Huberly," I say.

She squints at me. It's not her name, but it will signal to her who I am, if she remembers.

"I need a guy named Aaron Pursley," I say.

"I need a guy named George Clooney," she says.

I think she remembers. That's good. People here are suspicious of cops—federal or otherwise. But last time I came in looking for somebody, it worked out well. Maybe I won't have to establish my bona fides again. I take out my business card and write on the back "About Henry Tatlock" and hand it to her. "If you see him, perhaps you could give him this."

She takes the card. "Are you drinking?" she says. I wasn't planning to, but cash needs to change hands somehow.

"Granddad. Neat," I say.

She pours it. I down it. I drop fifty on the bar and leave.

Pursley calls me a couple of days later. I tell him what I want. He agrees to meet.

"Can I come?" Lizzy asks.

"No."

"Why?"

"Because the guy's a crook, and I shouldn't be meeting him myself."

I see her deliberating whether to argue. She doesn't.

The Elfin Grot is nearly empty. Huberly eyes me from behind the bar and tilts her head toward the very back. Pursley is waiting. I immediately dislike him. It's a pet peeve of mine: felons, crooks, and scumbags who wear business suits. Aaron Pursley wears a blue pinstripe. It's conservative. His tie is silver gray. He stands and I shake. His hand doesn't match the outfit. The hand is coarse, and he squeezes aggressively. He's screwing with me. "Henry Tatlock: very unfortunate business," he says.

"To put it mildly."

"An acquaintance of yours?"

"He was."

"And what do you want from me?" Aaron asks.

"I guess I want to buy out Henry's contract."

"Meaning?"

"Henry told me he hired you to find his biological family. I want whatever you found."

"If I haven't found anything, are you hiring me to continue the investigation?"

"No," I say. I know what this guy does. He pays bureaucrats and functionaries to provide him with confidential information. He intimidates and threatens those who won't play ball. When necessary, he hires someone to break in and get what he can't find through other means. Now the rumor mill has it that he's hooked up with some pimple-faced whiz kids who can hack their way into most anything. "I'll buy whatever you've already got," I say, "but I'm not interested in becoming your conspirator for more than that."

This pisses him off, but he doesn't walk away. I hold a few more cards than Pursley does. He knows that if I decided to investigate *him*, he'd be out of business, maybe even in jail.

He's cockier than I expected, though. He sits all comfy in his fancy threads. He wears a knowing smirk, like he's got something over me. Strange. Maybe the guy is protected somehow—why else would he feel safe taking Henry's case when Henry was still a prosecutor? And why else would he be here with me? I know he's not working for the Bureau, but maybe he's a confidential informant for the state. A stoolie: I bet that's it. I bet they have a deal with him that so long as he keeps it low-key and doesn't commit any violent crimes, they look the other way.

No matter. I can't do anything about it if he's got a deal with the state, but if the guy is doing business by mail or Internet, then it goes federal. I can have Chip or Isler look into it. It would be great fun bringing him in for questioning.

"I ended up carrying a balance for my work with Mr. Tatlock," Pursley says. "If you'll zero that balance, I'll consider you the client. I found a few things before his troubles began. Not a lot. Obviously, I discontinued my investigation when all that unpleasantness surfaced."

"*Obviously*," I say, mocking him.

He pauses to stare at me, then says, "Listen, Davis, you can buy what I've got or not. I don't give a shit. But you're starting to piss me off."

I consider this. The reason I feel so free to annoy him is that I *don't* really want whatever he's got. I *don't* want to know any more about Henry, I don't want to feel compassion for the monster, and I realize now that I agreed to do this only to give Lizzy the illusion of my willingness without actually being willing. I'm intentionally disrespecting Pursley to drive him away so I can go tell Lizzy I've struck out.

Now, having glimpsed my real motivations and intentions, I'm stuck. If I don't behave and make an honest attempt with Pursley, then I'm lying to Lizzy. Humble-pie time: "I apologize, Mr. Pursley," I say. "I'm repulsed by Henry Tatlock and I'm taking it out on you."

Pursley is gracious, which makes it worse. Now I'm hating myself for legitimizing the scumbag. "How much does Henry owe you?" I ask.

"Three hundred fifty should do it."

I'm incredulous. I expected thousands. Maybe I've misread him.

"I never had to really *do* anything," Pursley says. "No extraordinary measures." (By which I assume he means everybody's kneecaps are intact and no locks were picked.)

I hand him the cash and buy us both a drink. His is beer. Mine, again, is Granddad.

"Here's what I know," Pursley says. "Thirty-seven years ago, a kid of around two years old was brought to the ER at Milltown General. He had catastrophic burns on his face and hands. According to medical records, he should have died. Here's the sick part: Doctors could see that the burns were a day old"—my contempt for Pursley diminishes a notch; he is apparently human enough to be repulsed by this stunning cruelty—"and whoever brought him in just vanished. Poof. Never seen again. And that's why the first PI that Henry Tatlock hired didn't find anything. There's nothing to find."

"But the police—"

"I'll get to that. So the kid spent months in the hospital, then went into foster care, and after a few years, he got adopted. But who wants a kid that looks the way Henry looked and has all that medical shit going on? No, sir. Everybody wants a beautiful and healthy baby."

"I know the rest," I say. "He got adopted by a couple who were too old to adopt."

"Done some research yourself?"

I nod.

"Tatlocks," he says. "They just wanted some cheap labor. Maybe it was better than where he'd come from, maybe it wasn't. But it can't have been any bed of roses. Old man Tatlock supposedly raised hunting dogs, but the state kept seizing the dogs for cruelty. They were always malnourished. You kind of get the impression Tatlock treated the boy like one of the dogs. From what I learned about the Tatlocks, the good Lord knew what He was doing when He made them childless . . ." (*The good Lord?* Again I recalculate who this guy is.)

As Pursley talks, his enunciation and grammar become sloppy. He's obviously a guy who works hard at appearing refined, though it doesn't come naturally.

"Family services was always sniffing around the Tatlocks," Pursley says. "They finally removed Henry when he was, um, twelve, I think, on account of neglect. The old man died like a month later, so I guess the social workers figured it was safe to put Henry back with the mother. She wasn't exactly Mother Teresa or nothing, but at least she kept him fed and clothed and didn't beat on him."

It's a horrible story. The incomprehensible cruelty of not bringing him to the hospital immediately, the abandonment at the ER, the adoption into a loveless home of animal cruelty and neglect—it doesn't *excuse* anything, but maybe it begins to explain a bit.

Pursley goes to the bar and returns with a shot of whiskey for me. "Included in your payment," he says. He has another beer for himself. "Back to your question about the police. They tried to figure out who dropped the kid at the ER, but no luck. Nobody saw the car. Nothing about his clothes gave any hint. Today there'd be video surveillance. Back then there was squat. Cops tried researching fires around the state, but nothing turned up. Maybe it wasn't even a house fire. For all they knew, the kid fell into the fireplace or into a burn pile or something. So, zilch, zip, zero. Dead end."

"Dead end?"

"Dead end. End of the trail."

I expected more.

"I've got this," Pursley says. He hands me a thin manila folder. "It's what Mr. Tatlock gave me when I started."

Pursley and I shake hands. He doesn't squeeze as hard this time. I leave.

CHAPTER 59

I call Lizzy from the road and give her the news.

"Thanks, Dad," she says. "It's something."

"Yes," I say. "Something."

"What will you recommend to the judge?" she asks.

"Nothing. I take no position. I'll write up an objective narrative and submit it. That's all I'm willing to do. What will you do?"

"I don't know," Lizzy says. "I have to think. The poor kid. He really suffered."

"Lots of people suffer," I say. "It doesn't turn them into child killers."

"What's in the folder he gave you?"

"I don't know. I haven't looked."

"I'll look," she says. "Maybe there's something there. Can you bring it over? Mom's making dinner."

This sounds good. The Dunbar event did something to my mind, as if it created another room up there—a disturbed place I need to visit from time to time. A shrink would call it PTSD. I don't know, but I love going into Flora's kitchen, where Sabin took down Dunbar. I feel peaceful there.

I give Lizzy the folder. She takes it upstairs to her room. Bill-the-Dog lies in the living room by the woodstove. She has a big cedar-smelling bed and doesn't stand to greet me anymore when I come over, though she gets up for her dinner and to take care of business outside. I scratch her ears. One day soon Lizzy and Flora will have to decide what's most humane. My eyes water as I think about this: too much sadness. I sit down on the floor and stroke her for a few minutes before going back to the kitchen to help Flora with dinner.

Dinner is noodles with a mushroom stir-fry, salad, red wine. We get it on the table and Flora calls up the stairs to Lizzy, but we don't wait. She comes down ten minutes later with the Tatlock file.

"Not much here," she says. "It's mostly some notes that Henry made, and a few newspaper articles about house fires in the state when he was a baby."

"Dead end," I say.

"But there is this," she says. "Henry sent away to one of those companies that tells you about your ethnicity."

"He sent his DNA?"

"Yes. I guess so."

"How ironic," I say.

"I know, right? So here are the results: They didn't find any close relatives, but in this section called Ethnicity Analysis, it says he's most probably—like eighty-nine percent likely—of northern European lineage, especially from someplace around Latvia or Lithuania. The Baltics."

"Interesting," I say, "but it doesn't tell—"

"So I have a theory," she says.

I thought it was over. It's not over. She's pursuing it, and I'm still getting dragged in. "Okay, Lizzy, tell me."

"Northern Europe? Lithuania? Latvia? Think about it, Dad. He must be from Lukus County. Right? Those farmers who settled at Slippery River Valley back in the 1800s, you told me they were all from around there, right? It makes perfect sense: Where besides Lukus County could a two-year-old kid get burned up like that and nobody tells the cops and nobody takes him to the ER, right, Dad? You told me yourself how isolated and suspicious they were, and how it's only started to change recently."

I watch Lizzy as she says this, and for a moment the sound of her words feels disconnected from the movement of her lips. I have the sensation of watching a movie. I feel exhausted. The idea of going back into all of this sickens me. "No," I say.

"No what?"

"No. I can't do it anymore. I'm done. I don't want to hear any more. I don't want to know any more."

Nobody says anything. Maybe I was kind of shouting. They're surprised. After a few moments, conversation starts up again, but only on safe subjects. When we finish with dinner, I offer to help with dishes, but Flora says no. I kiss Lizzy and go home.

Lizzy calls a couple of days later. "About the other night," she says. "How you said you don't want to hear any more. Maybe I've found something."

I'm helpless to stop myself. She sounds excited. She wants to share something with me. I'm putty in her hands. "Found what?" I ask.

"I was thinking. Like I said before, what if it actually was Lukus County, and that's why it was never reported? What if they told people the kid died? What if they buried an empty coffin so nobody would know they just dumped him at the hospital?"

"But, Lizzy, the authorities—"

"What authorities? You've told me yourself . . ."

She's right. It was almost forty years ago: pre-Internet, pre–cell phone. There were even stories (though I don't know if they're true) of governmental officials going missing in the county.

"Lizzy, are you about to tell me you researched deaths?"

"I researched deaths in Lukus County. And guess what?"

"You found something."

"I found something. A twenty-two-month-old boy, William C. Tunis, died on October thirteenth, 1978."

"So?"

"So that's the day Henry was dropped at Milltown General."

"It's a long shot, Liz, but even if you're right, what difference can it possibly make? Who cares?"

"I don't know," she says softly. She's quiet. Then she says, "He was a human being before he was a killer—or a monster, as you call him. I just want to understand."

"You can't understand. Nobody can understand."

She's quiet again. I wait. Finally, she says, "I don't know."

"What do you want to do with all this, Lizzy?"

"I don't know. Can we, like, dig up the coffin or something?"

"Not a chance. Even if we could find it, you've got no evidence, and there's no crime other than maybe falsifying a death certificate. You're just trying to satisfy your curiosity."

"I guess," she admits.

We hang up. A small part of me understands. With Lydia, with Kyle Runion, with Nathan Miller, with Henry, with Calvin Dunbar, we have glimpsed the horror. Now it's too hard to turn away. It beckons with the terrifying and alluring promise of some deeper understanding: just one peek; one tiny momentary glimpse through the fingers covering your eyes. How can you not look? And how can you not wonder what makes Henry so different? He suffered unspeakable cruelty. Some people's suffering propels them into noble battle against oppressors and inflictors of pain. Others, like Henry, perpetuate the anguish, visiting cruelty upon the world as it was visited upon them. I wonder what makes the difference. Apparently, Lizzy wonders, too.

On the pretext of advocating one way or the other in Henry's sentencing (though she herself is unaware that it is a pretext), Lizzy is digging much too deeply into the tragedy of Henry Tatlock. She should run away from it, not toward it. She should run for her life.

This time I don't hear from Lizzy for nearly a week. It's Saturday when she finally calls. I'm at a playground with Barnaby, sitting on the grass watching as he and a passel of other kids slide through the tubular slide and cross the hanging bridge and climb up into the turret.

"I've done more research," Lizzy says.

"Why am I not surprised?"

"I've looked up a ton of stuff. Everyone is so nice. Court records. Vital stats. Even stuff like utility bills. So I've researched this William Tunis kid. And I found where they lived in Lukus County. Then this woman at the registry of deeds showed me how to research who owns what. If I did it right, the land has never been sold since way back then. Maybe someone still lives there."

"Who? Maybe who lives where, Lizzy?"

"Tunis," she says. "Whoever pretended to bury William Tunis— if he really was Henry."

"What do you want to do?"

"I want to go see who lives there. See if there are any clues. See if they'll let us dig up the coffin. Maybe he's got family still living. Maybe they'd want to know about Henry."

"Lizzy, stop and listen to yourself. It's probably just a fallen-down shack by now. And if anybody is there, the last thing in the world they want is to hear from you. They abandoned the kid and left him to die, for Christ's sake. If that's not enough, *nobody* wants to know they're related to someone like Henry Tatlock."

"Will you come with me, Dad?"

"No, Liz. We've done enough. I can't—"

"Because Chip said he'll go with me if you don't want to."

She plays dirty. How can I refuse to help her when her FBI-agent stepfather is willing? I agree to go along.

We combine the trip with a family cookout. Chip brings Flora and Lizzy. I take Kenny's truck with the canoe tied on top. Barnaby comes with me. We drive way out to the west side of the reservoir, nearly two hours from the city. We make a fire in one of the barbecue pits maintained by the state. We roast some corn and some hot dogs. We paddle the canoe around the reservoir after lunch.

It's a gorgeous day, and Barn is loving it, but it feels incomplete to me because Tina isn't with us. I invited her along, but she declined. "Just taking it slow," she said. Things *are* better with Tina, though. I think we're doing well, but she's still skittish, and the damn couples counselor seems to be calling the shots.

After lunch, Chip and I tie the canoe back on the rack. Flora takes Barnaby in her car, and they drive back to town while Lizzy, Chip, and I take the truck and go to snoop around Lukus County. We are looking for the former home of the long-deceased William Tunis, who, Lizzy believes, is alive and in prison under the name of Henry Tatlock. I drive while Liz navigates us southward through the windy web of dirt roads into the heart of Lukus County. This is really lousy land. What a tragedy it must have been for the Slippery River Valley farmers and settlers when the government closed the dam a hundred plus years ago. No wonder Lukus County is the way it is.

We pass shacks and trailers. We pass a sign for night crawlers and an old store that must have closed decades ago, the Coca-Cola sign still tacked to the siding. We pass engine blocks hanging from trees. A couple of times we have to stop and ask directions, even though Lizzy is consulting several maps in her lap. The roads seem aimless. There are no signs. We drive for an hour. Then we see a nearly un-noticeable road, barely more than a path, on the right.

"Wait," Lizzy says. "I think that was it."

I stop. We back up. She studies the map.

"Yes. I think it is," she says. "It's called Red Shed Trail. Drive up here and see if it takes a ninety-degree turn to the left."

It does.

"Drive a couple of miles. The house was on the left."

I do as she says, and ten minutes later, we come to a rutted path on the left. It bends around an old burned-out foundation and disappears into the willows. The shrubs aren't fully leafed out yet, and through the thicket, I can make out a structure. It's a mobile home way back off the road.

"Lizzy, do you know if anyone lives here?" Chip asks.

"No. If someone does, it's probably not the right people." She's studying the map again. The stack of research is on her lap, and she's suddenly hesitant. She created something in her mind that she never really expected to take this far. She's recognizing the overwhelming illogic. I should have put a stop to it all long ago.

"May I?" I ask. I take a handful of papers from her lap and start thumbing through. Some of the documents are in legalese. We lawyers forget sometimes how different and precise our vocabulary is. For example, "negligent" means something much different than "neglectful" in the legal universe. And there are all the Latin terms we use: Res ipsa, arguendo, corpus delecti, et cetera. It is a language of its own.

One word that has a unique legal definition is "issue," referring to someone's biological child (for example; *Baby Suzie is the minor issue of John and Mary Smith*). Many people are unaware of this definition. Most nineteen-year-old girls don't know it. Lizzy doesn't know it.

I'm looking at something that Lizzy has photocopied. The document isn't identified—just miscellaneous records about the Tunis family—and before I actually read the words, their meaning has registered in my mind: *Janet Tunis and her twin minor issue.*

"Well," Chip says. "Shall we?"

"Wait," I say. I hand Chip the photocopy and point to the sentence. He studies it a second. He starts to say something. He stops.

"Lizzy," I say, "the mother of the boy whose death notice you found: Was her name Janet Tunis?"

"I don't know," she says. "I think so." She senses the change in atmosphere. Chip has a hand over his mouth in disbelief.

"What's going on?" Liz asks.

I don't answer at first. I'm still thinking my way through.

"Tell me."

It probably doesn't mean anything. Lizzy's whole theory is unstable: *If* Henry was from Lukus County; *if* he was dumped at the hospital and reported dead; *if* Janet Tunis was his mother; *if* the "twin minor issue" were identical and not fraternal . . .

"What is it?" she demands.

I show her the document and point to the phrase: *twin minor issue.*

"What does it mean?" she says.

"I'm not certain," I say, "but what I think it means is that if you're right about Henry Tatlock being William C. Tunis, then Henry might have had a twin brother."

Chapter 60

If we were in town instead of here in the boonies, Chip would do a ton of investigating before making any move. The FBI could find out easily enough who lives here. But Chip *is* the FBI, and since we're already here, we decide to see what we can find out ourselves. We won't reveal anything. If somebody is home, we'll just ask for directions back to the interstate, or we'll pretend the truck is overheating and we need water, or we could say we're long-lost relatives of the Tunis family looking for genealogical information and maybe for directions to the cemetery to record gravestones.

That's it: genealogical information and directions.

I drive into the driveway. The place is tidy. It's relatively well kept, as trailer homes go. There's a car in the driveway. A yellow Lab barks twice and trots over to meet us with his tail going in circles. Chip and I get out. I tell Lizzy to stay in the car for now.

We have no grounds to search the place and no grounds to detain anybody. We don't even have grounds for suspicion. We don't know who lives here—we don't know much of anything. Our plan is to make conversation: *Hi, I'm Nick, and this is Chip. We're looking for genealogical information on the Tunis family.*

That's our plan, but the plan changes: I knock at the door. The Lab barks a few more times. We hear movement in the trailer, and through the silvery corrosion of the screen, I see a figure approach. It's a man, normal size, normal build.

"I'm coming," he says. "Who is it? I'm coming."

The door swings open. And I stand there gaping into the familiar face of Arthur Cunningham, whose dog supposedly found the body of Kyle Runion almost twenty miles from here.

CHAPTER 61

Arthur Cunningham was a keeper of mementos. He had locks of hair from Kyle Runion and Nathan Miller and two other boys. In the weeks before committing suicide in his jail cell, Arthur was quite forthcoming with state and federal agents who questioned him. He led them to the grave sites of the three other boys.

One of the interrogators, a woman, was a forensic psychologist and profiler. She was gentle with him. Sympathetic, even. She seemed maternal. Her clothing was feminine but not sexy. She offered him tea. There was a plate of cookies on the table. She said, "So about eight years ago, Arthur, you led police to where you buried Kyle Runion." She leaned in toward him when she spoke. I watched the questioning on a monitor from another room.

"Yes."

"Why?" she asked.

Arthur shrugged and looked at her with a befuddled expression. "I guess I just wanted to," he said.

She talked to him about how two different men, Daryl Devaney and Henry Tatlock, Arthur's twin brother, had been convicted of the crime. "Did you ever think about coming forward to save either of these innocent men?" she asked.

"Why would I do that?" Arthur asked, genuinely confused.

When the woman asked if he had known anything about Henry Tatlock before the DNA results became public, Arthur said, "My mom told me I had a brother who died when the house burned."

"After Henry Tatlock's DNA was linked to the boys you killed, didn't you figure out that he must be your identical twin?"

Arthur shrugged again. "Guess I didn't really think about it much," he said.

I'd watched one of the first interrogations of Arthur. Now, a couple of weeks later, it seemed he was regressing. He had obviously been intelligent: He'd been able to carry out these crimes and not get caught, and then he'd sat through Henry's whole trial. But now he was becoming more and more infantile. He seemed to have trouble understanding questions, and his answers were childlike. The psychologist probably has an explanation for this, but I haven't asked her yet.

"Your name was Arthur Tunis," the psychologist said, "but you changed it to Cunningham, is that right?"

"Yes. My mother's maiden name."

"Why did you change it?"

Arthur looked around the room for a few seconds, and he looked at his hands and finally said, "My dad was a mean person. That's why."

He didn't say any more. Another interview was scheduled for the next day, but late that night Arthur Cunningham twisted a sheet around his neck and cinched it tight.

CHAPTER 62

Nighttime: It has been two months since the verdict in the Henry Tatlock trial. Tina and Barn and I are leaving for the cabin in the morning, but tonight I'm at Friendly City. I'm trying to sleep, but the combined effect of a thunderstorm and the mischievous wanderings of my thoughts keep me awake.

I love thunderstorms, and I wish we were already up at the cabin, where I could hear the rain on the roof and see lightning lighting up the hills. I force my lids closed and pretend I'm there. But now everything is aloft in my mind like a flock of starlings startled from a bush: Henry, Daryl, Lydia, Philbin, and yes, Rachel Sabin.

I expected to be gone from Friendly City by now, but Tina and I seem to have hit a snag. Something spooked her. I'm trying to figure out what went wrong, both in the short term and in a bigger time frame. I've taken it on faith that it was mostly my fault, though Tina claims it was hers, and the counselor tells us both to get over it. Anyhow, I'm stuck in the mental labyrinth of figuring out what "getting over it" means in the context of my life at this moment. There are all these new realities to accommodate, and ever-present dangers to guard against. Bygones are not always bygones. Call me paranoid: Calvin Dunbar and Arthur Cunningham may be gone from the equation, but if there is anything I've learned, it is that evil can come at you from any direction at any time. So the first item on my to-do list is (metaphorically) barricading the door against any further trauma during the delicate period of Tina's and my rebuilding. I don't know what barricading the door consists of. Maybe it means that if I see something coming, I hurl myself between "it" and "us."

The next item on my list, and the one I'll spend the rest of my life pursuing, if necessary, is to be a friend to Henry Tatlock.

I don't think Henry blames me for believing he was guilty. In fact, I wonder if he questioned whether a dark shadow from his own soul—some unrecognized demon living within his body—might have killed Kyle. DNA doesn't lie; he must have wondered. Maybe he wonders still. Maybe he thinks of Arthur Cunningham not as a separate being but as that dark shadow, a part of himself that cleaved off in the nick of time: one self to take the fall and the blame and the death, the other to persevere.

My campaign to win back Henry's friendship won't be easy. He doesn't want me for his friend now, and maybe he never will, but I'll try. I'm not sure why it's so important to me. I have to admit, I wonder if it's selfishness: Am I simply wanting to believe that traumas can be overcome—that bad things can pass and life can get back to normal? Whatever. My campaign to regain Henry's friendship will be glacial and constant and one day, I hope, successful.

At about ten-thirty, I give up trying to sleep. I leave Friendly City and drive toward my house. I want to be near Tina and Barn, consoling myself that I really am father and husband, and that for tonight, at least, the Arthur Cunninghams and Calvin Dunbars of the world are held at bay.

I pull up in front of the house. The office light is on, but within a few minutes it goes out. I wonder if Tina looks out the window for me before going to bed. I have had the feeling that she is aware of my frequent vigil.

The pestering thoughts that didn't let me sleep at Friendly City are quiet now. I can feel Tina and Barn nearby. The rain on the truck roof is constant; crescendos of thunder come along intermittently. It's comforting. I pull the sleeping bag over me and doze, but I wake up when a car drives past. I'm slumped down against the door. The cab of the truck is dark. I doubt anyone can see me. I go back to sleep. Then awake: another car. Or the same car a second time. And now a third time.

The fourth time, it stops and parks on the same side of the street, maybe fifty yards in front of me. It's an old beater of some kind, but in the darkness, I can't make out any details. After about five minutes, whoever is inside opens the door. The dome light comes on. It goes dark again and nothing changes. Something doesn't feel right. I reach into the glove box for my Glock and flashlight.

I watch.

A few minutes later the door of the car opens again. No dome light this time. A figure gets out, seeming unfazed by the rain. It goes toward the house, and even in the dark, I recognize the gait. It's a sideways walk, one shoulder lower than the other.

I get out of the truck. He doesn't hear me. I angle toward him. "Hello, Smeltzer," I say in a voice just loud enough to reach him. He startles and turns toward me. "Unfinished business?" I ask. He has no idea who I am. I don't know if he can see my gun or not. I shine my light in his face. It's him. He has come to kill Tina. After everything we've been through, it seems unfair that more evil has come calling. In a flash of thought, I wonder if it is something about me, something in my soul that calls to monsters like Calvin and Arthur and Tony Smeltzer. I wonder if I somehow beckon this evil to my loved ones—to Tina, Barnaby, Lizzy, Lydia, and Flora. I want to roar. Rage rises inside me, rage that this convict trespasses on my home where Barnaby, in slumber, tries to reclaim his already corrupted innocence; my home where Tina struggles to extract herself from labyrinthine traumas; my home where even I am not allowed to show up unannounced. But Smeltzer, this putrid piece of shit, trespasses here to visit his rage-fueled vendetta upon *my* family? To make the extermination of *my* loved ones the final act of his worthless, toxic existence?

I shoot him. He falls. The crack of my gun is lost in the sounds of the storm. I walk over to him.

"How?" he asks.

I don't answer. He dies.

I drag him into the street. He can't weigh much over a hundred pounds. The colon cancer has done its work. He was planning his farewell: He would kill Tina, and perhaps some others on his list, with his last bit of strength. He was probably hoping to end it all with suicide by cop. I position him right in front of Kenny's truck. With headlights off, I drive forward until he's fully concealed underneath.

I sit in the truck trembling. I feel something I have no words for. With this act of gunning down Smeltzer, something has been severed. Ended. Maybe what I feel is no more than a flood of endorphins or dopamine, but tears stream down my cheeks. I welcome them, and I sit for some time in this perplexing euphoria that engulfs me like a mist. Maybe it is joy. I would love to stay like this forever, mythic guardian of all that is precious: I am perched atop my slain enemy, watching over the home where my loved ones sleep.

It is probably no more than a few minutes before I shake myself free of the reverie. Something needs to be done. I pick up my phone to dial 911. But I stop.

I have to think it through.

There will be an investigation. I'll be cleared, of course; even if it turns out Smeltzer has no gun, I'll get every benefit of the doubt. But there *will* be an investigation. Everybody will know that another assassin paid us a call. Tina will know. Lizzy will know. And whether he learns of the actual events or not, Barnaby will feel the reversal of our desperate attempts to recover normalcy.

I will lose Tina. She will careen back into the mental whirlpool of another near miss, another reminder of her own mortality and of her sister's murder and of our unceasing vulnerability. She must not know that this man—who's supposed to be shark shit in San Francisco Bay—came back from the dead to hunt her down. I don't want to be her hero. She wants no hero, she wants stability and consistency and safety.

It could damage Lizzy, too: She will retreat again, perhaps irretrievably this time, into her fears.

And Barnaby: One more trauma, one more land mine on the disturbed path of his childhood, could prove catastrophic. I wonder what the triggers were that sent Calvin Dunbar and Arthur Cunningham and Tony Smeltzer careening so far off the path of decent behavior. I must protect Barnaby at all costs. I must protect him from becoming them.

There must be no investigation. Nobody can know about this.

Upton doesn't answer his cell. I call on his landline and wake him up. "Who is it?" he says. "What's going on?"

"Upton, it's me. I need your help."

We lift Smeltzer into the backseat of his own car. "I know some guys," Upton says. "They're waiting for me."

He gets into the driver's seat. "I'll follow you in the truck," I say.

"No, you don't," Upton says. "Go back to your hotel. It'll be taken care of."

"Upton, I can't let you—"

"You can't stop me," he says. "I'll come back for my car later. If anybody ever asks, I spent the night on your couch at Friendly City."

"But it's my mess . . ."

"Which is why you need to be as far from it as possible."

He drives away. I go back to Friendly City. I'll never learn what happens to Smeltzer's body. Upton will protect me.

In my room at Friendly City, I shower and change and go to bed thinking that I'll never sleep. But I sleep like the dead.

In the morning I carry my things down to the truck, then I drive home and stop in the very spot where, just hours before, I sat in the truck above Smeltzer's corpse, waiting for Upton. The day is promising. Tina and Barn and I will be at our cabin up north in a few hours. Lizzy and Ethan will meet us there. Maybe Chip and Flora will show up, too.

I get out and walk toward the house. The door opens, and Barn runs out and jumps into my arms. "Daddy, you're late."

"Sorry, Barn."

Now Tina is at the door. I put Barnaby down.

"I was thinking about you last night," Tina says.

"I was thinking about you, too."

"Actually, I was missing you," she says.

"Likewise. Actually."

"It will be nice, all of us being together at the lake, now that everything is settling down."

"Yes," I say. "It'll be wonderful. Now that everything is settling down."

AUTHOR'S NOTE

Daryl Devaney and Tina Trevor are fictional characters, but the Innocence Project is real. In the late 1980s and early '90s, the development of modern DNA testing finally made it possible to prove innocence (or guilt) years, and even decades, after a crime was committed. But as the character Nick Davis says, "The justice system doesn't treat kindly continued claims of innocence once the jury has ruled and appeals have all been exhausted."

The Innocence Project was founded at the Benjamin N. Cardozo School of Law in 1992 to "assist prisoners who could be proven innocent through DNA testing." It is now a nonprofit, 501(c)(3) organization. Over the past twenty years, lawyers for the Innocence Project and its network of organizations have continuously chipped away at all the obstacles preventing the reversal of wrongful convictions, but it is still (as Nick says) a Sisyphean task.

At the time of this writing, DNA evidence has been used by the Innocence Project and its network of organizations to free 316 wrongfully convicted prisoners, 18 of whom spent time on death row. The average time of incarceration for these vindicated prisoners is about thirteen years. Also, many other wrongful convictions have been reversed through the work of the Innocence Project on grounds other than DNA evidence. Learn about the project and read some of the stories at www.innocenceproject.org.